In Harmony

a novel

Rosa,
Never doubt.
xo

Emma Scott

Acknowledgements

I always say "OMG, I have no time! How will I get this done? My schedule is so crazy!" And that's fine if it were just ME for whom my schedule is crazy. It's my responsibility to meet my deadlines, and my insanity should remain contained, except for the small fact that I cannot edit, proofread, format or beta my own book. I can *write* a book by deadline, but there is a team of extraordinary women who allow it to exist in the world. They go above and beyond to share with me their time, artistry, and feedback, taking on my massive crunch time with good cheer, support and unending generosity. *In Harmony* would have fallen to "my crazy schedule" if not for the following amazing women in this community:

Robin Renee Hill, Suanne Laqueur, Melissa Panio-Petersen, Grey Ditto, Joy Kriebel-Sadowski, Angela Shockley, Sarah Torpey, Kennedy Ryan, and Amy Burke Mastin.

To you ladies, I cannot thank you enough, from the bottom of my heart.

To my husband, who poured more time and love and support into our household so that I could finish this book; who never complained at the late nights or the time I spent eating dinner at my desk instead of with the kids; who took our girls on outings "to give Mommy time to write" when he had his own work to contend with; and who never,

ever faltered in the belief that I could do this...I could not ask for better partner in this life. Thank you, honey. All my love.

And to the readers and bloggers, all of whom also fall under the cloak of "extraordinary women in this community," I extend my deepest gratitude to all of you. Your support, encouragement and friendship is the fuel by which I live (that and coffee. Lots and lots of coffee.) This book is, in part, a story of women supporting women, of best friends, of hands reached out to say *I'm here if you need me.* This community is my inspiration. Thank you.

Playlist

Violet, Hole
Best Friend, Sofi Tukker
Legendary, Welshly Arms
I Feel Like I'm Drowning, Two Feet
Til It Happens to You, Lady Gaga
Imagination, Shawn Mendes
World Gone Mad, Bastille
Ophelia, Tori Amos
&Burn, Billie Eilish
Feeling Good, Nina Simone

Author's Note

There is a town in Indiana called New Harmony. That is not where this story takes place. The Harmony, Indiana of my book is purely fictional, as is the town of Braxton. But New Harmony was so inspirational, so beautiful, and so ingrained in my heart after a visit, I could hardly bear to change the name or move it to a different state. To the residents of New Harmony, Indiana, please consider my Harmony, with all its faults, a loving homage to yours.

Dedication

To every woman who has whispered, shouted, screamed, or said to a friend the words *me too*; and to every woman who has not yet said the words aloud, but will someday, and be heard, this book is for you.

For Suanne, for all the things. Let's always be us.

In Harmony

Act
I

"Words, words, words."
—*Hamlet*

Prologue

"Tell me a story."

Grandma smiled through a nest of wrinkles and brushed a lock of wavy blonde hair off my brow. "Another? Three books weren't enough?"

"Not a book story. One of your stories."

"It's late..."

Downstairs, my parents' voices rose as they argued about Daddy's job. Again. Grandma sat back down on the edge of the bed. The quilt was one she had stitched herself, with pink and red flowers. My favorite colors.

"How can I resist?" She touched a finger to the dimple in my left cheek. "Just a short one."

I beamed and settled deeper into my pillow.

"Once upon a time, there was a Little Light. She was born on the wick of a tall white candle and lived among a thousand other flames. Her world was filled with gold and warmth and good things. The Light danced and flickered, practiced stretching herself tall. And she was happy..."

"Until?"

Grandma's stories always had an 'until.' The problem that messed everything up but showed the characters what they needed or wanted most.

"Until," Grandma said, "a fierce wind gusted and blew out all the other candles. Alone in the dark, Little Light clung to her wick and

survived."

"I don't know if I like this story," I said, pulling the covers up to my chin. "I don't like being alone in the dark."

"The Little Light was scared, too. But she learned to grow tall again and shine."

"Alone? She was alone in the dark forever?"

"Not forever. But long enough."

"Long enough for what?"

"To discover that she may have been one light among many, but she had her own fire."

"I don't understand. She was happier with the other lights."

"Yes. But among them, she couldn't see herself, nor know how brightly she shone. She had to be cast into darkness in order to see her own brilliance."

I frowned, only a glimmer of understanding touching my eight-year-old awareness.

Grandma cupped my cheek. Her hand was strong. It hadn't yet begun to wither under the pall of cancer that would take her a year later.

"Someday, Willow, you might find yourself cast into darkness too. I hope that day never comes. If it does, it will be scary at first. But you will see your own brilliance. Your own strength. And you will shine."

I asked Grandma for Little Light's story many times. She said it was a folktale from her childhood in Ireland. Years later, I tried to look it up at the library. I searched book after book of Celtic legend and lore, but I couldn't find the tale of Little Light.

Instead, the dark found me.

Two weeks after my seventeenth birthday.

A cell phone photo I never should have sent. A party at my house. A dance with a boy. A spiked drink.

The dark was thick and suffocating as the boy, Xavier Wilkinson, made my own bed a prison. A mouth relentless on mine, stealing my air. A hand around my throat. His body crushing me. Smothering. Snuffing me out.

Alone in the dark, Little Light clung to her wick and survived.

I clung, too. In the morning, my mind remembered only slivers while my soul knew everything. I opened my eyes and even in the bright, searing sunshine, I was in the dark. Like feeling alone in a crowded room. A stranger in a new city. Forever detached and cast adrift from all that I was and all that I had hoped to be.

I saw no light. Not a day later. Or a week. Weeks that piled up into months.

Maybe not ever.

"We're moving," my father declared over his rare prime rib. His mashed potatoes were pink with blood.

"Moving?" I asked, pushing my own plate away.

"Yes, to Indiana," my mother said.

The tight anger in her voice told me she hated the idea of leaving New York City. I should've been pissed off too. A normal girl would be outraged. You don't *move* in December of your senior year of high school. Leave your friends you've spent twelve years making, and everything you know.

I wasn't normal.

"Why there?" I asked. Why not India, or Timbuktu, or the fucking moon? It was all the same to me.

My parents exchanged a look before my mother said, "Your father's been reassigned."

"Mr. Wilkinson wants me to head up Wexx's Midwest operations. They need me to sort out some of their more delinquent franchise owners. Reorganize and rejuvenate. It's a very lucrative promotion..."

His words faded out as the name stabbed me with a phantom pain, ripping through my midsection. A torrent of words—more than I'd spoke in a month—poured out in a current of irrational rage.

"Oh really? Mr. *Wilkinson* decided you should up and leave the city? Just like that? Around Christmas?"

My mother covered her eyes with a bejeweled hand. "Willow..."

"And of course, you said yes," I said. "No questions asked." I gave a mock salute. "Yes, sir, Mr. Wilkinson, sir."

"He's my boss," Dad said, his voice turning hard, the first sign that his short fuse was lit. "He's the reason you have food on the table and a roof over your head. It shouldn't matter where that roof is." He looked at my mother. "You should be grateful."

"Grateful." I scoffed.

"Since when do you have so much hatred for Mr. Wilkinson?" Dad demanded. "What's he ever done to you?"

Not him, I thought. *His son.*

"How about how he doesn't care that I'm being uprooted in the middle of the school year?" I said.

"Does it matter?" my mother asked, waving her spoon in the air, as if hoping to conjure the answer. "Since August, you've completely changed. You don't talk to your friends anymore. You've stopped wearing makeup, you don't care about your hair or clothes…"

I rolled my eyes, while inwardly I winced. Putting on makeup and caring about clothes both required looking in a mirror, something I didn't do much of anymore. And my blonde hair was probably too long—almost down to my waist—but it made a good shield to avoid eye contact. Like now.

I turned my head and let my hair fall, a wall between my mother and me.

She huffed loudly in her typical dramatic fashion. "What's going on with you? I'm so tired of asking this question and getting no answer. You used to be a straight-A student. You had your sights set on an Ivy League college, and now I feel as if you couldn't care less about anything."

I ignored her. "Where in Indiana?" I asked my father.

"Indianapolis," Dad said. "I'll be working in the city, but there's a little town called Harmony, just a few miles south. Your mother's right. You've changed, and the only thing we can surmise is that you've fallen in with a bad crowd. Moving you out of Manhattan to a small town seems the best thing to do, which is why I said yes to this opportunity."

Bullshit.

We were moving because Mr. Wilkinson told my dad he had to move. It had nothing to do with me. My parents loved me the way you'd love a piece of art: an object to keep in the house and admire with the hopes it will someday be valuable. Ever since the night of the party—a party I'd thrown without their knowledge—I'd become an eyesore to them.

The truth was without this job, my father would be sunk. He'd been at Wexx Oil & Gas for three decades. He was far too embedded to start over at another company. In his house, my father was strict and demanding, taking out his lack of control at his job on us. Because at Wexx, when Ross Wilkinson said, "Jump," my father jumped. This time, all the way to Indiana.

"And you, Willow Anne Holloway," Dad said, waving his fork like a tyrannical king with a scepter, "are going to find some extracurricular activities. And that's non-negotiable. Your college applications are a disgrace."

I didn't reply. He was right, but I just didn't give a shit.

"It'll be a nice change all around," he declared. "Instead of this townhouse, we'll have a huge house on a few acres of land. Lots of space. More than you can even imagine. And fresh country air instead of city smog…"

He kept talking but I tuned him out. Words had become so meaningless to me. I had to keep my most important ones locked behind my teeth. The time to tell what happened to me with Xavier Wilkinson had long passed. As soon as I washed my sheets and burned my clothes, it became too late. If I let the truth out now, it'd swirl into a violent storm that would raze my father's career and destroy my mother's lifestyle.

If they believed me at all.

"Are the Wilkinsons moving to Indiana also?" I asked.

"Of course not," Dad said. "Headquarters is still here. I'll be running their Midwest branch. And since Xavier is still at Amherst—"

"Can I be excused?"

Without waiting for an answer, I picked up my plate of hardly-touched food and carried it to the kitchen. I dumped it in the sink, then hurried through the living room. It was decorated for Christmas, complete with a glittering, elegantly decorated, completely fake tree. When she was alive, my grandmother insisted we get a live tree to fill the room with green scents and warmth. Garlands of popcorn and clay ornaments I'd made in grade school. But she was gone, and our townhouse looked less like a home and more like a department store decorated for the holidays.

I ran upstairs, the name Xavier Wilkinson chasing me.

I tried not to let myself think of him. He didn't even have a name in my reckoning. He didn't deserve one. Names are for humans.

X. That's what he was. An X. X marks the spot. If I were to draw myself, he would still be on me: five-foot-four with long thick wavy blonde hair, blue eyes, a dimple in my left cheek my grandma had loved, and a big black X scratched over the entirety of me. X marks the spot, on me, on the mattress, like a pirate's map. What was plundered. Pillaged. Ra—

(we don't think that word)

I locked my door and hauled the covers off the bed, onto the floor. I hadn't slept in my bed since the night of the party. There was a black X on it too. I didn't sleep much on the floor either. Horrifying night terrors assaulted me on the regular, and I'd wake up paralyzed, unable to breathe; the ghostly pressure of a mouth on mine, hands around my throat, and a body, pressing me down, crushing me, until I felt like I was being buried alive.

Bundled up on the hardwood floor in a plain gray comforter—X had ruined my grandmother's beautiful quilt—I lay on my side, staring at the stacks of books piled on the floor, the shelves, the windowsill. When I needed to escape, I ran into their pages. In them, I could be someone else for a little while. To live a life other than this one.

Maybe this move won't be so bad after all, I thought, my finger tracing the spines. *A new story.*

My sleeve pulled back a little when I reached to touch my books. I tugged it back further and examined the little black X's that marched in a wavy line from the crook of my elbow to my wrist. Like insects. I reached for the black Sharpie I kept hidden under my pillow and added a few more.

X marks the spot.

My hope that Harmony would give me something better died. So long as I was the main character, my horrible story would remain the same.

Until.

Chapter One

Isaac

I woke up shivering, wrapped tight in my blanket that wasn't nearly thick enough. Icy light fell across my bed, offering no warmth.

Goddamn trailer. Like living in a cracked eggshell.

I kicked off the covers and padded through the double-wide to the living area. Pops was passed out on the couch, instead of in his room behind the kitchen. A fifth of Old Crow—empty—stood tall amid the beer cans on the rickety, stained coffee table. An ashtray overflowing with butts still smoldered.

One day I was going to get the heat I craved in the form of a fire from one of Pops' smokes.

His snores filled the trailer as I crossed to the heater. We had to be careful about the thermostat—I made sure we kept it at sixty-five degrees—but the trailer had shitty insulation and no underpinning. I waved my hand in front of the vents. The heater was on and working, pissing our money away for all the good it did. A cold January wind whistled beneath us. I could feel it through the floor.

Outside the front window, the scrapyard lay under a cloak of white. Our Wexx-brand gas station at the far end, closed up today. Not that we had any customers. It was silent and still out there. The acre of rusted old cars were white mounds, pure and pristine over the tangles of metal. A graveyard.

All of Harmony felt like a graveyard to me, a place that buried you. But tourists loved it. In summer, they came from all over to step out of time and into USA circa 1950. Downtown Harmony was six square blocks of Victorian-era architecture, colorful storefronts, one ice cream and burger joint with a jukebox and posters of Elvis and Jerry Lee Lewis on the walls. A single traffic light hung over Main Street, and we had a five-and-dime that sold Civil War-era souvenirs. Some big battle had been fought in the rolling green fields between Harmony and the next real outpost of civilization, Braxton. The tourists came for the history and a milkshake and then left. Escaped.

I looked at Pops. Fifty-three years old and he'd been out of Harmony maybe twice. Once to the hospital in Indianapolis when I was born, and to that same hospital when my mother died eleven years ago.

He was like the cars we scrapped and the gas station he sometimes operated—old before his time, broken down, and reeking of his favorite gasoline. He wasn't getting out of Harmony, but I sure as shit was.

Someday.

I laid my palm on the cold windowpane. Icy tendrils of wind snaked their way in from cracks along the sill. I'd been saving up for better windows all summer—doing odd jobs for Martin Ford at the Harmony Community Theater when I wasn't manning the gas station. When October rolled around, Pops promised to get to the hardware store for the new panes. But I'd given him the money and he used it to go on a bender.

That's what trust'll get you.

Pops stirred, snorted, and blinked awake. "Isaac?"

"That's me. You want some breakfast?" Blowing on my chilled fingers, I moved to the small kitchen.

"Sausage," he said, and lit a half-smoked Winston.

"No sausage," I said, fixing us two bowls of cornflakes. "I'll go to the store on the way home from school. Before the show tonight."

"You bet your ass you will."

He hauled himself off the couch with a grunt and lumbered over to sit at the foldout card table that served as our dining table. I sat across from him and tried to ignore him slurping cereal in between drags off his cigarette.

Pops hunched over his bowl, the weight of his own life dragging him down. He was heavy with years of struggle and poverty, harsh winters, heartache and alcohol. His jowls were unshaven, drooping like the bags under his watery eyes. Unwashed hair fell like gray straw over his forehead. I dropped my eyes, determined to finish my food in ten bites or less and get the hell out of there.

"What's tonight? A show?" Pops asked.

"Yeah."

"Which is it this time?"

"*Oedipus Rex,*" I said, as if it hadn't been running for two weeks and in rehearsal four weeks before that.

He grunted. "Greek tragedy. I'm not all stupid."

"I know," I said, my hackles going up. He hadn't had anything to drink yet, so the meanness was still slumbering. It was mostly nocturnal—the Jekyll in him—and I did my best to stay out of its way until he passed out.

"And what part are you?"

I sighed. "I'm Oedipus, Pops."

He snorted, shoveled a spoonful of cereal into his mouth, dribbling milk down the gristle of his chin. "That Martin Ford really has taken a shine to you." He jabbed his spoon at me. "You watch out. Turn you into a fag if you keep up this acting nonsense. If he hasn't already."

I clenched my teeth and hands both but said nothing. It wasn't the first time he'd insinuated Martin—the director of the Harmony Community Theater—favored me for reasons other than my talent. Truth was, Martin and his wife, Brenda, had been more like parents to me than Pops could ever imagine.

But I didn't tell him that. You don't talk to a braying donkey and expect to have a real conversation.

"The play closes tomorrow night." I hazarded a glance up. I wasn't stupid enough to ask him to come, but the part of me that still wanted to believe he was a real father never fucking gave up. "Last show."

"Yeah?" Pops said. "But how many more after that? You been doing this shit for years. Turn you soft, is what. I'm not leaving my business to a queer."

The words bounced off me. I had a dozen girls' numbers I kept on rotation in my phone, and the idea of him leaving me Pearce Auto

Salvage or the Wexx franchise station was laughable. It had no business anymore, unless you counted the occasional stranded traveler who didn't know better than to go five miles farther up to the shiny, big-name places in Braxton. We lived off Pops' disability and my pay from the theater. Or rather, he lived and I existed. I didn't live until I was on stage.

I could take his words. It was his fists I had to watch out for.

More than once, after one of Pops' tirades that left us both bloody; I'd pushed my old blue Dodge pickup as hard as it could handle along the winding roads out of Harmony, intent on getting out of Indiana once and for all. Then I imagined Pops stuck here, alone, eating cold cereal for breakfast, lunch, and dinner until a bad winter gave him pneumonia. Or maybe he'd dive into a bucket of fried chicken and eat himself into a heart attack. Lay dead and rotting on our shitty couch with no one to check for weeks, if not months.

I turned my damn truck around every time.

That's what you did for family. Even if your sole family was a piece-of-shit-drunk who didn't give a damn about you.

"Gimme some more, yeah?" Pops said, as I rose to dump my bowl in the sink.

I poured him a second helping of flakes, then went to get dressed for school.

In my small room—bed, dresser, coffin-sized closet—I put on my best pair of blue jeans, boots, a flannel over my undershirt and my black leather jacket. I dug the wool cap and fingerless gloves Brenda Ford had knitted for me from under a pile of scripts and slipped a pack of my own Winstons from a secret stash Pops didn't know I had, or else he'd raid it. I stuffed them into the jacket's inside pocket.

Pops was peering blearily at the wall calendar a salesman had left us after a failed attempt at selling us homeowner's insurance. "Today's the eighth?"

"Yeah," I said, shouldering my backpack.

He turned to me, a glimmer of regret and pain floating in the bloodshot depths of watery eyes.

"Nineteen now?"

"Yeah," I said.

"Isaac?"

I froze, my hand on the door. The seconds stretched.

Happy birthday, son.

"Don't forget to get the sausage."

I closed my eyes. "I won't."

I went out.

My blue '71 Dodge, parked to the side of the trailer, was frozen up. I managed to get it started and left it idling to warm up while I scraped ice off the windshield. The dashboard clock said I was late for school. I puffed clouds of curse words in the air. Walking into a class already filled with students was low on my list of favorite things.

I took the icy roads from the scrapyard at the edge of town as fast as I dared, through the main drag and across town to George Mason High School. I slid into a parking space, then walked fast into the building, blowing on my fingers. The warmth inside eased some of my irritation. When I got the hell out of here, I'd move somewhere where it never snowed. Hollywood worked, but I wanted to act on stage more than film. Or I'd hit it big in New York and it could snow all it wanted; I'd keep the heater on in my place all the time and never think twice about the cost.

I strode down the empty hallway and into Mr. Paulson's first period English class. Thankfully Paulson was a little scatterbrained—he was still organizing himself at his desk and I slipped past him, eyes straight ahead and ignoring my classmates. Intent on the third-row desk where I always sat.

A girl was in my seat.

A breathtakingly beautiful girl in an expensive coat with a fountain of blonde, wavy hair spilling down her back. Sitting in my damn seat.

I stood over her, staring down. It was usually enough to get people the fuck out of my way. But this girl...

She looked up at me with eyes like pale blue topaz and a defiant smirk on her face that belied a sad, heaviness that hung over her. Her gaze darted to the empty desk beside her, and she raised a brow.

"Everything all right, Mr. Pearce?" Mr. Paulson called from the front of the room.

I held the girl's stare. She stared right back.

I snorted and slouched into the empty chair on her left, stretching my legs into the aisle. Doug Keely, the captain of the football team two seats over, hissed between his teeth to get Justin Baker's attention. Justin, a baseball player, looked around. Doug jerked his chin at the new girl, eyebrows up, and mouthed the word *hot*.

Justin mouthed back, *Smokin'.*

"All right, class." Mr. Paulson stood at the front of the room. It was only a few minutes after eight and he already had chalk dust on his pleated pants. "I trust you all had a restful holiday break. We have a new student at George Mason. Please give a hearty Mason Mavericks welcome to Willow Holloway. She comes to us all the way from New York City."

New York.

The classroom rustled as kids turned to give Willow the once-over. A few raised hands in a cursory greeting. A murmured "Hey," here and there. Only Angie McKenzie—the yearbook editor and queen of the geek squad—gave her a genuine smile that Willow didn't return.

She mustered a throaty "Hi" that sent a shiver up my spine. Willow Holloway looked like her namesake—beautiful, delicate, and weeping. Not on the outside, but on the inside. Martin Ford trained me to observe people by how they inhabited their bodies instead of what they said or did. This girl ran deep. Her eyes had given her away when we'd locked stares.

Of course she's sad, I thought. *She had to trade New York City for Harmony-fucking-Indiana.*

"Scorching," Doug whispered to Justin Baker, drawing the word into three syllables and Justin grinned.

Fucking meatheads.

But they weren't wrong. All through class, my eyes were drawn to Willow Holloway, keenly aware of how opposite we were. She wasn't immaculately put together—slightly disheveled, with long, thick hair that looked a little wild. But her boots and jeans screamed money. Her oval face was porcelain smooth, as if she hadn't spent a day in her life working under a harsh sun or biting wind. And as of that morning, she was likely a good two years younger than me.

Too young, I thought, even as my eyes stumbled on the swell of breasts under her cashmere sweater and got stuck there, along with that mass of just-climbed-out-of bed hair that my hands itched to touch.

Who's the fucking meathead now?

I shifted in my seat, reminding myself I had all the legal-aged ass I could handle, one text or phone call away. Still, for the rest of class, my entire damn body was acutely conscious of Willow beside me. When the bell rang, I lingered in my seat to watch her rise. She gathered her books with a lackadaisical confidence, as if she'd been at George Mason for years instead of minutes.

She turned to me with a dry smile. "You can have your seat back tomorrow."

I met her gaze steadily, silently.

She shrugged, and walked away, flipping that incredible mass of soft hair over her shoulder. It swished to one side, then the other, settling in a curtain reaching nearly to her waist.

Forget it, I told myself. *Too young, too rich, too…everything you're not.*

I'd been poor as shit for my entire life. I'd learned to roll with it most days. Other times, like this morning, it punched me in the teeth.

Chapter Two

Willow

"Please give a hearty Mason Mavericks welcome to Willow Holloway. She comes to us all the way from New York City."

I smiled blandly at my new classmates. The jocks in the letterman jackets, a clear agenda behind their friendly smiles. The girl with the dark curly hair and the freckles across her pale skin who was no doubt going to pounce on me the second the bell rang. The rebel-without-a-cause badass whose seat I'd taken…

Everyone was easy to ignore except for him.

Holy hell, I'd never seen a more stunningly gorgeous guy in my life. At least six-two with broad shoulders, lean muscle, and a movie-star face. Impossibly perfect features. High cheek bones, bristly chiseled jaw, thick brows, full lips. His eyes were gray-green, like the sea off of Nantucket in winter.

All of him was stormy and cold, with an undertow of danger. His black leather jacket smelled faintly of cigarette smoke and I wouldn't be surprised if he kept a switchblade down his boot. Even the way he looked at me felt dangerous. My body reacted instantly, all over, as if his scrutinizing gaze went deeper than skin. He looked at me like he could *see* me.

You're overreacting, girl. Like, a lot.

I fixed my eyes on the window and its bleak landscape of gray skies and dirty snow. This was all wrong. The first day of school was supposed to be at the end of summer, when the heat hasn't quite given in to chillier autumn breezes. Not the middle of winter with snow blanketing the ground and only a few months remained before graduation.

It would've sucked, if I still had the capacity to give a shit if I made friends or not. I was trapped in my own perpetual winter. Sealed in a cube of apathetic ice, like one of those mummies they show on the Discovery Channel. They looked so life-like but on the inside... Nothing.

I used to like school. I looked forward to the day. My friends could be moody and dramatic, but they were *my* friends. The workload was either overwhelming or mind-numbingly boring, but I took pride in my grades. In the months after the party, I hated watching my GPA sink lower and lower, taking my college prospects with them. I hated how I worried my parents, even if it was a peripheral kind of concern.

I looked around the classroom, safe in my ice coffin. I *wanted* to be friendly. But friendly led to friends. Friends led to phone calls and texts and late-night talks under the covers. Warm, dangerous conditions that made icy barricades melt and terrible secrets were liable to pour out on a torrent of never-ending tears.

Forget it. These kids could like me or hate me or ignore me—my preferred option—and I wouldn't feel the difference. Even James Dean next to me. He could have his damn chair back tomorrow. I didn't need him and his stormy green eyes digging under my skin.

I was right about the dark-haired girl. I avoided her after English, but she caught me coming out of Economics later in the morning. She sidled up, confident in boots, leggings and a slouchy black sweatshirt that read *My head says GYM but my body says TACOS.*

"Hi. Angie McKenzie, yearbook editor," she said. I half-expected her to hand me a business card, or flash me identification like FBI agents do on TV. "You're from New York? What brings you out here?"

"My dad's work," I said.

"Wow, sucky timing, right? Middle of your senior year?"

I shrugged. "I'll live."

She grinned slyly. "Look at you with your angel face and Disney princess hair…just a front for a secret badass?"

Despite my best efforts, a smile crept past my lips. Angie was one of those quirky, instantly-likeable girls, damn her. My best friend, Michaela (*former best friend,* I thought), had been the same.

I got the smile under control. "Yeah, that's me," I said. "The hair's a cover."

"A Pantene commercial-level cover," Angie said. "I'm so jelly. Nash, my boyfriend since, like, forever? He keeps bitching at me to grow mine out, but it wouldn't look like yours." She shook her hands in her mass of dark curls. "Can you say *humidity frizz,* children? I knew you could!"

A laugh burst out of me. "You're weird. I mean, in a good way," I added. I may have been in self-imposed cryogenic stasis, but I actually did give a shit if I hurt her feelings or not.

Angie laughed along, making her pink hoop earrings bounce. "Girl, weird is my life's mission."

We'd arrived at my locker at the end of the second-floor hall. Glass doors led to a small outdoor stairwell with brick walls and metal railings. The gorgeous guy from English class was out there, wearing a knit cap on his head and fingerless gloves, neither of which looked enough to keep him warm. He leaned against the railing, casual as hell, smoking a cigarette. The smoke thickened the plume of his breath as it was caught on the wind and torn away.

"Who's he?" I asked.

"Isaac Pearce," Angie said. "He's all kinds of hot, isn't he? But forget it. He only dates older girls. And by dates, I mean has epic, emotion-less sex with. I assume."

A phantom flush of heat swept through me, like the itch an amputee might feel for a limb that's been cut off. I leaned against the bank of lockers, adjusted my bag, then my hair, then my bag again.

"Oh yeah? He likes older women?"

Angie nodded. "Though it's hard to imagine him calling someone and asking them out. Like, on the phone. With words."

"What do you mean?"

"He doesn't speak," she said.

I blinked. "He's mute?"

She rolled her eyes. "I mean, he *can* speak. He just doesn't much. Unless he's on stage, acting…"

Her words trailed away, and I looked to where Isaac Pearce leaned against the wall outside the doors, braving the cold and smoking a cigarette in plain sight, not caring if a teacher caught him.

"He's an actor? He looks…" My own words dwindled away, none of them sufficient. *Hot. A bad boy. Manwhore. Chews girls up and spits them out. A different girl every night…*

"Tough," I finished.

"He has to be. His father beats the hell out of him."

My gaze jumped back to Isaac, trying to see if the signs of the abuse were written all over him, or if his worst scars, like mine, were hidden on the inside.

"His father beats him?"

"That's the word on the street. But no one's seen his dad in town for a while, so the current rumor is that Isaac killed him and hid the body in their scrapyard."

I scrunched my face at her. "What? Come on…"

Angie shrugged, her freckle-smattered nose wrinkling. "It's a dumb rumor, but I couldn't blame the guy. They live all the way on the edge of town, by themselves in that shitty trailer surrounded by a car graveyard." She shivered.

Now my eyes sought signs of Isaac's poverty and found it at once in his scuffed boots and faded jeans. Poor but proud. Not one thing about him begged pity.

"Okay, but he didn't *kill* his dad," I said.

Angie flapped her hands. "Charles Pearce will show up in town eventually. The rumors will rest for a few weeks then start up again. It's been this way since Isaac's mom died about ten years ago. He used to come to school all bruised up. Not so much these days. I mean, look at his build. He's strong enough to fight back now. Why wouldn't he?"

I had no answer to that. I didn't want to think about how horrible it would be, not only to be hit by your own father, but to have to fight back. To defend yourself.

"Onstage, Isaac's a whole different animal," Angie said. "An ungodly, sexy beast. He plays all these emotional parts—screaming and crying onstage. Couple of years ago, the community theater did

Angels in America, and he and another dude *kissed.* You'd think that would've been a death sentence but it wasn't. He's untouchable."

Untouchable.

The word sang to me like a lullaby. Everything safe was in those four syllables. Everything I wanted to be but wasn't.

Neither is Isaac, I thought. *He's not untouchable to his dad.*

"You should come to the latest play tonight or tomorrow," Angie said. "Watch Isaac act."

"He's good?"

She snorted. "Good? It's a transformative experience. I'm not a big fan of plays myself, but watching Isaac Pearce onstage…" She gave me a sly look. "Bring a spare pair of panties is all I'm saying."

"Maybe I will," I said. "*Go,* I mean."

"Let's go tonight," she said brightly. "It's *Oedipus Rex* at the community theater. I know, I know, Greek tragedy is a snooze, right? But trust me, with Isaac in the lead…" Her shoulders gave a little shiver. "I've already seen it twice. The show closes tomorrow but I can squeeze one more in. For you." She nudged my arm. "Aren't I the best welcome wagon?"

"I don't know, you're my first."

Angie fished a ballpoint pen out of her backpack, grabbed my hand, and wrote down her phone number on my palm. I flinched; her pen was inches from the concealed ink of my black X's on my wrist.

"Tonight at eight," she said. "Text me when you get the okay from your 'rents. I'll be waiting for you outside the theater."

I blinked at the sudden social engagement thrust upon me. My Friday night plans typically involved reading, drinking tea or binge-watching *Black Mirror* on Netflix. A quiet night in the ice palace.

I heard myself saying, "Yeah, okay. I'll text you."

"Brill." Angie beamed. "And come find me and my crew at lunch. You can avoid the usual New Kid Who Eats Alone bullshit."

"Thanks."

"Welcome wagon extraordinaire, darling."

The bell rang. She blew me a kiss and trotted off to class. I moved more slowly, my gaze lingering on Isaac over the open door of my locker. He looked up.

For a second, through the steamed-up glass doors, his eyes met mine. I was struck all over again by the dangerous beauty of this guy.

He was a sleek dagger. He'd cut you with a look if you didn't know how to handle him.

And I'd stolen his seat in English class.

Maybe let's not do that again...

Isaac tilted his chin at me, then ground his cigarette out and sauntered back into the building. He strode past me, smelling of smoke and the cold bite of winter, a hint of peppermint. He spoke to no one and no one spoke to him. But, like me, the students all stared. Everyone stared. Mesmerized.

I'd never learned to drive in New York City, there was simply no need. I didn't even have a learner's permit. So, I took the school bus home from George Mason. It lumbered and lurched toward the east side of Harmony, where the road started winding through small foothills. The houses were immense on this side of town, with wide, sprawling yards. More than one property boasted horse paddocks and barns. I'd never imagined having so much space around a house. Backyards, front yards, *side* yards. And trees everywhere. They were skeletal with winter, but it was easy to imagine them green and full in summer, or bursting orange and red in autumn. Easy and enjoyable. I found myself looking forward to that.

My mother wasn't as enthusiastic.

"I hope our homeowners' insurance covers Indian raids," she'd said to Dad when we first arrived. "And locust swarms."

He'd pretended she was joking, though I knew Mom was deadly serious. Country life wasn't going to suit her. She'd been a Connecticut socialite, a Wellesley girl and a fixture on the Upper West Side. I gave her six months in Harmony before she gave my dad an ultimatum: go back to New York or find a new place in Divorceville.

As the school bus let me off on my new street that first day, I inhaled the crisp air deep into my lungs. This was an entirely different kind of cold than New York. A cleaner cold. Probably just my imagination, but I felt like I could breathe a little easier.

Our old townhouse had been spacious by Manhattan standards,

but our new home was *huge.* No barn or paddock for Regina Holloway—she insisted we buy something entirely remodeled. Like Winona Ryder's stepmother in *Beetlejuice*, she wanted to tear the country charm out of a house and replace it with cold elegance. I would've loved an old country house with little flowers on the yellowing wallpaper and warm wood banisters on the stairs. The more polar opposite to our city home the better. No subconscious reminders or throwbacks to the illicit party I'd thrown and what had happened in my bedroom that night.

I unlocked the front door and stepped into the warmth. We had a grand entryway with a chandelier that belonged in a ballroom. I crossed the blond-gray hardwood floors, and I kicked off my snowy boots before heading through the maze of couches and chairs and rolled up area rugs—all still wrapped in plastic.

The house was quiet and empty. Our furniture from New York wasn't enough to fill this hulking space, and Mom was in Indianapolis buying more. Dad was at work, naturally, slaving away for Mr. Wilkinson to keep up with Mom's spending.

The kitchen was mostly unpacked. I made some strawberry tea and took it up to my room. My new bed was supposed to be delivered today. It was the only purchase I'd demanded for the move. I argued we had the space now and Dad, pleased as hell I wasn't bitching about Indiana, was more than happy to oblige.

I peeked my head into my room, then exhaled.

Yes.

My old bed with its X-marked mattress was gone. Consigned to the scrap heap or recycling. In its place was a queen-sized canopy bed with gauzy curtains.

I'm going to sleep in this bed, I vowed. *Like a normal girl.*

I set my tea on the table next to it and lay down on the plastic-wrapped mattress. I folded my arms over my stomach and closed my eyes.

"Untouchable," I whispered.

After countless nights of shitty sleep, it reached up quickly with clawed hands and took me under. Down into black darkness. Muffled, pulsing music through the walls and floor. A warm, beer-coated, peanut-smelling mouth on mine. Squeezing hands on my throat. And that weight. Xavier's crushing, smothering, destructive weight…

I bolted upright, a scream stuck in my chest, trapped between my tight, gasping lungs. My eyes blinked until my new room in my new house came into focus. The afternoon light was gone. The clock radio read 6:18 p.m. I sucked in deep breaths, wiped the tears from my cheeks and slid from the covers onto the floor.

No bed was safe anymore.

I sat, legs splayed out like a doll thinking that old song, "Living Dead Girl." I thought about bundling into my bedspread, cocooning myself in the comforter and spending the rest of the night there, waiting for morning light. Then I remembered Angie's invitation to Isaac's show.

With a nightmare still clinging to me, the idea of dragging myself out of the house to socialize, felt impossible. But maybe seeing a play was like reading—immersive and escapist. I could lose myself in ancient Greek times and get some goddamn distance from my own pathetic tragedy.

I wrestled my arm out from under the blanket and stared at the phone number on my palm.

Was I really going to the play? Why?

To make a new friend in Angie.

To see this so-called acting prodigy, Isaac Pearce.

To get out of the house.

To be normal.

I pulled my sleeve down and compared the blue ink of Angie's loopy print to the ugly black X's I'd scrawled below.

I grabbed my phone and shot Angie a text.

This is Willow. I'm in. See you at 7:45?

The reply was almost instant. **Make it 7 and we can grab burgers and shakes at The Scoop. You have a ride?**

I realized I didn't, and that Uber drivers or cabs probably weren't as plentiful in Harmony as they had been in New York.

No, pick me up?

Yes, Your Majesty. <3

I gave her my address then texted my parents.

Going to eat with friends then to the play at the theater. Be home 11-ish.

My mother wanted to know whom I was going with—she'd already formed the opinion that Harmony was entirely populated with rubes and hicks. Dad insisted on an eleven o'clock curfew and 'not a minute later.'

I ignored both of their texts as I got ready. It was none of Mom's business and I hadn't been asking Dad's permission.

Chapter Three

Willow

Angie honked from the driveway at ten to seven. I came out, bundled in my white winter coat and pink knit hat. Angie was craning her head out of the driver's window of her green Toyota Camry to stare at my house.

She let out a wolf whistle as I climbed into her car. "Chez Holloway ees verra nice-ah," she said in a terrible French accent and kissed the tips of her fingers. "Your dad's in oil?"

"Good guess," I said. "He's a VP at Wexx."

"Oh shit, yeah, we got those gas stations all over. Even Isaac's deadbeat dad runs a station at the edge of his scrapyard. So what's out here for you guys?"

I shrugged. "His boss told him to head up the Midwest operations. So, he did."

"You sound so okay with it." Angie drove carefully but not timidly along the winding, snow-drifted Emerson Road, which connected my neighborhood with downtown. Snow drifts piled on either side. "I'd be flipping out if I had to move senior year."

"Not like I had a choice. Have you lived here your whole life?"

"Born and bred," Angie said. "But I'm not staying. I'm applying to Stanford, UCLA, Berkeley—basically any school in California that will take me. I want sunshine and beaches, you know?" She pursed her lips at my silence. "What about you? Where are you applying to?"

"Nowhere," I said.

Angie slowed for a stop sign. "For real? You're not going to college?"

"No." I shifted in the seat. "I mean, I haven't applied anywhere yet. But I will. Soon."

"Girl, you gotta get on that. Clock's-a-ticking."

"I know," I said, gritting my teeth.

That was the bitch about life: it kept going even if you desperately needed it to slow down and wait a minute while you tried to piece yourself back together.

"You're going to be a Yale gal, right? Or Brown?" Angie said as we came to the bottom of the bend to see the lights of downtown Harmony straight ahead. "I picture somewhere posh and New England-y."

"Maybe."

"Hey, you okay?" Angie gave me a sideways glance. "I realize I don't know you very well—hashtag understatement—but you seem a little… I-D-K, down. Dimmer than earlier today."

"Oh, I took a nap and it left me kind of drowsy," I said. "And did you just *say* I-D-K?"

"I'm a child of the technological age."

"Is that what you want to do for a living?" I asked, mostly to keep the attention off myself, but curious too. "Something in tech?"

"Indeed," Angie said. "Robotics is my thing. I want to build prosthetic limbs for amputees. My dream is to be on a team that creates limbs like Luke Skywalker's hand, you know? Realistic on the outside, Terminator on the inside."

"You watch a lot of movies, don't you?"

"Geek: one hundred percent, certified fresh."

I smiled a little, but it faded just as quickly as I thought about Angie and her dreams. She was noble and kind, with ambitions of Stanford and doing some good in the world. I yearned to have that same spark. Some fire that fueled me toward a future with a career and goals and purpose. Some goal beyond making it through one more sleepless night.

You're out of the house now, said a voice like Grandma's. *Doing your best. That's something.*

I took some comfort in that and was rewarded with the picture-postcard sight of downtown Harmony. Garlands of Christmas lights were still strung along the Victorian-era buildings, their large facades fronting more than one shop. We passed a laundromat, the five-and-dime, Daisy's Coffeehouse and a beauty parlor. The neon sign of Bill's Hardware blared red beside the marquee of a one-screen movie theater. Snow had been shoveled into neat piles and a few people strolled along the sidewalks.

"It's beautiful," I murmured.

"Yeah?" Angie craned over her dash as we waited for the town's one and only light to change. "Yeah, I guess it is. Have you seen much of Harmony? I know it's buried under snow but we've got some cool stuff here for being a speck on the map."

"Like?"

"There's a cool hedge maze just north of us."

"A hedge maze?"

"It's not tall or complicated enough to lose a tourist in, but at the center is a cozy little shack with a windmill. Purely decorative."

Or romantic, whispered a thought.

"West of town, there's a really cool cemetery that dates back to the Civil War. And we have an outdoor amphitheater where town events and festivals are held. If you need outlet stores or fast food, Braxton is ten minutes north. And if you need a real city, Indy's twenty minutes beyond Braxton."

She pulled her car to the curb, alongside a building with a sign reading The Scoop.

"Here's your typical, John-Hughes-style, high school hangout," Angie said, shutting off the engine. "Be warned: it's a burgers, fries and ice cream place. In case you're a salad-and-sprouts kind of gal. I am not, if that wasn't readily apparent." She slapped her rounded hip with a laugh.

I followed her inside the restaurant. It was bustling with what looked like George Mason students, plus a few families with small children.

"Ah yes, I see the cliques—such as they are—have taken up their usual posts." With her chin, Angie indicated various groups clustered around tables or crammed into booths.

"There's my tribe," Angie said. "I hope you don't mind that I invited them."

"No, it's fine," I said, scrambling to recall the names of people Angie had introduced me to at lunch this afternoon. Her boyfriend, Nash Argawal—a sweet-faced guy of Indian descent. Caroline West, a petite brunette. And Jocelyn James, the towering blonde, captain of the basketball team.

"If I had to *Mean Girls*-classify us, we are the Greatest People You Will Ever Meet," Angie said. "The quirky, diverse science geeks and persons of undeclared sexuality." She leaned into me as we neared the booth. "We're all straight on paper, but Caroline once kissed Jocelyn at a party and in the immortal words of Ms. Perry, they both liked it."

I'd already classified Angie's crew as effortlessly likeable and Nice with a capital N. The kind of people it'd be really damn easy to get close to. The kind whom if you told certain ugly secrets, they wouldn't brand you a slut or ask you why on earth you sent a topless photo to an older guy. Or why you let that same guy into your bedroom. They'd even be horrified to find out you didn't remember allowing him in, in the first place.

"Hey all, you remember Willow," Angie said as she slid into the booth next to Nash. Caroline scooted closer to Jocelyn to make room for me. "I'm claiming her as ours before the cheerleaders grab her." She looked at me uncertainly. "Unless you want to be a cheerleader?"

She nodded at a table where a bunch of pretty girls with long hair and sparkling lip gloss talked at each other over their phones. Guys in letterman jackets sat at the next table, their eyes on the game blaring from a TV in the corner.

"No, I'm not a cheerleader," I said.

Not anymore.

In my old life, I'd not only been a cheerleader, but co-chair of the Junior Prom Committee, Class Treasurer and a member of the debate team. A whirlwind roster of activities that now all seemed like faded memories belonging to someone else.

"It's okay if you are," Angie said. "Our Plastics aren't all that Plastic."

"Everyone's pretty nice, actually," Jocelyn said, waving at a girl across the restaurant. "When you grow up with the same people since pre-school, it's pretty hard to be bitchy."

Nash smiled at me. "If you know the Homecoming Queen used

to eat paste, she doesn't exactly have a lot of leverage."

"Still, they might try to steal you from us," Angie said. "You're so shiny and new."

"Steal me from what?" I asked.

Angie exchanged glances with Nash. "I may have ulterior motives for calling the gang together. Motives that have nothing to do with Greek tragedy."

"She wants you for our yearbook staff," Nash said, and flinched as Angie elbowed him in the side.

"You didn't let me sell it," she said.

"The play starts in forty-five," Nash said. "We don't have that kind of time."

Angie rolled her eyes and dug into her bag. "Fine." She pulled out a yearbook from last year and slid it across the table. "As we discussed earlier, college apps are the thing now and you need extra-curriculars, right?"

I nodded, flipping open the glossy book of photos. "My dad commanded it, so it shall be."

"So?" Angie clapped her hands. "To paraphrase *The Breakfast Club,* are we not *exceptional* in that capacity?"

"Maybe," I said, flipping through the pages.

I had zero interest in being on the yearbook staff. Or a cheerleader again. Or obeying my dad's edicts at all. I looked at the faces in the photos—students laughing together, working on projects, singing in talent shows and winning ribbons for science fair exhibits. An entire book dedicated to normal kids doing normal things. I knew many of them—probably more than I could guess—had their own horrible shit to contend with, but they looked so much better at moving past it than I was.

I wasn't moving at all.

A waitress took our order, and I went back to browsing the yearbook while the others chatted around me. I turned to a page of Harmony community activities. And there was Isaac Pearce onstage. Frozen in a dramatic black and white shot. I leaned closer.

"Why, Miss Holloway," Angie said. "We're becoming awfully curious about Mr. Pearce, are we not?"

I ignored her and scanned the photos of Isaac with captions beneath each: *Angels in America, Buried Child, All My Sons.*

"He's been doing this a long time?" I asked.

"Since grade school," Angie said.

"Oh, I see," Nash said with a roll of his eyes. "Tonight isn't arts appreciation, it's inducting a new member into the Isaac Pearce Fan Club." He looked at his girlfriend. "I hope you told New Blood she's barking up the wrong tree."

"I'm not barking up any tree," I said, a deep ache clanging in my heart. The idea of being with a guy, ever again, was repellent. Having him stand close to me. Being in the closed confines of his car for a date. Being kissed. Or touched. A boy's body pressed close to mine and not knowing its intentions. Or its power.

I shut the yearbook with a snap, cutting off both the visual of Isaac and the thoughts that could send me into a level-10 panic attack.

"He's pretty to look at," Jocelyn was saying, "but a serial college-girl screwer. He won't even look at us children."

"Children?" I said. "He's our age."

They all shook their heads.

"No?"

"No. His mom died when he was eight," Angie said. "He stopped speaking for, like, six months or something, and had to be held back a year."

I frowned. "He stopped talking for six whole months?"

Angie nodded. "Maybe longer. He was in our third-grade class. Before he got pulled it was weird to see a little boy—what…? Eight years old? Not saying a word?" She shook her head. "Poor guy."

My mind conjured a little blond boy with smoky green eyes having the words punched right out of him by his tragedy. "What got him talking again?"

"Miss Grant, the fourth-grade teacher, directed a little show and convinced him to be in it." Angie raised her hands. "The rest is history."

I nodded slowly. *She gave him someone else's words to speak.*

"But he lost a year of school," Nash said.

Caroline nodded. "He's eighteen. No, wait…" She counted on her fingers. "He's probably nineteen by now, right?"

"That's got to be hard," I said.

Jocelyn shrugged and dipped one of her fries in ketchup. "It's paid off. His acting is going to make him famous."

"Speaking of which," Nash said, checking is watch. "We should get going. Oedipus isn't going to gouge his eyes out all by himself."

Angie whacked his arm. "Hello? Spoiler alert?"

"I know the story," I said, unable to keep from smiling. Unable to not like Angie, who linked her arm in mine as we strolled down the sidewalk. I flinched at first; I wasn't a fan of being touched, but Angie was warmth to my ice and I let her, as our breath trailed clouds down the twinkling winter streets.

"So, any thought about my offer?" she said. "Yearbook is heading into crunch-time and I could really use the help."

"I don't know," I said. "I don't think it's my thing."

She pouted. "You sure? Because—"

"Yeah, I'm sure," I said, my voice hard. I forced it to be soft again. "Sorry. We just moved nine days ago. I'm still getting my bearings."

"OMG, of course," Angie said with a wide smile. "I'm pushy as hell—"

"You think?" Nash muttered under his breath.

Angie scowled at him over her shoulder and leaned back into me. "You do your thing, Holloway," she said. "Whatever that is. But my door is always open. Always."

"Thanks."

Angie's words warmed me too, for the rest of the walk to the Harmony Community Theater.

Do your thing, whatever that is.

Chapter Four

Willow

Compared to the other shops of downtown Harmony, the building that housed the community theater was almost embarrassingly run-down. The turn of the century columns at the entrance were smudged with years of car exhaust. The cement steps leading to the entrance were cracked. Inside, dust motes danced in the soft illumination from the elegant stained-glass ceiling lamps.

After we bought tickets from a small box office, Angie and her friends talked amongst themselves while I strolled up and down the lobby, perusing the gallery of black and white photos. Some were historical shots of the building. According to the captions, HCT had been in operation since 1891, when Harmony was a small collection of sparse buildings separated by wide, unpaved roads. Horse-drawn buggies and women in dresses with big, feathered hats traversed the wide expanses of dirt.

One long wall was hung with photos of past performances—a time-lapse reel of styles, costumes and plays from 1900 to the present. Both my pace and my gaze slowed down at shots from the past five years. Nearly all of them featured Isaac Pearce. He wasn't always the lead, but he was in every one.

And he's different in every one, I thought.

Even in early productions, when his youth was evident in his softer, rounder features, he could make subtle changes in his facial expressions or change how he carried his body—tricks that transformed him into a completely different young man in each role.

"Peel your eyes off of those photos," Angie said, tugging my sleeve. "It's time to feast upon the real thing."

We entered the main theater with its two sections of plush seats. The velvet had once been vibrant red, but now it was dulled to a tired maroon. The red velvet curtain across the proscenium had also seen better days. Wall sconces sent columns of light climbing up the walls and into the interlocking arches in the ceiling.

Oedipus Rex had been running for two weeks in this tiny town, yet by my guess, the 500-capacity theater was three-quarters full.

"Hasn't everyone in Harmony seen this already?" I asked Angie, as we took our seats.

"More than once," Angie said. "Tomorrow's closing night and is sold out. People come from all over. Down from Braxton and Indy."

"Even up Kentucky," Jocelyn said from my other side. "Theater is big in the Midwest."

"Universities in Ohio and Iowa have prestigious schools for theater arts," Nash said. "Our little place draws some VIPs."

Angie polished her knuckles on the front of her sweatshirt. "We're kind of a big deal."

"If it's such a big deal, can't they afford to fix it up?" I asked, fidgeting as a spring in my chair cushion poked my ass.

Angie shrugged. "Martin Ford—the owner—took it over ten years ago from the previous guy, who ran the finances into the dirt. Nearly went bankrupt. Now Ford is doing his best to keep it afloat."

"Can't they get a grant or something? Some kind of endowment?"

"I'm sure Mr. Ford's doing whatever he can," Jocelyn said.

Caroline nodded. "He loves this place. He's not just an owner but he directs all the shows."

"Our citizenry is where he gets most of his actors," Angie said. "He wants to keep it organic." She pointed at my program. "He acts in the shows, too."

I looked down at the cast list and found the name Martin Ford playing *Tieresias, a blind prophet.*

"So he's the one who keeps giving Isaac all his roles?"

"More than that," Angie said. "He chooses plays he knows can showcase Isaac's talents. Isaac is his protégé.'"

"I think the word you're looking for is 'meal ticket,'" Nash said, absently and affectionately wrapping Angie's curls around his finger.

"That's two words." She leaned in to me. "Nash is jealous because he doesn't look as good in a toga." The house lights dimmed. "Speak of the devil."

The lights faded to pitch and when they came up again, the curtains had opened on a black, empty stage. Large white cubes and pillars framed out a room. A white backdrop of Thebes was sketched in rough, black strokes. A minimalist set to let the words capture the audience's attention.

A priest stepped onto the stage, surrounded by a crowd of men and women in white togas who pantomimed being afraid or confused or despairing.

Then Isaac Pearce strode onstage and a little buzz went through the audience; a surge of crackling anticipation.

There he is.

His beautiful face was partially covered by a fake beard, transforming him from a nineteen-year-old guy in 21st century America into a powerful and omniscient king. I'd never had a religious experience in my life, but at that moment, I'd swear the light pouring down on him came from the Greek gods. He was divine. Otherworldly.

Untouchable.

He raised his arms as he spoke, his booming voice demanding— no, *commanding*—our attention.

"Sons and daughters of old Cadmus,
The town is heavy with a mingled burdens of groans and hymns and incense;
I did not think it fit that I should hear of this from messengers but came myself—
I, Oedipus, whom all men call the Great."

I stared, slack-jawed.
Oedipus the Great.
"Holy fucking shit," I whispered.
Out the corner of my eye I could see Angie grin, though her gaze stayed riveted to the stage. "Told you so…"

We didn't speak another word until final curtain. Even with a cushion spring digging into my ass, I barely moved. A fire alarm wouldn't have stolen an ounce of my attention from the action onstage.

Like every other high school student, I'd read *Oedipus* in English with Spark Notes at my side and yawning, because who gave a shit about a dude who slept with his mother?

That night, I gave a shit. About everything. I lived it. With Isaac at center stage, I was there, in Thebes, watching it unfold, unable to look away. I held my breath as Oedipus hurled himself at his horrifying fate, seeking to unravel the mystery shared by every single person sitting in that theater. A mystery *I* was desperate to know.

Identity. Purpose. Self.

The truth, a voice whispered in my endless dark. *What's left of me?*

When Oedipus learned the traveler he had murdered years ago was his father, and the woman he married was his mother, the anguish was raw and powerful. Almost destructive. His tortured denial reverberated through the theater as if it could shake the foundations. Bring the whole building crashing down with him as he collapsed to his knees.

When Jocasta—his wife and mother—hung herself, the king's grief and pain sucked the audience in, uncomfortably close.

When he tore the golden brooches off her dress and used them to claw his own eyes out, the stage blood spurting from under his palms was as real as the horrified blood thundering in our veins. His agony saturated every scream, every syllable, every weeping gasp of breath. And we had no choice but to feel it too.

I was vaguely aware of sniffles from the seats around me, people passing tissues and exhaling ragged sighs. But it wasn't until Oedipus, purged of the terrible weight of the prophecy, was exiled from his home that tears broke free and streamed down my cheeks. The fallen king cast adrift in the dark, forced to wander alone.

The curtain fell and we all bolted to our feet in a thunderous standing ovation. The crowd roared louder when Isaac took his bow. Behind the beard and the streaks of blood, his expression was exhausted. Then he smiled. A brilliant, breathtaking, triumphant smile of someone who'd taken a dark journey and come out the other side.

I slammed my hands together over and over, tears streaming

unchecked as the dwindling, flicker of a fire in me stretched taller and reached for the stage.

Chapter Five

Isaac

The post-performance crush was always surreal for me. The congratulatory hugs and back pats from the cast seemed to fall on someone else's body while I looked on from a corner, still lost in and connected to Oedipus. Some actors called it being in the zone, but Martin called it the flow. A current of creativity where performance stopped being performance and became real.

The flow was my drug. I craved it as soon as I left the theater. Like a junkie, I'd sell off everything I owned to live in that place where painful emotions trapped inside me were set free. It let me be exposed and raw, yet kept me protected under costumes and shielded by sets.

Lorraine Embry, the forty-year-old school teacher who played Jocasta, pulled me in for a long hug. Tears stood out in her eyes when she pulled away.

"Every night," she said, her hands holding my face. "How do you give so much every night?"

I shrugged. "Just doing my job."

We headed to the dressing rooms to change and wipe off stage makeup and, in my case, fake blood. Changing into street clothes, the guys shot the shit and talked up the show, lamenting how we had only one more performance. They waved goodbyes and headed out to greet friends and relatives who'd come to see them. As usual, I felt a fleeting curiosity if Pops was among the crowd in the lobby. As usual, I shot it dead.

Only if every ticket came with a bottle of Old Crow.

The dressing room was now empty except for me, Martin and Len Hostetler, who played the role of Creon.

"You guys want to grab a beer?" he asked. Then he laughed. "Shit, Pearce, I keep forgetting you're only eighteen, O king, instead of thirty."

Martin, a slender man with a shock of graying hair and wide blue eyes, beamed. "Actually, today is—"

I shot him a warning glance through the mirror, shaking my head slightly.

"—not a good time," he finished. "Thanks, Len."

Len saluted. "What's the play after this, Herr Direktor? You make your decision?"

"Yes, I've decided it's going to be *Hamlet,*" Martin said, meeting my stare in the mirror.

"Good choice," Len said. "It begs the question, what came first—the play or the actor you had in mind for it?" He laughed and chucked me on the shoulder. "I kid, kiddo. You were brilliant. As usual." He turned to Martin. "We gotta use this guy's talents before Hollywood or Broadway snatches him up, am I right?"

"My thoughts exactly," Martin said.

"Have a good one, fellas."

The door shut and Martin and I were alone.

"The entire cast would throw you a birthday party if you'd let them," he said, tying his shoes.

"We have a party," I said. "A cast party. Tomorrow night after closing."

"That's not the same—"

"It's not a big deal," I said. "Turning nineteen and still being in high school is fucking pathetic."

Martin's face folded into concern and I immediately wished I'd kept my damn mouth shut.

"It's not your fault," he said, holding my gaze in the mirror. "You got the wind knocked out of you, kid. They held you back so you could catch your breath. You shouldn't be ashamed of that."

As usual, I didn't have a decent reply, so I changed the subject.

"*Hamlet?*" I said. "I thought you were leaning toward *Glass Menagerie.*"

Martin held up his hands. "Len's right. I have to use the talent I have and you need to be on bigger stages. *Hamlet* is the ultimate role and it's going to get you noticed professionally."

"Maybe."

"Not maybe. Guaranteed. I've been reaching out to a few talent agencies. A couple of bigwigs from New York, one from Los Angeles. The LA guy has already committed to seeing you this spring."

I sat back in the chair. "Are you shitting me?"

He put his hand on my shoulder. "I hate to lose you, Isaac, but I'm kicking you out of Harmony with this one. I want *Hamlet* to be your grand finale."

I stared. Martin knew the score with me and my old man. He knew I was saving up to get the fuck out of town. Our scrapyard and gas station didn't make shit. Between minimum wage to clean up the theater as Martin's unofficial handyman, and pulling $30 per show to perform in it, it'd be another nineteen years before I had enough. Never mind that the idea of leaving Pops to drink himself into a stupor in that shitty trailer always soured my getaway plans with guilt.

"You have to take care of yourself, Isaac," Martin said. "You're meant for something bigger and better than what you have now. And I know this is the part you don't believe, but you *deserve* something better."

I looked away to the mirror and wiped the last streaks of dried blood from under my eyes. "I have to audition first," I said, my voice tight in my throat.

Martin swatted me between the shoulder blades. "Yeah, you do. Don't blow it."

I made a noncommittal sound and slid out from under his hand on my shoulder to pull on my boots.

"Heading home?" he asked. "Or a hot date with one of your women?"

I rolled my eyes. "I'm going to work."

"No chance," he said. "You have the night off."

"I can't afford to take the night off."

"You think I'm going to dock your pay? On your birthday?"

Martin hauled his bulky, scratched up leather bag onto the

dressing table. He dug around and came up with a thick red envelope. "Happy Birthday, kid."

I stared for a moment, then took it from his hand. It was gift-card heavy. Probably for the clothing store in Braxton. My heart sank in my chest under the weight of everything Martin had given me tonight. Not just the card.

Hamlet, the role of a lifetime.

The talent agents.

A real shot at getting out of here.

The gratitude overwhelmed me, filling me up, and mangling what poor words I struggled to utter.

"You didn't have to do this. Any of it. But... I'm grateful." I cleared my throat and stuffed the envelope in the back pocket of my jeans. "I mean, really. Thank you."

"It's from both Brenda and me," Martin said. His smile tightened. "How's your old man going to be tonight?"

"He's probably got the surprise party all ready to go."

Martin crossed his arms and pressed his gaze.

"You know how he'll be, Marty." I shrugged on my leather jacket. "Passed out or on a rampage, itching for a fight."

"You watch yourself. And remember, our door is always open."

"Yeah, okay. Tell Brenda I said thanks."

He let his arms drop with a tiny sigh. "You bet."

Martin's concerned gaze followed me like a warm wind at my back to the cab of my old blue Dodge. An icebox. My breath steaming as I turned the engine over and let it idle to warm up. I turned Martin's offer over too, tried to get it to warm up in my mind.

The Fords lived in a large, brick house on Front Street. Huge maple trees out front, a wrought-iron fence along the sidewalk. The house was built in 1862 and had been redone and renovated. The inside was filled with eclectic sculptures and paintings they'd collected over the years from artist friends, and from their own extensive travels.

I'd been over there a hundred times, and on a few occasions, when Pops got really violent, I stayed in their spare room. On those nights, I thought plenty about living with Martin and Brenda permanently. I knew they'd have me. I was nineteen and I could live where I wanted. Pop couldn't say no. And yet...

Lying in the soft bed in the Fords' guest room, with the heater working perfectly, surrounded by comfort and sturdy brick walls instead of cheap siding, I hadn't been able to sleep. I'd imagined my dad alone in that shitty trailer, and remembered when I was a kid, before Mom died, and how he'd play ball with me. Or let me pretend to shave in the bathroom mirror with him in the morning.

Pops was a broken down drunk, but he was my family.

In my truck's front seat, I fished out the red envelope from the back pocket of my jeans. The card was fancy—probably from that expensive stationary store up in the mall in Braxton. Gold drama masks, tragedy and comedy, adorned the front. Inside was a fifty dollar bill, a gift card to The Outpost clothing store—also in Braxton—and a handwritten message in Martin's neat scrawl.

The money is for what you want. The card is for what you need.
Happy Birthday,
Martin and Brenda

My vision blurred. "Fuck, Marty."

Pops might be blood, whispered a thought. *But Martin and Brenda are family.*

I got my shit together, revved the engine a few more times and rubbed the last condensation off the window. From my parking spot across the street from the theater, I could see a few people still congregated, talking to cast members.

And then I saw her.

Willow. The new girl. Standing with Angie McKenzie and her crew on the steps. Her hair spilled out from under her pink hat and over her white coat. In her gloved hands was a rolled-up *Oedipus* program.

"She saw it," I heard myself say.

Like a dope, I touched the window. Safe and hidden in the dark confines of the cab, I stared as Willow glanced up at the glowing marquee. The light illuminated her stunning face, a perfect oval of smooth skin and large eyes. Then her friends tugged her arm, and they headed down the street in the opposite direction.

I didn't know this girl for shit, but I added Willow Holloway seeing me perform tonight to the birthday presents from Marty already in my pocket.

And for the first time in my life, I felt rich.

Chapter Six

Isaac

I left the lights of Harmony in my rearview while the road ahead grew bumpy, dark, and cracked by ice. The homes on this side of town were small, surrounded by chain link fences and bare trees scratching at the sky.

My shoulder muscles tightened as I pulled up in front of our trailer—the lights were on inside the living area. I took a deep breath to calm down. Pops might be passed out instead of prowling, I told myself. It wouldn't be the first time.

I killed the engine and tucked the envelope with my gift card and cash in the glove compartment. Bringing evidence of Martin Ford's generosity into the trailer was asking for a shit-load of trouble.

I turned my key into the lock and cringed as the door squeaked. I peeked my head in, a lion tamer preparing to walk into the cage. Pops was sitting on the couch. Sitting up and passed out. Chin to chest and snoring wetly. The TV blared the news. A second bottle of Old Crow had joined the first on the coffee table, also empty. The air was thick with cigarette smoke.

I eased a sigh of relief. Creeping on silent feet, I shut off the TV and lights. I thought about laying my father down and covering him with a blanket, but I'd learned the hard way it was safer to leave him alone. I didn't want to perform the final *Oedipus* with a busted nose.

The heater whirred quietly but the initial warmth from stepping inside was already wearing off. In my room, I kicked off my boots and jacket, then climbed into bed fully dressed.

My thoughts drifted back over the performance. Lorraine was right: I gave so much every night on stage—so much rage and regret. It was cathartic, letting it all out in that theater. Letting Oedipus' pain be a conduit for my own. I gave so much because I had so much to give since Mom died.

I rolled over on my thin mattress, trying not to think how Mom would've been at the show tonight, and every night. Maybe Pops would've been with her, and the hard, tough streak in him wouldn't have turned rotten and ugly if she was still with *him*. We'd still be living in one of those little houses I'd passed on the way here like we did when I was a kid, instead of this run down trailer. Instead of Pops' drunken bellowing and rage, the air would be filled with Mom's humming as she worked in her garden, or she'd sing aloud to the radio as she drove me to The Scoop for ice cream "just because."

When Mom was alive, I loved Harmony. Its soundtrack was her sweet voice playing in the background of life. But she'd been silenced forever, and when she died, some part of me went dead silent too.

I rolled over, putting my back to bullshit fantasies and burrowing deeper into my blankets. Done was done. She was dead, Harmony was Hell, and the only sure way to escape the misery and find my voice again was to get the fuck out.

Martin invited talent agents to see me.

My acting could take me somewhere else. I didn't perform for accolades. Compliments nauseated me. But now I recalled tonight's applause, the standing ovation that went on and on and on. The repetitive clapping reverberated in my head, blocking out the cold wind whistling under the trailer.

And just before sleep took me, I remembered the gold of Willow Holloway's hair as she stood under the theater marquee, staring up at it as if it held the secrets to the universe.

Pops was out of the trailer early the next morning. I watched him through the kitchen window, walking the far rows of junked cars in the yard. He was hardly more than a bulky blob of army green jacket and red hunter's cap. Smoky breath pluming from his mouth.

He often walked the graveyard of his business, like a mourner walking among the headstones of a cemetery. Grieving his hopes and dreams. Grieving my mother. I could almost sympathize, if I didn't know damn well he'd come back inside, pissed off at the failure of his business and the shitty hand the world dealt him, and he'd take it out on me.

My fingers touched a scar on my chin, mostly concealed by my light beard, where Pops had hurled a lamp at me. Another time he'd brought in an iron bar from the yard, demanding I find more and get to the recycling. When I didn't hustle fast enough, he broke my arm. I'd done *Death of a Salesman* in a cast.

The last time he took a swing at me, I hit back and left him with a black eye that he showed off at Nick's Tavern. Then the rumors at school started. I was violent, high-tempered and heavy-fisted, just like my old man. But no one fucked with me, which was exactly how I liked it.

I turned away from the window and took a shower in the trailer's one tiny bathroom, freezing my nuts off as the cool air slithered in through the cracks in the windowsill. I dried and dressed quickly, putting on the same jeans as last night. I pulled on a clean T-shirt, layered a sweatshirt over that, then shrugged into my jacket.

Pops was coming in just as I was going out.

"Where are you going?" he said, blocking the doorway.

"Out," I said. "Then to work at the theater. Then the show."

"Out." A smoke-lined exhale snorted out his nose as he backed me inside the trailer. "Does *out* include spending one damn minute at the gas station?" He flipped a thumb over his shoulder, indicating the yard. "Or checking the answering machine for part requests? Good product is rusting away out there while you prance around a stage."

I gritted my teeth. We hadn't had a call to the yard for parts in six months. Our only business was Pops sitting in the Wexx gas station every Sunday, and me stripping useable parts out of the rusting junk in our yard. No one came for gas, and I'd already been through what we had a hundred times.

"I can't strip 'em when they're iced over," I said.

"Bullshit. We got acres of potential profit going to waste because of your lazy ass."

My jaw ticked. One load of scrap in my flatbed wasn't going to buy a pack of smokes. With the shitty rates, it would take me weeks to load and haul enough down to the metal recycler to make anything decent.

"I make more money at the theater," I said. "When the snow melts, we can start up the recycling again."

And maybe you could run the station like your franchise contract says to.

Pops' face turned ruddy, and I wondered if he was going to try something. I drew myself up to my full height and tilted my chin. At six-two, I towered over him. Since the broken arm three years ago, I'd been lifting weights to ensure he'd think twice before fucking with me.

But he was sober. Whatever scrap of decency he had in him—and it wasn't much—wasn't drowning in booze this morning. Yet. He pushed past me, whiskey fumes and stale cigarette smoke filling my nose.

"Get the fuck out then. Useless. I don't want to look at you."

Feeling's mutual, I told myself, and slammed the door behind me as I left. Unscathed, but feeling like he'd hit me anyway, right in the goddamn chest.

I drove up to Braxton. At The Outpost clothing store, I bought two new pairs of jeans, socks and underwear. The lady at the register said I still had fifty dollars left on the gift card.

Jesus, Marty.

I left my purchases with her and went to the kids' section. I found a weather-proof winter jacket—a good one, not some cheap crap—in bright blue, and on sale for $45.99. I held it up to judge the size, then took it to the register.

"For your little brother?" she asked as she brought the card balance to zero.

"Yeah," I said.

She smiled. "How sweet."

At the mall food court, I grabbed a slice of pizza and a Dr. Pepper, then headed back to Harmony. I still had an hour before I was due for work at HCT; I veered back to my end of town, taking the customer road that flanked the eastern edge of Pearce Auto Salvage. At the far end, where the scrapyard's fence served as the backyard to a row of small houses, I parked and got out.

An old rusted out pickup truck, upside down, lay against the chain link. Like a forgotten prop in an action movie. From inside the cab, I heard a voice softly singing Nina Simone's "Feeling Good."

I put two fingers to my lips and gave a low whistle.

The singing stopped and Benny Hodges climbed out from the truck. His grin flashed, bright white in the dark of his skin, before he dialed it down to a thirteen-year-old's bored nonchalance.

"What's up, my brother?" he said, wiping his hands on his jeans then offering me a fist bump. "Happy Birthday."

"Thanks."

"Mama made you something. Hold up, let me get it."

He ducked through a tear in the chain link fence, his too-small coat flapping behind as he ran across the snow-deadened grass. He went into his house and came back out with a small, round cake on a plate under plastic wrap. Forks stuck out of his pocket and jangled as he ran.

He climbed back under the fence and held out the cake to me. It was white with cream cheese frosting and *Happy Birthday Isaac!* in a boy's messy orange lettering.

"Carrot cake," he said, beaming. "Your favorite, right? And I did the words."

"Thanks, Benny," I said, my heart clenching. "Thank Yolanda, too."

"She's at work, but told me to tell you Happy Birthday." He peered up at me, undisguised eagerness in his deep brown eyes. "We're going to bust into that now, right?"

I chuckled, "Yeah, let's do it. But first…"

I set the cake down on a semi truck tire, and held out the bag from The Outpost. Benny peered at it suspiciously.

"What's that?"

"A jacket."

"Is it my birthday or yours?"

I held out the bag. "Yours is too small. Take it."

He hesitated, pride keeping his hands at his sides.

I sighed. "Your ma keep a roof over your head?"

"Yeah."

"And food on your plate?"

He nodded.

"Damn straight," I said. "And how often does she make something for me and Pops?"

Benny scratched his chin with one finger. "Once a week?"

"At least. That's her looking out for us." I held out the bag. "This is us looking out for you. Take it."

He took it.

"The kids at school were giving me shit..." He shrugged out of his old coat and put on the new. Zipped it to his chin and smoothed down the sleeves. He smiled and for a moment, he was an ordinary kid, not a young man forced to grow up fast without a father.

"It's warm," he said.

"Good."

We shook hands, and then he gave me a half-hug and a manly thump on the back.

"Thanks, bro," he said thickly, holding on a little longer than necessary. I let him.

I met Benny three years ago. Or found him, rather, out here by the fence. He was huddled against the semi tire, sobbing over his father—killed in Afghanistan when Benny was five. He wanted to cry somewhere away from the house. "Where Mama wouldn't see and worry," he'd said. He told me it was his job to take care of her now. I told him I took care of my Pops the same way. We'd been friends ever since.

Benny let go of me and left the sentimental moment to blow away in the cold air.

"How was school this week?" I asked as we dug into the cake.

"Aight," Benny said. "Science test."

"And?"

"Eh."

"You're too smart for 'eh'. Work harder. You staying out of trouble?"

"Yeah. Are you?"

I glanced down at him with raised eyebrows. "Always."

He laughed. "Yeah, right. Who's your new girl this week?"

"Don't have one."

"Bullshit. You're the king of booty calls."

"Your ma know you talk like that?"

"No."

"My ass."

He shrugged. "She don't care."

From what I knew of Yolanda Hodges, she cared plenty. She cared too, about what kind of example I was setting for her son. But I'd let him mess around with my phone one night and he saw an age-inappropriate text from one of the girls I sometimes hooked up with. To take the edge off.

Naturally, Benny asked a thousand questions. I didn't bullshit him then, and I wasn't about to start now.

"Listen," I said, trying to form a few smart words, my jaw working like a rusted hinge. "You got to treat all girls right. No matter what. No matter *when.*"

"I will."

"I'm not fucking around. The girls that I—"

"Bang? Screw? Nail?"

I glanced down at him. He grinned up at me.

"Yeah, okay," I said. "Those girls. We have an understanding. It's okay that I don't stick around and take them out or call them all the time. They're not my girlfriends and they don't expect to be. Sometimes girls like to…"

"Bang? Screw? Nail?"

I chuckled. "Yeah. They do. Nothing wrong with it so long as everyone's down, okay?"

Benny peered up at me, his brows furrowed. "Why you getting so after-school-special on me?"

"It's important."

He thought about this, then shrugged. "Cool."

We ate our cake as the sun broke through the gray and glinted against the rusted pickup. Benny started humming "Feeling Good."

"Since when do you know Nina Simone?" I asked.

He blinked. "Who?"

"The song just now."

"I don't know any Nina. I got that from the Jay-Z video."

"That works, I guess."

"Tonight's your last show?" he asked.

"Last Oedipus, yeah."

"You sad about that?"

"Not really," I said.

For whatever reason, the memory of Willow Holloway came back to me, when she was standing outside the theater with a program in her hand.

I glanced over at Benny with frosting smeared over one cheek and smiled a little. "It was a good birthday."

Chapter Seven

Willow

Monday morning in English class, I sat in the only available seat—in the back row next to Isaac Pearce. He was already in the one I'd taken last week—slouched back, arms crossed, legs sprawled. He looked straight ahead as I came down the aisle and I tried to keep my own gaze restricted to a quick snapshot. Leather jacket, jeans, boots. The hard, angular features of his face no longer godly under stage lights, but no less devastatingly handsome.

I tucked myself into the desk beside him and stashed my backpack under my feet. Isaac's otherworldly performance had stayed with me all weekend. Taking a seat next to him in something as ordinary as English class felt odd, though I began to see why Isaac saved his words for the stage—he sat in his chair like it could hardly contain him.

He's too big for this town.

I stole a glance at him and caught him stealing one of me. My heart jumped in my chest. We both looked away and I sat perfectly still until the electric tingle subsided.

Holy shit.

"Hey," a voice hissed to my left.

I looked around to see Angie hanging over the back of her seat staring at me, amusement in her brown eyes. Her sweatshirt had a graphic of a rhinoceros and said, *Chubby unicorns need love too.*

"Have we met?" she asked. "You look familiar? Did we hang out last Friday or did I imagine it?"

"Oh, hey," I said, finding a smile for her. "What's up?"

She glanced at Mr. Paulson, who was still shuffling through a mountain of paper on his desk, then motioned me closer. We huddled together, whispering, just like I used to do with Michaela and the girls back in New York. Before X crossed them out of my life.

Angie tilted her chin at Isaac behind me. "It's like sitting next to Kit Harrington, right? Or Brad Pitt circa *Legends of the Fall.*"

I bit a smile between my teeth and shrugged. "I think I can handle it."

"You sure about that? You didn't even remember I existed until a second ago, which normally would have broken my heart." Her eyes widened and she hunched closer to me, her whisper turning to a hiss. "Are you into him? I keep telling you it's a lost cause, but maybe not. Maybe he's into you. You should tell him you saw his show. Tell him you *cried.*"

"Shh." I whacked her hand, a jolt of heated embarrassment surging through me. "I didn't cry."

Angie raised her eyebrows.

"Shit. You saw that?"

"Don't feel bad," she said. "He has that effect on everyone." She jerked her chin at Doug Keely across the room. "Sometimes the jocks beat their chests and toss a rude comment his way, but Isaac shuts them down quick. Like a pouncing lion. Or a jaguar?" She tapped a fingernail to her front teeth. "What's the sexiest genus in the big cat family?"

"Panther," I whispered, then rolled my eyes. Still, it felt good to gossip about a boy with a friend. Normal.

Except the boy in question is actually a man and sitting right next to me.

"Panther, *yes,*" Angie said, entirely too loudly. "Anyway, what was I saying?"

"Jocks giving Isaac shit?" I whispered.

"Mm. It's glorious to behold. I'm not a fan of violence, but watching him in *any* kind of action is hot. He's so...electric." She gave me a lascivious look. "It makes you wonder what he's like in bed. You know?"

A little thrill shot down my spine before turning ugly and heavy in my chest. Tightening my lungs, turning my breath shallow. The idea of being in bed with a beautiful man like Isaac—or any man for that matter—was a sweet ache of want that rotted under the black X. A swift sadness filled me, how such an innocuous comment and such a natural part of human nature could become so tainted. I sat back, away from Angie's warm energy.

Boy talk, apparently, was another thing to put on my list of things Xavier had X'd out of my life.

Angie misread my reaction and her friendly smile fell. "Oh, don't get me wrong. I'm one hundred percent Nash's girl—"

"No, I'm not…" I stammered. "I know you are. I just—"

"Good morning, class," Mr. Paulson said, moving to the front of the room.

I turned my attention to him with relief, though Angie's perplexed attention lingered on my left. On my right, Isaac was staring straight ahead, his face a stone. All at once, I was sure he'd heard every word of mine and Angie's conversation. Embarrassment swamped me and I tried to dismiss it. He was probably used to girls whispering about him and anyway, I was too young to be worthy of his attention.

"Couple of announcements," Mr. Paulson said. "The Spring Fling tickets go on sale next week. The dance will be held in the gym on March…" He peered at the paper in his hand. "March fifteenth. Also, if any of you read the *Harmony Tribune* instead of Twitter, you'll know the Harmony Community Theatre announced its next show will be Shakespeare's *Hamlet.*"

As if there were another *Hamlet.* Immediately, all eyes turned to Isaac, who didn't move an inch under the sudden scrutiny.

"I know many of you have seen our own Mr. Pearce's unbelievable performance as Oedipus," Mr. Paulson said, beaming like a proud dad. He pointed a thumb at himself. "This classics lover saw it twice. Bravo, Isaac. I'm sure I speak for many of us when I say we look forward to seeing you take on The Bard's most iconic play."

Isaac made no response but to nod slightly. I frowned, wondering if Isaac even needed to audition for roles any more. Then I remembered him falling to his knees in agony, fake blood pouring down his cheeks.

He probably didn't.

"On that note," Mr. Paulson said, "the HCT is holding open auditions next Wednesday, seven p.m. at the theater."

My head snapped up. Out of my peripheral, I saw Isaac's head jerk my way in response. We made eye contact and again I felt that zap of electricity, this time laced with curiosity before he looked away.

"I'll leave the info on the bulletin board for any eager thespians who want to give it a shot," Mr. Paulson said. "In fact, I'll give extra credit for our Poetry and Drama unit at the end of the year to any who lands a part. Or volunteers to help with the production."

This news didn't send anyone rushing to the bulletin board, and Paulson began the day's lesson about the symbolism in *Crime and Punishment*. I stared through the blackboard, my thoughts filling with possibilities.

Open auditions.

Deep within me, the flicker of light that reached to the stage Friday night, wanting what Isaac could do, reached up again. It burned straight and clear for an instant, then cowered again. What the hell did I know about acting? The last time I'd been on stage was my riveting portrayal of Monkey #3 in Ms. Mellon's kindergarten production, *Meet the Jungle Animals!*

Bad idea, I thought. *This is a real theater with real actors. And it's Shakespeare. People train for years to do Shakespeare.*

When the bell rang, I lingered by Mr. Paulson's bulletin board, long enough to mentally grab HCT's website address. Angie's eagle eyes noticed, though. Leaving the room, she linked her arm in mine with a familiarity I wanted to both lean on and squirm from.

"Why, Miss Holloway," she said. "I had no idea you were a fan of old Bill Shakespeare."

"I'm not," I said. "I'm just...curious. And my dad is all up my ass about extra curriculars."

"Uh huh. Or is the idea of spending time with Isaac Pearce the motivation beneath your subtext?"

"I am *not* interested in Isaac," I said.

I disentangled my arm from hers a little too forcefully and my ankle turned in my short-heeled boot. It didn't hurt, but I stumbled right into someone. Someone tall, built like a brick wall, and wearing a black leather jacket. A strong hand shot out to steady me, and I tilted my head up to see Isaac Pearce looking down at me.

Of course.

"Hi," I said.

"Hey," he replied.

He speaks…

We stood close, too close. Like a couple-at-a-dance-close. I smelled his soap, a hint of peppermint, the leather of his jacket, and the smoky undertones of his cigarettes. He was impossibly good-looking. My eyes swept over his features quickly, as if afraid to miss anything. When my eyes met the green of his, another of those little jolts shot through me again. I stepped back.

"Yeah, so… I'm sorry for…bumping you."

Oh my God get a grip. He's not a priceless statue.

I could feel Angie's amusement behind me and my cheeks flushed pink.

Isaac's grey-green eyes softened. For a split second I thought he was actually going to say something. But his expression hardened and he strode away.

"Okay," I said to his back. "Nice chatting with you."

I turned to see Angie watching me expectantly, her brows raised.

"What?"

"You touched him. He touched you. Is your life changed forever?"

I had to laugh, all my irritation at her draining out. "You're a pain in the ass, you know that?"

She grinned. "I've been told."

We stopped at my locker and Angie leaned against the bank while I exchanged my English notebook for economics. One bank of lockers down, Isaac was turning the dial on his padlock. I kept my eyes on my belongings, trying to ignore the pull to look at him.

Well, come on, he's gorgeous. I should want *to look at him. It's normal.*

"So," Angie drawled the word into seventeen syllables. "I'm going to throw this out there one last time then leave you alone, I promise." She batted her eyelashes and pouted like a begging puppy. "Yearbook?"

It would've been so easy to say yes. Yearbook was safe. Something I could do from the sidelines. Documenting other kids living their lives would be like a science experiment: What Normal Looks Like. But the memory of Isaac's acting the other night—the catharsis of emotion—called to me. *Hamlet* felt like the first thing I could *do*—a step toward getting me out from under Xavier's black X. Or at least try.

I shut my locker to look at Angie and sucked in a breath.

"I know you won't believe me that it has nothing to do with Isaac, but I'm going to audition for *Hamlet*."

There. It's out there. No going back.

"Yeah?" Angie pursed her lips. "Have you ever acted before?"

"Never," I said. "It's stupid, right? I'm not going to get a part. I don't know what I'm thinking."

"Way to be positive, Holloway," Angie said, then softened. "For real, if this is what you want, then go for it. I'll help."

"You will?"

"Duh." She rolled her eyes. "I mean, honestly, you'd make a killer Ophelia."

"Ophelia," I said, rolling the name over my tongue like a sweet candy, and racked my brain for what I knew of *Hamlet*. Which wasn't much. "Doesn't she go crazy and kill herself?"

"That's the one. Big, juicy role. Iconic. My queen, Kate Winslet, played her. And Julia Stiles. Helena Bonham-Carter…"

"Yeah?" I asked, my hopes rising, then crashing again. "If it's an important role, they're not going to trust it to a noob like me."

Angie blew a small raspberry. "The director, Ford, casts talent, not experience. Why else do you think *Oedipus* was full of grocers and hairdressers instead of grad students? You need a killer monologue to audition with." She dramatically jabbed her finger down the hallway. "Get thee to the library."

"Um, what?" I laughed, grateful for this quirky, kindhearted gal for pushing herself into my life.

"Get thee to a library?" Angie said. "Get it? Like, the 'get thee to a nunnery'? From *Hamlet*?"

"Oh. Right."

She narrowed her eyes at me, then began ticking off items on her fingers. "You haven't acted before. You don't know the play. You don't think you're going to get a part. *And* you're not trying to hang around Isaac Pearce every night for the next two months." She threw up both hands. "Girl, what the heck are you auditioning for?"

I shrugged, not looking at her. "I have to do something."

"It's getting a little late in the college app game."

"It's not that…"

"Then what is it?" Angie's soft face morphed into concern. She put her hand on my arm. "Hey. I'm here."

The simple declaration was almost enough to yank the truth right out of me. Tears threatened, but before I could speak, a huge guy with a blond buzz cut, wearing a navy blue George Mason windbreaker, walked by with some of his buddies. He stopped when he saw me and looked me up and down with pale blue eyes.

"Hey there, Princess. You're the new girl, right? I been seeing you around. And I like what I see."

A normal girl would've rolled her eyes at the cheesy line. Or told him to fuck off. Or maybe been flattered, if this guy's brand of meathead was her type. But my chest tightened and the air seemed thinner, harder to take in with his hulking presence so close to me.

Angie leaned in to me. "Willow, meet Ted Bowers. 'Roided out captain of the wrestling team."

Ted's face scrunched with anger. "Shut up, Angie. Dork." He turned back to me, his expression smoothing out into an overly friendly smile. He took a step closer. "We should hang out sometime. I'll show you around."

I felt my head nod while every particle of me recoiled from his obvious intentions. I'd gone mute, hardly able to draw a breath. Begging whatever gods would listen to not let me have a full-blown panic attack right in the middle of the hallway.

"Are you scared of me, Princess?" Ted said, looking back to laugh with his buddies, then back to me. "I don't bite. Unless you want me to."

My throat started to close and lights danced in front of my eyes. Distantly, I heard Angie tell Ted to shut up, and then Isaac Pearce was there.

He pushed between Ted and me like a shield, towering over the wrestler. His smoke-and-soap scent was like smelling salts, bringing me back around. I pulled in a deep breath and the lightheadedness faded a little.

"Oh look, it's Oedipus," Ted said. "What's up, motherfucker?

Get it? A mother...fucker?"

"Great joke, Ted," Angie said. "Very original."

He ignored her, kept his eyes locked on Isaac. "Back off the little princess, Pearce. She's too young for you."

Isaac cocked his head to the side. Ted had a good thirty pounds on him but I was suddenly afraid for the dickhead. Danger radiated off of Isaac, making the hairs on my arm stand on end.

"Well?" Ted said. "You got something to say, motherfucker?" He was on a roll now, nudged one of his buddies who didn't look nearly as confident. "Hey, how come you're still in high school? Aren't you, like, thirty now? Or are you on a prison work release?"

Standing this close to Isaac, I could feel the tension humming off of him. The panther ready to pounce. Angie's hand dug into my arm and the small crowd that had gathered held their breath. Watching.

Ted wasn't done. His laugh turned dark and ugly. "Haven't seen your old man in a while, Pearce. Where did you bury the body? Next to your mother?"

RIP Ted Bowers, I thought.

Isaac drew himself up but Ted struck first, ramming at Isaac's chest with both hands to shove him back.

At the same time, a classroom door shot open down the hall and Isaac, in a flash of black leather, lobbed a right jab into Ted's face. The sound of knuckles hitting bone snapped through the hallway, followed by a gasp. Ted reeled back, blood leaking out of his nose.

The crowd erupted with *oohs* and laughter and murmured talk.

"What's all this?" Mr. Tyler, the biology teacher, stepped into the hallway and pushed through the growing crowd. "Break it up, now, fellas." He took one look at Ted's bloody nose and whipped around to Isaac. "Whoa, hey now. Pearce. Principal's office. *Now.*"

Isaac didn't move, but waited calmly for Ted to recover. Possibly to retaliate. Isaac's hands weren't even balled into fists anymore, but he looked ready to strike again.

"You're a dead man, Pearce," Ted said, shoving his friends' helping hands off of him. "I'm sick of your bullshit, walking around like you own the goddamn place."

"That's enough, Mr. Bowers," Mr. Tyler said, holding his arms out between the two guys. "Isaac. *Go.*"

In no rush, Isaac cracked his neck, leaving no doubt who really owned the hallways at George Mason. Girls stared at Isaac as he shouldered his backpack and glanced down at me a final time before turning and heading to the principal's office.

"Enjoy your suspension, asshole," Ted called after him, trying in vain to regain the upper hand.

The crowd dispersed and it was clear that the murmurs and whispers weren't about Ted's bravery for taking on Isaac. Ted realized it too and tore out of his friends' grasp and wiped his bloody nose on his sleeve before stalking down the hall.

"And that, ladies and gents," Angie said, "is why you don't fuck with Isaac Pearce."

I turned to her. "Will he get suspended?"

She shrugged. "Wouldn't be the first time. Though I've never seen him defend a girl's honor before. That's new."

Angie watched my gaze linger to where Isaac had gone. "Hey. For real, girl. You like him? Because…" Her words trailed off and she shook her head.

"I'm not interested in him like that," I said. "And even if I were…"

"Yeah?"

"Nothing."

"You sure?" Her face melted into concern. "Is there something you want to talk about? I keep getting this vibe…"

I bit the inside of my cheek. "No. There's nothing."

Nothing I could tell her with my own voice and words. The odds I'd actually get a role in *Hamlet*, never mind Ophelia, were slim to none. But I had to turn the nothing into *something* before I flickered out for good.

Chapter Eight

Isaac

"Well, Isaac?" Mr. Dillings, the principal, leaned back in his chair, fingertips drumming his chest. "As an educator, I'm not in the habit of encouraging students to forgo finishing the year and taking the GED…but aren't we about done here?"

I met his gaze without blinking. It wasn't the first time we'd had this discussion. When I turned eighteen in the middle of my junior year—and gotten in a fistfight with three members of Ted Bowers' crew—Dillings proposed the GED. I could've gotten a full-time job to help pay the bills with Pops, and the humiliation of being held back would've disappeared with me.

But the GED wasn't the same as graduating. It screamed "dropout." Anyway, I *wanted* an education. My mother's death had tossed me out of the stream of life to flounder and gasp like a fish out of water. I'd climbed back in with hopes of having a little piece of a normal life. Instead, poverty, a drunk for a dad, and being held back a year all compounded until acting was the only thing protecting me. Acting onstage to exorcise the demons that screamed in my heart. Acting like a criminal at school to keep from being torn to pieces.

My mother wanted me to finish school.

Stay in school, baby, she said, over and over. *This world will try to take things away from you, but it can never take your mind or what you put in it.*

I wanted to quit a thousand times, but her words kept me going. And I wanted to set a good example for Benny. What would it say to him if I became a dropout?

"It's time, isn't it?" Mr. Dillings said. "Only six months to graduation. You can still walk with the seniors if it's important…" His words trailed off, leaving the truth dangling between us: *We don't want you here anymore.*

"Yeah," I said, standing up. "I'm done."

Dillings eased a sigh of relief and rose with me. He straightened his cheap suit jacket. "I think it's best. You're a bright young man with a brilliant talent. I have no doubt—"

I walked out and shut the door, cutting off whatever piece of life advice he'd been about to lay on me.

The hallways were empty. No one saw me as I walked out of George Mason High, leaving all my shit in my locker, and crossed the parking lot to my Dodge. I started the engine but let it idle, not knowing which direction to go, which road to take.

Pops would expect me to work at our dying business, but there was no money there. I doubted Martin could afford a full-time guy at the theater. I could probably work for an auto shop in Braxton, make some decent money to grow my pathetic savings account…

I glanced back at George Mason.

"So fucking what?" I said, as if speaking the words could solidify them in my heart. "There's nothing at that school I give a shit about."

Willow Holloway…

Of course, a beautiful girl like that shows up three days before I get kicked out. I didn't know her and she didn't know me, but she was the first bright thing in my shitty world outside of the stage. There was never going to be anything there, but I'd started to look forward to sitting next to her in English class. To smell the sweetness of her perfume and watch the soft fall of her hair over her shoulders. My eyes followed her everywhere, and they immediately saw how Ted and his gang scared her shitless.

Fucking Ted Bowers. He'd looked at Willow like she was a meal he was going to devour. Was *entitled* to devour. I'd wanted to slug his obscene smile but I restrained myself until Ted made a comment about my mom and my control snapped.

I lit a cigarette and flexed my aching knuckles. Getting kicked out school made me feel like shit. But I punched Ted Bowers for both my mother and Willow Holloway, and that made it bearable.

I put the truck in drive and tore out of the parking lot.

Back at the trailer, I parked in the yard but didn't get out. The idea of going inside and confronting Pops made me so goddamn weary. He'd been bitching at me to quit school and work more, but getting kicked out was just going to give him an excuse to vent his bottomless well of rage.

Instead of heading inside, I walked over dirty snow and slush toward the eastern edge of the property. At the semi truck tire, I tapped a fresh pack of Winstons on the heel of my hand. A low voice stopped me. It was only nine in the morning but Benny was under the overturned truck, rapping in a soft, sing-song tone under his breath.

I tucked the cigarettes away and whistled. Benny peeked out from under the truck, and took the earbuds out of his ears, his eyes widening.

"Yo, Isaac. What are you doing here?"

"I could ask you the same." I fixed him a hard look. "Why aren't you in school?"

He stared right back. "Why aren't you?"

I jammed my freezing fingers into the pockets of my jacket. "I'm done. I'm going to take the GED instead."

Benny came out from under the truck. "You're dropping out."

"I'm nineteen," I said. "I'm an adult. It's the right thing to do. You, on the other hand, are ditching and could get your mom in trouble for truancy."

He scowled, but I saw the guilt in his eyes. "I didn't feel like going." He tugged at the hem of the jacket I'd gotten for him. "When you got no money, you can get ragged for wearing new stuff as much as for old stuff."

"Uh huh. You do this a lot?"

"No."

"That the truth?"

"It's the truth," he said, and I believed him. It was our thing—me and this thirteen-year-old kid and our weird friendship. We were honest with each other, no matter what.

I took a seat on the semi-truck tire. Benny sat beside me.

"So what happened?" he asked.

"I punched a guy."

Benny's dark eyes widened to show the whites. "You did? Who? Why?"

"Some asshole was giving a new girl a hard time."

"Ohh, a girl?" He nudged my arm.

"Yeah. There are girls at GM."

"Who is she? What's her name?"

"Doesn't matter. Probably not going to see her again. Or maybe I will…" I trailed off, remembering how Willow sat up straighter at Paulson's announcement about *Hamlet* auditions, like someone had called her name.

"You want to see her," Benny said, grinning. "You want to baaaaad. You like her."

I shoved him with an elbow. "How the hell you figure that?"

"You got kicked out of school for her, for one thing," he said. "For another, your face just got all soft and mushy."

"It did not," I said.

"What's her name?"

"Willow."

He wrinkled his nose. "That's the whitest white girl name I ever heard."

I chuckled. "She's super rich too. And young."

And completely off limits.

My smiled faded. "Why the fuck am I talking about her with you? You need to get your ass to school. Tomorrow, and the day after that. I'm going to be around more to make sure."

Benny rolled his eyes. "Okay, okay."

A silence fell.

"You going to miss school?" he asked.

"No." I glanced at him sideways. "Yes. Some of it."

"Yeah?"

I nodded. My hands twitched for a Winston. Benny knew I smoked, but I kept it away from him.

"What part?" he asked. "'Cuz I can't think of nothing I'd miss."

"You'd miss doing kid stuff. Being in a club after school or doing sports with friends. Going to dances."

"Yeah, I guess," Benny said.

"I'm not going to be hanging around all day doing nothing. I have to work now." I tugged his sleeve. "And you have to go to school. Right now. I'll drive you."

"No way. They'll call Ma at her work. I don't have a note."

"I'll write you one." I stood up. "Come on. It's cold out."

He sighed and dramatically hauled himself off the tire. "Hey, is your dad going to be pissed about you leaving school?"

"Probably."

"Will he try to beat on you?"

"Maybe."

"Isaac." Benny stopped walking and looked up at me fearfully. "You're going to leave Harmony soon."

Honesty. Both onstage and with Benny. These were the talismans I held onto.

"Yeah," I said. "I am."

Benny swallowed hard, swiped a hand over his eyes, and then nodded. "Good."

Chapter Nine

Willow

That afternoon, Angie helped me pore through plays and books of audition monologues. While she searched, I flipped through *Hamlet* itself, scanning Ophelia's scenes. The words were English, yet I needed a translator. What the hell was Shakespeare *saying?* I couldn't connect to anything in Ophelia's lines.

"Focus," Angie said, pulling the play away from me. "You can't audition for *Hamlet* with *Hamlet*. It's bad form. Find another Shakespeare monologue to show you can handle him."

"I can't *handle* him at all," I said. "I don't know what the hell I'm doing or what this play is even about."

Angie took on a fake Spanish accent. "Let me e'splain. No, there is too much. Let me sum up: Hamlet's the prince of Denmark. His dad, the king, died and though it's only been two months, his mom married his dad's brother, Claudius. Now Claudius is king. Hamlet thinks that's whack."

"Sounds just like Shakespeare."

"One night, three guards see a ghost and they tell Ham. Ham sees it too. It's Dad. Dad says Claudius poured poison in his ear and killed him. Hamlet's mind is blown. But hold up, he's been dating Ophelia, daughter of Polonius. Polonius is Claudius' right-hand man. Polonius tells Ophelia that Hamlet's losing his marbles and she has to break up with him.

"Ophelia and Hamlet are in love but, like, the fucking *patriarchy*, right? She caves to the pressure and agrees to break up with him. Ham's devastated and rants that all women are traitorous bitches, and Ophelia should go to a nunnery and never reproduce. Then Ham confronts his mom while Polonius eavesdrops and—whoops!—Hamlet kills Polonius.

"Ophelia, having lost her man *and* her dad, proceeds to lose her mind. She goes nuts, sings a bunch of dirty, sexy-time songs, and drowns herself in the river. Then a bunch of other shit happens until pretty much everyone else in the cast is dead. Curtain." Angie sucked in a breath, her smile bright. "Got all that?"

I stared a moment, then begun a slow clap. "Angie, I can't even..."

"I know," she said, laughing. "I amaze myself sometimes."

Even with Angie's verbal Spark Notes, Shakespeare still looked like a foreign language. I was certain to crash and burn if I tried to audition with one of his monologues.

I was ready to scrap the whole endeavor for the millionth time when I read a synopsis for a play called *The Woolgatherer.* The lead characters were Rose, a shy young woman and recluse, and Cliff, the lonely truck driver she brings home one night.

Tears stung my eyes when I read Rose's climactic monologue, a recollection of a night at the zoo. She went there to watch the elegant cranes stand in the still, dark water. A group of rowdy boys came through the zoo one night, blaring music and talking loudly. They threw rocks at the birds, breaking their legs and killing them while Rose screamed and screamed...

I read it again. Then once more, my heart aching.

I had my audition piece.

Dinner silverware clinked against dishes. Dad held a fork in one hand, his phone in the other. Mom picked at her soufflé, then exchanged her fork for the wine bottle and poured herself a third glass. I ate more of my dinner than usual. I couldn't remember the last time I felt this hungry, not just for food but for the days ahead. I had something to look forward to, even if it were only making a fool of myself in front of the director of the HCT.

But I'm going to try. That's something.

I smiled a little, thinking Grandma would be pleased. For the first time since X marked the spot, I wasn't sitting in a block of ice, merely trying to get through dinner so I could make a half-ass attempt at my homework, then curl up on the floor of my room in my comforter and hope for a decent night's sleep.

"So, I decided what I'm going to do for an after-school activity."

My parents' heads shot up with comical sameness.

"Really?" My dad chewed his food slowly and swallowed. "This is encouraging."

"A tad too late," Mom muttered. "College deadlines for the best schools have come and gone. The best she can do is community college—God help me—and try for a spring enrollment."

"What's so terrible about community college?" I asked. "Besides, I'm not sure I want to go to college in the first place."

She looked stricken. "Of course you have to go to college. Why wouldn't you go to college?"

"Regina," Dad said in a warning tone. He looked at me. "We can talk about college later. First, tell us what you've decided to do. Debate? You were always quite good at debate."

"I'm going to audition for the play at the HCT."

My Dad stared harder, his jaw working in a way that meant he had a lot to say on the matter, though I couldn't imagine what.

Mom sniffed as if smelling something distasteful. "Acting?"

"Yes."

My father slowly chewed a bite of green beans almondine from side to side, then wiped his mouth with a napkin. "Hmm. That's not exactly…academic."

"It's what I want to do," I said.

"*Why?*" Mom asked, as if I'd said I wanted to join a circus.

"I just told you why," I said. "As an after-school activity."

My father held my gaze with his hardest stare. "It's not because of that boy, is it?"

I froze.

He knows. He knows about X. And the party. And what

happened...

Mom gaped between us. "What boy? Who...?"

My dad set his napkin down, my petrified silence seeming to confirm for him the truth of everything he was about to say.

"A fellow at the office has a daughter at George Mason. When he found out I did too, he gave me an earful about a boy named Isaac Pearce."

A sigh of relief loosened my tensed limbs and I sagged in my chair a moment. Then indignation flared through me, making my hands strangle my napkin under the table. My father, who would've been hard-pressed to name a single one of my friends from New York, now pin-pointed Isaac Pearce. Why should he interfere in my life now when it was too late? Why the fuck didn't someone at his office give him an earful about Xavier Wilkinson?

"Who is Isaac Pearce?" Mom demanded.

"He's a guy at school," I said. "I hardly know him—"

"Gary Vance, my coworker, says Isaac's a senior, but much older than the kids. He was held back a grade and there's talk about some trouble with the law—"

"He was held back because his mother *died* and he stopped talking for a year," I snapped. "You make it sound like he's a moron or a degenerate. He's neither."

My father pursed his lips, and nodded to himself, as if I'd just confirmed his worst suspicions. "Gary says he lives with his alcoholic father in a trailer in a junkyard, and worse—his father is one of our franchise owners. Gary says his station is a disgrace."

My mother's hand flew to her throat. "Jesus, Willow."

"What?" I gaped at my father's smug expression. "Judgmental much? So he's not rich off dirty oil money like we are, so what?"

"Dirty," my mother said with a sniff. "Who's being judgmental now?"

"Business aspects aside, the boy has a reputation," Dad said, as if he were the official Pearce Family Historian. "Apparently, he's something of an actor. He does plays at the community theater."

He deals drugs to small children, would've sounded the same in my dad's mouth.

Mom whirled on me. "Is that why you want to act? To follow this boy around?"

"That's the first thing you think of?" I cried. "Guess what? Isaac Pearce isn't a criminal. He happened to defend me today from some meathead jock, and even so, *even so...*" I was shouting over their knowing looks now. "He's not why I'm auditioning. Jesus, give me some fucking credit, why don't you. You wanted me to do something, so here I am, doing something."

"You watch your language," Dad said, his voice hardening. "And let's keep in mind you've never acted a day in your life. Suddenly you want to be on stage in front of the entire town?"

"Is *Isaac Pearce* going to audition too?" Mom asked, saying his name like it was a dirty word.

"Yes," I said, fighting to control my anger. "Probably he'll get the lead because he's brilliant. And back to the point, I probably *won't* get a part. Because, quote, *I've never acted a day in my life.* So just forget I said anything."

"We don't want you hanging around boys like him," Mom said, deaf to everything I'd just said. "We came here so you could get a fresh start, but of course, you immediately latch on to the worst elements—"

"Oh my God," I said, rolling my eyes. "Do you hear how ridiculous you sound? Assholes come in all shapes and sizes, Mom. City or country. Poor and rich, alike."

Sons of CEOs especially.

"And I'm not *latching on* to anyone. I'm trying to…"

Find myself in the dark.

Dad and Mom exchanged glances in which she silently pleaded with him to put a stop to this. Dad folded his napkin on the table in his signature I've-just-made-a-decision-move. "I'm not going to forbid you to audition if you think you want to. But no matter what happens," he said, "at the theater or at school, you're to keep your relationship with that Pearce boy strictly professional. He's legally an adult. You're seventeen-years-old. Do you understand what that means?"

"It doesn't mean anything," I heard myself say aloud. "Jesus, you're a worse gossip than the kids at school."

I inwardly cringed when I thought what would happen when Dad's informant told him that Isaac had been suspended for punching Ted Bowers. My parents held no moral authority over me; one of the many things I'd ceased to care about after X was done with me. But he could make things hard if by some miracle I got a role in *Hamlet*.

I lightened my voice. "It's not a big deal," I said. "I'm auditioning because I want to try something new. It has nothing to do with any guy."

"Let's hope not," Mom said. "It's not as if this town has a plethora of good families to begin with."

"For God's sake, Regina," Dad said. "Have you looked out the window? You live on a street of houses just as big and beautiful as ours."

"There's New York City well-to-do, and then there's country-well-to-do," Mom said, putting her wine glass to her lips. "There's a difference and you know it."

"So you're biased against the entire state of Indiana," I said. "And Dad's biased against a poor guy who lives in a trailer. Congratulations, you're both equally shallow." I stood up, gathering my plate. "And I've lost my appetite."

I'd never spoken this way to my parents. Ever. Yet I ignored Mom's gasp at my rudeness and ignored Dad's hollered order to sit back down. I stomped to the kitchen and dumped my dish in the sink.

Then I felt like shit.

I sighed. If things were different, I'd have been just as snotty and prejudiced about Indiana as Mom. No question. I was a Manhattan girl, born and bred. The old me would've looked down her nose at George Mason and made up her mind about everyone in it, before stepping one foot in the place.

X changed all that. You can't look down on anyone when your own self-worth is ground into the dirt, shattered into pieces, and then pissed on.

I *liked* Harmony. I liked Angie and her friends. I liked Isaac for standing up for me today at school and for the possibilities he'd shown me with *Oedipus*. After months of frozen apathy, caring about anything or anyone was like holding something fragile. I had to protect it before it slipped out of my hands and shattered too.

I went back to the dining room. "I'm sorry I spoke to you that way. I promise I'm not auditioning because of any boy, but because I want to. May I be excused to go upstairs and do my homework?"

My parents stared.

"Homework?" Mom said. "This is the first we've heard you say the word—"

"Yes." Dad said, cutting her off. "But another outburst like that and there will be no play. Understood?"

"Understood."

And I did. My dad had zero control over his work under Ross Wilkinson but in our house, he was the boss, ruling with an iron-clad fist that hadn't bothered me before, because I'd always fallen in line. Daddy's little girl.

Xavier X'd that out too.

I hurried upstairs. Behind my locked door, I dug the photocopied *Woolgatherer* monologue out of my backpack. I read the words over and over, losing myself in Rose's world. Letting her words be mine.

It was easy.

They gave Rose a needle to make her stop screaming. She screamed on the outside the way I screamed on the inside. On and on, all day long, every day, screaming from somewhere way down deep. Screaming like vomiting. Screaming until the sound exploded my bones. Mustering the courage to look into the mirror and being shocked I was still in one piece. I'd read books about people going fucking crazy. How was I still doing this one-foot-in-front-of-the other bullshit?

You still burn, Grandma whispered.

I grabbed my laptop and opened it, punched in the URL for the Harmony Community Theater. The site loaded to a flattering shot of the brick building under a blue, cloudless summer sky. Photo stills of the latest show, *Oedipus Rex,* were posted below, almost all of them showing Isaac Pearce, bearded and bloody, his naked emotions spilling out of the screen.

At the bottom of the page was an audition sign-up sheet for *Hamlet.* I typed in my name and contact info and hit *send.*

Chapter Ten

Willow

Two weeks later, Angie dropped me off at the audition.

"Looks packed," I said, staring out the passenger side window at the crowd in front of HCT.

"*Hamlet*'s a big play," she said. "They need to cast lots of gravediggers and guards and traveling jesters." She nudged my arm. "Break a leg."

"Thanks," I said, my mouth bone-dry. "I'll meet you at The Scoop when I'm done."

"I'll have chocolate waiting."

The theater lobby was bustling with auditioners, college age to seniors. I recognized a few people from Harmony, as well as a few college students I didn't. I spied a couple of older girls hanging out together, talking with their heads bent. Ophelia wannabes, maybe. They gave me a shared glance and turned their backs.

A middle-aged woman with dark hair in a loose bun was behind the sign-in table. She peered at me through thick-rimmed glasses. "Name?"

"Willow Holloway," I said, my heart pounding.

She made a check mark on her list. "And what role are you reading for?"

"Ophelia. Where are the auditions being held?"

"Through there," she said, jerking her thumb at the main theater entrance.

"We're all auditioning together? Onstage?"

"Correct."

"We're not being called in a room to read alone? For the director only?"

"Mr. Ford doesn't do it that way," she said, her expression placid. "He likes to keep things open and transparent. Break a leg. Next?"

I stepped inside the theater and saw the seats were two-thirds full with prospective *Hamlet* cast members.

Holy shitballs.

I nearly turned around and walked back out. No way I could perform my monologue in front of all these people. I couldn't even do it in front of Angie, no matter how many times she'd pestered me over the last few weeks.

If you can't perform a monologue in front of people, how can you perform an entire play?

"I can't," I whispered behind my teeth. "This is stupid. I shouldn't be here."

Yet I forced myself into a seat in the back row, near the door. This dumb audition was my best and only plan to dispel the darkness or crack the ice around me. Doing nothing hadn't worked. I had to try.

And if I humiliate myself, so be it.

I closed my eyes and thought about the opening words to my monologue.

I couldn't remember them.

I opened my eyes, heart now crashing in my chest. The director, Martin Ford, was setting himself up onstage. I recognized him from the HCT website. A lanky guy with flyaway hair and large eyes. He looked friendly. Welcoming. I still felt like I was going to puke.

My eyes darted around, searching the crowd for anyone who looked as nervous as I was.

My gaze landed on Isaac Pearce.

He stood against the back wall, alone, hands jammed inside the pockets of his leather jacket. Instead of nervous, he looked bored, like he was waiting for the bus. His handsome, chiseled face was expressionless. Then it turned toward me and stared. A flicker of disbelief, as if he couldn't believe I was there. Then he blinked and his gaze darted away.

"I see you, Isaac Pearce," I muttered under my breath. "Time to share your wisdom with the newbie."

I got up and went toward the back of the theater. As I came closer, his stormy eyes flared with surprise before shifting back to neutral.

Holy God, he's beautiful.

Looking at Isaac Pearce was like window-shopping: sighing over something you desperately wanted but couldn't afford. And yet...the impossibility of my being with him—or any guy—made it easier to be bold.

"Hi," I said.

"Hey," he replied, looking straight ahead.

"I don't think we've officially met. I'm Willow."

He glanced at me, then away. "Isaac."

"So." I put my back against the wall, mirroring his stance. "Last time I saw you, you were punching that asshole, Ted Bowers."

"Sounds about right."

"That was two weeks ago." I lowered my voice. "The rumor mill says you were kicked out."

He shifted against the wall. "I left. My decision."

"You weren't expelled for punching Ted?"

He glanced down at me. "Does it matter?"

"I guess not. Anyway, I'm sorry."

"For what?"

"Ted was getting all up in my space and you made him back off. I feel a little responsible."

Isaac shrugged. "No big deal."

"It was to me," I said. "I've been wanting to thank you."

"Okay."

I blinked. "So...Thanks."

"Sure."

I sniffed a laugh. "Has anyone told you that you talk too much?"

His gaze slid to me slowly. "No."

The blood drained from my face as I remembered why Isaac had been held back for a year.

"I'm sorry. Bad joke. I'm just nervous as hell."

"So am I."

I glanced up at him, eyes narrowed. "Yeah, right. You look calm as…something really calm."

His lips twitched again. "It's all an act."

"*Groan*," I said, and laughed.

So Mr. Pearce, you have a sense of humor.

"Thanks, I needed that." I heaved a shaky breath. "I wasn't expecting us to audition in front of each other. I thought we'd be in a room alone, not in front of a firing squad."

"Martin likes to keep things open," Isaac said.

"So I've heard. You've worked with him a lot, yes?"

He nodded.

I bit my lip. Under normal circumstances, his reticence would've chased me off. Tonight, my nerves jangled so hard they loosened my jaw, and I couldn't *stop* talking.

"I saw you in *Oedipus* last month," I said.

"Mm."

"You probably hear this constantly, but you were incredible."

His sigh sounded irritated, as if he'd expected better from me. "Thanks."

"You do hear that a lot, I suppose," I said. "One more compliment just bounces off of you, right?"

"I said *thanks*."

He doesn't want to hear it. Shut up.

"How about this?" I squared my shoulders to him. "Watching you act was like looking through a doorway into another world. A place where extraordinary things happen. I got to escape by watching you. So instead of a general compliment, I want to thank you for taking me somewhere else for a couple hours. I needed it." The last words wobbled in my throat. I blinked hard, my eyes suddenly stinging with tears. "Is that better?"

He looked down at me. I felt him in my cells. A connection. A piece of his power or magic or charisma directed entirely at me. As the moment held and wavered, I wondered what it would be like onstage with him, wrapped entirely in that energy. Going somewhere together.

Impossible, I thought and looked away, breaking the moment. *He's a genius. I'm less than an amateur.*

Isaac's deep voice cut into my thoughts. "Thank you."

Two slow words. Nothing more. Yet they seem to say

everything. Now when I looked up, his angular face had softened and the storm behind his gray-green eyes was calmer. I stared, trapped in his gaze once again, wrapped in that energy.

"You're welcome," I said.

Martin Ford called the group's attention and asked everyone to find their seats. Without a word, Isaac and I pushed off the wall and moved toward the rows of worn, red velvet chairs. He stood in the aisle and gestured me in, as if he were holding a door open for me. I shrugged out of my jacket, and we sat side by side, his elbow resting on the armrest between us, his shoulder inches from mine. Unlike when Ted Bowers was in my space, I felt none of the suffocating tension being this close to Isaac. The scent of cigarette smoke and masculine shower soap wafted over me, and my rampaging nerves were calmed.

Martin Ford strode into a yellow circle of light on the stage, His gray hair stood up slightly in places, and his shirtsleeves were rolled up to his elbows. His smile was friendly and reassuring, but his voice was all business.

"Thank you all for being here. I'm so pleased to see such a turnout. When I call your name, please step to the center of the stage, introduce yourself and tell us the monologue you'll be performing. We'll give no feedback tonight. Callbacks will be sent by email tomorrow morning. Anyone called back will be expected to be here tomorrow night, same time. If you can't make it, you'll forfeit any spot you might've had in the show. Similarly, if you cannot commit to the rehearsal schedule posted on the website, you won't be considered for a role." He clapped his hands together. "Enough with the boring technicalities. Let's get started."

I expected alphabetical order. Or perhaps a system of seniority with the veteran actors going first. Instead, names were called at random, with unknowns following people I'd seen in *Oedipus.* The woman who played Jocasta performed a riveting monologue from *King Lear.* Another man performed a piece from *Midsummer Night's Dream.* A female college student auditioned with Juliet's "What is a name?" speech from *Romeo and Juliet.*

I leaned in to Isaac. "Did I miss the memo that said we had to audition with Shakespeare?"

The barest flicker of a smile touched Isaac's lips, but before he could answer, Martin Ford called his name.

The entire theatre craned to look back, like a spotlight trained on him the entire time it took him to stand and walk down to the stage. There, the actual light spilled over him, glinting gold in his brown hair. His hands were still in his jacket pockets and I wondered if he was going to act like that. A prizefighter tying one arm behind his back to give everyone else a chance.

"I'm Isaac Pearce." He turned his head in my direction. "My monologue is from *A Streetcar Named Desire*."

I let out a slow breath of relief.

Not Shakespeare. Thank you.

My inhaled relief reversed in a shocked gasp as Isaac tore his hands from his pockets. His face morphed from neutral to arrogant rage so quickly, I had to blink to remind my eyes they were seeing the same man. One of his hands balled into a fist, the other jabbed accusingly at the air above the audience's head as he began his monologue.

I watched, riveted, as he stalked the stage like a predatory animal. He tore off his jacket and flung it to the ground as if it were holding him back. He wore nothing but a white wife-beater underneath and the sight of his body clothed in that tight scrap of cotton stirred something in me that I thought had been suffocated to death.

Light filled in the lines of his muscles. A tattoo darkened his right bicep. Another on the inside of his left forearm. Skin and bone and power, stripped bare under the stage lights. Isaac turned inside-out, acting from the depths of his soul, with every atom in his body, every muscle, every sinew. He thundered that he was the "King around here" and everyone in that damn audience, including me, believed him.

When the words ended, the passion flowing out of Isaac shut off like a faucet. A brief bow, a muttered thanks, and he grabbed his jacket. He strode offstage, back up the aisle to reclaim his seat next to me.

His body was calm, yet it crackled a little. I could sense the last vestiges of his energy dissipating like steam. I stared as he laid his jacket over his knees. Stared at the bare bicep that was inches from me.

He kept looking straight ahead, then finally glanced at me.

"What?"

"Sorry," I whispered back. "Can't hear you over the ghost of Marlon Brando crying his eyes out."

A tiny smile crooked Isaac's lips. Twice I'd made him smile now. Come to think of it, the only other time I'd seen him smile was taking his bows after *Oedipus*.

"Willow Holloway?"

I froze.

You've got to be fucking kidding me. I have to follow that?

I swallowed the lump of raw nerves in my throat and started to rise to my feet.

"Any last words of advice?" I whispered.

I wasn't expecting an answer and so had kept moving out of my seat, but Isaac's hand wrapped around my arm, gently but firmly holding me back. A jolt of electricity rocketing through me again, settling warm in my belly. His hand was warm through my sleeve, and instead of feeling trapped, my nerves were growing quiet under his touch.

"Don't think about the words," Isaac said. "Even if you fuck up or forget the lines, keep going." He let go of my arm. "Just tell the story."

Martin called my name again, and the audience started to look around for me. My eyes still held in Isaac's.

"Tell the story," I whispered. "Thanks."

He nodded, and his gray-green eyes flicked toward the stage. *Go.*

I reluctantly broke away and walked down the aisle between the seats.

Tell the story.

That's exactly what I didn't do. I never did. I never could.

I took the three stairs to the stage and stood under the spotlight. Martin Ford, his stage manager, and the assistant director—the woman with the thick glasses who'd been signing us in—sat behind a table facing me. Behind them, the audience blurred into a sea of faceless spectators.

My own nervousness came roaring back on that stage with so many people watching me, rattling along my limbs, making my left leg tremble.

Fuck it, my character Rose was a nervous gal. I'd use the fear instead of fighting it.

"Hi, I'm Willow Holloway. I'll be performing a monologue from William Mastrosimone's *The Woolgatherer*."

I bowed my head, took another breath and when I raised it again, I stopped pretending I knew how to act. I forgot about the "scene beats" and "breath technique" from the acting book I'd grabbed at the library. I took off the invisible jacket that was Willow and did what Isaac said.

I just told the story.

I told the audience my favorite thing was to sneak to the zoo at night and watch the elegant cranes stand in the still water. I put myself there, with the birds and their gentle quiet. My heart pounded as the loud boys with loud music came and threw rocks at the birds. I watched in horror as the birds' legs "bent like straws", and I shouted to make it stop, but the boys couldn't hear me. They kept throwing rocks and tears streamed down my cheeks as I told the story of blood staining white feathers—

(*blood on my white sheets*)

—red, and of dark water growing still and quiet.

I told the story of how I ran to get the guard but when I came back it was too late. They were all dead. I told how I'd screamed and screamed—

(*X threw the stone of his body against mine, and I broke, while inside I screamed and screamed*)

—and didn't stop until they took me away, stuck a needle in my arm and then I slept.

I finished the story of how they never caught the gang, my voice trembling in Rose's soft, shy lilt, and how even if they did, it wouldn't make the birds come alive again.

(*I never told anyone because it won't make me come alive again.*)

Silence. I came back to myself, on that stage. I wiped my cheek and bowed my head to show the monologue was over, and when I looked up, they were all staring at me, mouths agape.

"Okay…thanks," I said.

I hurried off the stage, not looking at anything but the nearest way out. I pushed through the side emergency exit, into the cold, bracing air.

I did it.

I didn't care whether I got the part or not. All that mattered was that for the first time, I'd told the truth. Cloaked in other words, but still my truth.

I slumped against the wall. Tears streaked my cheeks and I couldn't tell if they were mine or Rose's.

Maybe it didn't matter.

Chapter Eleven

Isaac

Holy shit.

Willow exited the theater, her long hair flying behind her. I grabbed her forgotten coat and hat and got out of my seat. My goddamn legs felt weak as I shouldered out the front of the theater and circled around to the back. I wanted a cigarette and she'd want her coat. She was probably freezing out here.

Not that I care.

I could practically see Martin rolling his eyes at that line delivery and telling me to try again.

I found Willow in the narrow alley between the theater and Nicky's Tavern, leaning against a wall. Shoulders rising and falling and clouds of breath around her head. Her eyes widened when she saw me, and she wiped her sleeve over her face.

"What do you want?" she said. She hugged her elbows, not looking at me. Her body shivered in jeans and a soft pink sweater.

"You left these." I held out her coat—heavy, expensive wool—and her pink knit hat.

"Oh. Thanks."

I turned to go.

"Wait a sec." She drew on her coat and hat. "Thanks for the advice. It worked. I wasn't expecting what happened up there. Or maybe I was," she added, almost to herself. "Maybe it was exactly what was supposed to happen, but I wasn't... I wasn't ready for it."

"I get it," I said. "You mind if I smoke?"

She shook her head. I lit a smoke and the flame from my lighter lit up the side alley where we stood. The only other light came from the tavern next door. I took a drag and exhaled, struggling to find words.

"You okay?" I finally asked.

"Yeah. Just...took me by surprise."

I nodded. "You were..." *Powerful and raw and fucking real.* "...Good."

I winced at the flimsy, pathetic word. She deserved better feedback. But it was either tell her, *You shook me to the bone in a way I've never felt before and I couldn't take my eyes off you.* Or tell her, *You were good.* Nothing in between.

"Thanks," she said. She shivered, even though her coat was buttoned up now. "I should go."

I moved out of the way to let her pass, suddenly aware I was a virtual stranger cornering her in a dark alley.

She started past me, then stopped.

"Is that why you do it?"

"Do what?"

"Save all your words for the stage?"

I stared.

"Because it's a catharsis, isn't it?" she said. "It's telling your story without really telling it."

What story lay behind the one you told tonight? I wanted to ask. But whatever subtext Willow'd been operating off of to give us that performance, it wasn't a story for a casual talk behind an old theater. Or for me. Still, I wanted to tell her something of my truth too. Give something back.

Forget it. Also not for casual talk behind a theater.

I stuck my cigarette between my lips to keep from saying more than "Yeah, I guess."

"Is that why you don't talk much?"

"Maybe," I said, taking another drag, "Or maybe I just have nothing to say."

"I doubt it," she said. "But I get it too."

"You're going to get Ophelia," I said.

"Really?" Her eyes lit up, and right then, she was beautiful with the hope radiating off her. Rays that bounced off me, filling my head with possibility. If she were Ophelia, I'd spend the next two months rehearsing with her. *Acting* with her. Having this untouchable beauty on *my* stage.

And that was too much hope for a poor bastard like me.

"Yeah, you might get the part," I said, putting a hard edge in my voice. "But one monologue isn't the same as an entire Shakespeare play. You'll have to show up to every damn rehearsal. You'll have to take it *seriously*. Because it might've been a whim or something for you, but it's fucking important to me."

She bristled a little, her chin thrusting out. "It's not a whim," she said, an edge in her own words. "It's important to me, too. And cocky much? What makes you so sure you're going to get a part?"

My edge crumbled and I laughed around my Winston. The ugly yellow light from Nicky's Tavern turned Willow's hair to gold. The urge to bury my hands in that hair was so strong, I had to take another drag.

"I'll get it because there's no one else Martin will trust with it."

"That's not the only reason," Willow said. "You have to know how good you are."

I sighed and chucked my cigarette down and ground it out with my heel.

She cocked her head. "You don't want to talk about that either?"

"No, because it's boring. It is what it is. Acting is how I'm going to get the fuck out of Harmony. Beyond that?" I held up my hands.

"Oh," she said, her face falling. "You want to leave?"

I peered at her curiously. "You want to *stay*?"

She shrugged, rubbed her chin with her shoulder. "I don't know. Maybe. I like it better than I thought I would. It's quiet here. Peaceful."

"There's nothing for me here."

"No, I suppose not," she said. "Your talent is too big for this little town."

I'm counting on it. It's all I have.

A silence fell, and then she said, "Okay, well. I'm supposed to meet a friend. Mr. Ford will tell us what comes next?"

"He'll email the callback list," I said. "You'll need to be back here tomorrow night at seven."

"If I get called back."

I smirked. "See you tomorrow night, Willow."

"See you tomorrow night, Isaac," she said. "If *you* get called back."

I smothered the chuckle that bubbled up my chest, watching until Willow got to the street safely. Then I pushed off the wall and walked out of the alley, away from the theater. Away from my real home. It was good practice for when I left Harmony for good. I'd walk away from all the shit memories. My mother's ghost and my father's rage. The poverty and the cold and the constant hunger for something more than I had. I'd leave it behind and never look back.

Willow could stay here if she wanted. More power to her.

I'd walk away from her, too.

Chapter Twelve

Willow

Getting ready for school Monday morning, I stopped to read the email on my phone for the hundredth time since it arrived on Saturday morning.

<martinford@HCT.com >
Date: January 28th
Re: Hamlet, Final Cast List

Congratulations and thank you for being a part of the Harmony Community Theater's production of Shakespeare's Hamlet. *Please find the rehearsal schedule at the bottom of the list, and notify myself or Assistant Director, Rebecca Mills, or Stage Manager, Frank Darian if you have conflicts and can no longer participate.*
Thank you, and I look forward to creating stage magic with you!

Hamlet: Isaac Pearce
Gertrude: Lorraine Embry
Claudius: Len Hostetler
Polonius: Martin Ford
Ophelia: Willow Holloway
Laertes: Justin Baker

Other roles and names scrolled on and on, but my gaze kept stuttering and jumping back up to *Ophelia* and my name across from it.

"Holy shit."

The shock kept slamming me from one side while a flicker of pride burned the other side. I'd been happy with my audition and relieved I didn't embarrass myself during the callbacks, but I still didn't think I'd get the part. Now I had the kind-hearted Martin Ford trusting me with a small but pivotal role in one of Shakespeare's most famous plays. A play that would be performed in front of the entire goddamn town.

"And the school," I muttered. "They'll come to see Isaac…"

My gaze moved up from my name to Isaac's across from Hamlet. Of course, he was playing Hamlet.

And I was playing Ophelia.

Fuck. What the hell were you thinking?

This was too much. Isaac was a genius who deserved to act alongside actual talent. And Martin Ford was a good man just trying to put on a good show. I was a hopeless amateur who'd only auditioned to try to find some relief from my own fucked up situation.

The stupidity of it bowled me over. Then my eyes landed on the bundle of blankets on the floor beside my untouched bed. I'd spent another mostly-sleepless night, breaking in and out of dreams of shadowy weight pressing down on me, crushing the air from my body. My arm was still blackened with X's from my Sharpie.

Doing nothing didn't work. I have to try something else.

"I got the role, didn't I?" I said to the bedcovers. "I can do this."

I just have to tell the story.

I stuffed my phone into my bag and went out.

I took over Isaac's old desk in Mr. Paulson's English class. I told myself it was to be across from Angie. Really, I hated seeing it empty. Hated the daily reminder of how the system had failed Isaac. Literally kicked him out.

"I got the part," I said, sliding into my seat.

Angie's head shot up and she brushed a mess of black curls out of her eyes. Today's sweatshirt read, *I do marathons...on Netflix*.

"Are you serious?" she said. "Ophelia? And you're just now telling me this?"

"Not so loud," I hissed, glancing around at the classroom. Students either had their heads together talking, or their heads on their desks. Mr. Paulson was busy organizing himself. Nobody looked at us.

"When did they tell you?"

"Saturday." I pulled out my phone and called up the email.

"Saturday?" She was practically shrieking. "Two days is like two months by Angie Standard Time. That thing you're holding? It has this cool *text* function you should try."

"I wasn't sure if I was going to go through with it," I said, and handed Angie my phone. "It's crazy, right? I don't know what I'm doing."

Angie used her finger to scroll down the list, a slow grin spreading over her lips.

"Look at you, Miss Thang, acting alongside the great Isaac Pearce."

"Shh, don't say anything. Not around here. The last thing I need is everyone thinking I'm following him around like an idiot."

"Why would they think that?"

"*You* thought that."

"Guilty as charged." She tapped her finger on her teeth. "So why are you doing it? I'm not trying to give you a hard time, I honestly want to know."

I started to blow off her question with a bullshit reason. Instead I shrugged, dropped my gaze. "I had...a rough time last summer and I need a change."

Angie's round, open face was soft with concern. "A change from what?"

From what I've become.

"Nothing, just a change. A fresh start. Since we moved, I figure it's a good time to try something new."

Angie nodded slowly, her dark eyes warm. Then she smiled brightly and went back to the cast list. "I'm proud of you. And I promise to keep it amongst The Greatest, but looky here." She held the phone to face me and pointed to Justin Baker's name. "Your big brother, Laertes, is sitting right over there."

She inclined her head to a blond guy sitting in the front row. His face was turned to profile, talking with Jessica Royce, one of the Plastics. Justin was exceptionally handsome with a tall, baseball player physique clothed in expensive jeans and shoes. The kind of guy the old me would have noticed the first time I'd walked into the classroom, instead of weeks later. That Willow would've taken a seat as close to him as possible and asked him what the homework assignment was, even if I'd already written it down.

He leaned to say something to Jessica, and then they both turned to look at me. I quickly averted my gaze.

"Relax," Angie said. "Why would anyone think you auditioned just to follow Isaac? By that logic, so could Justin." She grinned. "Anyone who asks, tell 'em you did it for Mr. Paulson's extra credit."

The blood drained from my face. "Mr. Paulson..."

Who was at the front of the class now, beaming a smile right at me.

"Happy Monday, folks. Some announcements; so happy to report that our very own Justin Baker and Willow Holloway have both landed roles in the HCT production of Hamlet."

He started clapping his hands, encouraging the others to do the same. Half-hearted applause went around but for Angie who slapped her palms together and let out a *whoop.*

I gritted my teeth. "For real, Angie?"

Mr. Paulson beamed. "You will both be awarded extra credit toward our Poetry and Drama unit this spring." His smile fell. "And if you could please extend congratulations to Mr. Pearce on our behalf, I would appreciate it."

He was looking right at me, and the class saw it. I wanted to slink under my desk, my cheeks burning.

You don't give a shit what anyone thinks, remember?

Only I did. A little. I blamed the thaw in my detachment on Angie. The girl was impossible to dislike and oddly, she'd made me feel normal by doing nothing at all.

I sat up and nodded faintly at Mr. Paulson. Justin craned around and gave me a friendly smile and an inquisitive look, his brows raised.

He was gorgeous—nice eyes, strong jaw.

And while he didn't have the meathead douchebag aura of Ted Bowers, something about him made my stomach tighten instead of tingle with butterflies.

At lunch, I sat with The Greatest People You Will Ever Meet, and they crowed over my casting news.

"Congrats," Jocelyn said, sitting beside Caroline. Their hands were on the table next to each other, not touching but as close as they dared. "Your first time onstage?"

"Shakespeare, straight out the gate," Caroline said when I nodded. "That's not going to be easy."

"Especially on stage with Isaac," Nash said, and winced as Angie elbowed him. "What? I'm just telling the truth. The entire cast is going to have to up their game."

"But Mr. Ford won't let me fail, right?" I asked. "He'll put me out of my misery if I'm in over my head." I looked around. "Right?"

"You're not going to fail, you're going to do great," Angie said. "Won't she?"

The others agreed with enthusiasm, and then we all fell silent as Jessica Royce approached our table with two of the Plastics. She flipped a lock of silky dark hair over her shoulder.

"Hey, Willow. Please pass on to Mr. Pearce our *sincerest* congratulations," she said, echoing Mr. Paulson almost word for word. "And congrats to you too, on getting a part."

"Thanks," I said, trying to channel Isaac's stony expression.

Jessica's smile was wide, but it didn't come anywhere near her eyes. "You have to hand it to her, ladies," she said to her friends. "Some girls would just ask for a guy's phone number. Willow takes it to a whole new level."

The girls tittered and moved on, Jessica twiddling her fingers at me in farewell.

"I thought you said your mean girls weren't so mean," I said.

"We're stale and boring," Nash said. "You're fresh blood."

"I still don't get why my being in the play has anything to do with Isaac."

"Jealousy," Angie said. "The only reason they go *see* the plays is because of him. He never gave anyone here the time of day, but you just scored yourself a front row seat to the Isaac Show."

I rolled my eyes. "For fuck's sake, he's just a guy. Jesus, even my dad gave me an earful."

Angie frowned. "What does he know about it?"

"Some guy he works with has a daughter here. She told him all sorts of shit about Isaac's home life."

"Let me guess, Tessa Vance?" Caroline rolled her eyes. "Her dad works at Wexx. Last year, she got a hold of Isaac's cell phone number and asked him out over a text. He shot her down, and her little brother stole her phone, screenshotted the exchange, and posted it on Facebook."

I froze up at the thought of a guy, however young, using screenshots to humiliate a girl. It hit way too close to home.

"What happened to Tessa?" I said.

"Mass humiliation," Jocelyn said.

"What did Isaac say in the text? Was he a dick to her?"

"Worse," she said. "He wrote, *No, thanks.*"

I blinked, my chest loosening. "That's it?"

Angie nodded. "That's it. And when Tessa asked if he might want to expand on that, he never replied."

"Tessa's been talking shit about Isaac ever since, to recover," Caroline said.

"She's relentless," Nash said. "Always the first one to whisper 'murder' whenever Pearce senior isn't seen around town."

I wrinkled my nose. Apparently country high school bullshit wasn't all that different from city high school bullshit. In a lot of ways, it was worse. My high school in Manhattan was big enough to hide secrets in. Here, you coughed and half the student body heard it.

"Well, whatever," I said, relieved Isaac hadn't been a complete asshole in this scenario. "I'm not in the play to follow Isaac unless he's giving advice. I don't know what I'm doing. And I have no idea how I'm going to get to and from rehearsal every night."

"Your parents can't help?"

"It was like twisting my dad's arm to get him to sign off on the paperwork since I'm a minor. He works late most nights anyway and my mother was never the 'carpool and cupcakes' kind of mom. She's not about to start now."

"I'll help when I can," Angie said, "but you need to learn to drive, girl."

"Or get a ride home with Isaac," Nash said, and caught Angie's pointed stare. "What? I'm being practical."

"What about Justin Baker?" Angie said, jerking her chin to where Justin sat with Doug Keely, Ted Bowers, and couple of other jocks. "Your Laertes."

"He's super-hot," Jocelyn stared and caught Caroline's pointed look. "If you're in to that sort of thing. Which I'm not."

I smiled at the cuteness of the couples in front of me with a wistful kind of ache. I glanced over at Justin Baker and found him watching me. He smiled that friendly, curious smile and I quickly looked away.

"Who is Laertes again?" I asked Angie.

"Ophelia's brother," she said and rolled her eyes. "Girl, you need to get to work on that play. Maybe start by *reading* it."

That afternoon, Angie gave me a ride to downtown Harmony after school. "What's the rehearsal schedule again?"

"Monday, Wednesday, Friday nights and Saturday afternoon," I said. "It'll be every weeknight and all weekend as we get closer to opening night."

"I got you covered on rides down here, and we can hang out at The Scoop sometimes, but you still got a lot of ground to cover between now and seven o'clock." She leaned an arm on the steering wheel. "Why don't you want to go home?"

"Because I can't get back here," I said. "I'm fine, I promise. My parents are self-absorbed assholes but it's not worse than that."

"Okay," Angie said. "You know, when you first walked into class with your Disney princess hair and Manhattan clothes I thought you'd be a self-absorbed asshole, too. But you're okay in my book,

Holloway."

"Thanks, McKenzie." I gathered my stuff. "I'm going to kick it in the library for about four hours."

"A suggestion about how you can spend that time...?"

"I'm going to read the damn play."

She laughed. "Text me if you get stranded."

"Thanks," I said, climbing out of the car. I bent between the door and the interior. "Thanks a lot, Angie. For a lot of things."

She smiled. "Don't get soft on me now, girl. And I want a full report of what it's like watching Isaac Pearce in action."

I rolled my eyes. "I might even do some acting too."

She made a fist. "Power to the women people."

I shut the door and stepped out into bright, icy sunlight. Winter felt like it was releasing its hold and the air was clean and biting. I hopped over an exhaust-tinged pile of snow at the curb and headed toward the public library, about a block and a half from the HCT. I found a table under a window and settled in with a copy of *Hamlet* and my laptop open to Sparks Notes for when I got stuck. Which was frequently.

The old Willow was a straight-A student who considered going to college for something to do with English Lit. But *Hamlet* hadn't been a part of school curriculum and I'd never seen one of the film adaptations.

I scanned Ophelia's scenes and was relieved to see nothing overtly romantic on the pages. Hamlet and Ophelia's happy relationship existed prior to the start of the play. Their first scene together was essentially her—under pressure from her father—breaking up with him.

Hamlet torments Ophelia, kills her father.

She goes nuts, kills herself.

The End.

No romance. No declarations of love. No *touching*.

I breathed a sigh of relief.

File this under: things I should've investigated before *auditioning.*

I might've been the greenest of actors on that stage, but at least I wouldn't embarrass myself by having a panic attack in front of the cast from having to kiss or touch anyone. The black X across my body would stay invisible while I used Ophelia's scenes where she descends into madness to exorcise some more demons and find a little peace.

It was an innocent, naïve hope, and one that would eventually shatter into a million fucking pieces.

Chapter Thirteen

Willow

After a well-balanced dinner of fries, salad, and a chocolate milkshake at The Scoop, I walked the half block to the Harmony Community Theater. The front entry was eerily quiet, but a woman manning the front office directed me to a staircase that led to a second level above the stage.

The rickety steps smelled of dust and time. I passed closed offices and reached a large, dark room with one mirrored wall, like a dimly lit dance studio. A circle of chairs was set up in the center and the cast of *Hamlet* milled around them, talking and laughing.

"There she is." The woman who played Jocasta in *Oedipus* waved at me. "Our ingénue. Welcome. I'm Lorraine Embry, but you can call me Queen Gertrude." She wore bulky jewelry and flowing, silky clothes. I got the impression she enjoyed being dramatic on and off the stage.

"Hi, I'm Willow Holloway," I said. "Or…Ophelia? I guess?"

The man who'd played Creon strode forward—tall with freckles, rust-colored hair and a wide smile. Dressed in an athletic suit, I pegged him for a university basketball coach, or the owner of a sporting goods store.

"Len Hostetler." He engulfed my hand in his and gave it a shake. "My dear, your audition was really something. *Really* something."

"Agreed," Lorraine said. "Marvelous performance. So much

heart and pure, organic talent."

"Thanks."

They stood beaming over me like proud parents. Since my own parents neither saw my audition, nor had any reason to be proud of me lately, their pride was like a shaft of sunlight on a cold day. But the silence stretched to breaking while they waited for me to say something.

"Um…do we sit anywhere?"

"Sure, sure," Len said. "Herr Direktor will be in shortly." He rubbed his enormous hands together. "Isn't this exciting? Nothing like the first rehearsal for a new show, is there? Or is this the first of your first?"

"No, but it's been a while," I said.

"How long's a while?" Len asked.

I'm so fucked. "Kindergarten."

"Well…" Lorraine laughed. "If your audition was any indicator, you're a natural. I'm looking forward to seeing what you can do with poor, sweet Ophelia."

You and me both, I thought.

As I shed my jacket and took a seat in the circle, I tried to keep the warm welcome and the unexpected praise around me. The energy in the room revved my stomach with a little thrum of anticipation. Despite a dire case of Imposter-itis, I felt good here. At least, it was better than being huddled alone on my bedroom floor wrapped in blankets, with only a book, a Sharpie, and the dark for company.

Isaac Pearce stood in the corner where the mirror met the wall, staring through and beyond the room to some private place. The angle duplicated him—two handsome, contemplative profiles and four arms crossed over a red, three-ring binder.

He looked at me then, blinking as if he were waking up. I gave a small wave and a smile. The corners of his lips started to turn up in return, then his gaze cut away again and his aloof mask dropped down.

Well, nice to see you, too.

"Hey." Justin Baker now stood over me, slicing Isaac off from view. He indicated the empty chair next to mine. "You mind?"

"Uh…sure. Go for it."

As Justin sat, a tiny whiff of cologne wafted from his clothes. He wore jeans, Timberlands, and a blue T-shirt under a blue North Face jacket. He looked sleek, expensive and relaxed. Like he owned whatever room he stepped in, or would, eventually.

Old Me would've been thrilled to sit beside Justin. New Me felt more drawn to worn out jeans, black leather, and stormy gray-green eyes.

But both guys were inaccessible. Walled off by the ice coffin Xavier had left me in. I clicked my ballpoint and drew an X under the heel of my hand.

"You're Willow, right?" Justin said. "I'm Justin. We're in Paulson's class."

"I'm aware." It came out bitchier than I intended.

Justin chuckled. "Of course. Dumb opener, right? You ever acted before?"

"Once. Long time ago. You?"

"I've done a few shows. I blew out my knee a couple of years back, so instead of playing second base, I ended up in *Death of a Salesman.*"

"Cool." I managed a smile.

"Your audition was really good."

"Thanks. I…didn't see yours."

He shrugged. "I did okay. I think I got the part because of my hair."

"What?"

He grinned and tugged a bit of his blond hair. "Same color as yours, so boom—I get to be your brother."

I laughed a little. "I'm sure that's not why you got it."

He held up his hands and wore an easy smile. "I'll take it."

I smiled too while I drew a line of X's down the side of my notebook. His friendliness almost scared me more than if he were a dick.

My gaze flickered to Isaac.

He hadn't moved from the corner to take a seat, and the chair on the other side of me was unoccupied. I wished it were filled with Isaac's faint scent of cigarette smoke and soap, rather than Justin's expensive cologne. But Isaac was X'd out in other ways: my father signed HCT's release form, only under the condition I had nothing to do with Isaac beyond the stage. Dad would yank me out of the show if he found out I was socializing with "that troubled dropout who lives in a junkyard."

That had hurt, as if it were directed right at me. Isaac helped me at the auditions when I was ready to puke from nerves. He'd been kind of a jerk, but it was on the surface. Like a suit of armor with a million cracks in it that you couldn't see from afar, but up close …

You have a flame too, don't you? I silently asked him. *You guard it with your life. Mine gets blown around in the slightest breeze. You don't let anything near you. You're not a criminal, you're on duty. All the time. Why?*

My X's on the page had turned to question marks. Why did I care? I didn't. Couldn't. I snapped my notebook shut.

Martin Ford strode in with the assistant director, Rebecca Mills, their arms laden with red notebooks identical to Isaac's.

"Official scripts," Martin said as the cast took their seats. "We all need to be on the same page. Literally."

I put my library copy away and took the heavy binder on my lap. Once we were all seated, Martin stood in the center of the circle, turning to address us all as he spoke.

"My first command as your director—"

Veteran cast members finished in unison: "Get. Off. Book."

"That's right," Martin said. "Get memorized. You cannot act with a script in your hand. You can *emote,* but not act. Two different things." He spread his arms, as if the room were as wide as an African savannah. "We want to look outward and explore the vast, rich landscape of Shakespeare's words instead of being trapped—" he bent over, hands framing his face, "—our eyes cast down, noses stuck to the map."

I shifted in my seat. This shit was real. Martin Ford was a legit director and this was a serious show, and…*Oh my God, I'm going to fuck this all up.*

"Make sense?" Martin asked. "I give you three weeks and then I start elevating understudies. So, let's get started."

Martin gave a little bit of his background and a short speech about why he chose *Hamlet*—not merely just to play Polonius, he joked—then he had us go around and introduce ourselves, and state the role we were playing.

When the circle came to Lorraine, she sat up straighter.

"I'm Lorraine Embry, and I'm portraying Gertrude, Queen of

Denmark, mother of Hamlet."

I bit my lip and out the corner of my eye, I saw Justin doing the same. We exchanged short, amused looks. I felt Isaac's icy stare before I saw it—his glare wiped my smile off quick, replaced by hot embarrassment. The kid who got caught passing notes.

"Isaac Pearce. Hamlet," he said.

I stared at my feet until it was my turn. "Willow Holloway. I'm playing Ophelia." I said, certain that at any second they'd see this was a mistake and tell me I was in the wrong room.

Martin smiled. "Willow is new to Harmony and I'm so pleased to have her fresh energy here in our theater."

A round of spontaneous applause startled me, and I cringed farther back in my seat. I glanced at Isaac but he was picking at the hole in his jeans.

Justin was next.

"Justin Baker, and I'm playing Laertes."

"My stage children," Martin said, beaming like a proud father. He glanced around the room. "Done? Great. Unt now," he said in a German accent, "we read."

A flutter of pages as people opened their scripts. I glanced over at Isaac again. My damn eyes wouldn't or couldn't stay off him. This time, his gaze met mine then jumped away.

The read-through began. A lot of people took notes, Isaac scribbling the most. I wondered if I should be doing that, watching as the dialogue brought us closer and closer to Act 1, Scene 3. Ophelia's first lines.

Rebecca, the assistant director with the boxy glasses, read all of the stage direction. "Enter Laertes and Ophelia," she said.

Justin, as my brother Laertes, began a long diatribe against Hamlet. I mentally noted he was telling Ophelia not to sleep with the prince—to be afraid of sex and wary of giving away her 'treasures' to a guy who wouldn't marry her anyway.

Then Martin, as Polonius, started in. Treating his daughter as if she were a clueless idiot. Completely helpless and naïve about the ways of men.

"*You do not understand yourself so clearly,*" Martin said. "*As it behooves my daughter and your honor. What is between you? Give me up the truth.*"

I knew Isaac's eyes were on me as I read my lines. *"He hath, my lord, of late made many tenders of his affection to me."*

He helped me at the audition, I thought. *He brought me my jacket when it was so cold...*

"Affection?" Martin scoffed. *"Pooh! You speak like a green girl, unsifted in such perilous circumstance. Do you believe his tenders, as you call them?"*

I raised my eyes to Isaac. *"I do not know, my lord, what I should think."*

Isaac held my gaze as Polonius went on to rant that Ophelia must obey him, as her father, and stay away from Hamlet.

I swallowed and kept my eyes on the script that was throwing my own life back up to me in black and white.

"I shall obey, my lord."

Four hours later, the play ended with nearly every character dead. A dozen red binders shut with a resigned thump. We all stretched and gathered our things. Justin leaned over as I pulled up an Uber app on my phone. Leaned far enough into my space to make me cringe. I took a step away, pretending to readjust my bag.

"You need a ride?" Justin asked. "Where do you live? I got you covered."

"Oh, uh…"

My gaze sought Isaac for some stupid reason, but he was talking to Martin. Justin was waiting for an answer. The weight of his expectations hanging over me. I heard myself blurt my address in that fucking ridiculous way girls have been taught since time immemorial—saying or doing things they're not comfortable with for the sake of accommodating a man's feelings.

"Awesome," Justin said. "I live in Emerson Hills, too. About three blocks down from you."

"Great," I said. "Thanks."

I walked up to where Martin and Isaac were talking. "Sorry to interrupt, but I wanted to say thanks again for having me. Justin is going to give me a ride home."

Now you know where I am and whose car I'm getting in.

Isaac slung his hands in his pockets and gave me a blank look as Justin joined us.

"Wonderful," Martin said. "Brotherly love in action. Have a

great night and good work, you two. I'll see you Wednesday."

"Thanks." I started to go, then turned to Isaac. "Bye."

His chin moved imperceptibly up and down, but he said nothing. *Like a text that says* No, thanks *and nothing else.*

Justin and I headed downstairs.

"Brotherly love," Justin said. "Martin takes this stuff so literally."

I smiled faintly through my pressed lips. My entire body was stiff and when we stepped into the bracing cold night, my muscles bunched together tighter, drawing my shoulders up to my ears.

Justin led me to his shiny black, Ford F150 in the parking lot across from the theater, and held the door for me on the passenger side. Stiffly, I climbed in and was a bombarded with Justin's scent—cologne, leather and the air freshener tree hanging from his rearview. He kept his truck immaculate. There was nothing in it to fear, but when he slid his large form into the driver seat, my heart took off at a gallop.

Calm down calm down calm down.

I put on my seatbelt with shaking hands.

"Cold?" Justin said. "The heater should get going pretty quick here."

He let the truck idle for what felt like an eternity, and then finally began the drive to our neighborhood. He chatted easily the entire time, not seeming to notice my one-word answers to his questions.

"This is me," I managed when he pulled on to my street. "Thanks."

"No problem." He parked and glanced up at our huge white house. "You don't have a car? I can give you a lift every night after rehearsal if you need it."

"Thanks," I said, climbing ungracefully out of the truck. "Great."

I practically ran for my front door as if chased by a serial killer, my keys fumbling in the lock, unable to breathe until I was inside. The warmth wrapped around me, thawing my stiffened muscles a little.

Mom was sitting in the living room, a glass of wine in one hand and an interior design magazine in the other. HGTV's *House Hunters* was on the flat screen TV. A young couple was wandering through a beach house, complaining mildly about everything.

"How was rehearsal?" Mom asked.

I stared. "You said you couldn't pick me up every night."

"And you said you'd find a ride."

"Because you said you *couldn't pick me up*."

She sighed and turned a page. "Willow, after a long day I'm not going be up for traipsing through the cold at eleven at night. If you can't get there and back, then you shouldn't do it. You shouldn't do it anyway. So silly and of no use to your college applications. Anyway, you clearly found a ride." She glanced up at me. "Please tell me it wasn't with that Pearce boy your father warned you about."

I turned and stormed upstairs, her voice calling me back and then letting me go. I slammed the door to my room. The constricting cold squeeze from sitting in Justin's truck had worn off, but I knew a night terror was going to get me. I could feel it at the edges of my consciousness, like a dark shape snickering and whispering.

I changed into my pajamas and bundled myself on the floor in my comforter beside my stack of books—strategically placed next to me—a makeshift wall of better stories than mine. As I drifted to sleep, I had the foolish belief they'd protect me.

But the pressing weight and choking lack of air came that night anyway. When I finally could draw air to breathe, I cried and cried.

Chapter Fourteen

Isaac

Of course, I thought, watching Willow leave with Justin Baker. *That's how it should be.*

"Isaac."

Martin nudged my arm. Too late, I yanked my gaze from Willow's retreating form. Martin kept watching her head down the stairs, then turned back to me, a small smile on his lips.

"So. Willow Holloway."

"What about her?"

"She's going to make a fantastic Ophelia, won't she? She's nervous and a little stiff right now, but she has so much raw talent. In Act Four, we turn her loose." His eyes gleamed as he waved at cast members as they filed out. "It will be magnificent."

I agreed, but the thought made my stomach twist. Willow's raw talent was born of something deep and dark. I witnessed it in her *Woolgatherer* audition. I recognized the heaviness in her eyes because I had it too. Loss and pain pressed down on her. She pushed through it with small smiles and a tough facade that wilted the second she turned away.

Willow was here for the same reason I was: to find some relief. To tell her story. For the first time in a long time I felt nervous about a performance, only it wasn't my own.

"I don't know, Marty," I said. "It might be too much for her. Too difficult. I mean, because she's so new to acting," I added quickly.

"I think she can handle it," Martin said, as the last player departed.

"If you say so," I muttered.

Why do you care anyway?

Willow was a distraction and it was getting fucking annoying. During the entire read-through, I'd tried to keep focus on the play while my damn eyes kept going to her, radiant in a soft white sweater and jeans. The amber overhead lights threaded gold strands down the long waves of her hair. When she read her lines, her voice had a soft lilt with an undercurrent of steel. Perfect for Ophelia.

Ophelia was stronger than her dipshit brother or conniving father thought she was, and judging from her reading, Willow knew it too.

Goddammit.

I dragged my thoughts away from her hair—again—and vowed to get my head on straight. Do my job. Martin's talent agents were coming for *me*. I needed to give them the best goddamn Hamlet they'd ever seen, not worry about the mental health of a high school girl.

Who is currently sitting in the front seat of another guy's car.

The room was empty now, and I helped Martin stack up the chairs. The silence crackled and I could feel him gearing up to interfere in my personal business. He couldn't help himself.

"Justin Baker seems like a nice young man."

I grunted a response as I stacked chairs.

"But sort of bland, if I'm being honest," Martin said. "He has a clean-cut earnestness that's perfect for Laertes."

"Okay," I said.

"You don't think so?"

I shrugged. "You're the director, Marty. I don't have a thought about him one way or another."

"You sure about that?" Martin smiled gently. "I saw you looking at him and Willow—"

"For fuck's sake—"

"And I saw her looking at you."

I froze, six chairs in my arms. "What?"

Martin's smile widened and he shrugged. "I see everything. That's my job."

"Whatever," I said, and carried the stack to the wall. "I'm not in high school anymore."

"Does that matter?"

"Yes."

"Why?"

"Baker's her age. I'm not. He's got money. I don't."

"So you're interested in her?"

I let a stack of chairs slam down. "Mind your own business, Marty."

He sighed and shoved his hands in the front pockets of his cords. He wore a kind smile I'd never see on my own father's face.

"I can't help it, Isaac. Somewhere along the way, you went from being an actor I admire to a young man I care about." He shrugged. "I want you to be happy."

He said 'happy' as if it were something you just plucked out of the goddamn air anytime you felt like it.

"I'll be happy when I get out of Harmony," I said. "But if you really care about the play, you'll want me to be miserable. *Hamlet*'s a tragedy, remember?"

"I'm not worried about the play," Martin said. "But I am concerned that Willow won't always have a ride to and from rehearsal. Her father—"

"She has a ride," I snapped. "Justin Baker's her ride." I slammed the last stack together. "I'm done. I have work early tomorrow. Good night."

"Isaac—"

"Good night," I called again, already halfway down the stairs.

Martin's fatherly concern was something I craved and yet it chafed me. I was leaving Harmony. I needed to sever connections, not make them stronger.

Or make new ones with beautiful, talented girls.

I started my truck and let the engine idle. It would only stall if I tried to drive before it was warm. I supposed Justin Baker had a car built in this decade. Something sleek that didn't freeze up or belch black smoke at stop signs. With heated seats. Willow was probably used to heated seats. Used to guys like Justin, who hadn't spent a day in their lives worrying about money. Willow would be perfectly comfortable in his car, driving to her big house with a guy cut from the same wealthy cloth.

Good, I thought. Let her find her happy ending with Justin because it sure as hell wasn't going to be with me.

But as I drove my shitty truck to the shitty end of town, a thought hung on the horizon like a growing storm: at the end of the play, Laertes and Hamlet kill each other over Ophelia's grave, and no one gets a happy ending.

At Friday's rehearsal, Marty moved us to the stage. While he blocked a scene, the rest of the cast paired up to run lines. Willow and Justin worked together. Naturally. I swore I didn't give a shit, yet I studied her every move with my actor's eye. Was she smiling more? Did her eyes soften when she looked at him? Did she move more easily into his space?

You're turning into a goddamn lunatic, Pearce.

Marty was blocking Act 1, Scene 5, where Horatio and Marcellus show Hamlet his father's ghost. They warn the prince not to follow the apparition but he does anyway, leaving his friends behind. Then it's Hamlet alone onstage, speaking to an unseen spirit.

It's a scene that requires full commitment to witnessing something otherworldly, or it falls flat. I tried, but my attention was split in half: my body onstage, my eyes sweeping the theater to find where Willow and Justin huddled together in the dark.

"Take five, everyone," Marty said. He pulled me aside as the others hopped down from the stage. His fatherly smile was gone and his director's mask was firmly in place—lips drawn down, his eyes full of thoughts and ideas.

"What's going on?"

Out of professional courtesy, I never bullshitted him about acting. "I'm unfocused."

"You're angry."

I frowned. "What? No, I'm not."

"Yes, you are. So instead of trying to force the moment, let's work a scene where we can use it. We'll jump to Act Three, Scene One."

"*To be or not to be*? Already?"

"Not yet. We'll start just after the monologue."

When the cast returned from the break, Martin put a hand over his eyes to shield the lights and scanned the theater.

"Willow? There she is. Willow, come down here please?"

The overheads blared down on Willow, bathing her in a cone of gold light. She wore jeans, boots, and a long gray sweater. My stupid heart clenched at how goddamn beautiful she looked.

"We're going to give Act Three, Scene One a go," Martin said.

"Okay…" she said, drawing the word out and flipping through her script. Her eyes widened and she looked up to glance between Martin and me. "The nunnery scene? Already?"

"I don't work scenes in order," Martin said. "I work the scenes I feel the energy in the room needs. So. Hamlet has just delivered his most famed of speeches ruminating on whether to take his own life or not. Polonius has convinced the King that Hamlet's madness is his love for Ophelia. She's given Polonius a love letter Hamlet wrote to her, and she's ending the affair on her father's orders."

Willow bit her lip. "So…is Ophelia happy about this? Does she *want* to break up with him?"

Martin shook his head. "No direction right now. I just want your instinctual read." He looked at us both expectantly. "Well? Let's go."

As usual, Martin was right and anger was serving the right purpose. Hamlet was a complete dick to Ophelia in this particular scene, and I had no shortage of motivation. I was no longer the poor bastard with a shitty truck who lived in a trailer and worked his ass off to be here, while *she* waltzed in on Justin's arm with the scent of privilege flowing off her clothes like perfume. I was a fucking prince. She was nothing but a henchman's daughter.

"*Ha, ha, are you honest?*"

Willow recoiled at my withering, merciless delivery. The uncertainty in her eyes was real, until something caught fire and a line of hers that was supposed to meek and quailing came out with bite.

Martin listened and watched, one arm across his midsection, the elbow of the other resting on it, his index finger curled over his lip. Not two minutes later, he shook his head and stepped between us.

"Stop, stop, stop." He smiled faintly. "Okay, I take it back, I'm giving direction after all. This scene reveals everything about Ophelia and Hamlet. Some analysts contend the pair never consummated their relationship. Others say they were most definitely lovers."

Willow's lips parted in a tiny gasp, and a surge of heat swept through me.

"I hold to the latter idea," he said. "If they were lovers, so much more is at stake. It's a richer choice that holds more possibilities. Use that concept as actors: when confronted with yes or no, choose yes. Every time."

Willow and I exchanged glances.

"Hamlet truly loved Ophelia," Martin said. "It was all off the page, before the play starts, but that love needs to live behind every word that's *on* the page. The betrayal and agony of this scene is more potent if their love is dying here." He turned to me. "Your Hamlet is pissed off."

I shrugged. "He's *supposed* to be pissed off. Ophelia's dumping him and conspiring with Polonius and King—"

"Yes, yes, that's all true. But you're *only* pissed off and that's merely one layer of emotion in the scene. Ophelia's being forced to leave him and Hamlet knows it. She's squashed between her love for him and her duty to her father. But the love…" Martin's eyes were full of the zealous enthusiasm that made him such an extraordinary director. "The love was there first."

He smiled and put a hand on each of our shoulders. "This play doesn't work unless we feel that. So on that note, instead of coming to rehearsal this Saturday, I want you to go out together. Grab lunch or something."

My eyes widened while Willow's darted to me and back, her lips parted in another little gasp.

"I'm not asking anything outrageous," Martin said. "I want you two to hang out. Get to know each other. Be friendly. Become *real* to each other as human beings. I need you to see each other as more than co-actors on a stage."

Willow and I glanced at each other again and I noticed some of her stiffness had mellowed, her shoulders dropped a little, her frown loosened.

"Do this," Marty said, and looked to me, "and the next time we run this scene, every cutting word you say to her will cut you back." He looked at Willow. "Obeying your father, instead of staying true to

Hamlet, will be the hardest thing you ever do. You see?"

She nodded.

Martin beamed. "Great. Moving on." He clapped his hands once and moved off stage. "Act Two, Scene Two. Will someone please wake up Rosencrantz and Guildenstern...?"

He left us alone in the center of the stage.

"Is this a normal thing to do?" she asked, hugging her script to her chest. "Have the actors hang out together, outside of the theater?"

"You don't have to," I said. "I'm not going to force you."

"No one's forcing me," she said. "If Mr. Ford thinks it's a good idea, then...okay."

"Okay," I said. "So... What do you want to do?"

Fuck, why was this so hard? Usually I texted one of my hookups a time and a place and that was it.

Willow shrugged. "I don't know. "Lunch at The Scoop? Or maybe coffee if it's too..." She ran a toe along a crack in the stage floor.

"Too what?" I knew damn well what: *too expensive.*

"Too...Harmonious?" she said.

A smile tugged at me. "Something like that. Do you need a ride?"

"No, I can... I'll meet you here," she said, hugging her script tighter.

"Okay."

"One o'clock?"

"Fine."

"All right. So...see you then?"

"Yep."

It's a date, snickered a voice that sounded like Benny.

Still hugging her binder, Willow went down the stage steps. She passed Justin in the front row. He half rose from his seat, but Willow only gave him a fleeting wave before moving toward Lorraine and Len a few rows back.

Justin sat down, glanced up and caught me watching him. He stared. I stared back until he looked away and started gathering up his shit.

It was a stupid, meaningless win. Willow still left with him at the end of rehearsal.

When the last cast member had gone, Martin locked the side door and crossed the stage. He stopped when he saw me sitting in the front row, arms crossed, my boots kicked up on the lip of the stage.

He held up his hands. "I know what you're thinking, but it's for the good of the show, I swear."

"Really."

"Yes, really." He came to the edge and sat on his heels. "You can turn your Hamlet into a jerk who rants and raves against Ophelia and chalk it up to his madness. And ninety-nine percent of the audience won't know the difference. But two people will."

He pointed at himself and then me.

"I know you have more than that in you. And yes, I've seen the way each of you looks at the other when the other can't see…" He rubbed a hand over his incoming beard. "I'd love to see something happen there."

"Jesus, Marty…"

He held up his hands. "None of my business. The quality of the play, however, *is* my business. At the very least, you two need to be on stage in a way that says, 'this is not the first time we've been in the same space.' Right now, you both look like boxers getting ready for a match." His hands became fists, protecting his face.

Despite myself, a little laugh snuck out. He laughed too and knocked my boot with his hand.

"Come on. Let's get out of here."

We closed and locked up the theater. As we headed to our cars, he tripped on a crack in the cement. My hand shot out to grab him before he could fall.

"Yikes, thank you," he said clutching my arm. "That'll take ten years off a guy." He glanced down at the crack, shaking his head. "It's bad. This entire block, actually. It all needs work."

We walked on, my gaze fixed on the sidewalk. He was right: cracks snaked along much of the cement, like black lightning.

"How are things with the theater?" I asked, a sudden lump of worry sitting heavy in my gut. "Money-wise?"

"*Things*," Marty said with a smile, "are fine. You concentrate on your part." He headed to his older model Lexus. "And have fun tomorrow on your date."

I sighed. "Marty."

"Your *working* date."

Chapter Fifteen

Willow

Mid-morning on Saturday, I grabbed my phone and typed a text to Angie.

Help!

Are you being held for ransom by pirates? she texted back. **Because I sleep in on Saturday, Holloway.**

I have to spend the day with Isaac.

My phone lit up with Angie's number. I hit the green button and answered, "Yes, I'm serious."

"Why? When? How did this happen?" Her voice was equal parts sleep and indignation. "Whoa. Is this—pause for dramatic effect—a date?"

"Absolutely not," I said, making my firm voice belie the flutter in my stomach. "Martin Ford asked us to hang out and get to know each other better. So we're not so awkward on stage."

"A likely story," Angie said. "Ok, what's with the S.O.S.?"

"I need a ride into town to meet Isaac."

"Doesn't Isaac drive? He's got an old blue pickup, if I'm not mistaken. Hold up." Her voice dropped. "You're not ashamed to be seen in his truck, are you?"

"For God's sake, I'm not a *completely* shallow bitch."

"I know, but us plebes need to stick together against the bourgeoisie."

"You've seen *Marie Antoinette* too many times."

"No such thing. Sophia Coppola is a goddess." She yawned. "What were we talking about again?"

"My imaginary prejudice against Isaac's truck," I said. "The real problem is my dad. He won't let me see Isaac outside rehearsal. If I tell him we're hanging out all day because the director told us to, he'd never believe me. He'll yank me from the play."

"Hmm, a legit dilemma. Very well, Cinderella. When do you need me?"

"I'm meeting Isaac at one o'clock."

"Your carriage shall arrive at quarter 'til, but girl, I got yearbook shit to do the rest of the day. I can't be schlepping your booty back home when your non-date with Isaac Pearce is over."

"I'll figure something else out. Thanks, Angie."

I sat on the windowsill in my room, overlooking the neighborhood. Green things were starting to grow again. The snow was gone and the sun was golden and bright in a clear sky I'd never seen in Manhattan. It splashed long stripes across my hardwood floors and the pile of blankets still there.

I'd had a rocky sleep last night, but no terrors. Instead, whenever I woke, my thoughts were filled with the rehearsal.

And Isaac.

He'd been cold and rude to me in rehearsal. No, correction, *Hamlet* was rude to *Ophelia.* But the scene called for it and I had to take it. That's what I signed up for. I could be a professional and not take it personally. There was nothing between us—he was acting a part. And besides, the more realistic he was, the better the show.

The love was there first.

I pulled my script on my lap and wrote those words—just an actress taking notes from her director, that's all—at the top of Act Three. Black X's crawled along the side margin, looking like they were swarming up the page to overtake those defenseless words floating at the top.

I drew a protective bubble around *The love was there first* with arrows stabbing out to keep the X's away… Then shut my script.

You're going to be as crazy as Ophelia by the time this thing is over.

Angie honked from the driveway at quarter of one. I breezed past my parents in the living room. They were bickering about some work function in Indianapolis Dad wanted Mom to attend with him.

"Where are you going?" Dad said.

"Out with Angie." I grabbed my white jacket from the hook in the mudroom. When I came back out, Dad was peering through the kitchen window to the front drive.

No, Dad, it's not Isaac. Aloud I said, "Be back before dinner."

Dad nodded. "Glad to see you're making friends."

I hurried down the drive to hop into Angie's car. Her unruly curls were held back by a colorful headband. Her black sweatshirt read *I'll stop wearing black when they make a darker color.*

"Don't you look so pretty and fresh for your non-date with Mr. Pearce," she said, taking in my light jeans and pink cashmere sweater. She leaned closer. "Nice perfume. And are you wearing lip gloss?"

"Shut up. My lips are chapped."

She grinned. "His might be too. You should probably share."

"Stop." I rolled my eyes but that silly flutter was in my stomach again. I turned on the music to avoid having to talk about it.

It was just before one when Angie dropped me off in front of the HCT.

"Thanks so much, Ange," I said, hopping out. "I appreciate it."

"One last thing," she said.

"What's that?"

"Kiss him."

A jolt shot through me. "What?"

"With *tongue.*"

"What the hell for?"

"Ophelia and Hamlet were *lovers,* right? So, for research or Method acting or whatever you call it."

I rolled my eyes. "Isaac's not into me. And judging by his pissy mood in rehearsal last night, babysitting the newbie actor all day is the last thing he wants to do."

Angie shrugged. "We'll see. I want a full report. *Tonight.* Not on Monday morning or I'll be dead from curiosity."

"Bye, Angie," I said.

"*With tongue,*" she called just as I shut the door on her.

I turned and nearly tripped over my damn feet. Right in view of Isaac, who leaned against the brick wall next to the theater's box office, smoking a cigarette. My heart crashed against my chest then dropped to my knees.

If there is a God, Isaac did not hear that.

"Hi," I said, moving toward him slowly, like a lion tamer walking up to a big cat.

A panther.

He wore his usual jeans, boots, and black leather over a white shirt. His dark hair was wet from a shower and his gray-green eyes watched me with a bored detachment.

"Hey," he said. Nothing more.

"I brought my script," I said. "If you wanted to run lines or something."

He exhaled a plume of smoke, dropped his cigarette butt and ground it out with his heel. "Whatever. Did we decide coffee or food?"

"Coffee's good."

"Okay."

We walked the block and a half to Daisy's Coffeehouse without talking. Isaac held the door for me.

"Thanks," I said.

No reply.

Not into this. Got it. Message received.

Daisy's was a cute little place with warm wood flooring and tables that were half-filled with patrons. They chatted over steaming cups, typed on laptops or read books. Nina Simone crooned over the sound system.

"What do you want?" Isaac asked.

"I can get my own," I said, reaching for my purse. Isaac gave me a stormy glare and I met it with my own pointed look. "Listen, it's obvious you don't want to be here. No sense making you pay for it, too."

He opened his mouth and then snapped it shut. He turned away, looking around the café. When he spoke, his voice was softer.

"There's a table over there," he said, indicating a two-seater tucked in the corner near a small shelf marked *Free Books*. "Tell me what you want to drink and then grab it."

"Medium latte," I said. "Please."

He nodded and I went to the table. He came back a few minutes later with a latte for me and what looked like black coffee for him, both in mugs instead of to-go cups.

He started to sit, then stopped. "You need sugar?"

"Two, please."

Female eyes followed as Isaac went to the little station of creamers and stir sticks, and a small smile spread over my lips. Date or non-date, it didn't suck to have a hot guy sitting across from me.

Not a date, I thought. *We're just sitting.*

"Something funny?" Isaac asked, sliding into his seat.

"Nothing," I said, taking the sugar. "Thank you."

He sipped his coffee and the silence stretched until it itched.

"You take your coffee black?" I asked, a painful crank of the engine to get this conversation going. "I could never. Too strong for me." I rolled my eyes. "I'm sure this is exactly what Mr. Ford had in mind when he sent us out here. 'Hamlet, go find out how Ophelia likes her coffee.'"

Isaac's lips twitched, then finally smiled and the tight tension between us cracked a little. "Call him Martin or Marty," he said. "He won't answer to Mr. Ford."

"Good to know," I said. "You've worked with him for a lot of shows, right?"

"Five years now."

"You have a favorite?"

His eyes on me were steady and unblinking. "*Oedipus.* So far."

"That's funny. That's the only one I've seen." I cleared my throat and tucked a lock of hair behind my ear. "So, will you really be off-book in three weeks? You carry half the play."

"It's a lot," he said. "I have help though."

"Yeah?" It was the first time he'd offered something of himself.

"Yeah. Kid who lives next door to me helps me run lines."

"Lucky you."

"Yeah," Isaac said. "I'm really lucky." He put a subtle filter over the last word, tingeing it with bitterness but not enough to invite questions.

The conversation sputtered out again. After a few excruciating moments, I reached for my bag. "I brought my script. Not sure what Mr. Ford... I mean, Martin, had in mind, but we can run lines now if you want. I don't want you to lose the day."

Isaac crossed his arms and leaned back in his chair. "Why do you keep apologizing?"

I bristled. "I'm not apologizing."

"You are."

"Well, it's not like you're super thrilled to be here so—"

"I am," he said. "I mean, I'm *here*. Now we can run lines or whatever you want to do. But stop worrying if this is a waste of my time. It's not."

I folded my arms and leaned over the table at him. "You know, it would be a helluva lot easier to not feel like you're here against your will if you didn't act like *you're here against your will*."

He pursed his lips. "I don't make a lot of conversation."

"I can see that," I said. "But I need this assignment, or whatever you call it, to work. You have this whole acting thing down, but I'm scared shitless. I need all the help I can get."

The front legs of his chair came down. "You don't."

I blinked. "Sorry?"

"You don't need that much help. I saw your audition. And being scared is a good thing."

"How do you figure?"

"It's how you know you care."

I turned my coffee mug around. "Being scared doesn't feel like care. It feels like danger."

"It is," Isaac said. "It's dangerous to put yourself out there. To rip your heart out and throw it to the audience. What if they hate what you're trying to say? What if they don't understand it? Or worse, what if *they* don't care? The validation of your entire life is tied up in your art. So yeah, that's pretty fucking dangerous. And scary."

I glanced up at him over my cup as I soaked up his little kernels of knowledge I desperately needed. "You don't seem scared. You seem cool as shit, all the time."

He smiled faintly. "It's all an act."

"You said that before. At my audition."

"I remember," he said, only this time his short answer wasn't a wall to the conversation but an opening.

"You also said I'd get Ophelia," I said. "And you were right, because I took your advice. I told the story."

He nodded. "It's the only thing to do."

I went back to my coffee, thinking he couldn't be more right. I ran my finger along the edge of my coffee mug's handle. "So, since we're here, can I ask... Does it help?"

"Does what help?"

"Acting. I mean, why do you do it? For relief?"

He nodded. "Yes. For a little while. But there's always more there. More story to tell, so to speak."

"What's your story?" As soon as the words left my mouth, I wanted to snatch them back. They were so horribly invasive.

And I couldn't give mine in return.

"Well," he said.

I waved my hands. "No, forget it." I grabbed for my coffee and took a long pull to keep my mouth occupied.

He shrugged. "It's sort of what we're here for, right?" His lips pressed together and relaxed, as if he couldn't decide to release the words behind them. His long fingers tapped the stirring stick I'd used in my coffee, his eyes far away.

Maybe he was like me. Maybe under the bravado and aloof manner and don't-give-a-fuck, Isaac Pearce only wanted a little piece of normal. To sit over a cup of coffee and just *talk*.

"My mom died when I was eight," he said. "She had a stroke. She was too fucking young to have a stroke, but... It was a blockage no one knew about. It killed her instantly."

A slow horror crept under my skin.

Did he see her die? Please tell me he didn't see it.

"I was at school," he said, as if reading my mind. "I went to school with a mom and came back without one."

"I'm so sorry."

His smile was hard and quick. My stirring stick moved through his fingers, turning over and over.

"Sounds dramatic, but losing my mom so suddenly was like having the wind knocked out of me for an entire year. No way to process what happened. She wasn't sick. One minute she was there, totally healthy, and the next minute she was gone. It was so fucking meaningless." He shrugged, a casual, bitter acceptance of something terrible. "So I stopped talking. I didn't see the point."

"For a whole year?" I asked.

He looked up at me, his features hardening. "You heard that, huh?"

I sat back. "Well…yes. At school."

He waved a hand. "It's okay. There's some weird shit floating around about me. My dad isn't well. You probably heard that too."

He deserved honesty, so I nodded.

"He didn't take Mom's death well either. Drove him to drink. Talking to him never got me much but a fist or a boot after that anyway."

I swallowed hard and Isaac noticed.

"Sorry. I don't know why I'm telling you that shit. It doesn't matter."

"Yes, it does," I said. "Of course, it does."

He didn't reply but I saw my words land on him and sink in.

"Then you found acting," I said, and it wasn't a question. "I heard it helped you find your voice again." Shame burned my skin for sucking up rumors and gossip as if there weren't real people on the other side.

"Fourth grade," Isaac said. "When I went back to school, Miss Grant was the only teacher who didn't demand I talk. She put someone else's words in front of me one day and said, *This character needs a voice. If you could lend him yours, that would be great.* Like I was doing her a favor." He glanced at me. "So I did. It wasn't me talking. It wasn't my words. And that made it okay."

"You've been acting ever since?"

"Yeah."

"And it helped you."

He nodded. "That's the funny thing about art. If it's really good, you can see yourself in it. Sometimes a little bit. Sometimes a lot."

"Do you see yourself in Hamlet?" I smiled faintly. "Seems like the exact kind of question Martin wants us to ask each other."

He didn't smile back. "Yeah, I do. Hamlet hates that his mother married Claudius so soon after his father died. In Hamlet's eyes, Claudius is an imposter king, sitting in a chair that doesn't belong to him. I lost my father when my mom died. An imposter sits in our shitty trailer now, drunk and unrecognizable, pouring the poison down his throat."

Now I had to bite the inside of my cheek. Angie told me by doing this play with Isaac, I'd have a front row seat to his incredible talent. Sitting across from him at this little table, I realized he had an incredible mind, too. Poetry in his own words, though I doubt he knew it. His quiet observations about his life were a thousand times more potent and raw than anything I'd seen him do onstage.

He raised his eyes to mine and slowly they came back to the here and now. And my awestruck expression.

"Shit," he said. "That was probably way more than you wanted to hear—"

"Don't apologize," I whispered.

His eyes widened slightly, drawing me deeper into their gray-green depths. A storm-tossed ocean, miles deep. Icy and choppy on the surface. Warm stillness beneath.

We stared. And in the short silence, something settled between us. An agreement or understanding. He'd shared himself, yet asked nothing in return. I was free to float in the intimate closeness between the storyteller and the listener. I wasn't trapped or weighed down by him.

I could become the storyteller…

Except I couldn't. My own story had to stay locked behind my teeth. Unfair, but how could I tell my acting partner what I hadn't been able to tell my own parents or best friends? Risk a mental breakdown in this cute little coffee shop?

No, the time to tell the truth had long passed. What happened to me could only manifest through the words and acts of a character written more than four hundred years ago. The safest way to tell my story was to cut, distill and refract it through the prism of Ophelia's madness.

"I'm still trying to find the connection to Ophelia," I said, not looking at him. "I haven't done this before. Dialed deep into a character, I mean."

"Yes, you have," Isaac said. "Your audition piece."

"That was three minutes. A single moment. *Hamlet* is so much bigger." I arched a brow at him. "I distinctly recall you telling me as much at the audition." I tapped my chin. "How did you put it? Ah, yes. You politely requested I not *fuck this up for you.*"

A small smile ghosted over his lips. "It's my standard request," he said. He crossed his forearms on the table and leaned on them. "Start with the basics. What do you and your character have in common?"

"I don't know." I sat back in my seat, thinking. "You could say my father's an overbearing ass, like Polonius."

Isaac nodded, his expression thoughtful. "It was his idea to move you out here in the middle of your senior year?"

"Yeah. Well, no. His boss transferred him. Even though my dad's a senior VP, he obeyed without question. My mom loves Manhattan but even that wasn't enough to keep us there."

"Do you miss New York?"

"Not really." I swallowed hard. This was veering a little too close to a spot marked X. "Turns out I like it here," I said. "Something about Harmony feels secluded, and I think that's what I need right now."

"Why?" Isaac asked, his voice softer than I'd ever heard it.

I can't tell you that, Isaac, I thought. *Not ever.*

I shrugged, as if a flick of the shoulder could disperse the weight I carried. "Manhattan's busy and kinetic and I guess I got tired of the pace. Things move slower here. Maybe that's why you don't like it?"

Ball back in his court. Good. Except Isaac didn't answer. He only looked at me for a long time. And I knew. I knew he could see right through my pathetic segues and my clumsy subject changes. He knew I wasn't telling the story. Yet I sensed he respected the not-telling. The kind of respect for silence only someone who hadn't spoken for an entire year could have.

"Yeah, I'm leaving Harmony," Isaac said finally. "Martin has some talent scouts coming to the opening night of Hamlet."

I set down my coffee mug hard. "He does? Oh my God. Isaac, that's amazing."

He shrugged. "We'll see. I keep thinking it's like a guaranteed ticket out but…"

"It will be," I said. "They're going to shit their pants over you."

"Maybe."

"Not maybe. There will be much shitting of pants."

He smiled with one side of his mouth. I had yet to see a full-blown grin or hear a hearty laugh from this guy. I wondered if I ever would before he moved out of Harmony.

He's leaving Harmony, I thought, as if test-driving it. I didn't like it.

"The theater won't be the same," I said, tucking a lock of hair behind my ear. "Martin will miss you."

"He'll be okay."

"Won't you miss it here? Even a little?"

Isaac met my gaze steadily. "No," he said, and stared hard at something over my shoulder. I turned to look.

Outside, two Plastics and their boyfriends walked past the window. They slowed when they saw us, snickered to each other and continued on.

"Great," I muttered. "Commence milling of rumors."

Isaac's expression darkened.

"Not about you," I said. "Me. Jessica Royce and Company is under the impression I auditioned for the play just to follow you around."

Isaac's eyebrows went up. "Oh?"

"It's total bullshit," I said. "I don't do anything I don't want to do."

Not anymore.

I straightened and drank the last cold dregs of my latte. "Anyway, I don't give a shit what they think. Do you want to get out of here?"

Isaac frowned. "And go where?"

"I don't know. Let's get out and walk. I didn't see much of Harmony when it was under the snow. You can show me the highlights."

"Harmony has no highlights."

"Impossible. Every place is famous for something."

Isaac nodded. "Yeah, I guess so," he said. "I know a place."

Chapter Sixteen

Isaac

Willow and I stepped out the coffeehouse into the chilly air. As I blinked under the bright sun, it hit me how I'd told this girl—a virtual stranger—everything about my mother. Without feeling like I should be choking it all down. Telling secrets was part of Marty's assignment, I supposed, but it didn't explain why the words fell easily from my mouth. As easily as they did when I was performing. No acting this time. I'd been myself for a few precious minutes and it didn't suck. It was bearable.

Willow made being myself bearable.

I hunched deeper in my jacket and glanced down at her, no longer seeing the Manhattan rich girl living a perfect, pampered life. She closed her eyes, turned her face to the sun and inhaled a deep, cleansing breath.

She needed Harmony in her veins. She left something behind in New York. Something that was destroyed or taken away from her. It wasn't her idea to come to this town, but once here, she found her escape. Her chance to hide. Or maybe rebuild?

She wouldn't tell me but she didn't have to. She'd given me so much already.

"Where are we headed?" she asked.

"Just up here," I said.

We turned a corner and I led us north, out of downtown. The

shops and buildings lining the street were replaced by tall trees—maple, oak and dogwood—just starting to turn green again.

We passed through a small neighborhood, row after row of one-story houses, each no more than eight or nine hundred square feet. Kitchen gardens and low fences separated the lots. Children's toys lay scattered on the grass, spilling onto the sidewalks, as if they belonged to everyone. Wind chimes played a hollow tune.

"These houses are so cute," Willow said, her eyes lit up. "What is this neighborhood?"

"It's called The Cottages. Artsy-type folk live here."

"Is this what you wanted to show me?"

"No." I glanced down at her. "You like it?"

"I love it," she said. "So quiet. And peaceful."

We passed a house with a pottery wheel in the front yard. Another with small wrought iron sculptures of Kokopelli with his flute, sunbursts and small horses.

"Can't you picture it?" Willow said. "Having a little house like this? You come out in the morning with a script, drink your coffee and watch the sun come up?"

I nearly stopped walking as her words punched me in the chest. I passed by The Cottages hundreds of times—thousands of times. All the years I lived here, I never thought anything except how lonely it would be to live in this corner of the world.

As we passed the last row of little houses, I saw them through Willow's eyes. The curtains of my imagination opened on a scene: sitting on a front porch with a cup of black coffee, a script in my lap. Watching the sun rise over the green of the trees and spill between the leaves. Soft arms went around my neck, a lock of long blonde hair fell over my arm and soft lips brushed my jaw, whispering, "Good morning…"

I shook myself out of the reverie.

Nice fantasy, dumbass.

Another curtain rose: me spending another twenty years living in Harmony with my shitty home life dogging me. Half the town afraid of me, the other half judging and whispering. My father's drunken rampages more famous than my acting. The Pearce name associated with a rotting junkyard sign, not lit up on a marquee.

Fuck this place.

Willow didn't miss the dark expression on my face this time. "Not a fan?"

"No," I said. "I want out."

"Which do you think?" she asked. "Hollywood or Broadway?"

"Whichever will take me."

She frowned. "You don't care? Wouldn't it be really different to act on film as opposed to being on stage? Wouldn't you miss the energy of a live audience?"

"Yeah, I guess I would," I said. "But I've never really thought about acting beyond as a means to an end. Using it to get out."

"Really?" Her face scrunched up as if she had just smelled something rotten. She fell silent, but with more questions behind her eyes.

"Go ahead," I said. "You can say it. I'm egotistical. Or ungrateful for what I have."

She shot me a look. "Now that you mention it…"

A small laugh ground out of me like a rusty gear. Instead of feeling insulted, I loved that I didn't intimidate her.

"I get it," I said. "But I don't think of what I can do as talent or a gift. It's an escape."

"But can't you feel what it does to the people who watch you act? It's like a gift of transportation. An escape for us too."

I stopped walking and looked down at her. "I'm glad it can be that for you. For anyone watching. But for me…" I shrugged. "It's all I have."

"I feel the same," she said. "Like I was a little bit lost and then *Hamlet* fell into my lap. To help me find my way again." Her laugh was nervous. "That sounds all kinds of dramatic. And probably silly."

"It's not silly," I said. "Things happen for a reason, I guess."

"You think?" Her voice suddenly went sharp. She stopped, her expression twisting in confusion and disbelief. "*Everything* happens for a reason?"

I blinked at her sudden fury. "I don't know. Martin's always telling me—"

"Your perfectly healthy mom having a stroke and *dying* happened for a reason? You said yourself, it was meaningless."

My jaw clenched, my own blood rising. I jabbed a finger at my chest. "*I* get to say what that meant to me. Not you. Not anyone."

"Exactly," she fired back. "It's *your* story. I hate 'everything happens for a reason.' Like someone's pain doesn't mean anything *yet,* but someday it will and then everything will be all right again. It's bullshit." She looked up at me, and her expression changed again, tear-filled eyes almost begging me. "What do we do in the meantime?"

"I don't know," I said. "Try to get by. To survive."

She held my gaze a moment, then nodded. "I'm sorry but…" She ran her fingertips beneath her wet eyes. "Some things *happen* and it's like the power going out. Or the volume turns down to mute."

I nodded. "Yeah, it is."

"Until."

"Until?"

"It's something my grandmother told me once. She said every story has an *until.* Something bad happens that shows the character what they want most. But where is the *until* that puts everything back together? When does the character actually get what they want most?"

"When they allow themselves to have it," I said. My hands itched to brush the lock of hair that had fallen over her cheek. "Or when they go and take it."

"That's why you're leaving Harmony," she said.

"Yes."

She nodded, then huffed a sigh. The strength returned to her voice. "I wish I was as brave as you."

"Auditioning for a part in Shakespeare's most famous play without having acted a day in your life sounds pretty brave."

"Or stupid," she said, with a small laugh. "I'm sorry for what I said about your mom."

"Don't be."

"Too late. I am." She was smiling again and my eyes were drawn to her full lips that glistened with a touch of gloss.

I wondered what it tasted like…

Willow jerked her chin down the street. "*That* must be what you wanted to show me."

I followed her gaze to the Harmony Amphitheater across the street.

"Yeah," I said, snapping my eyes away from her. "Yeah, that's it."

We crossed the quiet street and passed under a freestanding

square arch of white stone. The theater was a circle made of tiers of cement stairs that wrapped all the way around with a stage in the center. Random, free-standing cement blocks were placed here and there around it, as a kind of abstract decor. Green grass surrounded the amphitheater, or it would be green once spring came. Now the sun beat down on muddy patches in the brown and yellow turf.

"I come here sometimes at night," I said. "To smoke and be alone."

"I can see why." She held out her arms. "Why didn't Martin stage *Oedipus* out here?"

"Too cold in January."

"Oh, right. But summer time? Does he do shows?"

"No. Too expensive to rent."

"Bummer," she said. "Can't you just see it? Shakespeare-in-the-park?"

"I can," I said, easily imagining Willow building a life here. A house in The Cottages and a summer of Shakespeare in her backyard. While I ran as fast as I could in the opposite direction.

"So can Marty," I said. "He dreams of expanding the theater program to outdoor productions."

"Why doesn't he?" Willow said, climbing up on one oblong block of cement. She sat and dangled her booted feet over the edge.

"No funds," I said. I leaned against the block, my shoulders level with her waist. "He won't tell me much, but the previous owner of HCT didn't manage the books very well."

"Is it serious?" Willow asked. And the genuine concern in her voice made my damn heart swell.

"I don't know. But it's another reason I need to get out of here. I can't make any money here. But out there," I waved my hand to indicate basically anywhere but Harmony. "I have a shot. I can help him out."

"You won't forget where you got your start," Willow said, her voice softening.

I shrugged, but smiled to myself and reached for my Winstons. "You mind if I smoke?"

"Yes and no."

I glanced up at her, squinting. The sun was behind her, turning her long, wavy hair into a golden halo around her.

She looks like goddamn Lady Godiva.

I cleared my throat. "Yes and no?"

"Yes, I mind because it's not good for you. No, the smoke won't bother me."

I nearly put my smokes away.

Do not start with that changing-yourself-shit, Pearce. You're leaving.

I tapped a cigarette out of the pack, put it between my lips and lit it with my silver Zippo. As I exhaled my first drag, I noticed a small black X inked on the knee of Willow's jeans. "What's this?"

"Nothing," she said, a little too fast. "I doodle when I'm bored. Paulson was putting me to sleep the other day."

I nodded. I wasn't an expert on clothes, but I could tell her jeans didn't come out of the bargain bin at The Outpost. Designer brands ran at ninety bucks a pair. Not something you wanted to mark up with black ink.

Let it go.

I took a drag and looked over the amphitheater. I liked coming here at night, when the white stones glowed in the moonlight. My own Stonehenge. In the light of day, the space echoed with all the activities it hosted in Harmony: the fair in summertime, the occasional wedding ceremony and the high school graduation I wasn't invited to.

"I heard George Mason High holds graduation here," Willow said, apparently reading my mind. "Are you going?"

"No."

"Does that bother you?"

"Nope."

"What about all the other school events and experiences? Football games…" She kicked her feet against the cement block. "Dances."

I shrugged. "I'm nineteen. I've had enough of high school." I glanced up at her. "I remember there's a Spring Fling or something coming up. You going?"

Oh shit. It sounded like I was asking her. I didn't even go to the school anymore; I couldn't ask her. Could I?

"No, I'm not going," she said slowly.

"There might be rehearsal that night," I said, tossing my cigarette on the ground. "Is why I mention it."

"True. And anyway, no one's asked me."

"Justin hasn't asked you yet?" My voice was casual and I slouched as I looked out over the amphitheater. Just a guy making conversation. Oscar-caliber acting.

"What? No. Justin and I are only friends."

"I got the impression…" I shook my head. "Never mind."

"The impression I like him?"

I looked back at her. "That he likes you."

"Oh," she said, her brows coming together. "God, I hope not. He's nice enough. I mean, he gives me a ride after rehearsal. But…"

I felt myself craning forward for the rest of her sentence, my ego gleefully throwing out suggestions.

He's dumb as a brick.

He secretly can't read.

He farts when he laughs.

"It feels more brotherly to me than anything else," she finished. "I suppose because he's playing Laertes."

"Yeah," I said and my ego high-fived itself.

"I'm so…*not* into being with someone right now," Willow said with a nervous lilt to her words. "Not for a while, anyway."

I heard a whisper on the breeze, *or ever again.* A heaviness in her eyes hinted she had lost something and had almost given up trying to find it.

She hasn't given up, I thought, a fierce admiration welling in me. *That's why she's doing the play. To find it again.*

In that moment, I vowed to try to cut out all the egotistical bullshit and jealousy over Justin. The dance was out of range now anyway. I couldn't ask her to go even if I wanted to. Which I didn't. My job was to help her find what she was looking for in *Hamlet,* however I could. Even as it dented my eagerness to get the hell out of Harmony.

Willow shielded her eyes from the sun and squinted at me. "So what about you?"

"What about me?"

"Do you like anyone?" she asked, her voice a half tone higher than usual. She laughed. "That's such a high school thing to ask."

"No," I said. "If all goes to plan, I'm leaving Harmony, remember? Stupid to start something now."

"Sure. Makes sense."

A silence fell.

"Yeah, so I probably won't go to the dance," Willow said. "I'm not good in that kind of situation anymore."

"What kind of situation?"

She shook her head. "Never mind. I should get back."

Willow started to scoot down off the block. I held my hand out to her to help. She hesitated for a fraction of a second and then took it. I held my other hand out and she took that too. I steadied her as she hopped down and then we were standing face to face. Close enough I could see her pale blue eyes had lighter shards of blue in them, like a topaz. Close enough to smell the sweetness of her breath—coffee tinged with sugar. Close enough to dance if we wanted.

"Thanks," Willow said, gazing up at me.

"Sure," I said.

I still held her hands. She didn't let go.

"So," she breathed, still not moving.

"Yeah."

I glanced down at our hands. I hadn't touched something this soft and good in ages. The sleeve of her coat bunched up and I spied a black mark on the inside of her forearm, close to her wrist. Willow drew in a breath as I turned her hand over. An X, about the size of a quarter, was stark on her pale skin.

She tugged her hands away. "I really need to get back."

Every instinct cried out to take her hand again, to ask her what the X meant. To lick my thumb and erase it off her skin. I didn't know what it meant but the sight of it made my stomach feel heavy.

"Willow—"

"I doodle when I'm bored. I told you that." Her voice was sharp but her smile wobbled. "Let's go."

We walked the short distance back to town wordlessly. Back in front of the theater, Willow shouldered her bag and glanced around. "Thanks for today. I think Martin would be happy with our progress."

"I do too."

God, would he, I thought.

"So, I guess I'll see you Monday?" she said.

"You have a ride home?"

"Oh, uh…" She still wouldn't meet my eyes. "I was thinking of walking."

"To Emerson Hills?" I said. "That's a mile and a half and it's getting dark soon."

She raised her brows. "I'm not allowed to walk in the dark?"

"You're allowed," I said, "but I don't want you to."

Willow's expression softened. "Oh. Okay. If you don't mind."

"I don't."

As we walked toward my truck in the theater parking lot, every dent and scratch in the blue paint screamed for attention. Once inside, Willow sat with her eyes locked on the view outside her window. Her hands clutched her bag tight, her coat sleeves tugged far over her wrists.

We were silent on the drive to Emerson Hills, where the flatness of Indiana was broken by a few rolling hills. We passed a small overlook with a view of downtown Harmony. Most of the houses here were huge. No cottages or trailers allowed. Stables and trees in the backyards instead of piles of rusted, twisted metal.

Willow directed me down one street. "Right here is good," she said with a vague wave of her hand.

"Which one is yours?" I asked, pulling to the curb in front of a house built in brown brick and gray stone.

"This is great, thanks," she said. She grabbed her bag and reached for the door, then paused, her hand white-knuckled on the handle. "Thank you. Not just for the ride, but for showing me the amphitheater and for our talk. I think it helped."

"You're welcome."

"Was it helpful for you, too? I mean, as far as what Martin wanted from us?"

"Yeah," I said. "It was."

I scrambled to think of something else to talk about, anything to keep her in the car for one more minute...

"Okay, then," she said, grabbing her bag. "I'll see you Monday night."

"Yeah. See you."

She climbed out of the truck and shut the door, then waved at me from the curb. And didn't move.

She's waiting for me to drive away.

Normally, nothing could've budged me from the curb until I

knew she was safe inside her house. But I made an exception and flipped the truck around to head back to the western edge of town, to my shitty trailer. In my rearview, I watched as Willow fidgeted with her bag. Maybe she was digging around for her house keys, but I doubted it. And by the time I turned the corner, I *knew* the brown and gray house I'd pulled in front of wasn't hers.

Chapter Seventeen

Willow

Monday morning in English class and Mr. Paulson was at his usual spot, rifling through papers. Angie was at her desk, wearing baggy jeans, Dr. Martens boots and a black T-shirt that read, *I'm pretty cool but I cry a lot.*

When she saw me, she pulled out her phone, shook it and put it to her ear with a perplexed look on her face.

"Hello? Hello? Is this thing on?" She let her hand drop and gave me a pointed look. "That was a rhetorical question, in case you were wondering. How do I know this? Because my *real* friends, Caroline and Jocelyn, called me over the weekend."

"Sorry," I huffed, slouching into my desk. "I didn't feel like talking okay? I don't always feel like talking on the phone. In fact, I hardly ever feel like talking on the phone."

"I get that. Most people don't like talking on the phone anymore. That's what the *text* function is for." She turned in her seat and leaned over her arm toward me. "You told me you'd call after I dropped you off downtown. I assumed that meant *you would call me.* But you didn't. So I had to call you. You didn't answer. I then spent the weekend thinking Isaac Pearce murdered you and dumped your body in a ditch."

"You did not think that," I said, rolling my eyes.

"Does it matter to you what I thought? My guess is *no.*" She whirled in her seat to face front, then she whipped back around. "Look, I don't know how they do things in New York, but here friends don't just go silent on each other whenever they feel like it." She held up her hands, empty palms facing me. "I'm not a stalker, I'm not your mother, I'm not your babysitter. But you could've texted me. That's all I'm going to say about it."

She turned around. And that was all she had say to me for the rest of the class too.

So what? I thought, trying to find my protective layer of I-don't-give-a-fuck. I'd stopped putting effort into friendships long ago. My New York friends told me the exact same things Angie did. Told me a hundred times until one by one, they gave up on me. Michaela, my best friend, stuck it out the longest. She suspected something had happened that summer, but I refused to talk to her at all, about anything, afraid the worst story would come tumbling out. By Thanksgiving, she stopped calling me. Her last text was the week before Christmas break:

Please talk to me.

I didn't respond. When we moved to Indiana, we got new phone numbers and I cut off everyone who knew me before. X'd myself out of their lives.

Angie's back to me hurt more than I was prepared for.

The bell rang and she hurried out of the classroom without a glance at me. I grabbed my stuff and followed her to her locker.

"You're right," I said. "I'm sorry. I truly am. You've been such a good friend to me and I just... I forgot what that's like."

She gave me a funny look then turned to her locker to exchange one textbook for another. "You didn't have friends in New York? I find that hard to believe."

"I had friends," I said. "Then I didn't. And that's the way it's been for a while now. Until you."

Angie shut her locker and turned to look at me, clutching her binder to her chest. "Why has it been that way?"

I couldn't look at her. "It just had to be."

Angie wilted with a sigh. "You know, if there's something you want to talk about... I'm here. Okay? Whenever you want." Her dark eyes met mine. "Or...whenever you're ready."

I started to tell her I had nothing to say. "Thanks, Angie," came out instead on a low whisper of breath.

She nodded briskly, her long black curls bouncing around her shoulders. "Great. And if we've dispensed with old business, can we now move onto new business? Namely, the great non-date with Isaac Pearce?"

A small smile came over my lips without my permission as we started down the hallway together. "It was really good," I said. "Isaac's not what people think he is." She gave me a look and I nudged her elbow. "I know how that sounds, but I'm serious. People around here paint him as criminal or acting savant and that's it. But he's actually a complete human being. He's really smart and he thinks on different levels…"

"Sounds like you guys hit it off. Why do you sound so sad when talking about him?"

"We were doing fine until two of the Plastics saw us having coffee together. I'm worried one of them was Tessa Vance and that she'll tattle. If my dad finds out, he'll pull me out of the play."

"Sounds like a legit concern," Angie said. "But we're *sad* because…?"

"I can't explain that to Isaac. He'd know I heard the gossip about him and Tessa. Worse, he offered me a ride home. When we got to my street, I told him to park half a block away from my actual house because I didn't want my mom to see him. And I *know* he knew it wasn't the right house. I'm making him feel like shit for all the wrong reasons, but I'm afraid he'd be more hurt by the truth. That my dad forbids me from associating with him outside of the play."

Angie opened her mouth to speak and then nudged my arm. She leaned into me. "Tessa Vance is standing right over there," she said through her teeth. "Reddish brown hair."

I followed her eyes to the Plastics, standing together near the drinking fountain, and immediately recognized two of them from Saturday.

"Shit, that's her."

"And shit, they see us eyeballing them now," Angie replied.

Tessa gave me the fakest of smiles and then pointedly leaned to whisper to her friends. They all turned to look at me with wide-eyed amusement and disdain.

"And I'm fucked," I said.

"Come on." Angie hooked her arm through mine and pulled me down the hall. "Don't look back."

"I'm totally fucked. I don't give a shit what they think, but if she tells her dad…"

"So what? Angie said. "Just tell *your* dad she's a lying little bitch—" she turned to shout over her shoulder, "—*who can't mind her own business.*"

My laugh degenerated into a groan. "What am I going to do? I need this play."

"You *need* it?"

"I've just…grown attached to it. To the director and the actors."

"And Isaac."

"Yes, okay? But he's leaving Harmony in a few months so we're just friends. We can only ever be friends."

Angie rolled her eyes. "Famous last words."

As the day wore on, I became more and more convinced Tessa would rat on me. The silly paranoia fed on itself, fueled by my fear of Dad pulling me out of the play. I'd told Angie the truth. I needed the play. I still hadn't found what I was looking for in Ophelia, but it was there, on the horizon, like a hint of dawn on a new day. An optimistic sun rising against my ever-present darkness.

And what about Isaac? Starting over with a new Ophelia might throw him off his game. I didn't want to be responsible for anything disrupting his flow or whatever process he had. Talent agents were coming to see him. He already had enough to contend with. The last thing he needed was drama from my dad's ridiculous prejudices.

As the last bell rang, I grabbed my homework out of my locker and shut it. I jumped back with a little cry to see Justin Baker standing there, leaning casually on a shoulder.

"Hey," he said. "Missed you Saturday, but you'll be at rehearsal tonight, right?"

"Yeah, of course," I said.

Right after I recover from the mini-heart attack you just gave me.

"Cool." He looked out over the hallway and the milling students going here and there. A lazy prince surveying his kingdom. "Listen, there's a dance coming up in a few weeks. The Spring Fling?"

"Yeah," I said slowly. "I've heard of it."

"Cool." Justin said again. "You think Martin will give us the night off from rehearsal to go?"

"I…I don't know."

I stepped back. My eyes took in Justin's handsome face. Blond hair, blue eyes and an easy smile. There was nothing threatening about him, but then there'd been nothing threatening about Xavier either.

Over Justin's shoulder I saw Tessa, Jessica and a couple the other girls watching us.

"So? You want to?"

"Do I want to what?"

He laughed, perplexed. "Go with me."

It wasn't even a question.

"Go to the dance…?"

A dance. Bodies writhing in the dark. Pulsating music. A hand on my hip. A voice in my ear, "Can I get you something to drink?"

I pushed the black memories away. The longing to be normal and have normal experiences was a hunger in my stomach. I wanted to go to a dance. I wanted to go shopping for a pretty dress and feel a tingle of anticipation in my stomach when my date came to the door, with a corsage in a plastic box.

But in my short-lived imagination, Mom opened the door and cooed over how devastating my date looked in a tuxedo. My father shook his hand and welcomed him inside his home. I came down the stairs, and it was Isaac who was waiting for me, and he smiled…

I blinked and came back to Justin's expectant grin.

"Oh, I'm not really… I'm not looking to be with someone…seriously. Not that you're asking me to be serious. I mean…"

His smile widened and he leaned deeper against the lockers, as if he were used to girls stammering over their words for him.

"Great," he said. "We can go as friends, and just…see what happens."

My stomach clenched at the momentary gleam in his eye, and the ceiling suddenly felt like it was an inch above my head.

"We need to ask Martin…"

"What's up, guys?" Angie asked, sidling up beside me. She gave Justin a hard look, which he returned with his easy-going smile.

"Not much," he said. "Just working out Spring Fling details."

Angie's eyes flared and her finger moved between us, pointing. "*You* guys are going to the dance together?"

I opened my mouth to speak.

"Yeah, we are," Justin said. "We'll talk more at rehearsal. I gotta go." He jerked his chin at me in a kind of farewell. "See you tonight."

"Yeah…see you," I said.

"See you," Angie echoed and dragged me outside. "I am *so* confused. Justin?"

The early-spring afternoon was brassy and cold, bringing me around.

"Well…sure. Why not?" I said, fighting for my equilibrium. "Now there's nothing for Tessa to blab about. Right? And…when Justin shows up at my house, my dad is going to hump his leg, he'll be so happy. I won't have to worry about him pulling me out of the play. Yeah. Perfect cover."

Angie looked doubtful. "I guess, but for a second there it looked like you got railroaded—"

I stopped walking. "I did *not*," I said, too loud. "*I* get to say. I can go to the dance with whomever I want."

Except Isaac.

I fought for calm. Isaac flat-out told me he was done with high school. If I wanted my normal, I'd have to go and take it. Just like he said.

"Okay, okay," Angie said. "But Willow—"

"We'll just go as friends. All of us. Together. You and Nash, and Joe and Caroline, right? We'll all go together, okay? Please?"

Angie's brows came together. "Yeah, sure," she said slowly. "If that's what you want."

"That's what I want. Yes, of course it is."

To be normal. That's what I want. That's all I'll ever want.

"Willow, dear," Martin called from the stage. "Come up here?"

Rehearsal hadn't started yet. The cast milled in the audience, chatting in low voices. Isaac stood onstage with Martin. As I took the steps to join them, my eyes took in Isaac's tall body, slender yet packed with lean muscle. He stood with arms crossed over his chest, his long legs in jeans and scuffed black boots. His biceps strained at the sleeves of a white T-shirt.

Why do I notice these things about him? Why can't I stop looking?

"I was just chatting with Isaac about your outing on Saturday," Martin said. "Not too torturous, I presume?"

"I survived," I said and ventured a small smile for Isaac.

He returned a faint, disinterested nod but his gray-green eyes were intense as they looked me up and down. His lips—always pressed together—parted slightly. Then he abruptly tore his gaze from me. "Yeah, it was good," he said. "Really good."

"Really good?" Martin said, his eyebrows raised in comical disbelief. "You hear that, folks? On this day in history, Isaac Pearce found something to be *really* good."

"Knock it off, Marty."

Martin winked at me. "I have a good feeling about this." Louder, he said, "Let's run your dialogue for Act Three, Scene Two."

Thanks to afternoons in the library with my script and a Spark Notes translation, the play was no longer blocks of vague poetry. I was familiar now with every Act. The scene Martin wanted to run was a play-within-a-play—Hamlet's scheme to have a troop of actors reenact his father's murder. During the performance, Hamlet tortures Ophelia with bawdy jokes and sarcasm.

Two rows of chairs were set, facing stage left and cheated out so they weren't in profile to the audience. The King and Queen were to sit in the front row. I sat behind, beside an empty chair. Isaac waited offstage for his cue.

I was off-book for this scene, as was Isaac. Dialogue committed to memory, it was the first time we'd be acting without the buffer of scripts in our hands and I didn't know what to do with mine.

"From your entrance, Hamlet," Martin said. He'd slouched into his usual pose—one arm across his middle, the other elbow resting on it, fingers over his mouth.

Isaac slipped out of the shadows of backstage. Eyes wide and with a loose, jangly smile he never wore in real life.

Martin cued him with Gertrude's line, *"Come hither, my dear Hamlet, sit by me."*

Isaac's manic gaze fell on me and softened. *"No, good mother. Here's metal more attractive."*

He rushed toward me and slid to his knees at my feet. His expression was pretended innocence, and his eyes storm-tossed and wicked.

"Lady, shall I lie in your lap?"

I startled and sat up straighter, face forward, hands folded. *"No, my lord."*

"I mean, my head upon your lap?" he said and did exactly that, resting his cheek on my thigh.

A shiver rippled out from where he touched me. Half danced down my calf, the other rest rocketed between my legs and settled there warmly. My first intimate male touch since X. Instead of tensing up or shutting down, my body liked the weight of Isaac's head in my lap. The dark brush of his stubble so stark against the white of my jeans.

A blush burned my cheeks as I whispered. **"Aye, my lord."**

Isaac turned to prop his chin on my thigh. The scene called for him to show mocking disdain hidden under false humor, but his delivery bordered on flirtatious.

"Do you think I meant country matters?"

I already knew from Spark Notes that country matters = sex.

My flush deepened and I sat up straighter. *"I think nothing, my lord,"* I said, my thoughts full of his thick brown hair and wanting to sink my fingers in it.

"That's a fair thought to lie between maids' legs."

God, another flush of heat swept through me, settling between *my* legs, as if his voice had commanded it.

"W-what is, my lord?" I asked, stammering Shakespeare's words.

"Nothing," he said.

I tried to remember Hamlet was toying with Ophelia, but my line came out on a small, provocative laugh. *"You are merry, my lord."*

Isaac smiled knowingly. *"Who, I?"*

"Yes, merry indeed," Marty said, breaking the moment like a sledgehammer. "A little too merry, methinks. I'm going to give a little direction here."

Isaac lingered a moment more, then lifted his head from my lap and sat in the empty chair beside me. I put my hand where he'd been, to touch the warmth there a little longer.

Martin rubbed his chin with one hand. "I love the progress you two have made. I can feel the difference in how you relate to each other, the familiarity." He turned to Isaac. "But you're too nice."

Isaac sniffed. "I'm nice?"

"First time for everything," I said.

He shoved his shoulder against mine playfully, not looking at me, but his Oedipus curtain call smile slipped out, and it put a crack straight across my block of ice. A sliver of light in the dark. I knew he forgave me for not showing him my house, while I hated even more that I'd had to hide him.

I don't want to hide him. I feel good with him.

"Last time, Isaac, you were too pissed off," Marty said. "This time, too nice. Go back to pissed off and layer it over the feelings you have for each other. Build on what we worked through last Saturday."

Isaac nodded. "Yeah, sure."

Martin turned to me. "Willow, I love the nervousness. Ophelia's a proper lady and Hamlet is being quite inappropriate for a prince. Your initial stiff, shocked reaction was brilliant. But later, you... How do I put this delicately? You looked turned on."

My eyes widened and a tingle of electricity shot down my spine.

Martin turned to Isaac. "You look smitten too, come to think of it. Right now, this scene plays like something out of *Romeo and Juliet*."

Unable to look at Isaac, my eyes sought refuge in the audience. They found Justin sitting in the front row with Rosencrantz and Guildenstern—two college actors he'd become friends with—watching me blankly.

"If you're building an emotional castle in this scene," Martin said, pulling my attention back, "the foundation is the love. The ruin of that love is the ground floor. Upstairs is his madness. And in the attic, a healthy dose of sexual tension. Okay?"

Martin checked his watch. "Damn. The Equity actors need their break." He clapped his hands. "Okay, everyone. Take five."

Isaac and I were left alone on the stage, a thick silence between us where words whispered.

The feelings you have for each other...

You look smitten...

More like Romeo and Juliet...

"Well," I finally said. "Martin's a very...colorful director, isn't he?"

Isaac rubbed the back of his head. "Yeah, he gets some wild ideas."

"I like his ideas," I said. "I mean, him. I like him."

Isaac met my gaze. "Yeah. Me too."

The moment shimmered. His gray-green eyes so warm in mine and the yellow stage lights shining down. Then Martin clapped his hands to call attention, making me jump in my skin.

"Martin also likes to clap," Isaac said. "A lot."

I laughed. "I noticed."

"Just a friendly reminder about memorization. It's been two weeks." Martin said. "How is everyone doing getting off-book?"

A few murmurs and nods, a few groans. Len Hostetler grabbed his own throat with both hands and mimed being choked to death. Then he smiled brightly and gave a thumbs up. "Going great, Marty."

Justin raised his hand. "I have a question. Willow and I are going to the Spring Fling dance next Friday night at the school. Are we going to be able to get the night off?"

An icy cold bloomed in the pit of my stomach and spread out. I looked at Isaac. He stared back. For half a second, the hurt was evident in his eyes. A little boat floating in the green-gray waves, then swiftly sinking. His face closed up and he looked away.

"You have to say yes, Herr Direktor," Len said in his booming voice.

"Indeed," Lorraine said. "A spring dance is a milestone in any high school experience."

"I will make an exception this time," Martin said, frowning a little. "But one night is all I can spare. Anyone else? Put your hand down, Len."

Everyone laughed and Justin looked pleased with himself. The weight of my guilt and embarrassment was so heavy I couldn't lift my eyes to meet Isaac's.

Why do you feel guilty? He's leaving town. He said he's done with high school...

"Okay," Martin said, with a clap of his hands. "Let's get back to work. Willow? Isaac?"

We ran the scene again, this time with no flirtation. No niceness. Isaac delivered his lines with barely-concealed disdain. A wounded prince mocking the lover who betrayed him. His head in my lap was a heavy stone. We weren't playing roles now. We were just being ourselves.

It had only taken one Saturday afternoon to make a connection. Isaac shared private information with me. I let him come closer to my story than anyone. The time we spent together was the foundation of the scene. My going to the dance with Justin was the betrayal. Hamlet's pain was Isaac's. Ophelia's regret was mine.

When it ended, Martin clapped again and this time it was applause.

"Perfect," he said. "That was perfect. It adds so much more dimension to the scene. Good work everyone. Moving on…"

At the end of rehearsal, I hurried to grab my stuff and get out. Then I remembered Justin was my ride home. He was waiting for me at the theater entrance, looking smug and triumphant. I hated him a little for that.

I tried to jam my script into my bag too quickly, dropped it and the three-ring binder busted open as it hit the floor. Pages spilled out and I kneeled to gather them up. A figure crouched beside me and I smelled gasoline, aftershave and cigarette smoke.

"I thought you said you weren't going to go," he said, muscles showing in his clenched jaw.

You said you were done with high school, I wanted to shout.

"I changed my mind," I said, thrusting my own chin out. "I'm allowed."

He sniffed a short, hard laugh. "Yeah, you are."

He started to hand me the stack of papers, then froze, his brow furrowed over the crawl of little black X's in the margins, like an infestation of insects.

"Are rehearsals that boring?"

"They're not. It's just doodling."

"You said you doodle when you're bor—"

"Give me those, please."

The hard angles and lines of his expression softened as he handed over the pages. Almost reluctantly. As if he didn't want to give all those black X's back to me.

"Night, Willow," he said softly, and rose to his feet.

"Good night, Isaac," I said, but he'd already walked away.

Chapter Eighteen

Isaac

"What the fuck was that, Marty?" I asked, when the last cast member left for the night. "Smitten? I looked fucking smitten?"

Martin just regarded me placidly. "I'm not going to change how I direct my show," he said. "I call it as I see it. But I was hoping…"

"Cut it out with the hoping. Direct the show however you want, but keep your matchmaking bullshit out of it."

His eyes hardened and he crossed his arms over his chest. "I call it like I see it," he said again. "If you give it to me, I'm going to incorporate it into the scene." He took a step toward me. "Nothing you can do about that, but there's something you can do about *her*."

"It's too late, Marty," I said, the anger draining out of me. "I'm moving out of Harmony. Whether your talent scouts take me or not."

"I hope you find whatever you're looking for when you do. But I also hope you don't miss what's right in front of you." He clapped my shoulder. "It's never *too late*. Those two words are the greatest, most powerful killer of hope mankind has ever invented for itself."

I opened the door to my trailer and found Pops passed out on the couch, a lit cigarette still smoldering in the ashtray on the coffee table. A pile of unpaid bills served as a coaster, stained by beer and whiskey and the remnants of his fast food dinner. If hopelessness had a smell, it was stale beer, grease and an overflowing ashtray.

"It's not too late to get the fuck out of here," I muttered.

But instead of packing my shit and heading over to Marty's place, I stubbed out the lit cigarette and turned out the lights.

The following morning, I poured milk into a bowl of cereal and ate it standing at the kitchen counter. Pops eventually snorted awake and sat up, blinking at me with bleary eyes and scratching the stubble on his chin. "You going to work?"

"I have the day off."

He sat back on the couch. "You're taking a day off?"

My body tensed, every muscle and sinew going on high alert. He was in a fighting mood and hadn't even gotten off the couch yet.

"I'm not *taking* the day off, Pops," I said evenly. "I don't work Tuesdays."

The body shop I worked at in Braxton wanted to give me full-time, but I alternated working there and helping Marty in the theater. No way in hell Pops needed to know that.

I ate my cereal faster.

"What are you going to do all day? Rehearse that stupid play? Prance around in tights and breeches while spouting off a bunch of bullshit no one understands."

"Yeah, Pops, that's exactly what I'm going to do," I said.

He stared at me for a moment and I stared back.

"Don't get smart with me," he said in a low voice, like the rumbling of thunder that warns of a storm.

He stared me down for another moment more, then grunted. He found his lighter and began rummaging around the cluttered coffee table for his pack of smokes. Frustration mounting, he scrounged faster, knocking over empty bottles and beer cans. Finally, with a muttered curse, he upended the entire table, sending cigarette butts, ash, bottles and cans across the floor.

"Jesus, Pops."

I set my bowl aside and grabbed a trash bag from under the sink. I kneeled beside the mess and began to clean up, putting cans and bottles into the bag.

Still sitting on the couch, Pops bent down for an empty beer can and tossed it into the sack. Then he took one of the bottles by the neck and slammed it into the side of my face.

"*You don't get smart with me,*" he bellowed, brandishing the bottle.

I stared, my heart crashing against my chest. My breath came fast and I felt the right side of my face start to swell. With every heartbeat, hot pain throbbed on my cheekbone and under my eye. Blood trickled down my cheek.

With a cry of rage, I knocked the bottle out of his hand, grabbed his wrists and pinned them to his chest. I pressed him back against the couch, leaning over him with all my weight, my face inches from his. The blood streamed down my cheek dripping onto his plaid shirt.

"Never again," I yelled between clenched teeth. "*Never fucking again.*"

He'd hit me hard, a lifetime working with heavy steel behind the blow. But my guard had been down. I was stronger than him now. He didn't bother to struggle and a glint of fear touched his eyes.

I gave him a final shove and stood up. I stared down at him for a few more minutes, trying to remember a time when he didn't look at me with contempt. A time when he and my mother and I were together and happy. I had a photo in my mind of the three of us, but now it showed only my mother and me. The man who'd been my father had faded out of the picture.

I headed toward the bathroom. Behind me, Pops gasped and caught his breath, muttering curses. I shut the bathroom door and looked at my reflection.

"Jesus fucking Christ."

My right cheekbone was swollen and puffy, the skin split by a half-inch gash still streaming blood. An alarming patch of red stained my white T-shirt.

I grabbed the hand towel by the sink, ran cold water over it and cleaned up my cheek. I probably needed stitches, but I wasn't about to incur a bunch of Urgent Care charges. I had a stockpile of butterfly Band-Aids for just such an occasion. It took me three tries to get one on fast enough before the blood made my skin too slick. I put a second one beside the first and a regular Band-Aid over both.

My whole face throbbed now. The swelling would probably last another couple of days. Another couple of rehearsals where the cast would stare at me with pity, but no one would ask me what happened because they already knew. Marty would pull me aside and tell me, yet again, his door was always open. His hospitality there for the taking.

As I stared at my reflection I wondered why the fuck I just didn't take it.

When I left the bathroom, I understood why. My father sat on the couch, his hands in his lap, staring at nothing. Sad and lost. Splotches of my blood dried to maroon against the green of his plaid shirt.

He looked up and his eyes went immediately to my wounds. I saw the pain and regret fly across his face before he looked away quickly.

I put my *Hamlet* script in my backpack, grabbed my car keys, my Winstons and my jacket. I went back to the coffee table to grab the TV remote and he flinched as if I were going to hit him. That hurt almost as badly as my face.

"You want the news?"

He nodded. I turned the TV on and went out.

I walked to the eastern edge of the scrapyard, toward the overturned truck by the chain link fence. I lit a cigarette as I walked and took a deep drag. I let it out slowly, willing my nerves to calm down. I stopped when I heard Benny's low singsong voice.

"Goddammit, Benny."

I heard a *bonk* followed by a curse. Benny came out rubbing his head.

"Damn, you scared the crap out of me."

"Why aren't you in school?"

He shrugged sheepishly at the ground. "I don't know," he said. "Don't want to go." Now he looked up from his shoes and his eyes widened. "What happened to you?"

"You know what happened to me," I said. "I want to know what's happening with you. You can't *not* go to school."

"Why not?" he spat back. "You don't go to school."

"I stayed in school until they kicked me out and now I'm taking a test to finish. You are in the eighth grade. You're fucking up your future if you don't go."

"Okay, okay," he said, no commitment in his tone. I hadn't gotten through to him. I didn't know how. I didn't know what to do or

145

what to say. I didn't have the words. I wasn't his dad. I was just the neighbor with the drunk father.

And suddenly I was so fucking tired. Weary to my bones.

"You want to help me run lines?"

"You're not going to take me to school?"

"I can drive you there every day of my life, Benny, and it won't matter if you don't know it's important. This play I'm doing right now? It's important to me. So yeah, I could use the help."

"Yeah, sure."

I handed him my script and he sat down on the semi-truck tire. "Where are you at?"

"I have it marked."

He found the dog-eared page and flipped it open. "To be or not to be?"

"Yeah, that's it," I said, taking a final drag off my cigarette. I dropped it, ground it out with my boot. "I'm not acting it, just running it for the lines."

"I'm ready," Benny said.

I stood in the middle of the scrapyard clearing and closed my eyes.

> *"To be or not to be, that is the question.*
> *Whether t'is nobler in the mind to suffer*
> *the slings and arrows of outrageous fortune,*
> *or to take arms against a sea of troubles*
> *and, by opposing, end them?"*

My shoulders sagged. *"To sleep. To die,"* I said my voice low. *"To die, to sleep perchance to dream."*

"You skipped a bunch of stuff."

"I know."

"What does it mean?" Benny asked, his voice hushed now.

"He's asking if it's worth it. To keep going or not."

"Is it?"

I don't know, I thought. *Sometimes I just don't know*

"What's the next line?" I asked.

"Ay, there's the rub," Benny said and wrinkled his nose with a small laugh.

I went through the rest of the monologue, Benny stopping me now and then to correct my mistakes. I got to the end, where Ophelia entered, and fell silent. My thoughts filled with Willow, imagining her stepping onto this stage with me—this crappy junkyard—looking beautiful and fragile, but strong and resilient too.

Benny thought I had forgotten my lines. *"In your orisons, may all my sins be remembered."* He wrinkled his nose again. "What are orisons?"

"Prayers," I said. "She can't hear him yet, but he's asking her to remember him in all of her prayers. Like saying goodbye."

"Is he going away?" Benny asked.

"Yeah, he is," I said, the words dropping from me like stones. "And he can't take her with him."

I walked over to Benny and took the script out of his hand to shut it.

"Benjamin, if you were ever my friend, you will stay in school. For me and for your mother. You have to take care of yourself because no one's going to do it for you. Your mom is going to try her best but it's up to you, in the end."

"Where you going?" Benny asked, blinking back tears.

"I'm going to go stay at a friend's house for a while and after *Hamlet* closes, I'm leaving Harmony."

"Will I see you again?" His voice trembled now.

"Yeah, of course. You'll see me around. And I'll come say goodbye before I go."

Benny sniffed and wiped his nose on the sleeve of his shirt. "Sucks, man," he said. "But I'm glad for you. I'll miss you."

I reached out, ran my hand over his close-cropped hair. "Come on. I'm taking you to school."

I dropped Benny off at Elizabeth Mason Middle School, then drove my truck back to the trailer, my thoughts still full of Willow and a page covered in little black X's.

I would ask nothing of her. She owed me nothing. But I'd give her the play as best as I could. I'd help her get through to the end, to tell her story and find the relief she kept asking me about. And when it was done, I would go.

Pops was in his room with the door shut when I came back. I went directly to my own small room and packed up a bag of my things. It wasn't much. Everything I owned fit in one small suitcase.

Outside my dad's bedroom door, I paused. I raised my hand to knock and then let it fall again. Instead I tore out a sheet from my script and wrote on the back:

I'll pay the bills and send you money. You don't have to worry about anything.

--Isaac

I set the note on the coffee table that was now free of debris except for one ashtray and a pack of Winstons. Just to be safe, I propped the paper against the smokes so he wouldn't miss it.

Then I left.

I drove across town to the neighborhood beyond the amphitheater. Streets of large, comfortable homes, most dating back to the Civil War. I knocked on the front door of the Fords' red brick house with the wrought iron fence. Brenda Ford opened the door, her hair and smock smudged with paint, a big smile at the ready. Her expression morphed into shocked concern as she took in my bloodied clothes and swollen cheek.

Her eyes dropped to the bag in my hand and the suitcase behind me. A myriad of emotions splashed across her face: sorrow, concern and finally, relief.

"Come in, Isaac," she said, opening the door wider for me. "Come right in."

Chapter Nineteen

Willow

Wednesday afternoon, Angie and I went to Roxy's, a women's dress shop in the Braxton shopping mall.

"Your mission," Angie said, "should you choose to accept it, is to find me a dress that doesn't make me look like I'm trying too hard."

"It might be hard to find a dress with a smart-ass quote on the front," I said with a nod at her T-shirt. It was gray with black lettering that read, *Sorry I'm late, I didn't want to come.*

"If I had my way, I'd wear this little baby," Angie said, plucking at the hem. "But I gotta pretty myself up for Nash. He deserves it. Although I try not to give him my full glory too often as it tends to overwhelm him."

I grinned. "I can only imagine."

"What's your style?" She held up a long, full-skirted yellow dress in shimmery satin. "With your hair, you can go full-princess easy, though you're more of a Rapunzel than a Belle."

"No princess dresses," I said. "I want simple. I don't want Justin to think I'm trying too hard either."

"Maybe you should give the guy a chance."

I held up a red floor-length with a low neckline and put it back immediately. "Give him a chance at what, pray tell?"

"Oh, *pray tell*," she said. "Someone's all Shakespearean up in here."

"Methinks thou art a nutjob."

"That's going on my next shirt," she said. "But for real. Justin is super cute. He's nice. Or seems to be."

"I'm not interested in anyone," I said. "Even if I were, it wouldn't be Justin. Yes, he's nice and his Laertes doesn't suck, but there's no…"

"Spark?" Angie asked.

I nodded. "I just want to go to the dance and have a good time and that's it. I don't want it to *mean* anything."

"Fair enough." Angie held out a simple black dress. "Oh my God, I love this. It's like something an ice skater would wear."

The jersey bodice was cut like a T-shirt only tighter-fitting and lower in the neck. From the fitted waist, a taffeta skirt flared out to just above her knees when she held the hanger under her chin.

"It's kind of plain now," she said, meeting my skeptical look. "But when I accessorize, like you know how I do, it'll be perfect."

"You'll look beautiful." I held up a navy blue halter dress. It also flared out in a full skirt above the knee. The bodice was intricate beadwork and sequins. "And this does not suck."

"Are you kidding?" Angie said. "This is going to be gorgeous on you. Come. Let us try."

We tried on our selections, posing in the mirror with silly faces and laughing. Dresses chosen, we each tried on hideously frou-frou gowns with bows and lace for the hell of it, and took selfies to text to Jocelyn and Caroline. And the whole time, I felt that feeling I'd been searching for. A little hint of excitement that comes from shopping with your girlfriend for a dance. But not enough. No spark. My thoughts kept wandering to Isaac. I wondered if he'd been telling the truth when he said missing a dance wouldn't bother him.

I wondered if he cared that I was going with Justin.

It doesn't matter, I thought. *I couldn't have gone with him, even if he asked me. Dad would ruin everything.*

Besides, I wasn't sure I could handle the dance at all. The thought of a guy's body pressed to mine, whether it was Justin or Isaac… A guy getting in my space. The potential to be alone in a darkened room and out of control…

I went cold all over and quickly pulled my street clothes back on.

"You okay?" Angie said. "You look pale."

"I'm fine. I just need to eat something."

We sat at the food court with our dress bags on our laps, eating pretzel bites from Wetzels and drinking lemonade. We took more selfies. We people-watched. We laughed. I remembered what it was to have female company again. The trust and safety. I'd cut it out of my life, X'd it out, but now, with Angie, I had it back and it felt good. I had a real friend.

"You sure you're okay?" Angie asked. "You're looking at me like you're in love with me. Which is cool, I get that a lot."

"Yes, Angie. You found me out. I love you."

We laughed and made jokes, but it was the truth.

Wednesday night, the good vibes of my shopping trip with Angie stuck with me, straight into rehearsal, I stepped into a theater that was only half-full with the cast. Justin and some of the others with smaller roles weren't called that night. I felt lighter somehow...until I saw Isaac.

The right side of his face was swollen and bruised. A white butterfly bandage covered a gash on his cheekbone. Covered most of it—the edges peeked out, dark red with congealed blood.

My heart ached. Until that moment, the abuse he suffered from his father had been only rumors to me. That and one single comment Isaac made during our outing on Saturday. It was vague and abstract and happened somewhere else. Now it was a raw, wincing wound and vivid, purple and blue bruising under his eye.

It's real.

This happens to him.

And no one is talking about it.

I supposed the veteran HCT actors all knew the score by now. They'd known Isaac much longer than I had. But their silence still angered me.

Doesn't anyone care?

But then again, Isaac wasn't exactly inviting questions. He stood alone, wearing his leather jacket like armor. His bruised face a stone wall, the gates locked tight. He probably didn't *want* anyone talking about it.

But what if he does?

I marked myself with black X's, my version of the Scarlet Letter, only no one knew what they meant. Maybe it was me crying out for someone to ask, even if I would never tell them. Isaac had asked. Now he wore the marks of the abuse he suffered full on his face where he could not hide it.

I moved to stand next to him. "Are you okay?"

"Yeah, I'm okay."

He hardly moved his mouth, his voice soft. And grateful.

"The Fords are letting me stay with them," he said. "I moved into their spare bedroom."

"Good," I said. "I'm glad."

"It's just for a little while."

"Of course."

A silence, then, "I can't sleep. The bed is soft, the house is warm and I have a hot dinner every night, but I can't fucking sleep. I lie awake and think of my dad, alone in that shitty trailer…"

I nodded. "I know what you mean," I said, and then more words followed without my permission. A little piece of my secret. "I can't sleep either."

Slowly Isaac's head turned. His gaze dropped down to my wrist, its black X concealed under a long-sleeved shirt. Then he looked me in the eye and his voice was like a hand held out to me, asking me to trust him. "Why can't you sleep?"

Staring back, I wondered what it would be like to actually tell someone. To smash the icy block once and for all, and let the words out into the world.

I turned toward Isaac, and he turned toward me so that we leaned against the wall, on our sides, like how a couple might, lying in bed. He bent his head to me, ready to hear me, and I tilted my chin up to him, the words climbing up my throat.

Martin clapped his hands together, slicing the moment apart.

"Act Two, Scene One," he called. "Ophelia? Daughter of mine?"

"Go on," Isaac said. "Maybe later?"

"Yeah." I said softly. "Maybe."

Martin set the other actors to work with Rebecca, the assistant director, then pulled me aside. "Come, daughter. T'is time you and I worked out Act Two, Scene One."

In Act Two, Scene One, Ophelia runs to Polonius, explaining that Hamlet came to visit her and was acting crazy. Instead of reacting to others onstage, I had to fly in, already terrorized, with a veteran actor and director as my scene partner and no motivation but what I created for myself.

This is going to suck...

"Whenever you're ready," Martins said from our corner of the stage.

Feeling like an idiot, I stepped backstage, took a deep breath, then flew back on.

"*O my lord, my lord, I have been so affrighted!*"

Martin whirled around with the perfect mix of shock and worry. "*With what, i' th' name of God?*"

"*My lord, as I was sewing in my closet...*"

I broke character with an unladylike snort of laughter. "I'm sorry, but sewing in the closet?"

"Closet merely means room," Martin said with a mild smile.

"I know, but it just sounds so..."

"Archaic?"

"Yes," I said. "I picture her locked away in an actual closet with hardly any light, sewing like a dutiful little woman. I'm just not feeling it. Hamlet came to visit her and she's explaining what happened? Why not just s*how* what happened?"

"Without dialogue?" Martin shot me a grin. "Shakespeare doesn't ever *not* use words. Words are kind of his thing."

I pursed my lips in a smile.

"Ophelia is explaining how Hamlet scared her, but Polonius takes it as a sign that Hamlet's so in love with his daughter, he's losing his mind."

My cheeks flamed. "Okay, well, I'm having a hard time with this. Finding the emotion. The pretty words make it hard to get into that mindset, you know?"

Ugh, actor fail.

Getting into Ophelia's mindset was exactly my job, but Martin smiled patiently.

"Why don't we try making it real?" he asked. "Perhaps if we

acted it out first, the lines would make more sense when you describe them to Polonius. You'll have a physical memory to draw from."

"Anything to help."

He scanned the theater and found Isaac running lines with Mel Thompson, who played Horatio.

"Isaac," Martin called. "Can I borrow you for a minute?"

My heart started pounding in my chest as Isaac came up the stage steps. Or came anywhere near me, I suddenly realized.

"What's up?" he asked.

"In this scene, Ophelia is describing to yours truly how Hamlet barged into her room with his clothes a mess, acting strange enough to frighten her."

Isaac nodded. "Okay."

"Willow's having trouble finding her motivation. So why don't we do this?" Martin turned to me. "Willow, I'll read your lines. Isaac, you act them out. It'll give Willow an idea of the severity of the situation."

Isaac looked at me as he answered, "If you think it would help?"

I nodded. "I want to get this right."

He looked reluctant, but we took our spots, me sitting in a chair pretending to sew.

"Very well," Martin said. "Hamlet has flown into your room, looking pale and disheveled, his knees knocking, et cetera."

Isaac took one step and somehow made it seem he'd rushed onto the stage. His eyes were wild in his bruised face. His breath came in short hard gasps, his fists clenching and unclenching.

As Martin read Ophelia's description of Hamlet's behavior, Isaac performed them.

He flew at me and grabbed my wrist, hard, hauling me out of the chair. I barely found my feet when he pushed me away, holding me at arms' length but his fingers still dug into my wrist. The wild intensity of his gaze flew over my face again and again, as if he were trying to memorize me. My heart began to pound, this time with a hard, panicked clanging that made me want to tear my arm out of his grasp. He moved close to me, bent his head toward mine, his nose in my hair, inhaling me. Then he exhaled and let it out on a soft groan of regret as he let me go.

I pulled my wrist to my thudding chest. Isaac backed away, his eyes locked on mine. He turned and walked off stage, all the while watching me over his shoulder, heedless of anything in his way. He melted into the curtains and I stared after, trembling, my legs weak.

Martin dropped the script to the floor, jerking my wild gaze to him. He was Polonius now, and he grabbed me by the shoulders, seizing the moment while I was still trapped in it.

"*Come, go with me. I will go seek the king. This is the very ecstasy of love.*" He gave me a slight shake. "*What, have you given him any hard words of late?*"

I stared at him, my eyes wide and unblinking, my mind translating the question.

What did you do to him to make him act that way?

My words emerged on a whisper. "*No, my good lord. But as you did command.*"

Polonius held me for half a second more. When he let go, it was Martin's face breaking into a jubilant smile. "You got it," he said and pulled me in for a hug. "You're a natural, Willow. Raw talent. I'm so grateful you found my theater."

"Thanks," I managed. "Can I use the restroom?"

I didn't wait for an answer, but hurried out of the theater to the ladies' room in the lobby, where I splashed cold water on my face a half-dozen times.

"You're okay," I told the girl in the mirror. "You're okay, you're okay, you're okay."

When rehearsal ended, I surveyed the remaining actors, wondering who I could ask for a ride home. I decided I could be a big girl and call an Uber. I booked the ride, then went outside into the chilly air. The days were getting warmer now, but the nights still held a little bite of winter.

"Hey."

I looked around and saw Isaac leaning against the wall, one foot flat against the bricks, a cigarette tucked between his lips. Hulking and battered in his black leather jacket, he'd look dark and dangerous to everyone. But not to me.

"Hey," I said. "Thanks for helping out tonight."

He looked away for a moment, his jaw hard, then back to me. "You were scared."

I tucked my hair behind my ear, shrugged. "You were intense.

Isn't that what's supposed to happen?"

"So it was all an act."

"They don't call it *acting* for nothing."

He snorted smoke out of his nose. "I didn't like scaring you like that."

"Why?"

"It felt real."

I crossed my arms. "You think we don't feel the same when we watch you? In *Oedipus* I was scared you'd actually gouged your damn eyes out."

"I'm being serious."

"So am I." I tilted my chin up in mock arrogance and flipped a lock of hair over my shoulder. "And maybe I'm just that good."

He nodded, not smiling at the joke. "I know you are but…"

"But what?"

He thought for a minute, took a drag off his smoke. "When I get really into a scene, it's because I'm connecting to some real emotion or memory within it."

"I'm familiar with Method acting, yes," I said, clinging to snark to keep the conversation from where Isaac was taking it.

He glanced at me, then looked away. "I don't want to get all up in your business, but tonight when I got close to you, when I grabbed you…" He ground his teeth. "The fear I saw in your eyes…"

And then it came again, Isaac's hand out to me, strong and sure, offering to be there while I crossed the great black chasm.

"I drew it out, but I didn't put it there to begin with," he asked. "Did I?"

"No," I whispered.

"Who did?"

I swallowed hard. "It doesn't matter."

"Matters to me," he said, his voice gruff. "It fucking matters to me, Willow."

I felt myself moving closer to him. He looked so strong and brave and unafraid of anything. And I felt so small and tired. I wanted to give up pretending I wasn't exhausted down to my soul and fall into his arms. Let him hold me up for a little bit, even if it was a cowardly thing to do.

"I should go," I said. "It's late."

He held my gaze a moment longer, then nodded and crushed out his smoke. "I'll drive you."

"You can't," I said. "Not because I don't want you to. I swear. It's my father. He'll—"

Isaac waved a hand, cutting me off. "You don't have to explain."

"It's why I had you drop me off at another house."

"I know." His smile was gentle. "It's okay. Marty insisted on putting my truck in the shop for some maintenance. I've got Brenda's Nissan this week. I can drop you off and your father will be none the wiser."

"I hate that it has to be like this," I said. "I hate that he's a bigoted ass, but I can't lose this play."

"I don't want you to either," Isaac said. "Come on. You're shivering."

He drove me home in Brenda Ford's Nissan Altima. Pink crystals hung from the rearview mirror. They jingled against Isaac's black leather sleeve when he reached to adjust it. The scent of potpourri clung to the leather seats, yet through it, I could still detect the cigarette smoke. All the feminine trappings of the car only made Isaac more striking and masculine. He was a formidable form next to me, yet I felt perfectly safe.

He pulled to the curb in front of my house, then leaned over the steering wheel to get a good look at it. Probably comparing it to his trailer. Maybe thinking I was just another spoiled rich girl who didn't appreciate what she had.

"You safe here?" he asked.

I stared, taken aback. Confused. Then it sunk in what he was asking and God, my heart ached. The simple consideration touched my bones.

"Willow?" His gray-green eyes pressed me, searching.

"I'm safe here," I said.

He nodded, satisfied. "You should go. I think we're being watched."

I looked to see a figure in the living room window, holding the curtains back.

"That's my dad," I said. "Right on schedule."

"Just tell him you got a ride with the director's wife."

"Right." And before I could stop myself, I leaned over and

kissed Isaac's cheek. His scruff was bristly under my lips, but his skin was warm and smelled of soap and tobacco. When I pulled away, his eyes were wide.

"Thank you," I said.

"For what?"

"For saying it matters." Tears suddenly choked my throat and filled my eyes. I threw open the door and got out. The cold air was bracing in my lungs. I caught my breath before turning back. "Good night, Isaac. See you tomorrow."

"See you, Willow. Good night."

I shut the door and hurried up my front walk. Dad remained at the window, watching until Isaac drove away.

"Who was that?" he demanded.

"Hello to you too, father dear," I said. "That was Brenda Ford, the director's wife."

"What happened to Justin?"

"He wasn't called to rehearse tonight."

"Your mother says you're going to a dance with him, and that he comes from a very fine family."

"Yes I am, yes he is, and I'm really tired—"

"And you're staying away from Isaac Pearce, yes?" Dad's eyes had darkened. "My coworker Gary's daughter thought she saw you with him on Saturday."

"Well Gary's daughter needs to mind her own damn business, doesn't she?"

My father put his hands on his hips. "I meant what I said about Isaac. I don't want you associating with the one boy in the entire town with a reputation like that."

Words rose up in my mouth like bile. I wanted to spit them at my father. Tell him he could take his pretend concern for me and shove it up his ass. It wasn't concern for *me*, it was concern for his own reputation.

But I was seventeen. A minor. If my father told Martin I wasn't allowed to do the play, Martin would have no choice but to kick me out.

"Well?" Dad asked. "Did you see Isaac or not?"

"No, my good lord," I said, biting out the words. "But as you did command."

Chapter Twenty

Willow

The night of the dance arrived. My parents, thrilled I was making an effort at socializing, had a spread of hors d'oeuvres and sodas fit for twenty people instead of six. Our marble kitchen counters were laden with little sandwiches, chocolate covered hazelnuts and cherries. Even crackers and caviar.

"Caviar?" I said to Mom.

"Protein, darling." She wore a frilly apron over her Chanel skirt and blouse, as if she cooked all this instead of ordering from a catering service.

"Are you serious?"

She sipped a glass of red wine. "I believe the words you're looking for are *thank you.*"

I sighed, mumbled a thank you and went upstairs to put my dress on. I would've been more grateful if I knew she was doing this for my friends, not to keep up appearances.

Several hours later, Nash and Angie, Caroline and Jocelyn all arrived together.

"Safety in numbers," Angie whispered as she hugged me. She gaped at the entry of our house. "Your foyer is bigger than my bedroom."

As I predicted, she looked beautiful in her skating-style dress. Her hair fell in soft black curls around her shoulders and she'd affixed a choker around her neck with a red silk flower. Nash and Jocelyn both wore suits. Nash had a red bow tie and vest to match Angie's flower. Jocelyn wore a pale blue tie and pocket square to match Caroline's flowing blue dress.

Mom's smile tightened when she swept into the foyer to greet my friends, her voice rising an octave as she demanded we huddle together to take a photo. My dad stood at the rear of the room, hands in his pockets, rocking back on his feet. His smile was stiffer than Mom's.

"My parents are not evolved," I said to Angie.

"A mixed-race couple and lesbians," Angie whispered back with a giggle.

"It's straining the limits of their tolerance."

"They got to get woke, son."

The doorbell rang. "Reinforcements," I said.

As suspected, my parents were thrilled to meet Justin Baker. He arrived in the rented limousine and I had to admit, he looked pretty dashing in a black suit with a navy blue tie to match my dress. But his handsomeness was like that of a sleek car in a showroom. Nice to look at but I had zero interest in taking it for a spin.

Why am I doing this again?

Mom fawned all over him and Dad shook his hand as if they were closing a business deal. The contrast between how he treated Justin compared to my friends was like a flashy neon sign: straight white people only.

"I'm sorry," I whispered to Caroline.

She gave me a smile and a shrug. "Not the first. Won't be the last."

Justin came over, carrying a blue rose corsage in a plastic box. "You look beautiful," he said.

"Thank you," I said.

For someone who had a hard time looking in the mirror and feeling good about what she saw, I thought I'd done pretty well. My mother insisted on taking me to a salon and they put my hair in a high, spectacularly messy yet graceful bun. Tendrils fell down here and there to frame my face, a few trailing down my back. I'd brushed sparkling pink makeup lightly over my eyelids and a darker pink gloss stained my lips.

I felt pretty but Justin wasn't who I wanted to be pretty for. I couldn't help but wish the eyes gazing down at me were stormy gray-green seas, instead of flat blue pools. I wanted the arm offered to smell like gasoline and cigarettes, not Drakkar Noir and money.

Justin slid the corsage up my wrist where I'd spent an hour scrubbing little black X's off my skin, but I felt as if they'd rise to the surface, like goosebumps, when he bent to give me a kiss on the cheek

What happened to just friends?

I took a step backward, into my own space again. Judging by Justin's smug, knowing smile, he took my reaction as being swept off my feet by his charm. A cold lump settled in my stomach, spreading outward, freezing the progress I'd made so far.

I can do this I can do this I can do this...

My mother took a million photos of the two of us, a few thousand group shots, and then it was time to go. We filed out of the house and down the driveway. Mrs. Chambers, our nosy next-door neighbor, watched the procession from her front porch.

Naturally Dad made a fuss over the limo Justin hired. It wasn't a stretch, but long enough to fit the six of us, with room to spare.

"Very nice," Dad said, as we climbed in. "Very nice, indeed."

"I'll have her back by curfew, sir," Justin said, shaking his hand.

"Take your time, take your time," Dad said to Justin. "Have fun." Again, to Justin.

I shot a look at Angie as we settled in, smoothing our dresses and making sure our hair didn't bump the limo roof.

"This is really nice," Jocelyn said, running her hand along the leather seat.

"Let us pitch in to cover it," Nash said.

"Nah," Justin said. "I got this."

"You don't have to," I said. "It's a lot of money."

He shrugged and smiled down at me. "You're worth it."

Another girl might have swooned, but I heard implications. Expectations.

You're being paranoid. He's being nice.

The weight of expectation fell on my bare shoulders and another shiver slipped down my back. Justin put his arm around my seat. I tried to relax. My thumb kept rubbing my wrist.

Angie leaned close and took my hand. "I feel like a damn broken record asking this, but are you okay?"

"Fine," I said.

"Yeah? Because you don't look fine. My man Nash looks *fiiiine.* You look like you just gave five pints of blood."

"I'm just cold."

"You don't have a wrap?"

"No, I…"

My jaw worked but no more sound came out. The limo was pulling into the roundabout in front of the high school. The dance was over at ten, but I heard Justin tell Nash we had it until midnight, in case we wanted to go somewhere later.

As I climbed out of the limo, I knew this was a mistake. If Nash hadn't pulled Angie aside for a romantic, private moment just then, I might've found the courage to tell her I had to go home. I wasn't ready. I couldn't be here.

"Let's go inside," Justin said. "It'll be warmer there." He put his hand at the small of my back, to gently steer me.

Inside the gym, a DJ was set up at one far end and a snack and drink table at the other. The rows of bleacher seats were folded back to make more space. The dance committee had strewn garlands of paper flowers with little LED lights around the perimeter, and three balloon arches stretched across in blue, green, pink and yellow.

As our group took a table, a few Plastics standing nearby turned to stare. I registered Tessa among them but then the dark, the music, the bodies…it all closed in. It was the party I'd thrown on a larger scale. A bigger stage and different actors, but my psyche was adding it all up and coming to the same conclusion.

Xavier…

Angie gave me a thumbs up. I nodded vaguely, but I no longer cared about this ridiculous ruse. I was already drowning in an icy black sea of memories.

The DJ played the throwback, "Do You Really Want to Hurt Me" by Culture Club. Angie and Nash hurried to the dance floor while Caroline and Jocelyn went to the snack table, leaving me alone at the table.

I stared around the dark, crowded gym and the crush of students dancing under sweeping lights. The Plastics and their dates stood at the edge of the dance floor. Justin stood with them, talking with some of his baseball buddies.

Plastics. I hated that name. I vowed never to use it again. With a low-grade panic attack humming in my veins and threatening to blow, the idea of hating on another girl felt like betrayal. I wasn't alone. I knew many of the girls out there on that floor had experienced something like I had. Maybe treated like plastic: cheap and disposable. Something you used once and discarded. Or they were harassed. Made to feel less than their worth. Ugly. Fat. Tease. Slut. Plastic.

Tessa could talk about me all she wanted, but I couldn't hate her. She'd been hurt too. Humiliated when her brother shared Isaac's *No thanks* text.

Isaac. My heart thumped and a surge of heat warmed me, remembering his head in my lap, and his chin on my thigh and a smile...

"Want something to drink?" Xavier murmured in my ear.

I flinched so hard my purse hit the floor and I bit back a scream.

Justin Baker gave a jolt. "What the hell? I just wanted to know if you were thirsty."

"No, I...I'm fine."

I had to get out of here. I rose to my feet slowly and Justin took my hand.

"Right on," he said. "Let's dance."

I let him take me to the floor. The crowd danced and laughed, their faces lit up by the sweeping lights. Angie and Nash were there, smiling and waving. Their mouths moved but I couldn't hear what they said over the music.

Justin leaned down and put his mouth to my ear. "Having a good time?"

I managed a nod. "Great."

"What?" he shouted.

"I said, *great.*" My stomach writhed and my breath came short. Sense memories lurked on all sides. Murderous and ready to pounce. Pillows in hand to snuff me out.

The DJ played "Best Friend" by Sofi Tukker and the crowd let out a collective *woot.* The energy in the room amped up and the dancing changed tenor. Couples moved closer. Girls rubbed their asses against the boys' crotches. Even those dancing in groups huddled closer, as if the song granted them permission to grind.

Justin moved closer to me, his smile eager. As he invaded my space, the weight of the room settled over me. His cologne filled my nose. The heat of his body emanated through his dress shirt as he slung his arms around my waist. Instead of warming me, it made me more aware of my own chill.

I can do this I can do this I can do this.

I turned around—hoping and praying it would be better if we weren't face to face. That I could dance and laugh and be sexy—if only on the dance floor— just like so many other kids in that gym.

Justin's hands landed on my waist. His breath gusted over my shoulder and I felt his chest press to my back. I was hardly moving. I must've looked like a corpse, but he didn't seem to notice or mind.

Inside, I'd begun to scream. I sucked in a breath but it wouldn't go further than my throat. The night was crushing me, pressing me back against Justin. Tears sprang to my eyes. It was stupid to think I could do this.

No, please. I just want to be at a dance like a normal girl...

The dimness of the gym was swimming now. Murky. I stopped moving, frozen stiff and flattened by the invisible force of remembering. Dark memories that had no shape or definition, except for X's crushing weight that stole my breath and left me paralyzed.

With a strangled cry, I broke free and shoved away from Justin to stagger through the gym. I had to get out. Escape. To save myself from nothing and everything.

I shoved open the bar on the side door and spilled out of the gym, stumbling and falling on my hands and knees. Cement scraped my skin and the pain brought me around like a slap to the face.

The weight lifted.

There was no shadow monster. Only me in the amber light above the door, sitting on the ground with blood trickling down my shins and my palms scraped raw. I inhaled sharply, then dissolved in wracking sobs.

I pulled my knees to my chest and hugged my legs, crying until I felt turned inside out. Any second the door would open and someone would see me, or Angie would follow me. Gasping for air, I got to my feet. My pretty blue dress was smudged with dirt and my knees were a mess. *I* was a mess. My purse was inside but there was no chance I was going back in looking like this.

I hauled myself off the ground and stumbled after one step in my heels.

"Fuck."

I took off my shoes and walked to the girls' room across from the gym. While the idea of walking barefoot in a bathroom didn't exactly scream 'dignified,' I didn't much care. I tore a few paper towels from the dispenser, ran them under cold water and cleaned up my knees.

When I straightened to wash my scraped palms, I let out a little gasp at the reflection in the mirror. My hair was falling out of the messy bun and my face looked as if I'd been driving at a hundred miles an hour with my head sticking out the window. Smeared makeup. Swollen, shining eyes. Ruddy cheeks.

"God," I whispered.

When? I wanted to scream. When could I go back to being myself? When would this mess of a girl in the mirror get better? Ever?

Never?

I splashed cold water on my face and dabbed it dry. Smears of mascara still smudged my eyes, but it seemed like too much effort to clean up and try again. Impossible to go back and face concerned questions from Angie, or confused expectations from Justin. I was too tired to make something up. Pretending to be okay was fucking exhausting.

My house was a good two miles away. I could call an Uber, but my phone was in my purse and my purse was in the gym. With my heels dangling from one hand and my left knee still trickling blood, I began to walk.

I trudged along the quiet streets of northern Harmony. The school wasn't ten minutes behind me when I realized the stupidity of my plan. My feet ached and were scratched by rocks and debris. I was on the verge of taking a seat on the side of the road to rest when headlights splashed in front of me.

A car pulled up. No, a pickup truck.

Isaac Pearce's Dodge.

Oh God, not like this. Don't let him see me like this.

I walked faster.

He drove slowly beside me and rolled down the passenger window.

"Hey, where are you go—"

His voice cut off as he took in my bloodied knees and dirt-streaked dress. He slammed on the brakes, killed the engine and jumped out of the truck.

"What happened?" He took my arm. "Willow…?"

I stared up at him, a thousand thoughts passing through me in a second. His hand on my arm didn't sent icy shivers over my skin. His presence felt like a shield instead of danger and his face… God, he was so handsome. He would've looked so amazing in a suit, and I would've felt so proud arriving in his truck instead of a limo. With Isaac as my date, the dance would've been perfect because he didn't make me feel like I was drowning in ice water…

"Willow, what *happened*?"

"Nothing," I said, wrenching free. "I fell. I'm fine."

Isaac's gaze swept my face with its swollen eyes and smeared makeup. "You fell."

"Yes, I fell," I snapped. "On my way out of the gym. It's not a big deal." I turned away from his scrutiny and started walking again. Limping now, as a rock had punctured my heel, but I wasn't about to let him see how bad it hurt.

"You went with Justin Baker, right?" Isaac said. "So where the fuck is he?"

I stopped and whirled to look at him. "What do you care?"

"Did he hurt you?"

"No and it's none of your business anyway."

"Willow…"

My anger rose, carried on a tide of frustrated tears. "Don't say my name like that," I said. "You had nothing to do with this. You don't go to dances, remember? You're done with high school. I'm not. And I was just trying to have a good time like any other *normal* girl and I…I had…"

"What?" Isaac asked softly, coming closer. "What happened?"

"Nothing," I said, fighting for control. "Nothing happened. I got…claustrophobic or something. A panic attack. It happens sometimes and it's so…stupid. So fucking stupid. And unfair." I wiped my eyes. "Never mind. It's not a big deal."

"Yes, it is."

"Is it? To who? If you cared so goddamn much about what

happened at the dance, then you should've…"

You should've told me on Saturday…

I bit the words back before they could escape and make things worse.

"You're right." Isaac's deep voice was low and quiet. "I should have."

My heart pounded and I stared, not knowing what to say or how to feel. I desperately wanted to recover one scrap of dignity. I wiped my nose with the back of my hand.

"Well, it's too late now."

For an instant he looked through me, as if my words reminded him of something. Then he jerked his chin toward my knees. "You're bleeding. Come on, I'll take you home. And I'll park where your dad can't see."

"No, thanks. I'll walk."

"You'll *what?*"

"Walk. I'm going to walk."

"Christ, Willow, will you get in the car?"

"I'm fine. And what are you doing anyway? Driving around town, looking for damsels in distress?"

"No, I…happened to be driving." He carved a hand through his hair. "Who gives a shit what I was doing? Get in the car."

"Don't tell me what to do," I said, and kept walking.

"Fine."

I heard the crunch of his booted feet on gravel. The car door opened and slammed shut. The engine roared and then settled to a low purr. And then Isaac was driving beside me at all of three miles an hour, eyes straight ahead. A hand casually slung on the steering wheel, the other arm stretched over the passenger seat.

"What are you doing?" I asked.

"Driving."

"Are you kidding me?"

"No."

I fumed. "Great. Have fun with that."

I kept limping for another few steps, until the utter stupidity of the situation became too much. I stopped and faced him, crossing my arms over my chest.

"I want to make sure you get home safe," he said in a low voice.

"That's all."

That's all he wants.

Tears sprang to my eyes again. I blinked them away and climbed into the Dodge.

Immediately I was saturated by the essence of Isaac permeating the interior. Gasoline, cologne, cigarette smoke and something sweet and woodsy that was *him*. It defeated the lingering vestiges of my panic attack and stirred something new in its place.

I cleared my throat. "Thank you for the ride."

"You're welcome."

Chapter Twenty-One

Willow

We drove in silence a few blocks. I eased a sigh and leaned my head on the window.

"What happened?" he finally asked.

"I told you," I said. "Claustrophobia."

We came to a stop sign. There were no cars in either direction. Not a soul around. The night was black and silent and cold. Isaac reached over and closed his large hand around my left forearm, turning it over. The faint black X was visible in the weak street light on the corner.

I caught my breath. Then let it out. Isaac kept his gaze on my arm while his thumb went back and forth over the faded ink.

"I wanted to go to be like other girls," I said, hating the tears blurring my vision, turning my voice high and flute-like. "I didn't expect much. Just one decent dance would have been enough."

Isaac said nothing. He rubbed his thumb over the X a final time, then let go to drive. I held my arm in my lap, touching where he had, trying to keep the warmth.

We turned up Emerson Road. It sloped up for a quarter mile before leveling off about fifty feet above town. Isaac pulled the truck over at a lookout spot and parked under a tall oak, standing like a sentry at the top of the hill. Harmony's tiny downtown lay below, twinkling with little yellow lights and the larger, gold light of the

HCT.

Isaac cut the engine but left the keys turned. Lights still lit up the dash and he fiddled with the radio knob, searching.

"What are you doing?" I asked.

"Not sure," he said.

Static crackled. He passed by a few blaring commercials and then the opening guitar strains of Shawn Mendes' "Imagination" came on.

Isaac looked at me, his green eyes deep and softer than I'd ever seen them. "How's this?"

I nodded. "It's nice."

Isaac got out of the driver's side and came around to open the passenger door. He offered his hand and I took it. His hand was rough and callused with work, but warm and strong. Just the touch of it made me eager to have both his arms around me. All his body pressed to mine.

I never thought I'd want that again.

He helped me from the car and I winced as my feet touched down on the dirt. He caught me as I stumbled, then stepped back to reached through the passenger door to turn up the volume. He took my hand again and we walked to the edge of the lookout, onto soft grass that grew around the oak tree.

Isaac wrapped his arm around my waist and held my other hand to his chest, over his heart.

"Is this okay?" he asked.

I nodded and slipped my arm around his neck. The scent of him, so potent in the car, enveloped me softly. I leaned into it and let my head rest against his chest, against the white of his cotton shirt exposed by his leather jacket. I inhaled as we swayed slowly to the music, the lyrics speaking for both of us.

After a few moments, I raised my head to meet his eyes. "This isn't an act, is it? This is you?"

Isaac opened his mouth, looking as if he might protest or deny. Then he nodded. "I didn't plan this, but… Yeah. This is me." He raised a hand to cup my cheek, his thumb brushing aside my tears. "Are you okay?"

"Yes." I rested my head back on his chest. "Right now, everything's perfect."

He said nothing but I felt him nod. His cheek rested against my hair. This was exactly what I needed.

Maybe he needed this too.

The song ended and a used car commercial came on. We stayed in each other's arms, with all of Harmony laid out below us. The real Harmony, with the HCT where we met and the amphitheater where Isaac touched my hands for the first time. Not the neighborhood behind us where my parents lived in a cold white house.

"I have to go back," I said, finally. "They'll start looking for me. The longer I stay out the worse it'll be." I glanced down at my bloodied knees. "It's already going to be bad."

"How bad?"

I reached up to gently touch the swelling under his eye. "Not like this. I'll be okay, I promise."

Reluctantly, he broke our protective circle and helped me to his truck. We drove back to my street and I told him to slow down a few houses from my own. Justin's limo was parked in front.

"Shit," I said. "Justin is there. Maybe my friends too."

"I hate letting you walk in there alone."

"You have to," I said.

"Do they know?" Isaac asked in a low voice. He reached over and gently took my arm again and turned it over to reveal the X. "Do they know what this means?"

"No," I said. "No one does."

I realized that wasn't entirely true. Xavier would know what it meant. He owned every single one of them. He'd marked me, maybe forever.

"I have to go," I said. "Thank you for the ride and the dance and for…just being there."

I slipped out of the car before anything else could happen and limped with my shoes in my hand to my house. In the driveway, I turned. Isaac hadn't moved his truck yet. I gave him a small wave and stepped inside.

Justin was in the living room with my parents. They all turned to look when I came in and the men bolted to their feet. My mother's hand flew to her mouth with a gasp, her other clutching a glass of wine.

"What happened to you?"

"Where did you go?"

"We've been worried sick."

"I'm here. I'm fine," I said. I looked at Justin. "I'm sorry I left. I had a...panic attack and I ran outside to get some air—"

"You had a panic attack?" Mom asked from the couch. "Since when do you get panic attacks?"

Since last summer...

"I don't know, it just...happened. I ran outside and fell. The gym door was locked from the outside and I was a mess and embarrassed, so I decided to walk home. I didn't have my phone or I would've called you." A thought jolted me. "Where is my phone?"

"Justin had it," Dad said, "along with your purse."

He held up my phone and the blood drained out of my face. I suddenly felt as naked as I had when I sent Xavier those photos. My personal property and thoughts and content out of my control again. Dad had scrolled through my phone tonight, I *knew* he had. I wasn't allowed to keep the passcode a secret from my parents—part of the conditions since I'd turned 'uncontrollable' last summer.

I mentally raced through every message Angie and I had ever sent. I couldn't remember if we'd texted about Isaac.

"Give it back." I reached for it but Dad held it high.

"First, you tell us where you've been. With Isaac Pearce?"

"He's bad news," Justin said.

I turned my glare on him. "Shut up."

He held up his hands. "I've lived here longer than you have, Willow. I'm just trying to watch out for you. I was worried sick."

"I wasn't with Isaac," I said. "I told you, I walked home. It's two miles and I was barefoot. You do the math."

"Why would you walk?" Mom asked. "Looking like that? You're a disgrace."

"Regina," Dad said.

"It's true. She looks like a streetwalker." The way my mother's mouth slurred around that word, I guessed she was working on her second bottle of wine. "What will the neighbors think?"

"Give me my phone," I said to Dad. "I need to tell Angie I'm okay."

"I drove them home," Justin said. "They were worried too."

"I'm sure they were," Dad said and handed me my phone.

I walked away from them and sank into an easy chair, quickly scrolling through my texts. I knew every single one of them had been read by my father. Maybe Justin too.

"She's been different since last summer," I heard Dad say. "Hard to manage."

My hands shook as I kept scrolling for any texts with Isaac's name. I found the S.O.S. to Angie I'd sent about hanging out with Isaac on Saturday and quickly deleted the entire convo.

He didn't see it, or I'd be dead right now.

"Nothing to apologize for," Justin was saying to Dad. Their voices lowered. I heard *Isaac* once or twice from Justin's mouth and I wanted to scream.

Here is the noble Laertes and Polonius, discussing what to do with their poor, frail Ophelia. Deciding what's best for her as she's been incapable since last summer.

My mother was the audience, drinking her wine.

I shot a text to Angie.

I'm okay. I'm home. I'll call you later. Promise.

The reply was instant. **Oh thank God. Where did you go? I wanted to text you but I knew Justin had your phone.** A pause. **Is this you? Tell me something only Willow would know.**

I smiled through tears. **Angie McKenzie is the best friend anyone could ever hope for.**

That's common knowledge. Try again.

My fingers flew. **At the mall, you told me that I was more of a Rapunzel than a Belle.**

And I was right. Call me when they let you out of your tower.

I will. Love you.

Love you too.

"Justin's leaving," Dad said loudly. "Given what a disaster this night has turned out to be, could you please walk your guest to the door and say good night? Thank him for his consideration?"

I got to my feet and obediently walked with Justin to the front door. Dad stayed at the edge of the foyer, arms crossed, watching like a coach who doubted his star athlete had it in her anymore.

Justin smiled benevolently at me. "Are you okay?"

I nearly flinched. The exact same words had meant so much more coming from Isaac. Isaac had asked me because he cared. Justin asked me as a segue to his own feelings.

"I really was worried about you. We all were. I dropped your friends off and then I tried to find you."

I hadn't been gone long enough for that to be true, but I was too tired, too drained to argue.

"I'm sorry," I said.

He smiled. "Forgiven." He bent to kiss my cheek but I moved out of his reach.

"Okay," he said, his smile tightening. "Good night then." He looked over my shoulder and waved to my father. "Good night, sir."

I could have puked.

"Good night, Justin. And thank you."

"Of course."

I couldn't shut the door on him fast enough.

My father stood with his arms crossed, now looking like an angry coach whose athlete had blown the big final match.

"That's how you treat him? He spent all that money on a limo for—"

"He didn't have to do that," I said, looking down at my bare feet. "I told him not to. I told him we were going as friends."

"Why? What's wrong with him? I had such high hopes tonight. For the first time since last summer, you were acting more like yourself. Granted, your friends weren't what I expected, but it's progress from having none at all. But you did the same thing to Justin that you did to Xavier…"

My head whipped up and I stared. "I did *what*?"

"Xavier's also a fine young man and I thought he was interested in you—"

"*Interested* in me?"

Once more, the blood drained from my face, this time from the memory of Xavier's benevolent smile. Spreading wide like the Cheshire cat's. *Let me get you something to drink…*

"He's my boss's son," Dad said. "It would've been smart of you to put some effort into that relationship."

"Dad," I said, my voice trembling with cold. "I'm tired and I want to go to sleep now."

I started toward the stairs, but he reached out and grabbed my arm.

"If I find out you were with Isaac Pearce tonight instead of Justin, I will call Martin Ford the same minute and tell him you're no longer able to perform in his show. Do you understand?"

"Yeah," I said, looking down at my arm where he held me. Little black X's spread out from under his hand, skittering over my skin like ants. "I understand perfectly."

Chapter Twenty-Two

Willow

I spent a sleepless weekend, mostly curled up on the floor in my room. I called Angie and told her what happened—that Isaac had given me a ride home, but nothing about our dance. Monday morning, I stood in a daze at my locker at school. I nearly jumped out of my skin when Justin tapped me on the shoulder with one finger. Gone was his friendly, put-one-on-for-the parents smile and instead he wore the angry mask of a popular guy who got stood up by his date.

"What really happened the other night?" he demanded.

I took a step back. "Didn't we go over this on Friday? I told you. Claustrophobia attack or something. The gym was too crowded. I didn't have my phone."

"Or did you leave to go see Isaac? You know I see how you look at him at rehearsal."

I slammed my locker shut. "That's none of your business."

"Stay away from him."

"Yes, brother."

"I mean it. He's trouble. I heard his dad was at Nicky's Tavern the other night, ranting and raving. Owners had to call the cops to take him home."

"Oh, his dad's *alive*?" I said. "I thought Isaac had killed him."

Justin shook his head. "Okay, if that's how you want it. I'm done with you." He started to go, then turned back. "You know, since you were the new girl and all, hanging around with a bunch of losers, I took pity on you. What a fucking waste of money."

"We offered to chip in. Remember? How much do I owe you?"

How, exactly, did you want me to pay you back?

He stared, then turned away with a disgusted snort and joined the group of girls formerly known as the Plastics. Their heads leaned in, then fell back in loud laughter. The girls' eyes widened over his shoulder at me, with mock pity.

Great. By lunch, I'd be the crazy girl who freaked out at the dance. I didn't think Justin was mean enough to make it worse than that, but who knew? I hurried to English class, wishing I could skip the day and get to rehearsal where I could be someone else for a little while.

"How are you holding up?" Angie asked as I slid into my seat. "You look tired." Today's t-shirt was white with black lettering: *If you don't have something nice to say...we have a lot in common.*

"I'm great," I said. "Considering the guy my dad wants me to hook up with is a complete douchebag and the guy I want to see is literally forbidden."

Angie's jaw dropped open. "Really? Isaac? You want to *see* him, see him?"

"Shh. I don't know. Maybe. It's so stupid because he's leaving Harmony in a couple of months. But I can't stop thinking about him. He doesn't make me feel trapped."

"Trapped by what?"

I plucked at the long sleeve of my dark green shirt. Underneath, a new army of little black X's marched along my forearm. "Nothing in particular," I said. "I just don't like feeling pressured by guys. And I don't feel that from him. At all."

"Holy shit," Angie said. "Do you think he's into you? He has to be, right? Picking you up in your time of need...?"

And dancing with me.

I played every detail over and over in my mind while curled up on my floor in a blanket, waiting for sleep that wouldn't come.

"I'm sorry I ruined your night," I said.

"It's—"

"I know, I know. You told me over the phone it wasn't a big deal. But I need to tell you in person. I'm trying to get better at this whole being-a-good-friend thing."

"You're doing all right, Holloway."

Her eyes dropped to my notebook where hundreds more little black X's crawled all along the margins.

She frowned, a fingertip tapping the paper. "What's all this about?"

"Nothing. Just doodles," I said. "Hey, did you start your poem yet? The one Paulson assigned us last week?"

"Yes," Angie said slowly, "I've been toying around with this one, tell me what you think. *Roses are red, violets are blue, when you're ready to talk, I'm here for you.*" Her bright smile dimmed with sadness. "Okay?"

I nodded and whispered, "Okay."

While eating lunch, my phone pinged an incoming text. Isaac's name and number flashed on the display, making my heart pound and my stomach flutter.

Hey, had a question about rehearsal tonight. RU free to talk?

Smart, I thought.

The coast is clear, I typed back.

Wanted to make sure you are OK. I would've texted earlier.

I'm OK. Thank you.

A pause and then he started typing again.

Do you want to run lines today after school?

Was this code for something else, I wondered? It didn't matter. I just wanted to see him.

He's leaving. Be smart. Don't try to crawl your way out of the darkness by falling for some guy who can't be with you.

My fingers flew as I typed a text. **Love to. Where?**

The same place as last time?

I remember. 3:00?

CU then.

A text from a boy I liked, and I had to delete the entire thread.

"I need two little favors," I told Angie after school. "I'm meeting Isaac at the amphitheater to run lines."

"Is *run lines* code for *sex* and no one told me?"

A shiver slipped down my spine but it was a heated one, not icy.

"It's code for running lines. Can you cover me?"

"Cover you how? Put a mannequin with long blonde hair in the passenger seat of my car and drive around town?"

"Now that you mention it…" I grinned. "Just tell anyone who asks we're studying together."

"Oh my God." She pinched my cheek. "Look at that smile. You love him."

"What? I do not."

"Mm. And I'm not the best friend anyone could hope for."

"Just let me be a little bit happy about this right now, okay?" I said. "He's leaving in a few months, and at the very least, I want to make this experience with the play special."

"Okay, Holloway," Angie said. "I got you covered. But girl, this town is small and Isaac Pearce is big. He gets noticed and if you're seen together…"

"I'll be careful," I said and kissed her cheek. "You're the best."

"That's the word on the street. What's the second favor?"

"I need a ride to the amphitheater, like right now."

She sighed for five whole seconds and rolled her eyes. "Oh woe is me, woe is me, my kingdom for a car for my friend." She slung her arm around my shoulder. "Come on princess, let's hit the road."

I got to the amphitheater first. I climbed up on the cement block and sat, waiting, remembering the feel of Isaac's hands when he helped me down. Hoping he'd do it again today.

"Hey." Isaac stood at the northern edge of the theater. He wore jeans that looked new, a white T-shirt and a hoodie with the hood pulled up. He had a backpack slung over his shoulder.

"Hi," I called, and my heart did that rabbit-y thumping it always did in Isaac's presence.

Neither of us spoke as he walked up to me. By now, I knew Isaac took a little time to warm up. He stood still and silent. Not climbing up next to me, or even putting down his pack.

"Did you want to run lines?" I finally asked.

"Not here." He glanced around at the wide-open space. "Anyone could walk by and see us. I know a better place."

"Okay." I started to scootch down from the block. Isaac offered me his hand again. Then his other. I took them and hopped down to stand in front of him as we had done a few weeks ago.

He held both my wrists and his thumbs ran back and forth along the delicate skin there. I wondered if he could feel my pulse point; my heart was beating so fast.

He looked down at me from under his hood. His gray-green eyes placid and warm. He no longer wore a bandage, and the cut on his cheek was still dark with congealed blood. Most of the swelling had gone down.

"Are you sleeping better?" I asked softly.

He shook his head. "Not yet. You?" He was still holding my wrists.

"Not yet."

Gently, he pushed up the sleeve a little to reveal a few of the black X's on my forearm. I held my breath, waiting for the cold shiver, and instinctive urge to snatch my hand back. Instead, I let him see them and then he raised his eyes to mine, concern darkening them and furrowing his brows.

"No questions," I said softly. "Not yet, okay?"

"Okay." Simple as that. He drew my sleeve down and let go of my hands. "We should get going."

We climbed back up the stone steps and started down a small, quiet street beyond the amphitheater. Bright spring sunshine streamed through the trees lining both sides of the road. We passed a small children's park, not talking as we walked side-by-side, the backs of our hands brushing now and then. The houses grew further apart. The streets grew quieter until the buzzing of insects was the loudest sound.

"What do you think?" Isaac said.

We stood before a hedge maze.

"I love it," I said, before even stepping foot inside.

The hedges were about five feet tall, their corridors branched off in two directions and covered thirty yards or so. In the center, I could just see the top of a small shack with a windmill.

"In the summertime, this place is busy with tourists," Isaac said. "But we should be good for now."

"Okay. How close are you to being off book?"

He shrugged. "Ninety percent?"

"That's not bad, considering you have approximately that much of the play."

"What happened after I dropped you off after the dance?"

"Oh…uh, nothing shocking," I said. "Justin played nice with my dad. They both talked over my head as if I were incapable of making any decisions on my own. Talk about art imitating life."

"When do you turn eighteen?" he asked.

"July," I said.

Isaac nodded. "Tonight at rehearsal, should I ask Marty to run the scene where Hamlet kills Laertes?"

"No," I said, "because Laertes kills him right back."

"Laertes kills him first actually. Hamlet just dies more slowly."

"Not as fast as Ophelia. I got you all beat."

A silence.

"You know it's a Shakespearean tragedy when you're discussing which character dies the fastest."

He smiled a little, but I watched it fade as his eyes held mine. I felt the moment thicken between us. It would've been nothing for him to bend down and kiss me.

I want him to kiss me.

The thought sent electric shivers dancing down my skin, but tangled my stomach in a knot at the same time. What would happen if he did? Would I freeze up? Would panic grip me, shake me and throw me to the ground? Would the shadowy memory of Xavier's mouth come through Isaac's lips?

I turned my head and brushed a lock of hair out of my eyes. "I'm ready to check out this maze."

"Sure, yeah," he said, with equal parts relief and regret too. "Let's go."

We faced the two entrances to the maze, each heading opposite directions.

"It's not hard," he said, "and you can see the center so you can't get lost."

Getting lost in a hedge maze with you wouldn't be the worst thing that could happen today. "Okay, I said. "Race you to the center?"

"I'll win," Isaac said. "I've lived here my entire life."

"So you're scared?"

He laughed. A small one but a real laugh nonetheless. "All right, let's see what you got. Ready. Set..."

I took off running down my branch of the maze before he could say go.

"Cheater," he called.

I laughed, feeling the warm sun on my face and the smell of spring coming back all around me. The maze was composed of dried brush, slowly turning green. Bugs chirped and small white butterflies fluttered across my path. It wasn't a complicated maze, and I kept my bearings by watching the windmill shack in the middle. Isaac, at six-foot-two, should've towered over hedges but he was nowhere to be seen.

"No way he's that fast," I muttered, reaching the clearing where the little windmill sat. A cutout door faced me, its faded red paint peeling away. Isaac sat on a bench inside, one ankle resting on the knee of his other leg, looking like he'd been there for hours.

"Okay, you win," I said with a laugh, but it died to see the way he was looking at me. He slowly got to his feet and stepped out of the windmill, his brows together as if he were in pain.

"What's wrong?" I asked.

He kept his hands to his sides as if it were an effort to do so. "Nothing. I can't do this," he said. "We should go."

"Go? We just got here."

"I realize that but it's not fucking fair to you or to me..." He sighed, dropped his gaze to the ground, shaking his head. "You have no idea how beautiful you are."

"Isaac..." I swallowed over the pounding of my heart.

"We should go," he said. "We should... I'm leaving in a few months. I have to. I have to get out of this town for myself and I have to get out to make some money for my dad and Martin and the theater. I'm broke as hell, but maybe if the scouts like me...?"

The desperate hope in his gruff voice broke my heart.

"I know you do," I said. "You have to go. It's your dream. The world needs your talent."

He swallowed hard. I watched his Adam's apple rise and fall as if he were choking down a jagged lump.

"It needs your talent too," he said. "Your Ophelia..."

"I don't know about that, but *I* need Ophelia. I need this play and I can't lose that."

Or you.

"I know," he said in a low voice.

"This play is how I keep you...keep hanging out with you," I said, louder. "Before you leave, we have this. *Hamlet.* My father will ruin it if we..."

He shook his head as if to cut off my words and nodded brusquely. "Yeah, I know. That's why we should go."

Without another word we walked out of the maze side-by-side. Isaac knew exactly which way to turn. We didn't hit a dead end until we came out.

Nowhere left to go.

"Are you going to be okay getting home?"

"I'll call Angie."

He nodded. "See you at rehearsal?"

"Yeah, I'll see you then."

He nodded again, then turned and walked away, while I turned and headed in the opposite direction.

I walked into town and got a ride home with Angie, and hardly spoke. I told her I wasn't feeling well in order to stave off her barrage of questions. It was the truth, anyway.

My house was empty. I went into the kitchen for a glass of

orange juice and found today's mail on the counter. On the top of the pile was a thick invitation envelope. The name on the return address read *Wilkinson.*

With a trembling hand, I turned the envelope over. It had already been opened. I pulled out the card inside. Fancy calligraphy swam before my eyes, focusing into words:

You are cordially invited to celebrate Wexx's highest fourth-quarter earnings in the history of the company. Grand ballroom, Renaissance Hotel 8 PM April 30, Braxton, Indiana

Below that, in handwritten black ink:

Xavier has the time off from Amherst. If he knew Willow was coming I could persuade him to come join us. I'm sure he'd love to see her again. Hope to see you all there!
Ross Wilkinson

Xavier. In Indiana.

The words on the invite swam again, until all I could see were little black X's.

Chapter Twenty-Three

Isaac

You're doing it, I thought. *You're walking away from Willow, just like you promised yourself you would. How's it feel?*

"It fucking sucks," I muttered.

It was a twenty-minute walk from the maze to the Fords' house. Twenty minutes under a sun that was getting warmer with every passing day. It shone so brightly over Willow when she emerged from the hedge maze. The cold pallor of her skin the other night was gone and she looked fucking radiant with the sun in her hair and a smile for me. All for me.

How did I let this happen?

I hefted my backpack higher on my shoulder and reaffirmed my vow: I would give her *Hamlet* and nothing else. She'd give her Ophelia to me and that's how I was going to get out of Harmony.

And I had to go.

The other night I hadn't been able to sleep, as usual. I'd gone downstairs for a snack, but froze halfway through the living room. Brenda and Marty were in the kitchen, talking in low voices. I was about to backtrack when I heard Martin say my father's name. I froze then, listening.

"…showed up at Nicky's Tavern… Made one hell of a scene… Cursing Isaac out… Telling everyone he has a faggot for a son…"

Dad was arrested and spent the night in the drunk tank. The

humiliation of it cut me to the bone. Not because of the gay slur—I was used to that. Pops wasn't only the town drunk now, but the town's ranting bigot as well. Our names back in circulation among the town gossips. I prayed Sam Caswell hadn't been at Nicky's that night. He and I did *Angels in America* two summers ago and he'd had felt so empowered by the experience, he came out to his friends and family. Now my dad was ruining that too.

God, I had to get out of Harmony, I thought as I walked, and lit a cigarette.

But Willow... Maybe, after I made my fortune as the heroes do in the stories, I could come back to Harmony.

The thought stopped me cold in the bright sunshine. In all the years of plotting my escape, *coming back* had never factored in.

"Shit," I muttered as I blew smoke out my nose. I was finally on the verge of getting out for good and I meet the one thing that could bring me back. The universe had a sick sense of humor.

Fuck that, I'd focus on *Hamlet.* I'd take all these thoughts about Willow and give them to Hamlet. *He* could pine for her and regret their separation. He could be angry at her father and murderous toward her brother. Keep all this shit onstage, where words written hundreds of years ago could speak for me.

That evening, when rehearsal began at seven, Willow wasn't at the theater.

Neither was Justin.

"We'll give her a few minutes," Martin said.

Twenty minutes later and still no sign.

A heavy feeling settled into my gut. I reached for my phone to text Willow, but she buzzed me a text first.

Isaaaaaaaaac I'm outside and OGM I am sooooooo drunk :D:D:D

"Oh, shit." I grabbed my leather jacket off the back of a chair. "It's her. I'll be right back," I told Martin.

I stood on the sidewalk outside of the theater, looking up and down the street in both directions. Finally, half a block away, in front of the liquor store, I saw her. She was standing with the group of guys—older men, not high schoolers—and laughing loudly.

I covered the distance between us in about three seconds. "Willow."

"Isaac," she cried, her face lighting up the way drunk people do, as if they hadn't seen you in ten years. "Oh my God, you're *here.*"

She slung her arms around my neck and I smelled a sharp bite of whiskey on her breath.

"You guys, this is Isaac. Isn't he beautiful? He is *so* beautiful." She placed her palm on my face and patted my cheek. "He's a genius actor. He's *Hamlet.* You see that big sign up there?" She jagged a finger in the general direction of the HCT marquee with HAMLET *coming soon* in black lettering. "That's him." She smacked my chest with her hand. "He's our Hamlet."

"Willow, what are you doing?" I eyed the three guys who watched her with amusement.

"With the help of these fine gentlemens, I am purchasing some beer," she said, with slow and careful enunciation.

I looked at one of the guys. He shrugged. "She gave my buddy fifty bucks for a six-pack of Heineken."

"And you think it's cool to buy underage girls beer?" I slipped my arm around Willow's waist to hold her up. "Come on, let's go."

"No." She pushed herself away from me, stumbling slightly. "I am not leaving here without my beer." Her angry expression melted into joy as another guy came out of the store with a black plastic bag. He stopped when he saw me watching him darkly.

"No, no, no." Willow wagged a finger at me. "No one tells me what to do." She took the plastic bag from the guy and peered inside. "Oh, yes. *Perfect.*" She chucked him on the shoulder as if they were old buddies. "Keep the change, my friend."

The guys moved on, laughing and shaking their heads.

"You gave him a fifty for twelve bucks' worth of beer?" I asked.

"So what?" she said. "Back home I drank more than fifty bucks' worth of my dad's million-year-old Scotch, I'll tell you that right now."

"You don't need to tell me," I said, her whiskey breath wafting over me. "Willow, what happened? What is going on?"

She gave me a funny look. "Isn't it obvious? I'm getting trashed." She started to rummage in her plastic bag trying to wrangle one of the beer bottles out of its container. "You want one? Nobody likes to drink alone."

"Not here, Jesus," I said and took the bag away from her.

Her happy drunk face morphed instantly into anger. "I told you, no one is telling me what to do. Give me the beer or I'll start screaming."

"You're drunk enough."

As fast as it had come on, the anger now disappeared and her face crumpled. "You don't get it, Isaac," she said, gripping me by my sweatshirt. "I need to get away from all of this." She waved her hand over her head, as if trying to dispel a dark cloud of thoughts or memories.

A cloud of what? Put there by who? I looked into her wide, frightened eyes and recalled black X's on her skin, and a deep fear uncoiled in my gut.

It's bad. Whatever it is, it's fucking bad.

"Please," she begged. "Just take me somewhere."

I looked back at the theater, then back at her, torn in two.

"The cemetery," Willow said, her glassy eyes lighting up. "Take me to the cemetery. It's really old right? Hundreds of years old? I want to go there. Please." She firmed her voice. "It's my choice. I'm getting plowed with or without you."

Shit. Helping her get drunk felt like exactly the right thing and exactly the wrong thing to do. But if she were intent on going on a bender, better I was with her.

"All right, let's go."

She hooked her arm in mine like we were going to take a stroll down the boulevard. I fished out my phone and texted Marty:

Willow's not feeling well. I'm taking her home. I won't be back.

His reply came a minute later. **Take care of her.**

I walked Willow to my Dodge pickup and helped her inside, then climbed behind the wheel. She was already trying to dig into the bag.

"You have to wait until we get there," I told her. "No open containers. Try not to get me arrested, please."

Then I can spend a night in the holding tank, just like my old man. Wouldn't he be proud?

"I don't want you to be arrested," she said with drunken solemnness. "That would truly suck."

I had to chuckle, despite myself. Willow laid her head back against the seat, her eyes closed, smiling and humming to herself. Her hair was loose, falling almost to her waist in long blonde waves. She wore a black, tight-fitting, long sleeved shirt. It highlighted the swell of her breasts and the elegant curve of her neck.

She was the most exquisite girl I'd ever seen, even drunk off her ass. But she *was* drunk, which altered my attraction. Put any physical desire on the back burner. My job was to take care of her and that's it.

And try not to get puked on.

"How much did you drink?" I asked. "What was it, Scotch?"

"Mm." Her head lolled toward me. "My father, unbeknownst to him, genuinely... I mean *generously* let me partake in his stash."

"How did you get downtown?"

She snorted wetly. "There's such a thing as taxis. Even in little Harmony, you know. So many things here you don't see."

"I've lived here my entire life," I said. "I've seen everything."

"With your eyes, yes. But there's so much more..."

She leaned forward to rummage in the back pocket of her jeans and came up with a small wad of cash. "My mother genuinely... *Generously* supplied me with funds for this little excursion. Here." She peeled off three twenties and stuffed them in my sweatshirt pocket. "Gas money, courtesy of Madame Holloway. So you can drive her daughter all over and see the sights."

"I don't want your money." I tried to give it back to her and she pushed my hand away, so I left it on the seat between us.

I pulled onto the street in front of the cemetery. It had no parking lot, and only a squat, brick mortuary, closed for decades, stood in front of the plots.

Willow was opening the door before I even had the truck in park. I ran around to the other side to help her. As I put my arm out to steady her, she gazed up at me.

"You really are...so handsome." The drunken slur of her words was changing, from silly to serious. Her thoughts diving deeper. "Beautiful," she said, "but not in a girly way. No. In a manly way. The way a man can be beautifully a man. This...?" She grazed her fingers over the stubble on my jaw, then traced my eyebrows. "And here..." Her touch gently trailed over my cheekbones, mindful of the still healing gash.

I closed my eyes under her touch; a rush sweeping through me as if I'd pounded a shot of Scotch myself.

Don't do this to me.

"And here," Willow whispered, her fingertip tracing my lips. "And your eyes, Isaac."

I opened them to her, standing so close to me, so beautiful…

"Do you know what I thought the first time I saw you? That your eyes were like the stormy sea off Nantucket in winter. Cold and wind-tossed but deep. But they're not cold now…"

She inclined her head toward me. She was going to kiss me. And if she hadn't been drunk, it would've been the most perfect moment of my life.

I turned my head away and held her by the shoulders. "No, Willow. We can't."

"We can't," she echoed. Her face clouded over. "No truer words, right? I want a beer."

"Only one."

"You can't tell me what to do," she snapped. "Remember?"

I bent to pull two Heinekens out of the bag. "No, but you can get alcohol poisoning. And that's not going to happen."

She pouted but made no further protest.

I pointed to the small brick building. "Let's go behind the mortuary before someone sees us."

We took a small gravel path around the mortuary where a single light still glowed yellow, probably to keep out trespassers. Crickets chirped a never-ending cacophony in the trees that surrounded the cemetery. They were the only boundary marking this place. No gates or fences, no formal entrance or exit. Just an uneven patch of earth. A black sea where tilted tombstones bobbed on the surface. According to the small placard on the mortuary wall, some graves dated as far back as 1830.

"This is perfect," Willow said, as I opened two beers with my keys and handed her one. She took a long pull from her beer, as if it were a potion she desperately needed.

"Drink slow," I said. "You don't—"

She grabbed at me then, one hand clutching her beer, sloshing it, and the other gripping my sweatshirt. She hauled me toward her. Her lips crashed against my cheek, trying to find my mouth. Her breath smelled of expensive whiskey and cheap beer.

"This is how I can do it," she whispered between the frantic kisses that both set my blood on fire and repulsed me. I wanted her more than anything, but not like this.

"Willow…"

"This is how it's done, right? Drunk and delirious and you can just take me, Isaac. It'll be okay this way."

"No…"

"Like before," she said, nipping at my neck and then slumping against my shoulder. "This is how I can do it. Probably the only way I can do it now."

A shadow of a thought slid down my spine like a cold sliver.

"What do you mean? Do what?"

"You know what," she said. "Do I have to spell it out?"

"Yeah, you do, Willow. What are you saying?"

"What am I saying?" she wondered. "I'm saying it, aren't I? I'm telling the story. Why? Because I like you, Isaac. So much and it's so fucking sad, isn't it? I want to be a normal girl who likes a boy and that can never ever, ever happen. Not for me."

"Why not?" I asked, my mouth whispering the words while my muscles tensed to brace myself for the answer.

"Because once upon a time…" Willow's head lolled and her bleary eyes were heavy with alcohol and shadows. "I had a party. There was dancing. We danced like sex and I felt sexy. And grown up. And he wanted me. He was older and hot and popular and he was paying attention to *me*. His name was Xavier."

She hooked a finger up her sleeve and pulled it back to reveal a swarm of little black X's covering every inch of her pale skin.

"X marks the spot," she said. "They're on my arm right now but I can put them everywhere." Her voice quavered. "He touched me everywhere."

She pulled the sleeve down and slumped against the wall while my entire being stared at her, vibrating with terrified anticipation. What she *had yet* to tell me.

Willow took a sip of her beer and then contemplated the bottle. "I drank beer that night. Out of a cup. I didn't drink much but I guess I didn't need to. Xavier put something in it…"

"Jesus…"

"I don't know what he used. Everything turned murky. My memories broke apart and shattered. Now I only remember the night in bits and pieces." She glanced up at me, half-remembered, fragmented pain filling her eyes. "I remember everyone had gone home and he stayed to help me clean up. He was being so nice. Thoughtful. *Let me get you something to drink,* he said."

She squeezed her eyes shut. "Then I remember being upstairs. In the bedroom."

I held my breath. My heart crashed against my chest, over and over.

"They say you're supposed to tell the truth," she said, opening her eyes. "But what if you know it happened but you don't remember how? I remembered the dancing. I wore a short skirt. I drank. And I went with him upstairs without a fight."

"Goddamn. Willow…"

"I didn't say yes," she said, her watery eyes holding mine desperately. "But I can't remember saying no. Not with my voice. I had no voice. But inside…" She shook her head. "Inside, I was screaming it."

The words hung in the air, terrible and unwavering. I swallowed hard, a jagged lump of pain and rage and helplessness. I fought for words. Something to say or do that would make this untrue. I wanted to wake her up from this nightmare. Grab her and take her far away. Get in my truck and start driving. Shift into a parallel gear, put it in overdrive and take us out of this world, into some magical fucking place called This Never Happened.

I want it to never have fucking happened…

The helplessness was a vice around my goddamn neck. I wondered how Willow endured it. Day after day. All day. All night. How was she still standing here? Drunk and wracked by pain, sure, but she was *here.*

She shrugged and wiped her eyes on her sleeve. "That's it, isn't it? I didn't say yes, but I can't remember saying no. Not out loud…"

"What happened after?" I said through gritted teeth.

Tell me the fucker's in jail right now. Getting his shit beat in every day of his life.

Willow shrugged again, a terrible, hopeless gesture.

"The next morning happened. I had a headache that felt like my brain was trying to break out of my skull. I burned my torn underwear. I scrubbed the blood out of the sheets. I took a scalding shower that lasted forty-five minutes. I tried to erase all the evidence and make like it never happened."

"You didn't tell anyone," I said.

"Tell someone..." She shook her head. "Impossible. Tell the police that Xavier Wilkinson, the son of a multi-billion dollar company's CEO drugged and...and...raped me?" A choked sob paralyzed her for a second over that word, and she swallowed it down. "My dad would lose his job. They'd send an army of lawyers after us. We'd be broke. Not to mention I'd have to explain what I was wearing and what I was doing. How much I drank and who saw me dancing with him, bumping and grinding in front of everyone like I *wanted* it."

"But—"

"No, there's more," she said. "We'd been flirting all summer. I'd met him at a Fourth of July party in the Hamptons. We started texting. And the texts turned...*more.* They went too far and until I..." She tried to meet my eye and couldn't. "I sent him a picture. Of me. Topless. He asked me to and I did. Now he has it. He still has it. He'll show everyone if he hasn't already and I...I..."

She bent suddenly and vomited the night's alcohol all over the cement. I hurried to her and held her hair back while she heaved. Knowing the violent purge had more to do with her story than the liquor she'd drunk.

When there was nothing left, she pushed me away and sagged against the wall, drained and tired and gasping.

I paced. Fire coursing through me, my hands balled into fists and my heart pounded hard. Blood thumping between my ears and clouding my vision red.

"*Fuck.*" I whirled and slammed my fist into the wooden mortuary sign, splitting my knuckles and scraping them raw. "I'll kill him. Where is he now? I'll fucking kill him."

Willow spit a bitter laugh out. "Oh, will you? You'll kill him? Or beat the shit out of him? Will that fix everything?"

"I just... I have to do something..."

"Will that make you feel better?" She wiped her chin with the back of her hand. "Yeah, well, good for you. But what about me? When do I get to feel better? *Never.* I get to carry this memory in my brain and this filth on my body forever. A chronic disease and there is no cure."

"It's not your fault…"

"I *know*, but can't you see? It doesn't matter. It's not my fault but *it doesn't matter.* Because it's too late. Too late. You can beat the hell out of him, or punch more signs until your bones break. But I'm still going to be right here." She jabbed her finger at the puke-splattered ground, tears brimming in her eyes. "I'm going to be right here, for always. Right *here.*"

The realization dawned in her, like watching a horrible tragedy unfold right before her eyes.

"Fuck…" she whispered. The tears spilled over her red cheeks. Her lower lip trembled and her breath started to come in short puffs. "Fuck. *Fuck.*" She hurled her bottle at the ground where it shattered in glittering green shards, then left the path and began stomping unsteadily up the hill, into the cemetery.

I followed in silence. I had no words she needed to hear. She was going to release some of the rage and agony and my job was to let her do it and be there for her after.

"Fuck him. Fuck him. *Fuck him.*"

Her voice rose louder and louder, clawing the sky ragged. "Fuck you," she screamed. "Fuck you! *Fuck you! FUCK YOU!*"

Her last cry imploded, along with her body. Her knees buckled and just in time, I caught her and held her, but carefully. Neutral. How could she want a man to touch her ever again?

But Willow dug at the lapels of my jacket, pressing herself to me, trying to get *in.* I wrapped her up. Pulled her close. Made my armor her armor. Her blonde hair spilled over my hands and I made fists in it, holding her so tight. Christ, I'd envisioned touching her hair a thousand times but not like this.

Never like this.

I held her, trying to absorb her pain. Even a little. I'd have gladly taken all of it. I could feel it shaking her bones apart. Even if her mind didn't remember more than a few drugged flashes, her body remembered *everything.* It was in her cells. In her soul. Every moment of that violation was ingrained into her. Imprinted on her.

And there was nothing I could do about it.

She wept against my heart, sucking deep, ragged breaths between each sob. The sobs tapered to shudders. Then a deathly stillness with her voice a croak against my chest:

"I want to go home."

I stroked her hair. "I'll take you."

"But where is home?" Willow wiped her eyes on the sleeve of her shirt, looking around the cemetery. The crooked rows of old headstones, some canting to the side and smudged with age. "God, I'm so tired."

She slipped through the circle of my arms, sinking to her hands and knees. She lay next to a grave, curled up on her side and pillowed her head on her arm.

"Willow..."

"You don't have to stay," she said, closing her eyes.

"But...here?"

"Yes," she said. "Us dead people, we rest in graveyards."

"You're not dead," I said, crouching down. "You're not dead, Willow."

I won't let you die.

"Not all of me," she said, sleepily. "But a part of me is dead and gone. And I'll never get it back."

And that hit me in the heart a thousand times harder than her screaming rage at the sky.

I moved closer to her and slowly, carefully, curled up behind her, spooning her. I moved as close as I dared, still hesitant to touch her. But she let me curl up against her, let my chest press against her back and my knees tuck behind hers. Her thick hair was soft on my cheek as I wrapped my arms around her. She melted against me and I thought she'd fallen asleep when her voice rose into the warm, quiet night.

"I'm sorry," she whispered.

"Christ, Willow, there's nothing to be sorry for."

"I'm sorry I can never be the kind of girl you want."

You already are the kind of girl I want.

The words lodged in my throat. Wanting to spill out, yet they remained locked behind my teeth. A backwards stage fright. I had no problem letting playwrights speak for me when I performed for strangers. This girl in my arms made me feel closer to my true self than I could ever remember.

Willow heaved a final sigh. At last she slept, in as much peace as she could find on the ground between headstones. Only then was I brave enough to whisper it.

"You're the girl I want, Willow."

I said it as me, as Isaac Pearce. Not a line in a play written by someone else. Me.

"You're it. You're the girl. I don't want anyone else."

She sighed again and settled deeper against me. And that's how we slept. The old dead and the new, with the sun rising and a morning mist coming to settle over us all.

Chapter Twenty-Four

Willow

I woke up with a headache thundering behind my eyes and a sour taste in my mouth. The smell of soil filled my nose. I opened my eyes to a tuft of grass and tried to remember. The alcohol had broken last night like a deck of cards, shuffling events and words out of order, dealing them back to me in random flashes.

I blinked. Row after row of crooked gravestones swam into view, a white mist hanging low and seeping between them.

Oh my God, I slept in a graveyard.

I came more awake, aware now of Isaac wedged behind me. His black leather was draped over my body, along with his bare arm, goosebumped from the chill morning air. I noticed the tattoo there, Old English script in black ink, in a line up his forearm.

I burn. I pine. I perish.

Shakespeare? Maybe. The words felt so very *him* in a way I didn't fully grasp yet, but maybe someday I would. His warm body was flush to mine. His presence—the hard, heavy reality of him—didn't terrorize my psyche. I slept all night. I felt safe.

And then I remembered.

I told him everything.

It floated back to me on a current of fear and humiliation. I told Isaac he was beautiful approximately six hundred times. I tried to kiss him. Offered him my body because I thought being half out of my mind with alcohol was the only way I'd ever be able to be physical with a man.

I told my story.

I screamed obscenities at the sky.

Then I threw up.

"Oh my God," I whispered.

The secret suffocating my life was out, and Isaac Pearce had it now. All of it. Every screaming, puking minute of it. Every sordid detail. He bore witness to the ragged agony pouring out of me. It was no longer a shadowy memory locked somewhere inside, leaking to the surface of my skin in little black X's. It was real. It was out.

Xavier Wilkinson drugged and raped me.

I'd said the words to Isaac. Said *that* word, out loud, in my own voice, and by doing so, I took away a little of its power. Not a lot; a drop in a vast ocean, but it was a start.

I sat up slowly and Isaac's jacket slid off my shoulders. My jeans were mud-streaked and damp from lying in the grass all night. My hair fell down around me in a tangled mess.

"Hey," Isaac said in a low voice.

I whipped my head around to stare down at him. All the words I'd spoken hung heavy in the air between us, and I could not take them back.

What if I don't want to?

Isaac knowing wasn't the same as Xavier having a naked picture of me. It wasn't all over his face. He wasn't turning it over and over in his mind, looking at it like a lewd photo. He watched me with furrowed brows, concern and uncertainty in his expression.

"Hey," I said, and winced. My throat was raw and hoarse from screaming. My thoughts such a jumble, I didn't know what to say except, "We slept in a graveyard."

Isaac smiled and his brow smoothed out. "Yeah, we did." He glanced at the gravestone. "I hope...*Joseph P. Bouchard, 'dear and loyal husband,'* didn't mind."

"Oh shit, what time is it?"

I felt around in my back pocket for my phone. The face was cracked, a casualty of my drunken exploits. The time read 5:17 in the morning.

I held my aching head in my hands. "Oh God, my parents are

going to be up soon. They're going to find out I didn't come home. I'll be fucked. I can't go home like this." I rose shakily to my feet. "I don't know what to do. What am I going to do?"

Isaac got to his feet and tilted his head back and forth to get a crick out of his neck. His white T-shirt was streaked with mud, his jeans damp from hip to ankle.

Quickly, I bent to grab his jacket and handed it back to him.

"Here," I said. "You look cold. "

He took the jacket from me and wrapped it around my shoulders. He held it shut in front, pulling me gently toward him. His gaze down at me held no judgment. He wasn't disgusted and repulsed by my story.

"Isaac," I whispered, swallowing hard.

"Don't," he said, and pulled me into his embrace. His arms wrapped around my back and held me tight. "Everything's going to be okay."

I shook my head against his chest. "No, it's not. It hasn't been okay for a really long time."

"Maybe last night was a start." He pulled back to meet my eyes, his voice lowering. "Where is he now?"

"College. Living his life. You can't tell anyone. It's too late." I said, panic rising. I pushed away from him. "I have to get home. I have to... God, they're going to know I slept outside." I flapped my hands down at my muddy clothes. "I can't hide this."

"I can take you to the Fords. Marty will cover for us."

"No. Not him. I can't tell him. I wouldn't be able to look at him in the eye for the rest of the play."

Isaac didn't debate me on that though I could tell he wanted to. "How about Angie? Does she know?"

I shook my head miserably. "No. And I hate that I keep doing this to her. Having her cover for me. I don't want to get her in trouble. I don't want to..."

Tell her.

"She's your *friend*. Willow..." He shook his head, raking his fingers through his hair. "What about your parents? Forget last night. Forget the booze, forget sleeping outside. Forget the play. They don't know what happened? Don't you think you should tell them?"

"No," I said, my voice hard. "I told you. And I'll...I'll tell

Angie. But that's it. No one else needs to know."

Isaac started to say something more, but I shook my head. "It's my choice. *Mine.* And I'm not ready. And even if I were, it's too late."

"You keep saying that."

I stiffened. "Because it's *true*."

"Maybe not," he said quietly. "Martin told me once that the idea of *too late* kills hope."

"They won't believe me," I said. "I waited too long and he's got that photo…" I shook my head harder. "No. I have to get to Angie's place, get cleaned up, and try not to lose the play."

I pulled up my phone and called Angie.

"Hello?" she said groggily.

"Ange, it's me."

"Willow? What time is it?"

I closed my eyes. "I need you."

The McKenzies lived in a modest-size house on the southern edge of Harmony. Angie met us at the back door, wearing baggy pajama pants and a T-shirt that read, *I solemnly swear that I am up to no good.* Her eyes widened as she took in my stained and muddy clothes, then she flew at me, arms wide.

"Oh my God," she whispered, hugging me tight. "It's okay. Whatever happened, everything is going to be okay." She let me go and eyed Isaac suspiciously. "My dad's away on business, but my mom is here," she whispered. "If she sees you…"

Isaac had retreated into silence, his usual stony mask on his face again.

"Give us a minute?" I asked.

Angie glanced back over her shoulder, into the house. "A fast minute."

I pulled Isaac aside on Angie's back porch and started to take off his jacket.

"Keep it," he said.

"I can't," I said. The tears were coming again.

"Willow," he said. "Don't."

"You said that before," I said. "Don't what? I don't know how I'm supposed to feel right now."

"And I'm not trying to tell you. I just want you to know that with me…it's okay. It's okay that you told me." He gritted his teeth. "I want to kill the fucker, I'm not going to lie. I want to track his ass down and…" He inhaled through his nose. "But I'm not going to do anything you don't want me to do, okay? I promise."

The tears spilled over and I heaved a steadying breath. "Thank you," I whispered.

Angie's patience ran out. She took me into her embrace and her voice was soft when she spoke to Isaac. "I'll take care of her."

He hesitated, as if he didn't want to leave me for a second. "Thanks." He turned to me. "Text me later."

"I will."

We watched him walk back to his truck into the cool morning, his hands stuffed into his pockets, shoulders hunched.

The second his truck was gone, Angie pulled me to face her. "Tell me the truth," she said, brushing the tangle of hair back for my face. I'd never heard her voice so hard or serious. "Is he the reason you look like this?"

I shook my head. "No. He's the reason I don't look worse."

My voice cracked open. The tears poured now. Angie's arm was strong around my shaking shoulders. "Come on, let's get you upstairs."

She hustled me up to her room on the second floor. From down the hall, behind her parents' master bedroom, the sound of running water could be heard. A dog, a beautiful Irish Setter with a flowing auburn coat, bounded up the stairs after us.

"Barkley, no," Angie said but he nosed his way in the room anyway.

"Mom's getting ready for work," she said as she closed the door behind us. I realized with a pang of regret I didn't know what her parents did for a living. I'd never asked.

Angie's room assaulted my aching head. It was exactly as I had pictured it: full of pop culture kitsch. Posters of obscure alternative bands I'd never heard of. One of Emma Watson as Hermione. Three separate bookshelves were stuffed with novels, comic books and row after row of Manga. Clothes lay discarded on the floor—all of Angie's lettered T-shirts.

She sat me down on the black bedspread of her bed. Barkley sat and watched his human pace in front of us.

"I don't know what to do here. I need a story to tell my mother, okay? You weren't feeling well after rehearsal? So you ended up here? And...?"

"I don't know," I said.

Angie knelt between my feet and took my hands and hers. "What happened, Willow? Forget everything else. *What happened*? Tell me everything."

I told her everything.

Unlike last night's combustive rage, the story came out between soft hiccupping sobs. Telling Isaac was a grenade thrown through the ice and numbness, shattering it in a messy explosion. Telling Angie was simply letting the words fall out of the hole left behind.

Angie sat next to me on the bed and cried with me. "You have to call the police," she said. "You have to press charges."

"I can't. It was nine months ago."

"It doesn't *matter*."

"I destroyed all the evidence, and he has that photo."

"Willow, you have to—"

"I don't have to do anything," I said. "I can't... God, I... I feel so dirty."

"*He's* the dirty one," Angie spat. "He's a disgusting, vile, despicable, inhuman monster. He's the one that should be ashamed. He's the one..." She broke off, shaking her head. She reached for one of her T-shirts to wipe her eyes, then handed it to me.

Barkley laid his long muzzle in my lap, and looked up at me with liquid brown eyes in that silent way dogs have of understanding everything.

"I've never told anyone," I said. "Ever. Not until last night. Please, just let me...process that it's out there. Okay?"

"Of course." She hugged me hard again. "God, I'm sorry. Whatever you need. Whatever you want."

A knock at the door and a woman's voice called from the other side, "Angie?"

The door opened to an older version of Angie. The same black curls, same plump roundness in a flowing dress.

"Honey, I'm heading out. Is Barkley in— Oh, I'm sorry, I didn't…" Her face morphed into shocked concern as she looked from me to her daughter and back again. "Hello…?"

"Willow, this is my mom, Bonnie," Angie said, her arms still around me. "Mom, this is my friend, Willow Holloway. She had a rough night last night. She needs to get cleaned up, have a shower and some food, and then we need to tell her parents she spent the night here with me, okay?"

"Angela," Bonnie said in a grave tone.

"Nothing illegal happened, I promise," Angie said. "She needs our help, okay? Please. You can trust me. You know you can."

Bonnie shooed Barkley away gently, and sat on the other side of me, brushed my long hair back from my face. "You've been drinking."

Angie bit her lip. "Okay, so one illegal thing…"

"Angie had nothing to do with it, Mrs. McKenzie," I said. "I promise. And I'm so sorry for showing up here like this. She's right, I had a rough night, that's all."

"Willow's playing Ophelia in the HCT production of *Hamlet*," Angie said. "It's a big deal. And she's brilliant. Her parents will pull her out of it if we don't help her."

"I don't like lying," Bonnie said, all the while stroking my hair as if Angie and I had been friends since preschool. "I'll make an exception if you both promise me that saying she spent the night here is enough to fix things. I don't want to find out there was more to the story and my lie made things worse. You get what I'm saying?"

We nodded.

"Okay. I'm going to trust you both." Her tone implied she better not regret it later.

"Thank you." I sagged against her and she wrapped her arms around me. A mother's hug, warm and comforting. "Thank you," I whispered again. "I'm so sorry."

"Is there something you want to talk about, honey?" she asked.

"No," I said, shooting Angie a look.

Then my phone rang, making us all jump.

"God, it's my mom," I said, my voice trembling. "She's going to tell my dad. I'll lose *Hamlet*." I swallowed hard. "I'll lose Hamlet."

Bonnie plucked the phone out of my hand and hit the green

answer button.

"Hello, Mrs. Holloway? My name is Bonnie McKenzie, I'm Angie McKenzie's mom." A pause, and she frowned. "Angie. Willow's friend?" Pause. "Yes, hi. Willow is in the shower right now. I answered her phone because I'm sure you're concerned about her." A pause. "Yes, apparently last night, after rehearsal, my daughter was studying at The Scoop. The girls met up and decided to come here. They stayed up too late talking and lost track of time. I'd assumed Willow called you, but learned this morning that's not the case."

Angie and I exchanged glances, listening with rising hope as her mom saved my ass.

"I know," Bonnie said with a short laugh. "Teenagers, right? We're always the last to know. But Willow's not feeling well. I think it'd be best if she stayed home from school today. I can drive her home or…" A pause. "Yes, of course," she said, shooting me a sympathetic look. "You can come pick her up from here." A pause. "Very good, I'll text you the address. Okay, bye now."

She pressed the button and handed the phone back to me. "I'd say you have about twenty minutes to get cleaned up."

"Thank you so much," I said. "Again."

"Mom, you're a straight-up rock star," Angie said.

Bonnie pursed her lips. "Well, I'm not doing that again, ladies. It may have worked, though. Your mother—I hate to say it—sounded more irritated than concerned."

"Sounds about right," I said.

Bonnie stood up and smoothed down her skirt. "Get showered, wash your hair, and make sure you use the mouthwash on the sink. Angie, maybe you could loan Willow some clothes. She's too tall for you, but perhaps one of your skirts and a T-shirt? I'll put your clothes in the wash and you can pick them up, later. Breakfast? I was going to do eggs and bacon."

I stared at this woman. It was like seeing a ghost or a UFO. A real mom doing mom things. I'd heard they existed but had never seen it for myself.

"Thanks, Mom," Angie said. "You're the best."

She made a *hmmmph* sound, then reached out to cup my chin. "Next time, if you think you're going to have a rough night, call Angie *first,* okay? And then Angie will tell me. Won't she?"

"Yes, she will," she said.

Bonnie patted my cheek and stepped out of the room, closing the door behind her.

I shook my head. "Your mom…"

"Yeah, she's a keeper. She's a therapist. Reading a situation and keeping it confidential is kind of her specialty."

A therapist, I thought. Immediately followed by Isaac's words: *everything happens for a reason.*

I took a shower in Angie's bathroom, washing away last night under the warm water and flowery shower soap. Mouthwash rinsed away the taste of vomit and booze. The reflection in the mirror showed puffy, bloodshot eyes. I gave more silent thanks to Bonnie's quick thinking by saying I was sick. There was no way I could've gone to school anyway.

When I came out of the bathroom, Angie gave me a long flowing skirt with green and red flowers on it, and an oversize green T-shirt that said, *IRONY, the opposite of wrinkly.*

Angie sized me up "Sloppy, but it'll do."

We went downstairs, and I had a few bites of egg and bacon while sitting on a stool at the kitchen counter. The McKenzie's house was as updated as mine, but on a smaller scale, and with all the warmth and comfort mine lacked.

Bonnie must be good at her job, I thought.

Twenty minutes later, my cracked phone buzzed a text. It was my mother.

I'm outside.

"I'll bet she regrets coming all the way over here after you offered to drive me home," I said, feeding Barkley a piece of my bacon. "Her suspiciousness wore off and now she's just irritated she had to come and get me."

Bonnie's mom raised her eyebrows at me. "Was she the reason for your rough night?"

"No," I said.

"Then I would go out there and apologize to her." She smiled behind her cup of coffee. "You know? For the inconvenience?"

I had to laugh. It had only taken one phone conversation, and Angie's mom had read the situation with mine perfectly.

I slid off the stool, and Angie and Bonnie walked me to the front door, Barkley in tow. Outside, my mother waited in her silver Mercedes. I rubbed the dog's ears, and then hugged Bonnie, hoping to take a little bit of her comfort home with me.

"Thank you," I said.

"You thank me by remembering what I said," Bonnie said. "I'm here anytime to talk."

Tears welled in my eyes. They spilled over as I hugged Angie.

"Us girls got to stick together, right?" she said, her voice quavering. "We'll talk more later, okay? After you've had some rest."

I nodded, exhausted down to my bones.

My mother laid on the horn, and I sighed. "That's my cue."

I walked down the driveway holding only my phone, Angie's skirt swishing about my legs. Angie and Bonnie and their sweet dog remained at the front door, waving. A picture postcard of warmth and friendship and *home*.

I waved back, before climbing into the passenger seat. I let my hair fall down the left side of my face, hoping my mom wouldn't see how bloodshot and swollen my eyes were.

"Hey, Mom. Sorry about last night. We got carried away and now I'm not really feeling well."

"I guess not. Your voice sounds terrible," she said as she pulled away from the drive. "But I don't appreciate this, Willow. It makes me look bad in front of your friend's mother that I didn't know where you were last night."

"She understands. She's a therapist," I added. "And I like her. A lot."

"A therapist." Mom sniffed. "Maybe I should send you to her."

"Maybe you should," I muttered.

My mom sniffed again and glanced over at me. Her frown deepened and I braced myself for a question. The one Bonnie would ask. The one I almost wanted to hear. I could feel the truth bubbling up again. I'd told it twice. I could tell it again to her. She just had to ask.

Mom: *What's wrong, honey?*

Me: *Mom, it was Xavier...*

But she fumbled her lines. "What on earth are you wearing?"

Chapter Twenty-Five

Isaac

You're the girl I want.

Wednesday afternoon, my confession resounded in my head again and again while I worked at the HCT. Willow may not have heard me say it, but *I* heard me say it. And there was no taking it back. The line could not be unsaid.

"Fuck," I said, pushing a broom around the scuffed black floor of the stage.

I should've just kept my mouth shut, starting that day in Daisy's Coffeehouse. Talking got me into this fucking mess. I'd been silent for more than ten years, and then Willow came along and I told her everything. Now I was stuck. Somehow, she'd gotten under my skin, into the marrow of my goddamn bones. Her happiness was becoming the air I breathed.

I didn't want to stay.

I didn't want to leave her.

Especially after what had happened to her.

God, Willow...

I stopped pushing the broom and rubbed my fist against my chest. Willow's story was a sledgehammer to the heart. Another slug every time I thought of it. Over and over, it ripped through my thoughts. Conjuring images of a faceless guy dropping something in her drink, leading her to a bedroom, sliding her clothes off her semi-conscious body, lying on top of her…

I closed my eyes and clenched my jaw until my teeth ached.

Xavier. His name was Xavier.

Hatred for the rotten bastard smoldered in me like a low flame ready to combust the instant I ever laid eyes on him. Beating the shit out of him wouldn't do anything for Willow. But he hurt her. In the worst way. Something deep and primal inside me demanded I hurt him in return.

"She's not your girl, for fuck's sake," I told myself, sweeping again. "The play. Stick to the goddamn play."

But now *Hamlet,* which had always given me a shred of hope, rang hollow too.

"*Fuck.*" I slammed the broom to the ground. It echoed through the theater with loud, hollow *crack.*

Martin came out of his office, and joined me on the stage, hands in his pockets.

"What's happening?" he asked quietly.

"Nothing." I bent to pick up the broom.

He watched me, waiting. I kept my mouth shut. I was fucking done talking.

Martin nodded to himself after a second and dragged two chairs onstage.

"Let's talk Hamlet," he said, taking one and patting the seat of the other. "A little character analysis before everyone gets here. I want to make sure you and I are on the same page through the rest of the rehearsal process."

I set the broom down and sat in the chair, crossing my arms over my chest, and my feet at the ankles.

"Now that we are this far along, what do you think of Hamlet?"

"He talks too much."

Marty sat back in his chair, lips pursed, thinking. "Can you expand on that?"

"He talks too fucking much."

Marty gave me a look.

"He over-analyzes every aspect of every situation," I said. "Instead of doing something, he winds up doing nothing."

"Act Two," Marty said with a nod of his head. "*What an ass am I…?*" He grinned. "But then he concocts the idea of having an acting troupe play out his father's murder. That's something."

"The ghost of his father told him to seek vengeance," I said. "Instead of walking up to Claudius in Act One and putting a knife in his ribs, he talks and talks and talks. Torturing himself. Hurting Ophelia." My hands tightened into fists. "All he needs to do is what he vowed to do at the very beginning of the play."

"Ah. But then there is no play."

I shrugged. "In the end, everyone winds up dead. No one gets a happy fucking ending, Marty. No one."

"That's the peril of drama, isn't it?" Martin said after a long moment. "You're constrained to the lines that are given, and the fate of the character the playwright has written." He leaned forward. "But you, Isaac, are not confined in that way. On the stage, yes. In real life, you're free."

Bullshit.

I didn't feel free. Harmony constrained me with a role I never auditioned for. The son of an abusive alcoholic. A loser with a failed business. A high school drop-out. A potential criminal. The fate I needed to make for myself was to get out. End of story. Scene. Curtain.

Martin observed my hardened expression and sighed.

"Come on. Rehearsal is about to start. Is Willow going to be joining us?" he asked. "The other night she wasn't feeling well."

"I think so," I said.

Willow texted me that Angie and her mom covered, but no other details. If Willow's dad hadn't found out about us and the cemetery by now, she was still in the play. And my stomach would stay tangled with nerves until she walked through the door.

Seven o'clock came and went, and no Willow.

When Justin Baker arrived, he shot me a look of contempt. Willow embarrassed him by ditching him at the dance and getting a ride with me. He didn't give a shit about the reasons why, or how she'd felt. Only his pride.

Laertes would ultimately deal Hamlet his deathblow, but Hamlet kills Laertes in return. I suddenly had an intense desire to rehearse that scene so I could disarm the smug little bastard and run him through with his own sword.

Jesus, get a grip.

Fifteen minutes after seven, Willow appeared at the rear of the theater.

My eyes fell shut with relief, then opened and stared at her. Stared until my eyes itched from not blinking. Blinking would make her disappear and I wanted to freeze her in time. She looked whole and healthy and fucking gorgeous in a dark skirt and gray sweater. She scanned the theater and when she found me, she smiled and gave a little wave.

She's going to be okay.

More than okay. Even all the way across the theater, I could see the tiniest change in the way she carried herself. Like some of the terrible weight pressing down on her had been lifted. Not all of it. I didn't know if it would ever leave her completely. But telling me her story had helped in some way.

And it changed everything.

I saw it in her smile and in the way she looked at me. You don't hear a story like hers and keep things casual. Even blind drunk, she'd trusted me. I was the keeper of her secret now, and nothing would be the same between us again.

That's not the truth either, I realized, my heart pounding hard in my chest. Nothing was the same after that day in Daisy's Coffeehouse.

"Sorry I'm late," Willow said. "My ride got a flat."

"It happens," Martin said mildly. Rebecca joined us and they bent over their clipboards.

"We're set to run Act Two, Scene Two," she said.

Willow furrowed her brow, reaching into her bag for her script. "Is that… Sorry, which scene is that?"

"You're not required, dear, but in spirit," Martin said. "Act Two, Scene Two is where your dear old dad, Polonius—" he gestured to himself "—tells the king and queen he's discovered the root of Hamlet's madness. Or so he believes."

He pulled a rolled-up piece of paper from his back pocket.

"The prop will look much better," he said, "but this will do for now."

"What is it?" Willow asked.

"A love letter from Hamlet to Ophelia."

Martin handed the paper to Willow.

Doubt thou the stars are fire,
Doubt that the sun doth move,
Doubt truth to be a liar,
But never doubt I love.

"That's beautiful," Willow said. She glanced at me, then quickly looked away.

"Indeed, it is," Martin said. "Love is always a beautiful thing." He shook the paper. "And this is Exhibit A that Hamlet can, when he wants to, put his money where his mouth is."

Martin beamed at my murderous glare, then clapped his hands to call rehearsal to order, leaving Willow and I alone for the time being.

"I love how Martin gets so into this stuff," she said. "I guess it's what makes him such a good director."

"I guess so," I said.

"Hamlet, Horatio, Fortinbras," Rebecca called. "To me, please."

"I gotta go." I said.

"Sure," she said, and I hated how *unsure* she sounded. "Break a leg."

"Thanks," I said, and we went our separate ways.

Just like we're supposed to, I thought bitterly.

An hour later, Rebecca took center stage and consulted her clipboard again through her dark-rimmed glasses.

"We need Gertrude, Claudius, Ophelia, Laertes, Horatio and Hamlet. Act Five, Scene One."

Ophelia's funeral.

From the prop room, they pulled a wooden stretcher and Martin had Willow lie on it, her hands folded over her heart. Her hair lay spread around her in golden waves. Four actors carried her to the center of the stage where Gertrude, Claudius, and Laertes were waiting. Horatio and I stood stage right, watching the procession in hiding.

The scene began to seep into me, erasing my conscious thought and transporting me into a desolate graveyard…

With tilting tombstones like white, crooked teeth…

Willow was ethereal, lying still with her eyes closed. The single light shining down made her pale skin glow. Lorraine, as Gertrude, mimed laying flowers over Ophelia.

> *"Sweets to the sweet. Farewell!*
> *I hoped thou shouldst have been my Hamlet's wife.*
> *I thought thy bride-bed to have decked, sweet maid,*
> *And not have strewed thy grave."*

As Laertes, Justin's angry rant was overblown next to Gertrude's dignified grief. He fell to his knees to curse Hamlet's name.

> *"Oh, treble woe!*
> *Fall ten times treble on that cursèd head,*
> *Whose wicked deed thy most ingenious sense*
> *Deprived thee of! Hold off the earth awhile*
> *Till I have caught her once more in mine arms."*

Then Justin got to his feet and threw himself on the bier. He slipped his arms under Willow and hauled her up to him. Her body, graceful and limp before, now stiffened. Her face contorted behind her still-closed eyes, into the expression of someone suffering in barely-contained silence. The struggle to stay still. Stay quiet.

Don't tell.

My vision clouded. Then sharpened and I saw a guy lying on top of Willow, touching her. She couldn't move. Couldn't stop him. He had her while inside she screamed and screamed…

I raced forward, my lines erupting incoherently. The blocking called for Hamlet to throw himself at Ophelia's bier as well. I went for Justin instead.

Rage coursing through my blood like fire, I tore him off Willow. She fell back with a little gasp, her eyes still squeezed shut.

Justin whipped around, his own readiness to fight boiling over. *"The devil take thy soul!"*

He flew at me, hard and fast. The stage direction called for him to wrap his fingers around my neck, but Justin wasn't acting. His

hands around my throat squeezed, cutting off my air, his face inches from mine.

"*Thou pray'st not well,*" I choked out, a sneer on my lips as I took hold of his wrists and gripped hard. "*I prithee, take thy fingers from my throat...*"

Justin's eyes flared and his jaw clenched as he squeezed harder through the pain. His eyes were flat with hatred.

Len, as King Claudius, cried his line with genuine fear. "*Pluck them asunder!*"

The ensemble actors struggled to tear Justin and me apart, and then held us back as we strained at each other like rabid dogs.

"*Hamlet, Hamlet,*" Lorraine cried.

Horatio was in my ear, taking hold of my arm. "*Good my lord, be quiet.*"

I seethed, glaring at Laertes, reality blurring. "*I will fight with him upon this theme until my eyelids will no longer wag.*"

"*O my son, what theme?*" Gertrude wailed.

Willow was on the bier now, eyes closed again, face pale and beautiful. The enormity of what had happened to her last summer welled up in me like a tremendous wave.

He drugged her. A deathless death that left her with relentless dreams, and I can't change it. Marty's wrong. I'm too late. The story is told.

I stood alone, my gaze on Willow and nowhere else, and spoke the line that was given to me to speak. "*I loved Ophelia.*"

No one spoke. No one moved.

Willow opened her eyes and her lips parted in a little gasp. A small intake of breath that whispered through the silent stage. She sat up slowly, a trembling smile over her lips.

"Okay, folks," Marty said. "Let's take a break."

Martin called us around the circle. The intensity of Act V was as palpable as the red marks around my neck and the bruises on Justin's wrists.

"The beauty of theater is it can be very real," Martin said. "And despite the battle scars, I consider tonight a tremendous success."

He had Justin and I shake hands.

"Sorry about your neck," he said, gripping my hand hard. "Hope it doesn't hurt too bad."

I gripped harder and his smug smile fell.

"Watch yourself, Pearce," he said, leaning in to my ear. "Her dad's company owns you. Make sure you keep on his good side, eh?"

With the equilibrium restored for everyone else, Marty gave the night's final announcements.

"My generous deadline for getting off-book has come and gone, my friends," Martin said after rehearsal. "It's do or die time. We're going to be starting run-throughs next week. If you haven't already done so, get yourself memorized so we can do some real work, okay? It's really coming together, and you're all doing a fabulous job. Yes, especially you, Len."

Len put his hand down and beamed proudly. Everyone laughed and the rehearsal ended on a positive note. The actors filed out, Willow gave me a last, quick glance before leaving with Lorraine, who was her new ride home now, ever since the dance.

Marty and Rebecca retreated to the offices upstairs to do some prep work, and I worked on the stage, stacking chairs and cleaning up.

Willow reappeared at the theatre entrance. I froze for half a second, then kept moving, saying nothing. I'd said fucking plenty.

"I didn't want to leave without talking a little bit," she said. "About the other night."

"You don't have to," I said.

"I know I don't. But don't you see? That's what I appreciate so much, Isaac. You've never pressured me. Ever. And...well..." She tucked a lock of hair behind her ear. "I embarrassed the hell out of myself. Slobbered over how good-looking you are. Then I puked on you."

"Nah, you missed," I said.

Her smile broke through. "Look, I know it wasn't easy for you to hear what I said. I'm sorry I chose you but... But despite all that, I think it helped me."

"I'm glad," I said.

Such fucking weak words.

You're brave. You're strong. You deserve better than me.

"Anyway, I wanted to thank you for being there. And for—"

"Willow," I said. "I'm going to leave Harmony."

She flinched a little, her brows coming together. "I know you are. It's your dream…"

"It's more than that. My entire life, I've been tossed around. My mother dying, my father turning into an alcoholic asshole. Being poor as shit and struggling every single day. I have to make some money. Some real money. For my dad, and the theater. And I have to make a name for myself that's not connected to this place."

"I understand," she said, looking away. "You have to leave and I want to stay. I know it sounds crazy, but I need this place." Her voice dropped. "I still can't sleep in my bed. I still wake up sweating and unable to breathe, reaching for a black pen…" She waved her hands. "I'm sorry, I shouldn't—"

"You should." I moved a step closer to her, my hands itching to touch her. "You should talk more, Willow. Tell your parents what happened."

She shook her head. "No, I can't. I'm not ready and… We should concentrate on the show, right? The casting agents are coming to see you. You need to be ready. No distractions."

"Right," I said. "No distractions."

Her expression looked as heavy as I'd felt, saying those words.

"Okay, so… I should go. Lorraine is waiting for me. Thank you again, for the other night. And for being one of the good guys."

She walked away. I waited for the relief to hit me that my life was going to get back on track. No more dancing, no more holding hands, no more holding *her*.

I kept cleaning up the theatre. I found a piece of paper on the floor, near the back. Hamlet's love letter to Ophelia in Martin's messy scrawl.

Doubt thou the stars are fire,
Doubt that the sun doth move,
Doubt truth to be a liar,
But never doubt I love.

I started to crumple it up and throw it in the trash. Instead, I folded it up and slipped it into my empty wallet.

Chapter Twenty-Six

Willow

Saturday afternoon, Angie and her mom took me to the mall in Braxton for a girls' day out.

"You looked like you could use the pick-me-up," Angie said.

We walked with linked arms, both of us with clothing bags from Urban Outfitters banging against our thighs. All of her smart-ass T-shirts were in the wash, so Angie's shirt was plain today. But she'd bought a new one that said, *If I was a bird, I know who I'd poop on.*

Bonnie had gone to buy a new set of pots and pans at Pottery Barn, and said she'd meet us at the food court.

"So what's the story with Isaac?" she asked. "You guys are still just friends? After everything that happened?"

"Yes, nothing's changed. He's leaving town as soon as he can and… That's it."

She gave me a look. "That's it."

"We'll have the play, so long as my dad doesn't fuck it up for us. Isaac has casting agents coming to see him on opening night. Did I tell you that?"

"Only about a hundred times," she said. "I'd say you were being smart about this if you didn't look so sad."

"I'm not sad."

I loved Ophelia.

God, Isaac's voice in that moment. I'd never heard anything like it. It drew me from my false death and when I opened my eyes, the expression on his face…

"It's stupid," I said, waving my hand. "The play is really intense, you know? I think it's clouding my feelings. It's getting hard to tell reality from fiction."

Angie frowned. "It's hard to tell reality from a million-year-old play about lords and ladies and gravediggers?"

"That's art," I said, remembering Isaac's words. "The better it is, the more you can see yourself in it."

She pursed her lips, nodded. "I can dig that. But he did a good thing for you the other night and I thought maybe…"

I shrugged, looked away. "Maybe it was a mistake telling him. I don't know why or how I chose Isaac at all. The alcohol, I guess."

"Or maybe because you felt safe enough with him," Angie said. "The booze was just the grease to let it slip. You texted *him* for a reason."

My mouth opened to deny, to say he happened to be in my contacts. But the truth was even in a drunken stupor, I knew Isaac was one safe place left in the world.

"What about later on?" she asked when I didn't reply. "When you turn eighteen, and he's gone off to make his fortune. Like Wesley in *The Princess Bride*." She stopped and grabbed my arm. "OMG you *are* so Buttercup. Is there a play? You should do the play."

"Focus, Angie." I sighed. "Given what happened with X, I don't know that anything could happen with me and Isaac. Physically, I mean."

Angie stopped walking. "Hold that thought. I need to tell you something."

"What?"

"I kind of, sort of, told my mom what happened with X."

"Are you fucking kidding me?"

"We just have that kind of relationship. I can't keep things from her. She wanted to know if you were okay and I started to cry." She tentatively brushed my shoulder with her hand. "She's not going to say anything, I promise."

"Doesn't she have to? Isn't she required by law?"

Angie shook her head, her black curls flying off her shoulders. "She doesn't work for the school or the state, and you're not her patient. She's not required to do anything, I swear." She squeezed my hand. "I'm really sorry. I didn't mean to break your confidence. I just couldn't help it."

I thought I'd feel more humiliated or betrayed or scared, but it felt almost like relief. Like I had one more person on my side.

"She's got one hell of a poker face," I said as we resumed walking. "The entire car ride over here, she treated me like everything was normal."

"That's her job," Angie said. "And you *are* normal. X is the heartless freak of nature."

"She's going to want me to tell someone, isn't she?"

"She won't pressure you, but I can't promise she won't ask a bunch of questions."

"That's exactly the same thing."

Angie gave me a hard hug. "My mom is awesome. And to be honest, I wanted to tell her. I felt like maybe you could use another person on your side."

I stared at Angie for a moment.

"What?"

"Nothing."

At the food court, Bonnie was sitting at a table for four with a lemonade and a plate of French fries in front of her. A large Pottery Barn bag sat at her feet. She stared intently at her phone, curling her lower lip over her teeth.

"Hey, Mom," Angie said and bent to kiss her on the top of her head. She peered at her mom's phone screen. "Should've guessed. Mom's addicted to Words with Friends."

"The fries are to share," Bonnie said absently, then sighed. "Here." She handed me her phone. "You want to give this a try? I don't know what I'm supposed to do with four A's and three E's."

"You can make the sound of someone yawning," Angie said plucking a fry and dipping the tip in ketchup.

My brain refused to cooperate as it really hit me. Three people had my secret now. I felt like Bonnie, Isaac, and Angie were playing a game of Hot Potato, tossing it back and forth among them. If it dropped, it would explode, sending shrapnel flying in a thousand directions, ruining everything.

"I got nothing," I said, and handed the phone back.

"Stupid game," Bonnie said with a muttered laugh, and tossed the phone back in her purse. "So, did you guys find anything good? Are you hungry?"

Angie exchanged a glance with me, then said in a low voice, "She knows you know, Mom."

Bonnie's expression immediately smoothed into what I assumed was her Therapist Face. Inviting, friendly and extremely calm. A look that made you feel like she had everything under control, even if you didn't.

"I was hoping to get a chance to talk to you about that, Willow," she said. "Although perhaps not at the *mall food court*." She shot her daughter a look, then Therapist Face came back. "We don't have to talk about it here."

"I don't want to talk about it at all," I said.

"That's fair," Bonnie replied. "Can I just ask one question? Are you close with your mother at all, Willow? Even a little?"

"You know the answer to that one," I said. "She's not really someone you get close to. She keeps herself walled off with wine."

"I see."

"And all she really cares about is appearances. How we dress, the house we have, the cars we drive."

The boys we like...

"Whether or not I go to the right college..."

"Do you have plans for college?"

"That's two questions," I said, with a small smile. "Not anymore."

Bonnie nodded. "I just have one more and I promise I'm done."

"Mom," Angie drawled.

"Is that little black X on your wrist related to your assault?"

I glanced down at the table at the ink below the meat of my left thumb.

"Yes."

A short silence fell.

"Okay, no more questions, Mom," Angie said. "Willow will hate me for telling you."

Bonnie smiled, and Therapist Face was replaced by Super Mom. "Angie said that you were playing Ophelia in the HCT's production of *Hamlet*. That sounds exciting. Are you enjoying the experience?"

"Yeah," I said. "I like it a lot."

"She *loves* it," Angie said. "The play, I mean. I'm just talking about the play, nothing else. I mean, what else *would* I be talking about?"

I whacked her in the arm.

"Have you ever acted before?"

"No, never," I said. "I just had this idea that it could help, you know?"

"Express feelings in a safe way?"

I nodded. "Yeah, exactly that."

Angie's eyes went between her mom and me. "Oookay, I'm just going to grab a slice of pizza. Willow, you want one?"

"Pepperoni please, and a Diet Coke?"

"Mom?"

"I'm fine, love."

When Angie was gone to wait in the Sbarro line, Bonnie reached across the table and took my hand in hers.

"This really isn't the right place, but I feel I need to tell you that I'm sorry. For what happened to you. It was a terrible crime, and it wasn't your fault."

I nodded. My hand squeezed hers to keep my tears back. "Are you going to tell me to report it?"

"No, I am not," she said. "I think the perpetrator belongs in jail, and in a perfect world, you could drive down to the police station right now, tell your story, and they'd question him as relentlessly as they would you. But in my experience with sexual assault survivors, sometimes coming forward can be as traumatic as the event itself. I don't say this to deter you. I say this because I believe you'll tell your story when you're ready. In your own time, and in the way that's best for you. Right now, that's all you should be concentrating on. Okay? What's best for you."

I nodded, not trusting myself to speak. Somehow, Bonnie had given me permission to stop holding my breath every minute. To just breathe.

"And if you ever want to really talk, I'm here for you." She turned my hand over and rubbed her thumb over the X. "I'd really like to see these go away."

"Me too."

Bonnie patted my hand and let go. She handed me a napkin, took a French fry and sipped her drink. And all at once, I was back to being a girl sitting at a table with her best friend's mom.

"What'd I miss?" Angie said, plopping a slice of pizza and a drink down in front of me. "Nope, never mind. Attorney-client privilege."

"Indeed," Bonnie said. "So back to this play you're doing. I saw *Oedipus Rex* back in January. Isaac Pearce is an incredible talent."

"Yeah, he is," I said, and nudged Angie again. "Shut up"

Angie's eyes widened over a mouthful of pizza. "I didn't say a word."

"He's the one who brought you to our house the other morning?" Bonnie waved her hands. "I'm not circling back to the circumstances. This is pure girl talk."

"Yeah, he was the one," I said. "I told him. And it wasn't pretty, as you saw. We've gotten kind of close. From the rehearsals," I added quickly. I still hadn't told Angie about our dance at the lookout point. I kept that memory for myself, like a little treasure.

"And now you have feelings for him?" Bonnie said, plucking a piece of pepperoni off her daughter's pizza slice. "Sharing personal experiences will do that. It's almost impossible not to feel closer to someone."

"I guess. But we can't get involved. He's going to be leaving Harmony soon. Casting agents are coming to the opening night of *Hamlet*."

"Oh. So you've talked about your feelings for each other?"

"*Mom*," Angie said. Her eyes started to roll but then abruptly stopped. "Wait a sec, I actually want to know the answer to this one."

"Yes, we talked about it." I struggled to keep my smile and my tone casual. "And it's for the best. To stay professional. Besides, he's older and more experienced and I'm...not." I smacked my hands to my face. "God, I can't believe I'm talking about this now too."

Bonnie smiled. "Sometimes talking is like pushing a heavy boulder downhill. It seems impossible at first, but once you get going, it's easier and easier."

"There's not much more to say about the situation," I said. "Except that it sucks."

She tilted her head. "You like this boy?"

I nodded then shrugged. "But it's not the end of the world."

"Maybe it's for the best," Angie said. "If he's leaving town. I don't want you to get hurt."

"That makes two of us," I said, feigning a lightness I didn't feel.

Neither Angie nor Bonnie pushed the point; I guessed I was becoming a really good actress.

That night, wrapped in blankets on the floor, I read my *Hamlet* script by the light of my phone. I was struggling with the little songs at the end of Act Four, which Ophelia sings after she descends into madness.

"It's hard to know what to do with these lines," I'd said to Martin at rehearsal.

"At the root of all madness is an unbearable truth," he said. "It is known only by the person suffering the delusion. Ophelia's songs reveal the truth. Think about what it could be."

In my nest of blankets, I pondered. Was the root of Ophelia's madness grief for her father? Was it her broken love for Hamlet? Was it both?

"In order to keep her father's love," I murmured, "she gives up Hamlet. Then she loses her father's love anyway. She's left with nothing. And it's unbearable."

It was unbearable she hadn't followed her heart.

I shut the script and pulled up "Imagination" by Shawn Mendes. The song Isaac and I danced to at the overlook.

I shut my eyes and sleep took me down along the current of the beautiful song. My blankets became Isaac's arms. The hard floor was his chest. My last thought was something else Martin had said: when confronted with yes or no, always choose yes.

Choose yes, I thought, drifting.

Isaac looked down at me, a question in his eyes.

I smiled.

Yes.

Chapter Twenty-Seven

Isaac

Sunday afternoon, I had lunch with Benny and Yolanda, then went over to the trailer to check on Pops and give him some money. He wasn't there, and the mess was worse. The coffee table top was completely hidden by bottles, cans, stubbed-out cigarettes and fast food containers. I did a quick clean-up, washed some dishes and set them to dry in the sink. Then headed out to the edge of our grounds, toward the gas station. God, it looked so dilapidated and shabby. I could practically feel the gravity of the unpaid bills and royalties pulling it down into a bottomless sinkhole, swallowing my father with it.

Pops sat at the gas station window, staring at nothing and smoking a cigarette. I slid a thin envelope under the glass—most of my paycheck from the auto-shop in Braxton. Pops' smoke danced and swirled against the glass.

"I'll bring more next week," I said.

He nodded and slid the envelope toward him, eased off the stool and disappeared in the back.

Conversation over.

He'd hardly spoken to me after the incident with the beer bottle. But I didn't like this silence, or the look in his eyes. Whatever light he had was fading. Or drowning.

Being poor will do that to you, I thought with sudden anger as I strode back to my truck.

The constant heavy weight of *want* and *need* was a giant hand pressing you down. I know what people in Harmony thought: if my dad got his shit together, he'd be okay. He was the boxer in the ring, and they were the spectators who didn't have to fight his fight. They lounged in seats, yelling, "Get back up!" As if it were easy after you've been kicked so many times.

I've got to get out, I thought again. I had to take care of my old man. He was blood. Family. That was all there was to it.

And Willow?

"Nope, not doing this shit today," I muttered, getting into the truck. My *Hamlet* script lay on the passenger seat. My plan was to run lines at the hedge maze. Alone. Learn all my lines cold and keep to the words. Be professional.

But when I got to the windmill shack in the center of the maze, Willow was there. Wearing jeans and a loose peasant blouse with flowers. Eyes lighting up in surprise as she called, "Hi."

Oh, Christ.

Her smile was full of expectation and possibility. Every nuance of her thoughts playing over her beautiful face.

Knock it off.

"What are you doing here?" she said.

"I came to run lines."

"So did I."

"Okay."

"Okay, well…" She twirled a lock of hair around her finger, shrugged. "I was here first."

"You were here first? I've lived here my entire life."

She held up her hands as if to say, "what are you going to do about it?"

She was so goddamn cute. She was stunningly beautiful, but sometimes she was just damn cute.

I tapped my script against my leg. "We might as well help each other out. Since we're both here."

"Might as well," she said. "We're professionals, right? You first. Where are you struggling?"

That's a loaded question.

"I have a giant monologue at the end of Act Four."

Willow flipped open her script, her blue eyes scanning the page. Her neck curved elegantly down into her collarbone, and the swell of her breasts beneath her shirt…

Professional. We're being professional.

She looked up. *"How all occasions do inform against me…?"*

"That's the one."

"I'm ready when you are."

I got up and started the monologue, pacing the area in front of the windmill. When I finished one shaky run-through, Willow cocked her head. "What's it about?"

"Hamlet's ruminating on war and what drives men to risk their lives for it. What's worth dying for. Honor. He's saying that Claudius is still the King, his mother is still married to a murderer and he's done nothing."

Willow read from my script. *"From this time forth, my thoughts be bloody, or be nothing worth."*

I nodded. "The time for talk is over. Now he must act and do what's right for the honor of his family and his name."

"He should."

I looked over her and found her watching me softly. "Now my turn."

I sat down on the bench and she plopped her script in my lap, pointing.

"All these little songs at the end of my mad scene," she said. "They're so hard to keep track of. I *know* I know them, but then I start to second-guess myself."

"Try this," I said. "Go to the beginning of the hedge maze and do your stuff as you walk it."

She scrunched up her face. "How will that help? I'll be lost *and* screw up my lines."

"You just told me you know your lines. Your brain needs something else to worry about. Let the words just come to you while you concentrate on getting through the maze."

"But how will you cue me?" she asked. "Gertrude and Claudius have a lot to say."

I shrugged. "You're going to have to shout and I'll shout back. That'll be good practice projecting to the back row."

She went back into the maze, her long hair swaying behind her.

"Are you sure no one is going to hear us?" she called.

"Shakespeare-in-the-park."

"Very funny."

The afternoon was still and quiet, the air warm but not yet thick with summer humidity.

"Can you hear me?" she called, her voice came like a bell.

"Yep," I called back projecting my voice toward her. "Go."

Willow began her lines. I smiled to hear them punctuated with cursing as she ran into a dead end of the maze.

*"How should I, your true love, know from another one? By his—*shit!"

I laughed silently. "That wasn't it."

"Goddammit," she muttered.

"Wrong again," I called, and laughed harder.

"You're not helping," she yelled.

Shakespeare echoed back and forth over the hedges until finally Willow arrived back at the windmill. The sun behind her lit up her hair like gold as she planted her hands on her hips. Her eyes were impossibly blue as she gave me a look.

"Well, I hope that was fun for you because…"

Her words died away and the fun-and-games mood between us downshifted into something deeper. The moment held, naked and obvious and lying between us, waiting.

The time for talk was over.

I closed the distance between us in three long strides, took her face in both my hands and kissed her. She gasped in surprise but didn't flinch or stiffen. It took all I had to keep my mouth soft on hers. Make it easy for her to get away. But she moaned softly, a sound full of ecstatic relief to my ears. Her lips parted, she pressed into me closer and her tongue ventured a tiny bit into my mouth.

Christ, it's too good.

She tasted so sweet, her tongue soft as it slid against mine. A growl in my chest as I sank deeper into the kiss, my tongue sweeping her mouth. Her body melted against me, and I held her tighter, kissed her harder. Every turn of my head, every move of my mouth in hers, she responded. Willing. Eager.

My hands dug deeper into the soft, silken thickness of her hair. I wrapped it up in my fists, careful not to pull. Like ocean tides, her mouth drew me and released. We moved in tandem, back-and-forth, opening and closing, shallower tastes and nips of our teeth, tongues tangling and exploring. The need for her grew hotter, more urgent. Finally I forced myself to slow down, kiss her deeply one last time, then break away.

We stood together, breathing hard, her hands gripping the lapels of my jacket. I was loathe to take my hands out of her hair, but I slid them down her back and let them rest on her slender waist. One more deep breath with my forehead pressed to hers, then I took a step back.

Her eyes were full of tears.

"Shit, I'm sorry," I whispered. "Was it too much?"

"No," she said, with a breathy little smile. "It was perfect. It was perfect. And I thought I'd never have anything perfect again."

She craned on her toes to kiss me again, soft, slow, and deep. Taking her time, indulging in the victory over her nightmares. And me, I kissed back, reveling in the sweet ecstasy of her mouth on mine. Even if every taste and touch was going to make it so much harder for us in the end.

"What are we doing?" she breathed between kisses. Her fingers were grazing through my hair and I'd never felt anything so fucking good in my life.

"I don't know." My mouth was on her neck, dragging kisses down her throat. "We were supposed to be professional."

She drew my mouth to hers, kissing me again. "Isaac…"

"God, Willow…"

We kissed until the erection in my jeans was painful. Pressed to me, she felt it and gasped. I pulled away.

"Sorry… It's got a mind of its own."

"Don't be sorry," she said. "It's okay. It really is."

Her face was flushed, and her lips swollen from my kisses, her chin pink from my stubble.

That's how she should be marked, I thought. *With kisses she wants, not fucking black X's.*

My desire for her twined with a need to protect her and suddenly, getting out of Harmony felt like death.

Her dreamy expression faltered then, as if she saw the conflict on my face. "No," she said, pulling me close to her again.

"No?"

"You have to go. It's your dream." She spread her hands wide on my chest, skimming over my shirt. "But I keep thinking about what Martin said when we first started rehearsals. He said Hamlet and Ophelia's story begins before the play starts. Remember?"

"I remember," I said.

"I don't know what's going to happen later. I know you need to leave Harmony and I'm not going to stop you. I would never try to stop you. So maybe it's selfish of me to want you now. Or maybe…it's just how the story goes."

She slipped her hands around my neck. Her touch was brave and unabashed, though I felt her heart beat fast against my chest.

"Maybe we could have this time," she said. "Before we take the stage and perform. Before you get discovered by big-time talent agents that take you away from here. Maybe we can live in the time before the play. Live where the story begins." She looked up at me, her blue eyes clear and bright and unwavering. "The love was there first."

I brushed a lock of her hair away from her face. "Yeah, it was."

Willow smiled then, and my breath caught. No girl ever looked at me the way she did just then. As if I were valuable. I kissed her again and again, wanting nothing but to hold her and keep her safe.

"God, Isaac," she breathed when we forced ourselves apart. "This is crazy."

"It's life," I said. "Off the page. But how is this going to work?" My hands were in her hair again to keep them from roaming the soft curves of her body. "If anyone sees us…"

"We'll use codes when we text in case my dad checks my phone."

"Codes?"

"I'll put you in my contacts as…Ham? Hammy? No, too obvious."

"The Dane," I said. "Or Dane."

"Dane." Her face lit up. "My new friend Dane. She's in the play. She's constantly forgetting which scene we're rehearsing. If we want to meet, say, at three-thirty, we text Act Three, Scene Three."

"Perfect."

She gave me a playful, wry look. "And if we want to say something sweet to each other, because girls like that sort of thing, y'know…"

"You don't say?"

"If you want to do that…" She bit her lip, thinking.

"Act Two, Scene Two. A2, S2." I pulled her close. "Remember?"

Her lips parted, and her cheeks turned pink. "Of course I do. The letter. Never doubt…"

"Never doubt, Willow."

I kissed her again. In that moment, it seemed so easy. So perfect, I could almost forget the words were written for a tragedy.

Act
II

"I must be cruel only to be kind;
Thus bad begins, and worse remains behind."
—Act III, Scene IV

Chapter Twenty-Eight

Willow

I woke up with a slant of bright, spring sunshine over my face. I lay on the floor in my blanket as usual, though I'd slept straight through with no night terrors. I'd been sleeping better for the last few weeks. Not in my bed yet, but I was getting there. I had hope.

My phone chimed a text from "Dane." I smiled as I bundled deeper into my blankets with the phone, shutting out the rest of the world.

Need to change up rehearsal today he wrote. **Act 4, instead of 3.3**

Translation: *Running late, see you at 4 instead of 3:30.*

My thumbs flew. **Sounds good.**

A2 he wrote.

A pleasant shiver rippled through me and I bit my lip over my smile.

S2 I typed back and tucked my phone away.

I showered, dressed in a pretty, pale pink sundress that came just above my knee, and jogged downstairs for breakfast. My mother sat at the kitchen counter, flipping through a magazine. It was only quarter after seven, but Dad had been at work for hours already. The Wilkinsons worked him hard, or maybe he didn't want to hang around my mother. I couldn't blame him.

"You're up early," I said.

"Spa appointment in Braxton at eight." She let her magazine drop as I set my bicycle helmet on the counter and rummaged in the cupboard for a glass.

"Really, Willow, that helmet looks so silly. Especially riding a bicycle with a dress on. We can buy you a car. We can *afford* a car."

"Don't want a car."

"You won't be saying that next December," she said. "You know how God-awful it is here in winter."

I rolled my eyes. *Right. Because New York in winter is super fun.*

"We've been over this a hundred times, Mom. I love the bike. It's a short trip downtown and to school, and you never have to worry about me needing a ride."

Not that you ever did before.

For me, a bike was a necessity. My days of using Angie as my taxi service, or to cover for me, were over. I loved her too much to risk getting her in trouble again. And as my body continued its slow thaw of recovery, being outside in the sunshine and getting exercise brought me closer to my idea of normal.

I'll worry about winter later.

My mother set aside the magazine and flipped through the mail on the counter. "I should've known," she said, an envelope in her hand.

"What's up?" I asked, pouring some juice.

"The party for Wexx that was set for next week in Indianapolis. It's canceled. A new one is scheduled in Manhattan over this weekend."

I froze, the glass at my lips. "Canceled?"

These past weeks, the only dark cloud over my happiness with Isaac was the Wexx party and Xavier Wilkinson being there.

My mother sighed. "I wouldn't be surprised if half the attendees RSVP'd no and Wexx came to its senses."

Usually my mother's prejudice against the Midwest made my skin itch, but today I hardly heard her.

"So," I carefully set the glass down. "The Wilkinsons aren't coming here?"

"Willow, are you listening to me? Why would they come here if the party's been relocated? It's back in Manhattan. We're all invited, of course—"

"I can't go. I have too much schoolwork and the play is getting close to opening night. You guys go ahead. Have a great time."

"Okay," Mom said, drawing out the word. "You're awfully agreeable. More like your old self."

I shrugged.

"In fact... The last time I remember you like this was...last summer? Right around the time of your birthday." She frowned, thinking. "Willow."

"Yeah?"

Her delicate brows came together, her manicured fingers drummed on the counter in that way she did when an unpleasant thought occurred to her.

I held my breath. I could almost see her—finally—putting together the events of last summer. Meeting Xavier at the Wexx Fourth of July party. Me telling her how we'd hit it off. How she'd been so happy because he was "the right kind of young man" for me. She didn't know about the birthday party I'd thrown for myself a few weeks later, of course, but she knew I didn't talk about Xavier anymore after that. It was all right there.

"Willow," she said, her voice trembling slightly. "You understand the Wilkinsons are very important to this family? Your father's been a loyal employee to Wexx, and despite the move here, they've been good to us."

My voice went dry, and I could only nod.

"With that in mind, is there anything that you want to tell me?"

It was painful to hear the words creak out of her mouth. What was I supposed to do with them? Tell her the truth and bring her entire lifestyle crashing down? For an accusation that had no evidence, not even my own clear memory?

There was nothing to be done about it, especially since Xavier wasn't coming anywhere near my adopted state anytime soon. I had grabbed a little piece of happiness with Isaac. I wasn't about to let it go.

"No, Mom," I said and kissed her on the top of her head. "Got to run, I'll be late for school."

She patted her hair where I'd kissed her with an irritated sigh. But her fingernails had ceased to drum. "Have a nice day. Don't be too late coming back from rehearsal. My God, it seems like you live at that theater."

"The show is in two weeks," I said. "We have tech rehearsals and full run-throughs coming up this week, and dress rehearsal next week…"

But she'd already gone back to her magazine.

After school, I killed time riding my bike around Harmony, waiting for Isaac to be done with work. I biked to The Cottages first. It formed one corner of my triangle of favorite places: The Cottages, the HCT, and the hedge maze.

Everything I could want in a two-mile radius.

I stopped in front of one of the cottages. A sweet little blue one with white trim. It had a For Sale sign in the front yard that looked as old and faded as the house. The real estate market around here wasn't great, but I was glad this one hadn't closed.

Someday, I thought.

I rode back to town and stopped in the bookstore to pick up a comic book for Benny. Isaac mentioned he'd been doing well in school. I'd yet to meet him, but Isaac spoke about him a lot and with warmth. I figured Benny deserved a reward, not just for his schoolwork, and for being important to my boyfriend.

Boyfriend?

The word had crept in, shooting a thrill across my heart. And though it was probably foolish, I kept it there.

A few minutes after four, I rode to the hedge maze, and set my bike against the informational placard out front. Isaac's blue Dodge was parked at the far end of the lot already. The sun was bright and warm, thickening the air toward summer humidity. I held out my hand to shield my eyes from the glare. Beyond the hedge maze was a field of tall grass and trees. We'd had to sneak there a few times when other people came to wander the maze.

I navigated the hedges easily now, and found Isaac sitting in the windmill, a script on his lap and a pen in his hand. The end of the pen was mangled—he chewed it to keep from smoking when we were together.

I stopped and watched him for a moment, my eyes drinking him in, my body taking note of every detail. His long legs in denim, a black T-shirt that highlighted the broad planes of his chest. The bulge of his biceps and his tanned forearms, one bearing the tattoo, *I burn. I pine. I perish.*

He'd told me it was from *The Taming of the Shrew,* and that he'd chosen it because that had felt like the entirety of his life. Burning talent, endless want for a better life, and the fear he'd never reach it.

He's going to reach it. But right now he's mine.

Isaac's face was hard-angled and unsmiling above his script. But I knew the man beneath the stony expression. He was brilliant and poetic and protective. He'd been hardened by his experiences but they hadn't broken him. He showed all his soft to no one but me.

He looked up. A tilted smile came over his lips. "Hey."

"Hi." A longing stirred deep within me. It had been waking slowly over the last few weeks, my body thawing from its freeze under Isaac's hands, though he'd never done more than touch me over my clothes as we kissed.

Or maybe *because* he'd done nothing more. Never pressured me, verbally or physically. He kissed me and the kissing was perfect. He touched me gently, until my body understood the difference between his hands and the shadowy phantom of X.

Now I wanted more.

Isaac got to his feet and crossed the short space between us. At six foot two, he towered over me and I loved how protected I felt standing beside him.

"I brought something for Benny," I said, my heart pounding. "For acing his science test." I showed him the comic book. "According to Angie, Luke Cage is a serious badass."

"According to Benny too," Isaac said. "I'll take it to him tomorrow morning."

"How's your dad?" It was Monday, which meant Isaac went to

the trailer yesterday to give his father money for the week.

Isaac's eyes darkened. "Not good," he said. "I think he's drinking more. I tried to talk to him about a treatment facility, but he won't go and I can't afford to put him somewhere nice. Not yet."

"You will," I said.

He bent to kiss me softly, but I deepened the kiss immediately, pulling him to me and exploring his mouth with mine until we were both breathless.

"Okay, I'm ready to work," I said abruptly, and moved to put my bag down. Isaac stared, his smile stunned, while I floated light above a heavy, warm stone of desire between my legs.

I want him.

The truth of it shocked me, crackled down every part of my body like electricity. I shook out my trembling hands.

"I'm really nervous about opening night. I'd like to work my last monologue in Act Three."

"Okay," Isaac said. "Whatever you want. Though after a kiss like that, you ruined my concentration."

A high-pitched laugh burst out of me. "I'm going to walk the maze."

"Go for it."

I went to the beginning of the maze and sucked in a deep calming breath. I tried to ignore the strange feelings pulling beneath my skin, but they were a magnetic force that wanted only Isaac.

I needed to put myself in Ophelia's place at that moment in the play: the beginning of her spiral into psychosis and sorrow. But at that moment, standing at the start of the maze, I was stepping into something good and real.

"Oh, what a noble mind is here o'erthrown!—
The courtier's, soldier's, scholar's, eye, tongue, sword..."

I recited my lines as I walked through corridors of hedges, spring-green and buzzing with life. By now I knew the path perfectly. Likewise my lines came to me by rote; I didn't have to think of them anymore. They came to me like song lyrics, and I added my own little tune to them.

I emerged from the maze. Isaac waited on the bench. My brooding Dane. Dark and dangerous to everyone in the world but me.

"Like sweet bells jangled, out of tune and harsh; that unmatch'd

form..."

My eyes trailed over his unmatched form. Lean muscle under smooth skin. Power under softness. Strength underneath his gentle touch. The magnetic pull was inescapable now. I needed his hands on me.

He was silent as I move to stand between his knees. His hands slid over my hips. My breasts were level with his chin, my nipples hardening as his breath wafted over them. I grazed my fingers through the hair along his temples and fell into his eyes, dark and dilated, the gray-green stormy with want.

"And feature of blown youth." I let my teeth and tongue taste the next words. *"Blasted with ecstasy."*

"Willow," he said, his hands sliding up my sides, his thumbs grazing my breasts and pulling a small sound from my throat.

"O, woe is me," I whispered against his lips. *"Woe is me…"*

Our lips touched and then clashed together.

Something was different this time. He tasted differently in my mouth and felt differently under my hands as they ran through his hair and down the strong muscles of his back. Our breath rasped in our noses as we kissed and even the air smelled different as every inhale sank down into the warm heavy ache between my legs.

Through my eyelashes, I could see Isaac's brow furrowed, his face drawn tight with restraint. His hand slipped up my stomach to cup one breast. I moaned and leaned into that touch, shocked at how good and right it felt. We kissed and clutched, the need mounting between us until his hand slipped between my legs. The tiniest brush of his palm and a jolt shot through me.

Isaac broke from the kiss. "I'm sorry."

"No, it's okay," I said, breathing hard. "It's just…new. I don't want to stop. Not entirely."

"There's no rush. For anything, Willow."

"I don't want to take it easy," I said, the words tangling in my mouth, suddenly awkward and embarrassed to tell him what I wanted. "I don't want *everything* right now but I want… I mean, I need…"

"You need to come."

A flush of heat swept through me, taken aback at hearing the bold words out loud.

"Yes," I whispered. Then again, louder. "Yes. Touch me, Isaac."

His mouth grabbed mine in a hard kiss, deep with a demanding tongue and biting teeth. His hands swept over my breasts, my waist, down around my ass to the backs of my thighs. I said yes to all of it and let out a little moan when he pulled me onto his lap, straddling his legs. I slipped my hand under his shirt, while he laid biting kisses across my neck.

My hands couldn't get enough. Hard muscle and warm skin and a light smattering of hair over his chest. He let me explore him, all the while the need burned in me like the brightest flame.

My hips rolled and his hands slid up my thighs, his face drawn tight. He gripped my hips as I ground down on the coarse material of his jeans, the hard heat of him straining beneath the zipper.

A deep ache of pleasure was expanding down in my belly. All my senses narrowing to the place where we rubbed together. I sat up, riding him, glorying in the sheer desperation, shamelessly grinding myself against him and it was all perfectly okay. I was safe with Isaac. He wasn't a shadowy monster. He was flesh and blood beneath me. His eyes locked on mine, his words coaxing me.

"That's it…"

"Oh God," I whispered, pleading.

"It's okay," he said between gritted teeth. "I want you to."

"Isaac…"

"I got you… Come for me."

"I need…more."

I took his hand from my hip and moved it under my dress, between my legs. I cried out into his mouth when the touch of his fingers reached my panties. The pleasure increasing and expanding as he gently rubbed and stroked me in the exact right place.

"God, baby." His breath was hot against my ear. "You're so wet."

The words sent me over. My body wanted this. *I* wanted this. The pressure building between my legs surrendered to him and a shockingly powerful wave of heated pleasure rocketed through me. My entire body tensed and tightened. My breath stopped dead in my lungs, then rushed out as the ecstasy flew through me freely, without shame or regret.

"Oh my God," I breathed, collapsing against his shoulder. "Holy shit, Isaac…"

"Come here." He pulled me close and I melted into him.

"I can't believe I did that," I said, and raised my head. "What about you? Shit, you must think I'm—"

"I don't think anything," he said. "I wanted that for you. You looked so beautiful, just now..."

"Oh God," I said, burying my face against his shoulder. "I still can't believe it."

"Believe it, baby," he said, laughing in my hair. "You are so fucking sexy."

"Six months ago I couldn't look at myself in a mirror. And now you..."

He took my face in his hands. "Six months ago I was fucking miserable. And then you showed up. When I'm with you, I don't feel the need to be somewhere else or to be someone else. I can be in my own skin without it hurting so fucking badly. That's a gift, Willow. One I can never repay you for." He brushed his thumb over my lower lip. "So stop looking at me like you owe me something. You don't."

I clenched my jaw and sniffed. "Don't make me cry over my first orgasm," I said. "But don't you want... How long will you be satisfied with just...?"

"I don't want to sleep with you," he said.

I crossed my arms.

"I mean, I *do*," he said, laughing. "God, of course I do. But you're seventeen."

"So?" I asked, my tone huffy even as relief slipped into my chest, calming my electrified nerve endings.

"We should wait until you're eighteen. Or whenever you're ready, but at least eighteen."

"Age doesn't make a difference."

"Yeah, tell that to an angry father."

"Ugh, don't remind me." I traced my fingers along his chin. "You won't get frustrated waiting?"

He shook his head. "I feel like I've waited my entire life for you, Willow. I can wait a little longer."

Tears filled my eyes and I swatted his shoulder. "Now you're doing that on purpose."

He kissed me softly. "Never doubt."

I shook my head. "Never."

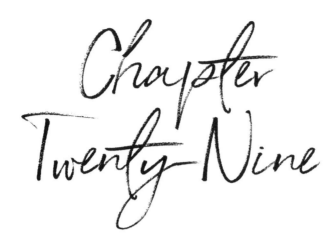

Chapter Twenty-Nine

Willow

In Paulson's English class the next morning, I slid into my desk beside Angie's. Today's T-shirt read *Don't read my shirt.* She mimed pulling down a pair of eyeglasses to peer at me.

"You look different," she said. "Bright and shiny. In fact, if I had to choose an adjective, I might say you look...*orgasmic.*"

The blood rushed to my cheeks and her eyes widened.

"*Noooo,*" she breathed. "Did you?"

"Shh."

She lowered her voice to a whisper. "With Isaac?"

"No, with Chef Boyardee," I said. "Of course with Isaac. But we didn't have sex. We did...other things."

Angie clapped her hands under her chin. "Oh honey, I'm so happy for you. And *other things* are underrated. Nash and I did *other things* for a year before the deed, and it was amazing. Like extended foreplay."

"Angie..." I glanced around.

She shrugged. "C'est la vie, ma chère."

"So..." I bit my lip. "You and Nash waited an entire year?"

Her expression softened. "Not all guys are assholes," she said. "In fact, most guys are distinctly *not* assholes." She pursed her lips, thinking. "Of course, there are guys in between who don't *think* they're being assholes. But that's because society has failed to educate them on what constitutes being an asshole." She sat up straighter and rummaged for a pen. "I should write that down for my blog."

I shook my head, laughing. "You're going to save the world, Angie."

"True fact," she said. Her eyes gave me an up-down and squinted. "Christ, Holloway, you're practically glowing."

Because my light's coming back, I thought.

"I swear to God, Angie I never thought I'd feel this way again."

"Happy?"

"*Normal.* Like I have a future where I can be just like any other girl."

Angie's smile dimmed down a notch. "Does this mean Isaac's plans have changed?"

I frowned. "No. And I don't want them to."

She gave me a look.

"I'm serious. Of course, it'll suck when he leaves, but he needs to go. For himself. He's going to be a huge success and we won't be apart all that long. I'll turn eighteen in July and then I can be with him as much as I want. My parents can take their horrible bias against him and shove it up their asses."

"But he hates Harmony and you love it. Won't that be a problem?"

"I don't know, okay?" I said, feeling my hackles rise. "Can I just have this little piece of happiness right now? You know what it means to have a man touch and kiss me. I thought that part of my life was over but it's not. I thought that Xavier was coming to Indiana in a couple weeks but he's not. Things are going really well. I have no reason to think they can't keep going really well."

Mr. Paulson called good morning and started droning about the poetry assignment coming up next week.

Angie leaned over for a final whisper. "I think it is very forward-thinking of you to let him go. I respect that. I just don't know if …"

"If what?"

"If you're ready for how bad it could hurt."

That afternoon, I sat on my parents' king-sized bed while Mom laid clothes in her Louis Vuitton luggage. Dad paced in and out of their walk-in closet, arms laden with ties and dress shirts.

"The play opens on Friday, remember," I said, plucking a thread on the duvet.

"Don't be so dramatic, sweetheart," Dad said. "We'll only be gone a week. We'll be back in time for your grand opening."

"Opening night," I corrected. "Why do you have to be gone for so long anyway? I thought the party was one night."

"Ross Wilkinson asked me to stay an extra few days to consult on an important project."

"And you just jump on a plane and go?"

"Your father is important and indispensable to Ross," Mom said. "Indispensable people jump on planes."

My mother's tone had the barest hint of sarcasm and my dad caught it. The tension between them always ratcheted up when talking about Ross Wilkinson. To me, he was like a shitty dog owner who hated dogs. He yanked on Dad's collar, dragging him around, dangling bones, taking advantage of his loyalty by uprooting him from New York. Maybe the salary was worth it. Still, I didn't get the sense my dad was indispensable. More like he was at Wilkinson's beck and call, and everyone in the room knew it.

My mother wagged a finger at me. "No parties. No boys."

Both sentences slugged me in the gut. "No," I said softly. "No more parties."

My dad stood over me, tying his tie. "Have you spoken to Justin Baker lately? He struck me as a stand-up young man."

The kind who flies into a violent rage and chokes his costars?

"I'm not interested in Justin," I said. "I'm not interested in anyone."

Dad grunted. "You know, part of my tasks here is to straighten out the lapsed franchise owners. A couple of them are behind on royalties, but Charles Pearce's station out on Calhern is the worst I've seen."

"Dad…"

"He's so in debt to Wexx, not even bankruptcy could help him. Legal thinks we have a pretty strong case for a lawsuit."

I tried to keep calm but couldn't help myself. "Wow, Dad. A

giant, multi-billion-dollar company smashing its fist on the little guy. You must be proud."

I rose to go but my dad caught my arm.

"Hey. First, you don't talk to me like that," he said, his voice hard. "Second, it's something I want you to think about. How bad choices lead to situations like this. No one forced Charles Pearce to drink his business—which is a piece of *my* business—into the ground. In this world, who you associate with says more about you than anything else. And in this town, who *you* associate with is a reflection of this family. Remember that."

He let me go and twenty minutes later, my parents headed out the door.

My mother kissed my cheek. "Be good," she said, then whispered in my ear. "Please."

My father looked back from the front door. "I want to remind you, Willow, that your mother and I trust you. And to break that trust would be a serious violation of our relationship. Do you understand?"

"Yeah, Dad," I said, rubbing my arm. "Loud and clear."

Chapter Thirty

Isaac

"First dress rehearsal tonight, boys?" Brenda Ford asked, joining Martin and me at the table with a plate of rolls. I dug the Fords' kitchen. Especially the eclectic jumble of art on the walls: small town Americana mixed with African tribal masks from their honeymoon in the Congo.

"First of many," I said.

"Nervous?" she asked. "Martin, you look like you're the one who's going to be on stage for four hours."

"I'm on for one and that's plenty," Martin said. He helped himself to fried okra and gestured at me with the spoon. "This one, as usual, is cool as a cucumber."

"You're awful quiet, Isaac," Brenda said. She glanced between her husband and me. "Is this part of your process?"

I blinked and came around. "What? No." My thoughts couldn't have been further from *Hamlet*. "I'm thinking of staying. In Harmony."

Martin's fork fell to his plate with a clank. "Say again?"

"Or coming back, I guess."

They both stared.

"I have to leave to make some money but then…" I nodded. "Yeah, I'm going to come back."

"Here?" Martin said, touching a fingertip to the table. "You're going to come back and live here?"

"Yeah. Not *here* in your house, but… Yeah, I'll come back."

"I just… I mean, you've always…" Martin laughed a little as he sat back in his chair. "You know, I was dreading opening night. I know those agents are going to snatch you up and I figured I'd never see you again. Not unless I showed up at your movie premier." He sat up straighter. "Speaking of which, the casting agent coming to see you has a role he might want to put you up for in Hollywood. Big time director. Big time money."

"Maybe that's it then," I said. "Maybe I get this movie, make some money to help Pops turn things around. Help you turn things around with the theater."

A slow smile spread over Martin's face. "And then you come back." He clapped his hands together, shaking his head at me with an awed smile. "Fantastic. I couldn't be happier. And Isaac…" He huffed a shaky breath. "Helping me out with the theater—"

"Is the least I can do," I said, meeting his eye and speaking with my own damn words. "You've done more for me than anyone. Both of you." I cleared my throat. "I don't want to hear any more about it."

"Well now," Brenda said, still smiling. "Perhaps it's not wise to spend money you don't have yet. Not that I don't fully believe in you, Isaac, but I thought you wanted to do Broadway. Stay on the stage?"

"I do, but Hollywood is where the big money's at. I figure I'll see what I can do out there. Then later, after I'm settled here, audition out east now and then."

I thought Martin's smile was going to spread into the next county. "That's right, by God. Dream big. Put it out there. And what do you do with the leftovers from this Hollywood fortune?" He laughed. "Marlon Brando bought an entire island—"

"I buy Willow a house in The Cottages."

Marty fell silent again and Brenda covered a smile with her fingers. "Willow?"

I nodded.

"How long…?"

"A few weeks."

"Is it serious?"

"As serious as I've ever been about anything in my life. Including acting." I smiled at their stunned expressions. "I'm not going to propose to her on opening night, if that's what you're thinking. But I know she wants one of those cottages, so I'm going to get it for her and…Jesus, Marty, get a grip."

Marty smeared his eyes with the napkin Brenda handed him.

My chest felt warm. He'd always treated me like a son and asked for nothing in return, except that I show up to rehearsal on time. The heat in my heart was pure gratitude, but also relief.

I don't have to say goodbye.

I leveled my fork at him. "You can't say a word about Willow to anyone. No one can know about us. Her dad will flip his shit and you'll be short one Ophelia."

"Lydia is a passable understudy…"

I gave him a look.

"Oh fine, Willow's extraordinary. But Isaac, she's…young."

"I'm behaving myself, Marty," I said. "I swear. I care about her a lot."

Understatement of the goddamn century.

Now it was Brenda's turn to wipe her eyes. She got up from her seat, reached to hold my cheeks and smacked a kiss in the middle of my forehead.

"I'm proud of you," Martin said. "And shocked. You and Willow. I never saw it coming."

"There's some straight-up bullshit," I said into my water glass.

"Language," Martin said laughing. "And I have no idea what you're talking about."

"Yeah, right," I said. I was going to make a smart-ass comment about his meddling and matchmaking, but I was too damn grateful.

Martin laced his fingers behind his neck, looking supremely proud of himself. "You and Willow. *Sweet lovers love the spring…* That's *As You Like It…*" He slapped his hand on the table. "*As You Like It.*" He looked at his wife. "I've always wanted to do that one. Can you not see them? Willow and Isaac as Rosalind and Orlando?"

I rolled my eyes and forked a bite of okra, unable to stop smiling myself. "Too soon, Marty."

"Well, since you're sticking around…" He grinned and shot me a wink. "But you'll have to audition first, of course."

That night, at dress rehearsal, I felt fucking invincible. The pieces of my broken life were falling into place. The only dark spot was my dad. I prayed to any god that was listening to watch over him, make sure he was okay until I could take care of him. I'd see him on Sunday to deliver the week's money, and I vowed to talk to him. Tell him everything was going to be okay. The silence of my shitty childhood and his abuse was fading. Because of Willow, I was learning to trust my own voice. Because she hadn't demanded that I be anything more than what I was.

And I love her for it.

The thought slugged me hard. I sat staring into space, flinching when Frank, the stage manager, knocked on the dressing room door.

"Three minutes," he said. "Three minutes to warm-ups."

"Hear that, thespians?" Len said, giving his fake white beard another dab of spirit gum. "Three minutes and this dress rehearsal is a go."

I looked in the mirror, darkening my own light beard and forcing my concentration through my pre-show process. I scrolled through Hamlet's evolution, mentally mapping his journey through every Act.

"Are you ready, Hamlet the Dane?" Len said. He clapped me on the shoulder, then cringed. "Sorry. You're doing your mental thing. I respect that."

I smiled a little. "You respect it, Len, but you never remember."

He laughed heartily. "I don't know what kind of happy pills you've been taking, mi amigo, but keep 'em coming."

Little by little, everyone cleared out of the dressing room, leaving only Justin Baker and me.

"I know you think you're hot shit," he said, straightening his vest in the mirror. "But you're just the son of the village idiot. And don't think I don't know what you're doing with Willow." His lip curled. "Happy pills, my ass."

Which was bullshit. If he knew something concrete, he would've spilled it. I stood up, towering over him by a good three inches and holding his gaze. Then I offered him my hand. "Break a leg."

"Fuck off, Pearce."

I shrugged and walked out. He wasn't worth my time. I was fucking flying on a pre-show high, or maybe it was just the exhilaration of making a plan for the future that wasn't based on desperation and regret.

Martin called us altogether on stage in a circle, and my eyes sought Willow.

She stood across from me, stunningly gorgeous in a simple white dress, square cut across her chest to reveal the swells of her breasts. Her hair was tied in a loose braid, tendrils escaping a gold circlet on her forehead. She was perfectly Ophelia, and I was perfectly Hamlet, and onstage, we were going to destroy each other.

But offstage, our story won't be a tragedy.

She flashed me a small smile, then looked away, her cheeks coloring.

My blood stirred. Now that I had my plan to be with her, I wanted all of her, all at once. My hands itched to touch her, to hold her, have her beneath me…

Calm the fuck down, I told myself, grateful the material of my costume trousers was thick.

Marty, in his Polonius costume of a purple robe with gold trim, gave us his usual pep talk, then led us through vocal warm-ups and breathing exercises. The tech crew had been in over the weekend loading lights and filters, the sound crew testing levels. The set was done but looked deliberately unfinished. Marty never used elaborate sets for his classic plays. He claimed he preferred keeping things simple and letting the words do the work. I knew his visions were thwarted by lack of funds. Ticket sales and concessions all went to handle rent and back taxes.

I'm going to fix that too, Marty.

An artist friend of his had painted a beautiful watercolor backdrop of Elsinore Castle. A local antique dealer donated a pair of elaborate, throne-like chairs. Everything else was easily brought off and on by a single crewmember in black, and props were minimal.

Including the love letter Hamlet wrote to Ophelia.

The props team designed the piece of parchment, tied with a red ribbon and affixed with a wax seal. Martin, always wanting things as organic as possible, had me write the words myself:

Doubt thou the stars are fire,
Doubt that the sun doth move,
Doubt truth to be a liar,
But never doubt I love.

The words were ours now. Mine and Willow's.

"Never doubt," I told her, always leaving out the rest of the line. My heart crashed against my chest again because that was something left to tell her too. How I would come back and live here with her, if that's what she wanted.

Frank called places. I waited backstage, watching the two armed guards take their places on the apron. Willow was somewhere in the dark of the opposite wing.

I closed my eyes and sucked in a deep breath. I didn't push away thoughts of Willow, or Justin, or my father, or anything else. I let it all in. Let my life's experiences meld with Shakespeare's words so I could give them life with my life.

The play began.

My scenes with Willow were exactly as Marty had envisioned: layered with pain beneath the mocking jokes and wordplay Hamlet used to confuse and outsmart everyone around him.

The love was there first...

Willow was astounding, but it was her scene toward the end of Act Four that blew the house down. When Laertes came back from Paris, ranting about avenging Polonius's death, only to find Ophelia unraveled by madness.

I couldn't take my eyes off her.

Her hair, out of its braid, was wild and unkempt, hanging in her face. Her dress was gone, leaving her in a white slip smudged with dirt and grime.

Like the night in the cemetery when she told me her story.

This night, she told her story through Ophelia.

My heart raced, my eyes nearly squinting at the talent radiating out of her. The second she was offstage, I raced around behind the set, nearly tripping on a coil rope to get to her, following her white shadow into the women's dressing room.

My blood was on fire, my hands clenching an unclenching because they were empty of her. I was thirsty and hungry for her.

Watching her onstage had ignited an entirely different kind of lust. One that had nothing to do with my need and everything to do with giving her whatever she wanted.

I threw open the door to the dressing room a few seconds after she'd stepped inside. She was alone.

Thank fuck…

Willow whirled around, pressed herself back against the dressing table. Her eyes widened and her lips parted as I shut the door behind me and locked it. We only had one other female cast member— Lorraine—and she was going to be tied up for at least five pages. I had eight or more pages before my cue.

Plenty of time.

"Can I help you?" she asked, pretending calm amusement, though her breathy voice gave her away.

I strode to her, kissed her once. Twice. And then we fell into each other desperately, kissing as if we were each other's food and water, and the air we needed to breathe.

"We shouldn't, not here…" she moaned, even as her hands tugged at me as if she couldn't get me close enough to her body.

"I want you," I said, backing her against the small dressing table. "God, I want you so fucking bad…"

Desire was in her every touch and kiss, twined with an edge of nervousness. I could feel it in her ragged breath.

"Not that," I whispered. "I just want you to feel good." I ran my mouth along her neck, biting the delicate skin there. "I want you to come. Hard…"

Her body loosened like water in my arms.

"Christ, Willow, you were incredible. I've never seen anything like it."

I lifted her and set her on the dressing table, stood between her knees to kiss her again, long and deep. My hands plunged in the tangle of her long hair, messy curls spilling over her shoulders and down her back. The eyes staring up at me were wide and dilated.

"What about the show?"

"We have time. I want to kiss you everywhere," I said against her neck, then raised my head to look at her. "Can I?"

Her lips parted and she sucked in a little breath. Her head bobbed. "Okay," she said. "I…okay. But hurry."

My eyes locked on hers, watching for any sign it was too much for her, I slowly slid my hands under her dress, up her thighs that felt like warm silk, and found her underwear.

"Isaac," she whispered, leaning forward to kiss me wetly. "Please…"

Slowly I slid her underwear down and pulled it off of her legs. I kissed her again slowly this time and then down her neck. Her pulse pounded against my lips. Down, over the tops of her breasts that were pushing out of her dress. Slowly working my way down until I knelt between her legs. My hand slid up her thighs again, pushing up her dress.

"You tell me to stop and I stop," I said. "Okay?"

She nodded.

"Say the word, baby."

"Yes." She held my gaze for a moment and the liquid blue of her eyes was full of trust. "Yes, Isaac," she said.

And again.

Yes, she said and I was at her knee.

Yes, she breathed and my lips trailed up the inside of her thigh.

Yes, she cried as I found the center of her.

Only *yes* until she had to bite the word back to keep from screaming as I tasted her for the first time. She gasped and her hips bucked beneath me. I slipped my arms underneath each of her legs, my hands on her hips, her legs over my elbows. Holding her open to delve deeper, taste her, suck and lick and bring her as much pleasure as she could handle.

Her hands made painful fists in my hair and my erection strained against my pants. I concentrated on her, even as the urge to take myself in hand coursed through me.

The climax was rising in her.

"Oh, my God, please let me…"

"Now, baby," I said against her flesh, and delved a final time, sucking the sweetness out of her.

She bit back a cry and arched her back. I stayed with her, kept my mouth on her with long slow strokes until she collapsed down, shuddering.

"My God," she panted. "Oh my God, Isaac."

I kissed a trail back along her thigh on the opposite leg this time and pulled her skirts down. Above me, she was so fucking beautiful, her face flushed, and the current of ecstasy only slowly draining from her.

"Come here," she breathed.

She grabbed me by the front of my doublet and kissed me hard. Her hand slipped down to my erection, feeling the size and shape of me through the material. "This isn't fair to you."

"It's plenty fair," I said, and quickly adjusted myself. "And I think I'm about out of time." I kissed her a final time and moved toward the door. "You're going to kill them on opening night. Fucking dead."

"Isaac."

I stopped at the door. "Yeah, baby?"

"I…" She swallowed and I saw tears glittering in her eyes. "Nothing. You should go. You'll miss your cue."

I rushed back to her, took her face in my hands. "Whatever you see happening between us, Willow, I see it too."

A little breathy gasp escaped her. "Really?"

I could've fucking cried at how happy she was. I kissed her quick, not trusting my own voice, and hurried out of the dressing room and straight into Justin Baker. He shook his head at me in the dark.

"You think a guy like you is going to keep a girl like that? The way her dad is?" He snorted. "Yeah, good luck with that."

I moved to him, loomed over him. "She doesn't like you, Baker," I said with detached casualness. "No matter what you do, or say, she'll never choose you."

He scoffed at me but had nothing more to say. I went to the edge of the backstage to get ready for my cue, and made it with one line to spare, my voice loud and booming now. I didn't fear Justin. Or Willow's dad. I feared nothing.

Until.

Chapter Thirty-One

Willow

When I walked into school Monday morning, I picked up a strange energy. The halls seemed to buzz as I passed, clumps of students standing together, talking intently. Some stopped when they saw me, and the girls formerly known as the Plastics outright stared as I walked past. A sliver of fear slid down my back that Isaac and I had been found out.

Get over yourself, I thought. *All this talk can't be for me.*

But why were so many people staring at me?

When I arrived at English class, the entire room swiveled to look at me. Justin ceased his conversation with Jessica Royce, and they both gave me a strange look. Justin's was quietly smug. Jessica's softer, as if she were ashamed and not hiding it well.

I found Angie's face in the crowd and hurried to sit beside her.

"What the hell is going on?"

"Is your phone on? I tried to text you, like, a thousand times this morning."

"It's in my bag," I said, reaching around to grab it. "I can't text and ride my bike."

Angie was waving her hands and shaking her head. She motioned me close and held my hand in hers. "I just found out this morning. Everyone did."

"Found out what?" A cold dread slipped down my back.

"Yesterday, there was an explosion at the Pearce Wexx station on Calhern."

I froze up. Tentacles of ice spread outward from my chest so I could hardly breathe.

"When?"

"Sometime in the afternoon. They say the whole thing blew. Huge fireball. Charles Pearce was gravely injured. Burns all over his body. They said—"

"What about Isaac?" I asked, gripping her hand until she winced. "He was there on Sunday. That's the day he goes to give his dad money… Oh my God. I'm going to be sick."

I pulled my phone from my bag and called up my text messages. Eight from Angie. None from Isaac.

"Oh God," I whispered.

"Now hold on," Angie said, swallowing hard. "No one said anything about a second person being there."

My mind immediately offered the worst possible scenario.

Because nothing was left of him. Huge fireball. They haven't found the body.

With shaking hands, I texted Isaac.

I just heard. Where RU? Are U OK?

No reply. The message read 'delivered' but not 'read.' I couldn't sit here, watching and waiting.

"Which hospital?" I asked Angie, grabbing my bag, my voice rising. Classmates turned in their seats. "Where did they take Mr. Pearce?"

"Braxton Medical." Now Angie was grabbing her things. "Hold on, I'll drive you."

We ran out of class, Mr. Paulson calling after. Which meant my parents would soon know that I ditched school. It didn't matter. Nothing mattered but Isaac.

"Call the hospital," Angie said, as we climbed into her Toyota. "Ask them how many patients were brought in from the explosion on Calhern." She glanced at my pale face and shaking hands. "Or maybe not. Honey, try not to panic, okay? The chances that he was there—"

"Are really high," I finished. "They're really high, Angie."

I looked up the phone number for Braxton Medical Center. It felt like an eternity to get someone on the phone. When I did, they told me only one person had been brought in so far, and that was all they could tell me.

"No help," I said, jabbing the *end call* button. "He might be okay. Right? Or he might not."

"You got to stop thinking like that," Angie said, as she navigated the quiet two-lane highway north toward Braxton. "What about your director? Isaac lives with him, right?"

"Shit yes, Martin." Panic was turning me stupid. I called up Martin from my contacts, but he didn't answer. I left a message asking him to call me and then sent him a text as well.

Is Isaac with you? Please tell me he is.

I clutched the phone in my hand, watching the scenery go by outside. The grass and corn had come back for spring. Everything was new and bright and green, while inside, the fear was turning me numb and cold. I was racing toward some terrible unknown future. One with Isaac, or without him.

Just as Angie pulled her car in the parking lot, my phone chimed a text from Martin.

He's w/me. We're at the hospital in Braxton. His father was badly burned.

The small sound that burst out of me was half sob, half sigh of relief.

Isaac is OK?

He's okay, sweetheart.

"He's okay," I told Angie, my voice bubbling up with tears. "I'm going to kill him, but right now he's okay."

We hurried inside and were directed to the third floor, the burn unit. The waiting area was set far away from the rooms to prevent infection. In a row of chairs, Isaac sat with elbows on knees, head in his hands, flanked by Brenda and Martin Ford on either side of him.

I crossed the waiting room to stand in front of him, my hands clenched to my sides. Wanting to touch him and make sure he was real, while floodgates of emotion I didn't know I had were pouring out of me.

"Isaac."

He looked up at me, his eyes bloodshot and shiny. Already he looked as if he hadn't slept in a week.

I'm so mad at you

I'm so glad you're safe
I love you so much

The last thought sprang out at me, from somewhere deep in my heart and the tears started to spill over. Out the corner of my blurred eyes, I saw Martin and Brenda stand up and move quietly away with Angie.

I sank down in the chair next to Isaac. "Is he…?"

"He has burns over eighty-two percent of his body," Isaac said. "They say if he makes it through the night, it'll be a miracle."

"I'm so sorry," I whispered. "What happened?"

Isaac shook his head and stared down at his hands. "Yesterday, I dropped some money off like I usually do. I told him not to worry, that I was going to take care of everything. I just needed a little bit of time. Two hours later Martin got a phone call from a friend of his at the fire station. I've been here ever since."

I nodded, fighting the tears and losing. "Isaac, when I heard what had happened, I got scared. Really fucking scared. I didn't hear from you and I thought…I…I don't want to tell you what I thought."

He raised his head miserably. "I'm sorry."

"No, it's okay…"

"You deserved at least a text," he said dully.

"It's fine," I said, my voice watery with tears. "Just don't go silent on me, okay?"

He nodded, but didn't say a word. I tried to comfort him as best as I could but every time a doctor came near the nurses' station, his head shot up, then sank back down when there was no news.

"Pops was so beat down," he said, his fingers fidgeting with his lighter. "Every time I saw him, it was worse. I should've known something like this would happen. I should've been there."

"You had to leave," I said. "He was hurting you."

Isaac's shoulders rose and fell. "I could take it. But he couldn't take being alone, I guess. Or it all just crashed down on him and he finally gave up."

I sat up. "What do you mean?"

He looked at me miserably. "It might not have been an accident." He sighed and went back to his lighter. "Wexx executives are at the site right now. We were already up to our ass in debt. But now…"

He shook his head.

I bit my lip, not knowing what to do or say for him.

"Whatever," he said gruffly, sitting up. "I'll handle it. Whatever we owe, I'll fucking handle it."

But despite his posture, something in him seemed to slump. The weight of the world settling on his shoulders. He had casting agents coming to see him, but that didn't guarantee success. Making a living at acting, even for incredible talents like him, wasn't a sure bet.

A surge of anger at my dad then rocketed through me. He could help Isaac out with a signature on a page to erase his father's debts, but he wouldn't dream of it. Not even for me. Especially not for me. Because Isaac wasn't the right kind of boy.

"Willow?" Angie said, as she and the Fords migrated back to us. "I have to get back to school. You coming?"

Isaac raised his head. "Go, babe. There's nothing to do here but wait."

"I want to stay with you..."

"If your dad finds out you ditched school to be here with me, everything will be worse." He shook his head. "I'll be okay."

"We'll stay with him," Martin said gently.

"Okay." I rested my cheek on his shoulder for a moment and then kissed the corner of his mouth. "I'll see you soon. Call or text me if there's news."

"I will."

I left with Angie, my stomach in knots.

"He's safe, honey," Angie said as we waited for the elevator down. "And we'll tell the school...something. My mom can help."

"Thanks, Ange," I said. "You're right. He's safe. That's all that matters."

The elevator opened on the first floor. Two men in suits with briefcases were waiting to get on. They stepped aside as we exited the elevator, and I caught the glint of a small tie pin. An orange W with gold outline. I'd seen it a million times on my dad's stationary, his computer screen saver, on every letterhead since I was a kid.

Suddenly I didn't feel Isaac was safe at all.

Chapter Thirty-Two

Willow

I trudged through the last hour of school and biked home to an empty house. My parents were due back in a few days. I loathed how my dad would come back to the news of the explosion and have even more ammunition to hate Isaac.

I flopped on our couch, ordered a pizza and flipped on the news. All the local channels were covering the fire. I watched yesterday's footage of a blazing inferno set against the night sky. The scene then changed to sometime this afternoon, Wexx executives milling around the blasted, blackened shell that used to be one of their stations.

The reporter, a pretty brunette, interviewed a Wexx executive who said the Pearce franchise had been "problematic" for a long time, and the company wasn't ruling out arson.

I shut the TV off, disgusted, and checked my phone for a text from Isaac. Nothing. He was going silent again, which was his version of little black X's.

I shot him a text: **How is your dad? How are you?**

No answer. The message remained 'delivered' but not 'read' no matter how long I stared.

I curled up on the couch, ate some pizza, and waited. I dozed fitfully and woke up to an incoming text. The clock said it was 11:36 p.m.

He's still in ICU, Isaac wrote. **I'm tired. Wexx people here for**

hours.

A pause, then a new message: **It's bad.**

Come over, I wrote.

Your parents would love that.

They're out of town until tomorrow night.

I don't think it's a good idea.

Why not?

You know why not.

Just to sleep.

I want to, he wrote back.

I don't want you to be alone tonight.

Another long pause, and then, **OK.**

A knock came at my back porch twenty minutes later. I deactivated our alarm system and opened the French doors. Isaac stood there, hunched over, hands jammed into the pockets of his hoodie. Looking so young, my heart ached. It was easy to forget he was only nineteen.

"I parked on the street behind this one," he said. "No one will see."

My heart ached at that too. Another slap to his face, to the shame he carried through no fault of his own. I opened the door wider to let him step inside. He looked like a thief in a diamond store. His gaze darted all around, certain my parents would jump out and catch him.

"You have a nice house," he said, as I led him through the kitchen to the family living room. His gaze roamed around once more, then came back to me. Some of the tension slid out of his shoulders as he took in my short pajama shorts and baseball-style sleep-shirt, white with pink sleeves.

"I shouldn't have come."

I didn't say anything but took hold of him by the front of his hoodie and pulled him to me. He wrapped his arms around me and we held each other for a long time.

"I needed this," he said finally. "You."

"Are you hungry?" I asked against his chest. "I have pizza."

He shook his head. I followed his gaze to the fireplace mantel and a service award my dad had received: a large glass Wexx symbol.

"I should go," he said.

And I should have let him.

"Stay," I said. "Talk to me. What happened with the Wexx people?"

Isaac hesitated, then slumped on the couch and rubbed his eyes.

"They gave me the 'big picture,'" he said. "My dad hadn't been paying royalties on the logo, and he was in debt up to his ass with the gas supplier. But I already knew that. What I didn't know was how much he owed in back taxes. There's a lien on the property. And because of the nature of the explosion, they suspect arson. Some kind of fraud, I guess, or willful negligence. What kind of person tries to commit fraud by blowing up his business when he's standing right in the middle of it?"

"You said you don't think it was an accident?"

"I don't know that he did it on purpose, but if he did, it wasn't to get out of debt. It was to get out of living."

I pulled Isaac to me and pressed my lips to his chin. "I'll talk to my dad. He has to help you."

"Willow..."

"I know, but I have to try. I can't let you take all of this on. It's too much."

"What will be the price I pay for his help? I can tell you right now, it's you. You'll be the price I pay." He shook his head slowly back-and-forth. "It's too much. I can't lose you on top of everything else."

"What are we going to do?"

"I don't know," he said. "I'm so tired."

I stood up and took him by the hand. I led him through my big, beautiful, cold house. Upstairs to my room, where his eyes immediately found the bundle of blankets on the floor.

"It's not the same bed where it happened," I said, "but I still can't sleep in it. I was thinking maybe I could give it a try with you."

Isaac nodded. He stripped down to his undershirt and boxers while I hauled my blankets up onto the queen-size bed. Isaac helped me smooth out the sheets and comforter, and then we climbed in together.

We lay curled on our sides, facing each other, our fingers intertwined, our legs tangled.

"I'm going to have to go away for a while," he said. "Probably longer than I thought. Seems so naïve to think I'd hit the jackpot right out of the gate, and make millions of dollars to fix everything."

"It could happen," I told him. "You're amazing, Isaac."

"So are you."

I shook my head against the pillow. "Not the same. Your talent is on a different level. It's like you cast a spell, tricking us into believing we're somewhere else. That's a gift. Sometimes people need a break from their own lives. You give that to them."

"That's why *I* do it," he said tiredly. "To get a break from my own life. Except for right now. With you."

I smiled, stroked his cheek, brushed the backs of my fingers across his stubble.

"You're going to be a star. It might not happen right away but it will happen. And I'll wait for you. However long it takes."

Isaac's eyes fell shut as if he were in pain. He kissed me. "Willow," he said, like a prayer or wish. He pulled me into the protective ring of his embrace, and we slept.

I dreamt of fire. A candle in the dark, a little light clinging to its wick. As I watched, the light grew and stretched—blue to orange to white—wavering but tall and strong.

And then it exploded in a fiery ball, hot and blinding.

I sat up gasping.

Just a bad dream, I thought.

But not a night terror. I could breathe. I was with Isaac.

I looked down at him. He was so beautiful in sleep, his brow smooth and untroubled. His lashes lay against his cheek, and I traced the line of them. The angular cut of his cheekbone, the hard line of his jaw under rough stubble. His full lips that had touched places I thought no man could touch again.

I thought I was lost, but he brought me back. He allowed me to find my way back to myself.

"Isaac," I whispered.

"Mm."

"I need to tell you something."

He opened his eyes slowly. "Hmm?"

"I'm sorry to wake you but it's important."

"What do you need to tell me, baby?"

I drew in a breath and let it out. "I love you. I'm in love with you."

His eyes focused. "Willow…"

"I love you. So much. You don't have to say it back but—"

"I love you too," he said. "I've been saying it for weeks with someone else's words."

"You do?"

"Yeay, baby. I do."

My chest felt warm and tears blurred my vision. "Say it again," I whispered.

"I love you," he said. "So much." His hand slipped behind my neck and he brought my lips to his. Kissed me softly, then deeper. "I'm glad you woke me up. There's something I wanted to tell you, too."

"Better than 'I love you'?"

"I hope so. I wanted to tell you… I *started* to tell you at the theater the other day but I ran out of time." He smiled a little. "I got too busy with other things."

"*Other things* were worth it."

He smiled briefly. "But I wanted you to know that whatever life you want, that's the life I want to give you. If you want to live in Harmony, I'll live in Harmony. It won't be the torture I always thought it would be. With you, I see it differently. I'm going to go and do something with my acting, to make you proud. To be worthy of you."

I put my fingertips to his cheek, to the scar where his father had hit him. "You'd really stay here for me?"

"For us," he said. "I want to do whatever it takes to make you happy. And besides, I hated the idea of leaving Martin and Brenda anyway. And not seeing Benny graduate."

"It might not be forever," I said. "I just want a little bit of quiet for a little while. I want to heal first. Here."

He brushed the hair back from my face. "I want that for you too. More than anything. I love you, Willow. So much."

"I love you, Isaac," I said.

We kissed until a small laugh burst from me, and I smiled

against his lips.

"What's so funny?"

"Nothing. Just happy."

"Me too."

I kissed him again and just as I settled my head against his chest to sleep, I heard it. A car coming down the quiet street. Isaac froze beneath me, his heart thumping in my ear. We listened as the car drew nearer, slowed, and the crunch of tires rolling into our driveway.

"Oh, God," I breathed, tossing the covers off. "My parents."

Chapter Thirty-Three

Willow

I flew to my window. Below, my parents were in the driveway, climbing out of my dad's dark gray BMW.

"Oh fuck, they're home. Why are they home?"

I spun around. Isaac was already putting his jeans on. "Fastest way out?"

"God, I don't know," I said. Adrenaline coursed through my veins, making it hard to think.

From outside, I heard loud voices. My clock radio read 3:30 in the morning but my parents were arguing, my mother's shrill voice echoing across the quiet streets.

Isaac had his boots on now. "Willow?"

"Wait," I said. "Hold on. They never come in here. We wait until they go to bed, and then I'll take you out the back door."

"Are you sure?"

I nodded and opened my door a crack to listen. The security system beeped at the front door and my parents carried their argument into the house. My dad spoke in hushed tones, my mom at the top of her lungs, and both their voices carried easily through our cavernous house.

"When is it going to be enough?" Mom said. "When? When they relocate you to the North Pole?"

Isaac gave me a look. I shrugged, shook my head.

"I'm a senior vice president," Dad said, sounding tired and strained. "It's an emergency situation, so I need to be here."

"And then? Canada, Daniel?"

"Look, Regina, if you wanted to stay in New York so badly, you should've stayed."

"What's that supposed to mean?"

Their voices roamed downstairs, from the kitchen into the den. I shut the door.

Isaac ran a hand through his hair. "They won't come in here?"

"They never have before."

"Canada?" he asked.

"I don't know what they're talking about."

Footsteps came up the stairs. I could hear my mother muttering to herself between deep sniffs. We held our breaths as she went past my room and slammed the door to the master bedroom.

"That means Dad's sleeping in the den," I whispered.

We waited for a nerve-wracking forty-five minutes, to ensure my dad was asleep, then I snuck downstairs to make sure the coast was clear. The den door was closed. The silvery-green light of a TV on in a dark room glowed along the crack beneath.

I crept back upstairs to take Isaac by the hand and lead him down. We hurried on silent feet through the dark house, not daring to breathe. At the back door of the kitchen, I kissed him quickly.

"I love you," I whispered, disarming the security system.

"I love you," he whispered back. "Never doubt."

"Never."

He slipped into the darkness, an inky shadow moving across the backyard. I shut the door, rearmed the security panel, then rested my head against the cool glass pane. I breathed a sigh of relief.

"What are you doing?"

A little scream burst out of me on a current of heart-stopping fear. I spun around to face my father, in an undershirt and slacks looking tired. A glass in his hand, something amber with two ice cubes floating in it. His drawn, tired face morphed from confusion to dawning realization to anger, like a spectrum.

"What are you doing?" he asked again, slowly enunciating each word. He rushed to the kitchen window and looked outside. "Who's that? Who was here?"

"No one, Dad," I said. "You and Mom were yelling and it woke me up. I came down to see…"

My reasons disintegrated under my father's hard stare.

"It was him, wasn't it? The boy from the junkyard."

"Stop calling him that. And no—"

"Why were you messing with the alarm?"

Before I could answer, my father seized me by the upper arm and dragged me away from the window. I gasped at the strength of his grip. He'd never grabbed me this hard before.

"Dad, you're hurting me."

He sat me down on the living room couch—hard—and stood over me.

"I have *had it*," he said, his face turning red. "I told you, you're not to see this boy. And now I find him here? *In my house?*" He craned his neck and shouted over his shoulder. "Regina, get down here." He turned back to me. "Give me your phone."

"I don't have it."

"Bring me your phone."

"No," I said, crossing my arms over my chest. "Nothing happened. You're being paranoid."

My mother came downstairs, tying a silk kimono robe around her waist. Her hair was still stiff from an updo and her face scrunched up from sleep. "What's going on here?"

"He was here," Dad said.

"Who? Oh God, not that boy?" My mother looked at me imploringly.

Yes, I thought. *That boy. Who is everything to me.*

"Yes, he was here," I said, my voice harsh despite the pulse pounding in my throat. "Justin Baker. I had Justin Baker over. Does that change things? Everything fine now? Great, I'm going to bed."

I started to stand, but my dad loomed over me. "Sit. Back. Down."

I sat.

"Was it, honey?" Mom asked. "Justin? Because he seems so nice…"

Something in me broke then. A dam bursting; all the hiding and lying flooding out and exhaustion pouring in. I was tired of hiding Isaac, tired of feeling ashamed of him, tired of listening to my parents' prejudice against him. The hope in my mother's eyes it was Justin. The look on my father's face as he pondered the possibility he had the wrong suspect... I sailed over the edge into the rapids below.

"You hypocrites," I spat. "You don't care that I might've fucked a boy under your roof. You only care if I fucked the *right* boy."

"Willow." Dad's voice was a sparking fuse, ready to blow.

"Isaac is not *that boy*. He's *the boy*. The only boy. He's good to me in ways you couldn't possibly imagine—"

"I don't want to imagine *anything*," Dad shouted. "He's nineteen. You're seventeen. He's an adult. You're a child. I could have him arrested for statutory rape."

My face drained of blood and my body felt boneless and heavy.

That unspoken, secret word I could never pin on Xavier. Now it was in my father's mouth, pinned on Isaac. I thought I'd be sick.

"No," I said faintly. "He didn't. He never..."

"He came over while we were out of town, skipped out of your room at four in the morning, but nothing happened?"

"Oh God, Willow." With a groan, Mom sank down on the chair beside the couch.

My eyes darted between the two of them. "What is wrong with you two? Why are you so angry?"

"Do you know why we had to cut our trip short?" Dad asked. "Because that boy's father put our company in the news. It alerted our stockholders to degenerate franchise owners running Wexx stations. My job—the entire *reason* we were sent here—is to clean up messes like the one Charles Pearce made of his business. He took our name and logo, smeared shit all over it, and then lit it on fire. And now his son, a high school dropout, is fucking my daughter under my roof?"

"Daniel," my mother said, her face pale. "Hold on a second..."

Dad whirled on her. "No, I will not hold on. You're perfectly fine with this? What were you doing every day while she was at *rehearsal*? You let this happen."

"No, Dad, you have to believe me," I cried. "He's good to me. He's—"

"Stop talking!"

I quailed against the couch. I'd never seen him like this, enraged, veins throbbing in his neck.

"You've been seeing him. All of this time. Making a fool out of me. Lying to my face every time we spoke."

A splash of blue and red lights lit up the front windows. My mother's eyes widened, and then she put her head in her hands. "Jesus, the police. What will the neighbors think?"

I went cold all over. The police. Isaac would be arrested. There'd be no opening night of *Hamlet*. No casting agents to give him a chance at a better life.

"Good," my father said. "We'll tell them what happened. Or maybe they caught him already."

"There's nothing to tell," I said. "He slept in my bed but that's *it*. We just slept."

"Stop lying to me," my father said. "Or maybe we can let the cops take a look around your bedroom for proof that he defiled you under my roof?"

As Dad went to answer the door, I looked to my mother, who sat statue-still, her face pale and her fingernails drumming the armrest.

I stared after my father, my entire body trembling, then turned tearfully to my mother. "Mom…?"

"You have to understand," she said. "He's under so much pressure."

"He's acting like a maniac."

"It's not his fault. You know how he gets when he thinks he's being pushed around. We just found out…" She pressed her fingers to her lips.

"Mom, what?" I swallowed hard. "What did you find out?"

My dad stormed back into the living room with two male police officers in tow. One tall, one shorter, both intimidating in size and uniform. The taller of the pair had Murphy on his pin, the other was named Underwood. Each had a gun strapped to his waist on one side, a baton on the other. Their glances went up and down my body, taking in my short shorts, my sleep shirt with no bra. Two men pinning me to the couch with their hulking presence and flat stares.

My dad crossed his arms and spoke. "Mrs. Chambers, next door, saw a young man leaving our house by the back door. She called the police, thinking we had a break-in."

I mustered my courage. "What was she doing watching our house in the middle of the night?"

"She heard your parents arguing, young lady," Murphy said.

"Would you like to tell us what happened here tonight?"

"And it better be the truth."

"Nothing happened," I said. "We were sleeping. That's the truth. Why is it so hard to believe, Dad?"

"Because he—"

"Because he's poor?" I cried, tears streaming down my cheeks now. "Because his father's a drunk? What if he were rich? What if he went to private school? What if his father was the CEO of a billion-dollar company? Would you believe me then?"

Mom went pale, staring at me.

My father's expression faltered, confusion in his eyes. "We're not discussing ridiculous hypotheticals," he said. "We're talking about what happened tonight."

"*Nothing happened tonight*," I said.

It happened last summer.

Call the police, Angie had said.

Now the police were here. Standing in my living room, large and imposing, detached and bored, dealing with a family drama at four in the morning. I felt no malice from them, but no sympathy either. No connection. No sense of safety. They filled up the room with a masculine indifference to the experiences of a seventeen-year-old girl. How would they react if I told my parents the truth about Xavier?

All at once, I could envision it perfectly from their perspective. A scared young girl who got caught with her boyfriend in the house, telling everyone that the real crime occurred almost a year ago, with a different guy, in a different town, in a different house with no evidence. It would look like the worst, most pathetic kind of deflection.

Telling them the truth wouldn't hurt Xavier. It would only destroy everything around me. It would open me up to invasive inquiry, endless interrogations to prove something that could not be proven. To answer question after question with *I can't remember.*

I looked up at my father.

"Nothing happened," I whispered. "I keep saying it and you can't hear me. I'm saying words with my voice and they're the truth and *you can't hear me.*"

My father sighed and turned to the officers. "Can't you just arrest him, or bring him in for questioning? He violated her in my—"

"*Stop saying that,*" I screamed from the couch. "He didn't hurt me. He never has."

Underwood held up the palm of his hand to me, his voice hard. "You need to calm down."

"It's not technically a violation, sir," Murphy said.

"But he's nineteen years old. She's only seventeen."

I stared as these men stood over me, talked about me as if I weren't there. I was *here.* Yet I wasn't. Half dreaming, half awake. Going insane because everything made perfect sense.

"The age of consent in Indiana is sixteen," Murphy was saying. "But if you want us to bring him in to answer a few questions, we could do that. They're still investigating what happened at the auto yard station, and it's not the first time his name's been on the radar."

I couldn't speak or breathe as a different scene unfolded. Isaac arrested for questioning. Brought to the station in handcuffs. Sexual assault added to a list of crimes he never committed. The final act in the tragedy of his life story. A story he never asked for.

"No," I said getting to my feet. Or tried to. My knees buckled and I sank on the carpet by Dad's feet. "You can't do that. Please listen to me. I won't...I won't see him again. I promise. He's leaving town. Casting agents are coming to see him in *Hamlet.* He's leaving Harmony. *Please,* Dad. He needs this show. Don't take that away. I promise I won't see him again."

The officers exchanged looks. "Sir?"

"Dad. I'm begging you."

A silence descended. My father's jaw worked side to side as he thought.

"Thank you, officers," he finally said, his eyes heavy on me. "I think we have this under control. *However*, I reserve the right to change my mind and have him hauled in. If I find the story is worse than what my daughter is insisting. Regina?"

My mother broke out of her reverie and roused herself, tightening the silk belt on her robe as she stood. Like a hostess at the world's worst party, she led the officers to the foyer. "Thank you so much for coming."

I sat on the floor at my father's feet, my hair falling all around me, tears drying on my cheeks.

"He's leaving town?"

"Yes," I whispered.

"With his father in the hospital?"

"*Because* he's in the hospital," I said to the carpet. "Isaac needs to go make money to help his father. Now more than ever."

"Make money *acting*?" My dad spat the word as if it were garbage in his mouth. "Him and ten million others? It's just that easy?"

"You could help him," I said, raising my head.

"Why would I do that?"

"For me."

"After both you and he disrespected me and my authority for God knows how long? Give me one reason I should."

I gave him the worst possible reason. The one thing I thought would soften my father's heart and save Isaac and me. Instead, I ruined us in three words:

"I love him."

My mother had returned from the foyer. She froze at my words, then gripped the back of the chair. Her eyes fell shut as her mouth closed with a *click* of her teeth.

The color drained from my father's face as the realization unfolded. This wasn't just sex anymore. Not a casual fling with the local bad boy. A reckless affair that would end with the season. This was love. This was the future. Isaac, a continued presence in my life and Dad having to tolerate someone he found unworthy of the Holloway name.

"No you do not," he said, pronouncing every word. "The last nine months, I've watched you throw your life away. Throw away your chance at a decent college when you were on your way to the Ivy League. I will not stand by and watch you ruin the rest of your future with that lowlife."

"Dad, *stop*," I cried, my heart breaking in my chest.

"This nonsense ends tonight. You are not to see him again. Ever again." He gave a rough exhale, running a hand through his thinning hair, satisfied. "I was disheartened earlier, Regina, but now I'm glad for the relocation. Given the circumstances, I think it's just what we need."

"What relocation?" I said.

"We're moving. Mr. Wilkinson needs me to run our Canadian

operation. We're moving to Edmonton at the beginning of June."

I sniffed. Then a laugh burst out of me. "Canada?" I laughed again. "No."

"Yes."

My laughter dissolved into fresh sobs. "No. We're not moving again. I can't…"

"You can and you will."

"I won't," I said, staggering to my feet. "I'll stay here. I can live with Angie until I turn eighteen. I'm not going."

"You are. And that'll be the last you see of Isaac."

"You can't do this. You can't stop me. When I'm eighteen—"

Dad gripped me by both shoulders. "I'm your goddamn father and I have the final word. You're *done* with him. If I hear that you so much as text him, I'll have him arrested for statutory rape and I'll let the entire *world* know it. Hollywood has zero tolerance for sexual predators these days. Whatever chance you think he has at a career will be demolished. I'll use every resource at my disposal, every press contact, every string I can pull…"

…pour poison in their ears…

"When I'm done, he won't be able to get a job in a Los Angeles McDonald's, never mind a movie."

"Why?" I cried in a croaking whisper. "Why would you do that to him? To me?"

To my shock, my dad's eyes filled with tears and his grip on my shoulders softened. "Because I love you," he said.

I shook my head. "You don't…"

"Willow, listen to me. I know his type. I've seen it before. I am sparing you a lifetime of pain. Alcoholism is genetic. It's only a matter of time before failure will drag Isaac down, and he'll drag you down with him." He sniffed and hardened his voice. "And I'll be goddamned if I stand by and let that happen. It's for your own good. I have experience. I can see the big picture. You can't, because you're a seventeen-year-old girl who thinks she's in love."

He let go of my shoulders, dismissing me and everything I felt or wanted, as easily as blowing out a candle.

"What about the play?" I managed to say. "I wanted…one show."

He shook his head. "Not with him in it."

"Just one show?" I said. "Please? Then he…he'll go and that will be…the end. And we're moving." A sob hiccupped out of me. "Dad, I promise, I'll… be better."

Mom finally spoke up, her voice a thread. "Dan, let her have one show. She's worked so hard. For months."

My father's jaw shifted back and forth again. The anger was draining out of him, the intensity of the night giving way to exhaustion. And perhaps, pity.

"Opening night," my father said. "You have opening night and no more. The next two days, you go to school and you come home. You go nowhere else."

"Okay."

"On Friday, we take you to the theater and we drive you home. That's it. You don't see Isaac Pearce after Friday. Or everything I told you will come to pass."

I nodded, feeling something inside me blacken and curl, something my grandmother had been proud of.

I clung to the wick but there was hardly anything left.

Chapter Thirty-Four

Isaac

For three days, Willow wouldn't answer any of my texts. When I called her number, it rang and rang. Thursday morning, I paced the Fords' living room, thinking I could go by the high school on the way to the hospital. Marty advised against it.

"If you think her father is the reason for her radio silence," he said, "stay far, far away from the school."

"What am I supposed to do?" I asked. "I need to know she's okay. If her dad found out about us, she's taking the shit for it by herself."

"Wait it out," Marty said. "Just have faith."

I had no faith. Or patience. Just a horrible sinking feeling that something terrible happened to Willow. It ate at my stomach until Friday night—opening night, when Willow arrived at HCT for costume and makeup. From the other side of the theater, I watched her speak a few words to Marty. I sagged with relief and for a moment, everything was all right.

Then Marty's bright, welcoming smile fell off his face. Her head down, her face drawn and pale, Willow quickly walked away to the women's dressing room.

I raced to Marty. "What's happening?"

"She's only doing one show," he said. "Tonight."

"What? Why?"

"She wouldn't say."

My fists clenched. "It's her fucking parents. Her dad must've found out I was there. Fuck."

Marty's eyes bored into mine. "Found out you were *where*?"

"I went to Willow's house the other night. They were supposed to be out of town—"

"Jesus, Isaac."

"Nothing happened," I said. "We slept together...I mean actual sleep. Real sleep for the first time in months. That's it."

Marty rubbed his chin. "I don't know," he said. "Maybe you should stay away from her tonight. Give her some space."

"To make sure your show goes off without a hitch?" I snapped. I immediately held up my hands. "Sorry. I'm sorry. I'm just fucking worried about her."

"I know you are. You have a lot going on, but you need to focus. The Los Angeles casting agent confirmed this morning he'll be here. Give it your best. Do it for you. And for Willow, since it's her only show."

I went to the dressing room in a daze. I didn't give a shit about the casting agent or putting on a good show.

God, I'm such a fucking asshole.

I *knew* I shouldn't have gone over there. But I'd needed her. I'd been so fucking exhausted, tired of telling everyone I was fine. I hadn't been fine, so I did a stupid fucking thing and went over there.

I ruined everything.

During the pre-show, vocal warm-ups and breathing exercises came and went, but Willow remained closed up in the women's dressing room. I pulled Lorraine aside to ask if she was okay.

"She looks pale and so delicate," Lorraine said, with a royal lilt to her voice. "I have to believe it's her process. She's quiet but flighty." She placed her hand over her heart. "I believe we're in for one incredible show."

None of that made me feel any better. I had no time left. The wheels of opening night were in motion. Warm-ups, Marty's last pep talk, final sound check, places, the audience filing in on the other side of the curtain. But no sign of Willow anywhere.

I forced myself to concentrate on my lines. The hundreds and hundreds of words I'd speak tonight. Words that had given me refuge.

Given me a voice.

Yet the only two words I wanted to say were *I'm sorry.*

Or… *I love you.*

I didn't see Willow until she stepped onstage in Act One, making her entrance with Justin, her brother. Laertes warned Ophelia to stay away from Hamlet, to be afraid of him. Hamlet couldn't give her the future he promised. He was trapped by his birthright, unable to choose his own fate. Whatever he said to her couldn't be believed.

Then Polonius, Ophelia's father, took the stage and took his turn unloading on her. Declaring she was too mentally feeble to know her own self-worth. Incapable of making her own decisions.

You do not understand yourself so clearly…

Affection! Pooh, you speak like a green girl…

Marry, I'll teach you. Think yourself a baby…

Ophelia bore the brunt of these exchanges on her face. Everything playing across her beautiful features. The audience was enraptured. She wilted under the pressure of her brother and father. Her love for Hamlet crumbled under the weight of their expectations. Willow was telling the story of the other night, of her life, as if Shakespeare had written it for her. My heart broke.

I took that pain onstage with me for the ghost scene, when the spirit of Hamlet's father tells his story. Betrayal and murder. Poison poured into his ear by his brother's hand.

I went looking for Willow the second I was offstage. I found her in the wings, sitting on an overturned bucket in the dark, her hands folded in her lap. She gasped as I took her arm, immediately pulling away. "No. Isaac, I can't talk to you."

"Shh." I moved her to a dark corner, dimly lit by an emergency exit sign.

"I can't talk to you," she said again, her voice rising.

"Willow…"

"I can't." Her gaze darted around the darkened area. I'd never seen her so frail and nervous. She'd blow away at the slightest wind.

"You can. Tell me what happened."

She shook her head, her eyes wide. "I can't. I promised I wouldn't."

"Promised who? Your dad?" I gently took her shoulders. "He's making you do this. Why? For what?"

Her mouth opened and shut. She looked almost panicked as she pulled from my grasp. "I have to go. I'll miss my entrance."

"Fuck the play," I said. "Talk to me."

"Don't say that," she said. "You have casting agents out there. This is your night to—"

"Is this about the money my dad owes?" I said. "If it is, forget it. I'll take care of it."

"No, you don't understand," she said, shaking her head miserably. "It's so much more than the money."

"Then *tell* me."

"He'll destroy you…"

"Fuck him," I said. "I'm not afraid of him—"

"You should be."

"Why?"

"Because you have no idea what you're up against." She was calmer now, stoic and resigned, which was worse than the frantic fear. "I've seen firsthand what privilege can do when it wants something."

I ran my hands through my hair. "You don't trust me to make this right? Is that it?"

"You can't do anything," she said, her voice breaking down to a whisper. "And he's taking us away."

"Away."

"He's been transferred to Canada. We leave Harmony in four weeks."

The words hit me in the chest. She couldn't go to Canada. She was just finding her way out of the cold. She needed Harmony to heal.

"He can't do that," I said, rage burning in my throat.

"He can. I'm not eighteen and even if I were—"

"You'll be eighteen in a couple of months."

She shook her head. "It doesn't matter to him."

"So what are you saying? It's… It's *over*? We're done? Forever?"

In the dimness, her eyes shone large and soft. "I hope not. But…"

"But what? We wait? Months? Weeks? How long? Goddammit, Willow…" I grabbed her hand, making her flinch. "Stay. Stay with me. Or Marty. He'll take you in."

"No, Isaac. You have to go too. Tonight is your chance for success." She struggled to pull her hand out of mine. "You're hurting me," she whispered.

I let go immediately. Pain whipped my skin. She was giving up. Choosing *him* over me.

I was losing her.

"I have to go?" I asked. "For what? To prove myself? What's it going to take, Willow? How much money do I have to make until I don't stink of the junkyard anymore? How much is good enough for your father? Good enough for you?"

"You know that's not true," she said. "You've always been more than good enough for me."

"Then why aren't you fighting?" I said through the wall of my teeth. "You're giving up. You're letting him win."

"He's already won. If I don't…"

"If you don't what?" I took her hand again, trying to squeeze from it the answers she wouldn't speak. "What's in this for him?"

"Isaac, don't."

"Tell me, Willow. Tell me now. What did you trade me for?"

"I have to *go.*"

I pulled her close to me, inhaling her, feeling her body one last time. "I would've done anything for you."

"I know," she said, her tears wet on my neck. "I'm sorry." She took a step away. Then another. "Goodbye, Isaac."

Then she was running toward the stage. Bursting like a comet under the lights and falling into her father's arms.

"*O my lord, my lord, I have been so affrighted!*"

As her lament poured out onstage, my old armor of silence locked around me.

Never again.

I'd never show myself like this again.

I told Willow things I'd never told anyone else. I gave her my best self. And for what? She wouldn't fight for us. Now I stood here, alone, helpless. I couldn't help her. I couldn't fight for us alone.

Part of me hated her. But a truer part of me loved her.

Understood her. I knew the truth of what was happening: it was all the wounds Xavier marked on her. They'd just begun to heal, and then her father unknowingly ripped them all open again.

It wasn't her fault.

My mother dying wasn't her fault either. But the loss was there. The yawning void of a life without Willow.

I lost her and so my own words meant nothing.

Chapter Thirty-Five

Willow

We reached Act Three, Scene One. The end of Ophelia and Hamlet.

A props person pressed a beaded necklace into my hand, then handed me a rolled-up parchment tied with a red ribbon. Hamlet's love letter, written in Isaac's own hand.

Never doubt I love…

I peeked through a crack in the side curtains, peering into the audience. My parents were somewhere in the dark theater, watching. So was the casting agent who could give Isaac a new life. I had to protect his chance. If anything good could come out of this nightmare, it would be Isaac finding the success his talent deserved.

And maybe someday…

I couldn't see someday. Everything felt hopeless. I could only picture a cold and snowy tundra sprawling in all directions. Me dropped in the center, a swirling icy wind whistling over me. And when I turned eighteen, what then? I had no money. All my life, I'd depended on my parents for everything. Now they had me trapped.

The only thing I could do was give Isaac this performance. Give him my best.

Just tell the story.

Onstage, Isaac was deep in his *To be, or not to be* soliloquy, tearing into it with naked rawness, leaving the audience pinned to their seats. The conflict within him burned bright in every word. The struggle to keep going when the desire was to give up. The ordeal of fighting when all you wanted was to sleep.

At the end, the audience held its breath until a single pair of hands began a spontaneous ovation that swept through the entire theater. I'd never heard of that happening before.

Isaac held still until it was over. I stepped onto the stage.

"*The fair Ophelia*," he said. His voice drew inward and he added, "*In thy orisons be all my sins remembered.*"

Hamlet strolled in a small circle around me, hands clasped behind his back. Black trousers, black boots, and a black doublet with a gold pendant sewn onto the front. Dark and dangerous. And unraveling. His hair askew, tousled and wild above his sleek, neat clothes. His lips bore a tight, mirthless smile. His eyes looked at me with a shifting sea of love, longing, anger, pain.

"*Good my lord, How does your honor for this many a day?*" My voice was already shaking.

"*I humbly thank you; well, well, well.*"

With a shaking hand, I held out the letter and the necklace. "*My lord, I have remembrances of yours, that I have longèd long to re-deliver; I pray you, now receive them.*"

Hamlet gave a small jerk of his chin, as if perplexedly amused. "*No, not I; I never gave you aught.*"

He continued his strolling around me as I thrust my hand out again.

"*My honour'd lord, you know right well you did; And, with them, words of so sweet breath composed as made the things more rich...*" I swallowed my tears... "*Their perfume lost, Take these again; for to the noble mind rich gifts wax poor when givers prove unkind.*" I put the necklace and letter in his hand. "*There, my lord.*"

Hamlet took them both, not breaking his stride. His lips curled up in a horrible sneer and his laugh was a mockery.

"*Ha, ha! are you honest?*"

"*My lord?*"

"*Are you fair?*"

His circling was making me dizzy as I fought to hold his gaze.

"*What means your lordship?*"

Hamlet shrugged, as if the answer were simple. "*That if you be honest and fair, your honesty should admit no discourse to your beauty.*"

"*Could beauty, my lord, have better commerce than with honesty?*" I asked.

He replied it was easier for beauty to turn a virgin into a whore, than honesty to turn a whore back into a virgin.

You're too late, he was saying. *The damage is done.*

"*This was sometime a paradox,*" he said, his voice growing soft, his steps slowing. "*But now the time gives it proof.*" He stopped his slow prowl around me and held my gaze, pain riding the surface of his face. Then he dropped his gaze to the letter and I watched his eyes fill with tears.

"*I did love you once.*"

Tears slid unbidden down my cheek. "*Indeed, my lord, you made me believe so.*"

The entire theater held its breath. The air felt crystalline and ready to shatter.

"*You should not have believed me,*" he said quietly. And tore the letter and its red ribbon to shreds. The pieces fell like snow and blood as he raised his head to look at me.

"*I loved you not.*"

His words slammed into my chest and sunk deep into my heart. I straightened to my full height, my lips trembling as the cold came back, turning me numb. Uncaring. And this time I reached for it.

Feeling nothing, I thought, would be preferable to the pain that was to come.

"*I was the more deceived,*" I said with as much nonchalance as I could muster.

Hamlet's eyes flared at my callous reply. His pent-up anger and pain flooded out on a current of ancient words. He strode to me, loomed over me.

"*Get thee to a nunnery: why wouldst thou be a breeder of sinners?*"

He gripped me by my shoulders, forcing a gasp out of me. My eyes were locked on his, unable to look away.

"*What should such fellows as I do crawling between earth and heaven? We are arrant knaves, all; believe none of us. Go thy ways to a nunnery!*"

His grip tightened, as he caught his breath, mastering his anger.

Up through his eyes rose a plea. One last chance for us.

"*Where's your father?*" Hamlet asked, his voice cracking open to show Isaac.

The play vanished. The stage and theater disappeared. The audience shrank to one single seat with my father in it. Watching from the dark as Isaac asked me—begged me one final time—to choose him.

He thought it was simple—disobey my father and love him. Love him no matter what. But he didn't know what he was asking. He didn't know what I knew. What my father could do to him. Staring in his eyes, I saw the love for me, but I also saw the ruination of everything he'd worked for. His dreams crushed by accusations my father could make. Endless resources and the influence of a multi-billion-dollar company behind them.

I'd die before I let that happen—before I let Isaac take on a crime he was innocent of while Xavier walked free.

The choice tore me in half. Whatever I decided would be *my* ruination. Live a life without Isaac. Or stay with him and watch him lose everything.

I had no choice.

My father was in the audience watching.

I drew in a shaky breath, my eyes pleading for forgiveness as I uttered the simple lie that unraveled us for good.

"*At home, my lord.*"

Isaac's eyes flared again. His fingers loosened their hold on my arms but didn't let go. He turned his face to the audience. The stage lights wouldn't let him find my father in the crowd, but I knew he spoke only to him.

"*Let the doors be shut upon him,*" he whispered, "*that he may play the fool nowhere but in's own house.*"

Isaac let go and I fell to my knees. I had a line but it was lost as I struggled to draw breath between the choking sobs that were strangling my throat. Isaac started to turn away, done with me. Done with us.

Then he whirled back around, shaking, unable to contain the pain any longer. He let it all out, spitting words that hit me like slaps to the face.

"*If thou dost marry, I'll give thee this* plague *for thy dowry. Be thou as chaste as* ice, *as pure as* snow, *thou shalt not escape calumny.*"

His voice rose, cracking, as tears filled his eyes. "*Or, if thou wilt needs marry, marry a fool, for wise men know well enough,*"—he jabbed his finger at his own heart—"*what* monsters *you make of them!*"

He stood over my sobbing form, breathing heavily. Gathering up his pain, calling it home and pressing it back inside. He spoke his final line in a voice devoid of all emotion. All pain. A tone that promised his silence from that moment forward.

"*Farewell.*"

Act III

There is a willow grows aslant a brook
That shows his hoar leaves in the glassy stream.
There with fantastic garlands did she come
Of crowflowers, nettles, daisies, and long purples,
That liberal shepherds give a grosser name,
But our cold maids do "dead men's fingers" call them.
There, on the pendant boughs her coronet weeds
Clambering to hang, an envious sliver broke,
When down her weedy trophies and herself
Fell in the weeping brook. Her clothes spread wide,
And mermaid-like a while they bore her up,
Which time she chanted snatches of old lauds
As one incapable of her own distress,
Or like a creature native and indued
Unto that element. But long it could not be
Till that her garments, heavy with their drink,
Pulled the poor wretch from her melodious lay
To muddy death.

—Act IV, Scene VII

Chapter Thirty-Six

Three years later…

Willow

I woke up to a sticky Indiana summer morning, the heat laying on me like a second, damp blanket. Air conditioning was on the long list of household improvements to my rental in The Cottages. I'd only been back in Harmony for three months, and food and rent ate up most of my little salary from the HCT. I didn't have much left over for home renovations.

I kicked the covers off to get some air on my skin. My bed was the same four-poster queen-size from my parents' house in Emerson Hills. It had moved with me to Canada, to Billings, Montana, and then to Austin, Texas. Three times in three years my dad was relocated, chasing the oil profits. My mother finally gave up packing and hauling furniture and insisted on pre-furnished homes with every move. It was wasteful and silly, but it was her way of protesting being dragged around North America.

I didn't protest. I had no voice. No money. Nothing. The only thing I asked was to take my bed, including the sheets and blankets. If I pressed my nose to the linens and inhaled, I imagined I could still smell Isaac there—gasoline and smoke, peppermint and aftershave.

"Isaac."

I let his name sigh out of me as I lay on the bed in my cottage, my hand pressing over my heart. No matter how often I thought of him—and it was constant—the ache in my chest never diminished. Missing him never got easier.

I shook off the sadness before it weighed me down, and got out of bed. I padded across the hardwood floors, through the living area, decorated with my own little touches. Wooden comedy and tragedy masks I found at a swap meet in Texas. A colorful Cheyenne throw rug I'd bought in Montana, soft under my feet as I crossed into the kitchen.

I started the coffee and my gaze lingered on the framed poem hanging next to the kitchen window. Angie wrote it for me in Mr. Paulson's English class in high school. She sent it to me in Canada, before she left for Stanford.

Willow Tree

Its limbs the long hair
of a sad girl,
reaching for the
ground.
'Sturdy as an oak,' they say.
A willow is stronger.
It bends to the storm.
Harsh winds whip it,
its leaves are torn
and carried away.
It bends but doesn't break.
It may weep
but it will
never
fall.

I smiled as I lifted my coffee mug, gratitude and anticipation in every sip. Counting the minutes until this weekend, when Angie would be at the final performance of *A Doll's House* at the HCT.

I hadn't seen my best friend in three years.

I showered, tied my long hair in a braid down my back, and dressed in a pale green sundress with yellow daisies on it. While Marty didn't enforce a dress code at the HCT offices, I liked to look as professional as I could on my little budget.

After a quick breakfast of toast, juice, and coffee, I grabbed my bike off my front porch and strapped my helmet under my chin. Greta, my neighbor, was already in her front garden with a smock and gloves, weeding.

"Morning, Greta."

"Guten Morgen, my girl." She stood up and stretched her back. "I have fresh peas for you," she said in her thick German accent. "When you come back from work."

"I'll trade you for some lemonade," I said.

"Yes, that would be fine."

I had a little lemon tree in a pot in my tiny backyard. It was my pride and joy, watching it grow tall and bear fruit. Bright yellow suns in a galaxy of green leaves. Greta said it wouldn't survive the winter, but I'd put it in a pot just for that; so I could bring it inside when it got cold.

I wouldn't leave it to die in ice and snow, but would take care to always keep it warm.

That afternoon, the sun was bright and warm on my face. People groused about Midwest humidity, but I basked in it. I craved being warm. I turned my face into the rays, let it seep into my bones and drive out the terrible memories of Canada when I was so lost.

Everything I loved—Harmony, Isaac, Angie—had been ripped away and trampled on. For long, agonizing months, I was a passenger in my own body. Feeling nothing, because allowing myself to feel anything hurt too much. Numbness was easier; and I'd returned to the dark, cold place I'd been the summer after Xavier had assaulted me.

My parents didn't know what to do with me. My eighteenth birthday came and went, but I had no money, no job, no savings, and no will to do anything. I stayed in my room for three solid months, hardly eating or bathing or sleeping. My mother tearfully begged and pleaded. My father sternly told me to stop acting like it was 'the end of the world' and to 'pull myself together.'

I had no sense of self to pull together. I was broken and scattered, the pieces of me spread out over a cold ocean floor. More than once, I imagined my robotic body transporting me out onto the small lake behind our house in Edmonton. Maybe the ice wasn't thick enough yet, and I'd hear a crack under my feet—a gun shot across the still, frigid air. A split second later, it would give way, and drop me down into the black water.

Bonnie McKenzie saved me.

My father had confiscated my phone and laptop for months, cutting me off from the world. When he finally permitted me a new phone, I called Angie one cold November night. She was home for Thanksgiving. One word in my cracked and trembling voice made her pass the phone to her mother.

It took months of late night phone calls and secret Skype sessions to break through the numbness. To pull myself together. By January, I got a job at a clothing store in Edmonton, and from that first paycheck to the last from a boutique in Austin, I saved for my return to Harmony.

Now I saw Bonnie twice a week at her downtown office on Juniper Street. She was kind enough not to charge me for her time, and I vowed to make it up to her somehow. On my own. If I were starving to death, I wouldn't ask my parents for a dime. I'd never be dependent on them or helpless without their money, ever again.

I rode my bike downtown. Past The Scoop, where tourists and locals crammed every booth, down to the theater. I locked my bicycle to a parking meter out front and glanced up at the marquee.

Henrik Ibsen's A Doll's House
Final Performances this weekend!

When I returned to Harmony three months ago, one of the first things I did was visit Martin. Stepping back into the theater felt like coming home, and Marty's arms closed me up like a benevolent, kind father. He was about to start auditions for *A Doll's House,* a play about a young woman who is tired of being treated like a precious doll by her older husband and bucks 19th century conventions and leaves him to find herself.

Martin thought I'd be perfect for the part. Nora was the opposite of Ophelia. Treated like a pretty toy by her father and husband, but instead of succumbing, she fights back. Fighting back was something I was slowly learning to do. The play gave me a road map. Bonnie's therapy was rebuilding my shattered self-worth. And Harmony had given me the peace to let it happen.

In the lobby's dim, coolness, I waved at Frank Darian, our stage manager. He waved back from the box office where he was preparing for this Friday's performance.

In the theater itself, the lights were low over the stage, casting spooky shadows on the sets. The chairs and tables of a 19th-century well-to-do home felt like a haunted house, waiting for Len, Lorraine, and myself to come give it life.

I found Marty upstairs in the offices with a pile of paperwork in front of him, as usual

"Hello, sweetheart," he said. Out of professional courtesy, he only called me sweetheart when we were alone. I didn't mind the fatherly endearment. Martin had been a better dad to me than my own.

And to Isaac.

"Hey, Marty. What's the news?"

"Nothing good, I'm afraid," he said. "The city council wants to move forward with the proposal to consolidate the entire block, including the theater. It'll attract investors for restoration."

"You don't think you'd get lucky with some benevolent investor who'd let you run the HCT like you want to?"

"I should be so lucky," he said. "I'm more concerned we'll get a callous corporation that doesn't care or understand what I'm trying to do here. It sucks, as you young people like to say. Especially since we just got back on track, thanks to Isaac." He glanced at me. "I'm sorry, does it bother you if I mention him?"

"You ask me every time and the answer is always the same," I said. "No."

Hearing his name hurt like hell, like pressing a bruise that would never heal. At the same time, I loved hearing how Isaac was taking care of the HCT from afar.

As predicted, after *Hamlet,* Isaac was snatched up by the casting agent and immediately went to California. He got a small role in a big movie, and his pay got HCT caught up on its back taxes and current with its rent.

I picked up a few bills to file, kept my gaze down and my words casual as I asked, "How is he? Still nothing?"

"Not a word," Marty said. "I guess we could open an entertainment magazine. That's the only way I get the news about him."

"His last movie did well. Rave reviews."

"Did you see it?"

Long Way Down had been playing at the Guild Movie House for weeks, but I could never muster the courage to buy a ticket.

"No," I said. "I'm not ready. Did you?"

He smiled sadly. "Six times." He reached over and patted my hand. "He went quiet on all of us, sweetheart. You, me, Brenda and Benny. I can't even thank him for the money. An LLC wires it every month and all the correspondence I've tried to send…" He shrugged. "Nothing."

"I'm sorry," I said. "I knew he'd be…upset with me, but I never expected him to cut you off too."

"It's not your fault, honey," Marty said. "It's what he does. How he copes with loss. He locks himself in his own mind and only lets the emotions out on the stage. Or the movie set, these days."

He watched the pain flit over my face. "I know it hurts. You did what you thought you had to do to protect Isaac. And now he has a brilliant career ahead of him, and he's making plenty of money doing what he set out to do. And you, my dear, have a brilliant career head of *you*. Your Nora is sheer brilliance."

"No."

"Don't take my word for it." He tossed today's copy of *Harmony Tribune* on my lap. "Vera Redding says you're a tour de force, and that woman hates everything."

I smiled and put the newspaper aside. "It's a good play for me. It's just what I needed."

The play, and the theater, and Marty Ford, were exactly what I needed; more steps in my healing process. The fear of potentially losing him or the HCT to the city council's renovation plans shook me to the bone.

"We have to fix this city council situation, Marty." I cleared my throat. "Can Isaac help?"

"The council says the project can cost millions. I don't know that he has that." He smiled sadly and held up his hands. "And even if I wanted to, I have no way of asking him."

As I biked home after work, my throat ached with tears. The pain of missing Isaac was slugging me in the chest with every heartbeat. I didn't have an appointment with Bonnie that afternoon, but I wished I did.

Back home, Greta and I sat on my little porch. We shared a pitcher of homemade lemonade and ate peas straight out of the pod. The sun was setting in Harmony, the lightning bugs flaring as they flitted among the juniper bushes that separated Greta's and my house. The cicadas were deafening—waves of buzzing that came and went like a tide. Children played in their yards. Neighborhood cats slunk here and there or dozed in the last of the sun's rays. Greta and I didn't talk much. We didn't need to. The evening was quiet. Warm. Peaceful. It was everything I needed.

Almost.

When the sun had set, Greta packed up her baskets and said goodnight. Inside my place, my phone lay on the kitchen counter, a notification flashing on the display: I had a missed call and a voicemail from Dad. After the stint in Texas, Ross Wilkinson had moved them back to Manhattan. They'd come full circle and arrived back where they started, this time without a daughter.

"Hello, Willow." Dad's voice always sounded strained on voicemails. As if he were forcing it over a boulder of guilt. "Mom and I wanted to see how you're doing. She told me about your work with the theater, trying to restore it and…such. A worthwhile endeavor." He coughed. "We're looking forward to flying in for the last performance of your show. And I hope this isn't too presumptuous, but we planned a little party afterward for you, your cast mates and director at the Renaissance Hotel in Braxton." A pause. "I hope you consider attending. Please let me know. All right, then. Goodbye."

I set the phone down. I didn't want a party. I wasn't even certain I wanted my parents at the show. We were slowly rebuilding a tentative relationship though I suspected deep down, we'd never be the same. Bonnie told me that forgiveness is for the giver's peace, not the receiver's, but I wasn't there yet.

And hearing Dad's voice piled more painful memories on top of the mess in my heart, and made Isaac's silence all the more deafening.

I sat on my small blue couch, opened my laptop and Googled his name. I scrolled past the articles about *Long Way Down*. Article after article raved about the breakout performance of Isaac Pearce—"an electrifying actor of raw intensity"—the *Los Angeles Times* raved. The text was broken up by photo stills. He was twenty-two now, and even more ruggedly handsome than before.

I checked articles on tabloid sites, because I had to know.

I found more shots of Isaac, caught at bars and clubs and events in Los Angeles. Always alone, a cigarette tucked in the corner of his mouth, a hard glint in his eyes. Comparisons to a dark-haired James Dean abounded, right down to the speculation that Isaac was gay. His lack of female companionship hadn't gone unnoticed by Hollywood.

Or me.

It was insanity to think he abstained from women for me. I'd broken his heart. More likely, he was being careful with his privacy. Guarding it against outside threats.

Who could blame him?

Still, hope burned in me, small and fragile. With shaking hands, I picked up my phone again and scrolled through my contacts for Isaac's phone number. It rang once before an electronic voice message played: *We're sorry, this phone is no longer in service.*

Though it was silly and hopeless, my fingers typed a text.

A2, S2

"Never doubt I love," I whispered, like a prayer.

I hit send.

The little red exclamation point in a bubble popped up immediately.

This message could not be sent.

The message *was* sent. It just couldn't be received. Not for three years now.

Still, hope burned.

I kept calling for him, sending my plea into the void.

No answer.

Chapter Thirty-Seven

Isaac

"Done deal, my friend," Tyler Duncan said. As he hung up the phone in his office on Wilshire Boulevard, my manager looked extremely pleased with himself.

"You are now seven-point-one million dollars richer." He ran a hand through his gold hair, his gold Rolex glinting in the bright gold Los Angeles sun pouring through the windows. Tyler reminded me of Matthew McConaughey—shiny, energetic, and always smiling. My polar opposite. Just being in his presence made me tired.

Then his words sank in.

"Seven million…?"

He grinned. "Less our fifteen percent, please and thank you."

"Jesus."

"Not bad, not bad, not bad," Tyler said. "Especially for only your second big studio movie." He pressed his palms together and bowed his head. "And let's not forget you have some points coming in off the backend later. That should net you a nice little surprise in your bank account when you least expect it."

"Seven-point-one million," I said again. "I have seven million dollars in my account? Right now?"

Tyler laced his fingers behind his head and kicked up his Ferragamos on his desk. "Yes, indeed, my man."

I nodded, thinking it was surreal. I'd made money on my first film, but not like this. When I came to Hollywood with the casting agent who saw *Hamlet,* he helped me land a small part in a high-profile movie, which netted me $1.5 million. A staggering amount to someone who'd never seen a bank statement with more than four figures in it.

But seven *million?*

It was even more astonishing, considering how much I fucking hated acting on camera.

I hated the constant retakes. The stops and starts. Telling the story out of order to an audience of camera crew and boom mic operators. During that first movie, I was sure my loathing of the process was evident on my face and captured in every frame. But the audiences loved me. Hollywood embraced me.

"And the women *really* like you," Tyler said when we first met. "You're a cross between James Dean and Henry Cavill. Hollywood handsome but with a bad boy, rough-around-the-edges danger. Pure catnip, my friend."

I didn't give a shit about the marketing plan, so long as I could make the money I needed to quit this fucking business.

Now I had.

I almost felt sorry for Tyler. He thought he had the Next Big Thing sitting across from him, but I was done. $7.1 million was more than enough to pay off my father's debts to Wexx. I personally wasn't on the hook for them but my father had died with those debts dragging him down, like Marley's ghostly chains. I was determined to cut him free. It wouldn't matter to Wexx. A drop in a bucket they forgot they were holding. But it fucking mattered to me.

"Holy shit," I breathed. I'd already paid off Benny's mom's mortgage. Now I could put Benny through college. I could make sure Marty had everything he could ever want for the HCT. And Willow…

Seven million was a number I'd dreamed of when I'd told her I'd come back to Harmony.

My chest hurt. Tyler saw me rubbing the spot.

"What's that, compadre? A little indigestion? Hard to swallow that you're a bona fide millionaire? Get used to it." He tapped his finger on a copy of *Variety* folded up on his mahogany and glass desk. "Have you read these reviews? My phone is ringing off the hook for you. Which brings me to the real reason for this little tête-à-tête today." He leaned over his desk. "Are you ready for this? Quentin Tarantino wants a meeting. Quentin-fucking-Tarantino."

I got to my feet. "Yeah, thanks, Tyler," I said absently. "I gotta go."

"Wait, what?"

"I'll be in touch."

Tyler stared. "Be in touch? What's that mean?" He broke into a Hollywood laugh—the kiss-ass kind that erupted when I hadn't said anything funny. I hated that too.

"Oh, I get it," he said. "You going out to celebrate? I'm down. Let's get us some female companionship and get plowed—"

"Some other time."

He called after me but I hardly heard him. I had to get the hell out of that office and think. I left the posh suites and hit the pavement under a hard, Los Angeles heat. Nothing like Indiana's thick humidity that promised green and growing things. This desert heat felt like it was trying to snuff the life out of you.

I jumped into my leased Land Rover. Tyler convinced me it was L.A.'s version of a truck. My Dodge was back in Harmony, put out to pasture at the scrapyard.

The Rover was a sweet ride, and my four-bedroom place in West Hollywood was a fucking palace compared to a junkyard trailer. But both felt like waste. I didn't need this much. I missed my truck. I missed Marty's old house and cemeteries with crooked tombstones and hedge mazes...

I missed Willow.

It hit me hard today. Harder than it had in the three years I'd been gone. Typically it slugged me from the outside like a hammer. Now it rose out of me from inside, from the place where I buried all the loss and pain in my life. Now that I had the means to return to Harmony, like I'd promised, it all came back on that current of possibility. The dream and hope was over and the reality was there for the taking if I wanted it.

I raced the SUV in and out of light traffic—by L.A. standards—to my huge place. Four bare walls and hardwood floors. A $12,000-per month storage unit with panoramic views of a city that didn't feel like mine. Los Angeles was good to me and I was grateful, but it wasn't home.

I went to my office, which was nothing more than the room where I kept my laptop. I had more rooms than I had stuff to put in them. I didn't even *want* a laptop but Tyler said I needed email access and a better cell phone as well. My old phone—the one Willow had the number to—I'd dumped in a trashcan in Dallas during a layover on my flight out of Harmony.

No email. No phone. No way for her to contact me, even if she wanted, and I hadn't lifted one goddamn finger to find her. I'd cut her out of my life entirely.

I held my head in my hands.

"What the fuck are you doing?" My voice echoed off the walls. "What the fuck have you *been* doing?"

It made sense back then. The pain was so raw and real. Losing Willow, watching her slip through my fingers on the opening night of *Hamlet* was like being shot in the heart all over again. After a life of so much misery, I finally had something good and perfect, and it disintegrated; I hadn't been able to do a goddamn thing to stop it. So I'd rolled with it the only way I knew how.

I got the fuck out and didn't look back.

The first few months were agony, but each day that passed was another brick in the wall between me and my old life and everyone in it—Marty, Brenda, Benny, Willow—until the wall was miles' high and years' thick. The only time I'd been back to Harmony was for my father's funeral. I'd stayed long enough to see him laid to rest beside my mother, and then I was gone again, back behind the wall.

Now it was crumbling to sand.

It's not too late, Marty always said. But what if it was? What if something terrible had happened to her?

I opened up my laptop and typed Willow Holloway into the Google search bar.

There she was. First hit, top of the page. My girl.

Goddamn tears stung my eyes. A review in the *Harmony Tribune* for *A Doll's House* playing—of course—at the HCT.

Willow Holloway (20), is miraculous as Nora. A delicate, almost frail young woman who stoically manages the patriarchal conventions of Ibsen's 1870 Denmark.

"Denmark," I murmured gruffly, even as hope and pride and love swelled my chest. "We haven't left Denmark, have we, baby?"

It is the final act of the play in which Miss Holloway's expressive face reveals the emergence of Nora Torvald. Not a daughter, wife, or young mother, but as a woman—a human being. The realization is stunning to watch, proving that Miss Holloway's debut performance in Hamlet *three years ago was no fluke.*

At the bottom of the article was a picture of Willow in a ruffled, high-collared dress that looked as if it were strangling her. Her smile for Len Hostetler, playing her husband Helmer, was sweet and passive, but fire burned in her eyes. She was still fighting.

I swallowed hard and shut the laptop.

"There you go, Pearce. Now you know where she is," I said. "She came home."

I left the office and flopped down on my empty, king-sized bed. A state-of-the-art luxury item that had never had a woman in it. When I first arrived in Los Angeles, I tried to date. To forget Willow and lose myself in someone else. But I'd sit across from a beautiful candidate and feel nothing. No desire. No interest. Not even base lust.

I miss her too much. I love her too much.

The closing night performance of *A Doll's House* was Saturday, four days away. I tried to harden my heart against the idea of jumping on the next plane out. Tried to ignore the possibility of standing in the same room with Willow. Self-preservation and yet I didn't know what was worth preserving. My life here was empty. But if I went back to Harmony, was there anything left between us to salvage?

She ended it, I reminded myself. *She cut you out and wouldn't tell you why. No recourse. No second chance. No defying her father's bullshit. She chose* him.

I'd mentally replayed our final scene on *Hamlet's* opening night a thousand times. No matter the hurt and anger it dredged up, the heart-breaking, agonized expression on Willow's face never changed. That night I'd been too blinded by my own pain to see hers. But she'd been dying on the inside too. Because she loved me.

The love was there first.

"Fuck..." I rubbed my hands down my face, then sat up and hurried back to the office.

Now that I knew where she was, the need to see her again was a ravenous hunger, and the simple truth was I'd starve to death without her.

She might hate me, or worse—ignore me, but…

If nothing else, I'll see her perform. Just that. Start there and see what happens.

I dialed up Tyler. He answered on the second ring.

"What's up, bro? Change your mind about hanging out?"

"No, man. Listen, I'm going out of town for a few days."

"Okay," Tyler said slowly, warily. "When are you coming back?"

I closed my eyes and conjured Willow in the hedge maze, with the sun setting behind her hair and her eyes full of love for me.

"Best case scenario?" I said. "Never."

Chapter Thirty-Eight

Willow

Saturday seemed to rush up to me. Marty added a performance of *A Doll's House* on Thursday night at the last minute to give myself, Len, and Lorraine—who played my best friend, Christine in the play—an extra night. It sold out within hours of the announcement. Friday night was packed too, and as the standing ovation washed over us, I tried to savor it and hold on. Only one performance left.

At noon, I went to The Scoop to meet Angie. My heart pounded in my chest and happiness bubbled out of me in a small burst of laughter as I locked my bike outside the restaurant. We'd been talking and texting, but between her packed schedule at Stanford and my father's constant relocations, we hadn't been face-to-face in three years.

I opened the diner door, and saw her sitting at a booth for two facing the door. I noticed she wore glasses now, and her curled hair was a little bit shorter, her skin a little paler from long hours of study.

Then I burst into tears.

She was a blur as she scrambled out of the booth. She threw her arms around me and I held her tight, crying against her shoulder as years of missing her overwhelmed me, so that I could hardly stand.

I pulled back long enough to wipe my eyes and get a good look at her. Her T-shirt read, *I will seduce you with my awkwardness.* I laughed, then collapsed in tears all over again.

We stood smack in the middle of the restaurant, holding onto each other until we heard a little girl in another booth ask, "Mommy, what's wrong with those two ladies?"

"Did you hear that, Holloway?" Angie said, finally pulling away and wiping her eyes. "The first and last time someone will ever call me a lady."

I laughed again but it threatened to turn into more tears. We quickly slid into the booth, grabbing for napkins, laughing and clutching hands across the table, then needing more napkins.

I shook my head staring at her. "Holy shit, Angie, I missed you so much."

"I missed you too, girl. It's so good to see you. To really see you. You look great."

"Thanks," I said. "It's been a long road just to get to presentable."

"How are you really? How are things with your parents?" she asked, bracing for the answer.

"Weird," I said. "My dad's in ass-kissing mode. I think once we'd been in Canada for a few months, his eyes opened and he saw what a mess I was. He finally grasped the damage that he'd done. He expected my pain would wear off. It never did. I never outgrew my feelings for Isaac." I shrugged, glanced down at my hands. "I'm twenty years old and I'm still in love with him."

"Oh, honey." Angie reached across the table and took my hand.

"Not that it matters, I suppose."

Her dark eyes flared with anger. "Isaac had to know you were being forced to break up with him, right?"

"I think so. I never told him what my father actually threatened. It was too horrible—so obscenely *wrong*... I was afraid it would make Isaac stay in Harmony. Stay and fight for us and end up losing everything. His future. I couldn't let that happen and have him resent me later." I sighed. "I'm glad he went, I just…didn't expect him not to reach out at some point. I guess it was too hard for him. He'd already lost so much."

"What about what you lost?" Angie burst out. She saw me through the dark months after my father moved us out of Harmony, and I knew she'd been biting her tongue about Isaac the entire time. "So that's it?" she asked, struggling for calm. "You forgive him? Just like that?"

"It's not that simple," I said. "It's not yes or no, it's…all tangled up. Yes, I'm hurt and angry with him. But we were both forced to do things we didn't want to do. Now we're coping. He's coping the only way he knows how and so am I. Finally. I made it back here. I'm away from my parents and I can start over."

Angie shook her head. "Three years, Willow."

"I know," I said. "I'm not denying it hurts. It does. I'm getting stronger every day, but pretending like I don't love him or don't miss him isn't going to get me anywhere."

"Sounds like someone's been talking to my mother."

I laughed a little and looked around. "Where is Bonnie? I thought she was going to join us?"

"She wanted to give us some alone time. But she'll be at your show tonight. Wouldn't miss it. I hear you're slaying some Ibsen."

"I don't know about that, but I'm enjoying it. It's helped too. But Christ, enough with my shit already. How's Stanford? How's Nash?"

We ordered burgers and shakes and ate while Angie filled me in on the details. Nash was at school in Pennsylvania. He and Angie were somehow making a long-distance relationship work while she was double majoring in robotics and pre-med at Stanford.

"I'll basically be in college until I'm eighty," she said. "I'll have one year to actually practice medicine until I croak."

"But it'll be a *solid* year."

"Oh, for sure. Like…golden."

As we talked and laughed the hours away, I felt another piece of myself, once broken and scattered across North America, were put back into place.

Out on the sidewalk, we hugged again.

"Bye, love," she said. "See you tonight, after you knock'em dead."

She started to go, but I grabbed her hand, blinking back yet more tears.

"Before I met Isaac, before I auditioned for *Hamlet*, before I had anything else that was good here, I had you. You were the first person to break through the walls I'd built up around myself from all that shit with Xavier, and I just want to thank you for that."

"Dammit, Holloway," Angie said, swiping her fingertips under her eyes.

"You're a life saver, McKenzie, okay?" I said. "You're a fucking life saver."

Angie pulled me close again. "Do me a favor?" she asked, sniffling.

"Anything."

"Tell Stanford that? Because it would save me a shit-ton in med-school tuition."

I met my parents in the lobby of the HCT at quarter after six. It felt uncomfortable to have them over to my little cottage. Now that I was no longer depending on them for anything, their iron-clad grip on me was slippery at best. As was my grip on forgiveness.

They greeted me in the theater lobby with too-wide smiles and loud talk.

"I'm so pleased that you're letting us throw the cast party after the performance," my father said.

"It's a thoughtful gesture," I said.

"Yes, it'll be quite nice, I think," my mother said. "The hotel—the Renaissance—is very nice. Doesn't that sound nice?"

Funny how everything in Harmony was *nice* now, as opposed to when everything Midwest was beneath her. All at once, I felt incredibly sorry for them both.

"It'll be great," I said. "Thanks for being here. I have to go get ready now. I hope you enjoy the show."

God, I sounded like a pre-show recording.

"Willow," my father said. He looked about to take my hand. "I just wanted you to know I'm proud of you," he said, stuffing his fist in his pocket. "Your reviews have been quite complimentary. And the work you and Mr. Ford are doing to keep the theater as a living piece of history in this town is quite commendable."

He glanced down and then forced his eyes to meet mine. "I feel it's important you know I recognize your accomplishments. And to that end, we'll have something for you at the party. A little bit of a surprise."

My mother's face wore a strange look, and she nudged my father with a nervous laugh. "Let's not ruin it now or make her nervous."

"Yes, quite," my father said. "After the show. Break a leg."

They hustled into the theater before I could tell them I wanted no surprises. The party was too much already. The only reason I'd agreed to it was because my cast mates deserved a better sendoff than burgers and fries from The Scoop.

I went backstage to prepare for the show—makeup, hair, and costume. The cast assembled onstage for warm-ups, led by Martin, who was playing Krogstad. On the other side of the closed curtain, we could hear the crowd beginning to file in.

"Standing room only," Marty said to me. "Break a leg tonight."

"I'll do my best."

He started to walk away, then stopped and looked at me closer. "Everything okay?"

"Sure, fine," I said forcing a smile.

"Closing night jitters?"

"This party my parents insists on having is kind of throwing me, I guess. Or... I don't know what. The energy feels strange tonight. You know how the air feels right before lightning strikes? Kind of tight and humming?" I gave my head a shake. "I'll get over it. It's been a wonderful experience, Marty. Thank you so much. I won't let you down."

"Thank you for your incredible Nora, my dear," he said. "And for seeking me out when you came back. For being such an amazing part of this theater."

"Marty," I said warily. "That sounded ominous. Did you get more news from the city council? Bad news?"

He chuckled. "As if I'd tell you something like that twenty minutes to curtain. No, I merely—"

Frank, the stage manager ran up to Marty looking pale. He whispered something in his ear, his eyes on me.

Martin's eyes widened and then darted to me as well.

"What?" I said. "What is it?'

Marty's face smoothed out and he said to Frank in a calm tone, "I'll be there in a minute. Thanks, Frank." He turned to me and patted my shoulder. "A theater manager's job is never done, even on opening night. I'll be right back."

"Marty," I said, grabbing his hand. "Tell me."

"It's nothing you need to worry about. I promise."

I would've believed him. He was a fantastic actor. But Frank was not, and Frank looked as if he'd seen a ghost.

Chapter Thirty-Nine

Isaac

Looking wild and anxious, Frank let me into Marty's office, then ran out to tell him I was here. I settled in to wait, feeling like a student sent to the principal's office: about to get my ass handed to me. These consequences would be far worse than detention. Marty was probably pissed mad as all hell. Who was I kidding—he was *hurt.*

I leaned against the desk in my expensive jeans and black jacket and tried to act like it wasn't a big deal. Like I had some kind of upper hand. Then Marty burst in, red faced and breathing fire. Anger crackled around him; I'd never seen him so pissed off in my life. And though I'd expected it, seeing so much outrage in Martin Ford was unsettling.

"Three years," he said without preamble, slamming the door behind him. "Three years without a word. Not one. You showing up for your father's funeral doesn't count. You said nothing to me then. You've said nothing to me since."

"Marty," I said. "I'm sorry—"

He took a step closer, his finger stabbing the air at me. "And don't get me started on Brenda or Benny or *Willow.*"

I gritted my teeth. "I know, I've been—"

"And now you just show up in my office *fifteen minutes* before I go onstage? What the hell, Isaac? Want me to hold the curtain so we can get a cup of fucking coffee?"

He stared at me, his jaw clenching. For a moment, I thought he'd have me hauled out of the building. Hell, maybe call the police. Or simply plant a foot in my ass and kick me to the street. As he took two steps toward me, I sort of wished he would.

Do it, I thought. *I don't deserve you, Marty.*

Instead, he grabbed my shoulders and engulfed me in a hug. My eyes fell shut with relief and gratitude.

"I thought I was too late. I thought you'd hate me," I said gruffly.

"I do hate you."

"I don't blame you."

Marty pulled back and held me at arm's length. "Are you here for real? To stay and talk? And be here?"

I nodded.

"Okay then, what I told you still holds. There's no such thing as too late. If you're really here then I stand by that. But Jesus, Isaac. What do I tell Willow?"

"I don't want her to know I'm here. Not until after the performance."

"She's the reason we're sold out," Marty said, crossing his arms and smiling. "I don't know where you're going to sit."

"I'll stand in the back. As long as I can see her, I'll be happy"

Marty's smile fell. "Why did you come back?"

"For her," I said. "For you and Brenda and Benny, but for her. To sort out what happened and—What?"

Marty was shaking his head. "No, no, no. I've grown very protective of her. *Very.*"

"I don't want to hurt her, Marty," I said. "It's the last thing I want to do, but she... Fuck."

"She hurt you too," Marty finished. "You're pissed off at her, but you don't have the whole story. Not by a long shot. Did she tell you what her father threatened?"

"No, she refused to tell me."

"You can't guess?" he asked, his tone heavy.

"I don't know. Yes, I can. He'd have me arrested for being at his house. He'd sue my dad into oblivion. He would've pulled her out of the show and we would've lost *Hamlet* but so what? I was willing to lose everything if it meant keeping her. She didn't believe me."

"It wasn't just *Hamlet* you'd lose," Marty said. "Her father threatened to have you arrested for statutory rape."

The word hung in the air, ugly and vile. The blood drained from my face and I swallowed. "Okay," I said slowly. "I should've expected that too. But even so—"

"Not even so. He vowed to use his position and power to destroy your reputation permanently. To label you a sex predator so no one in Hollywood would ever dream of hiring you. It wasn't only *Hamlet* she was trying to protect. It was everything. You, the money your father owed, your future."

"I never...I didn't realize he hated me that much. Or her."

"From what she told me, the night he caught you leaving his house was a nightmare. Beyond anything you can imagine. And I don't say this to make you feel worse..."

"Fucking Christ, Marty. Too late." I sagged against the desk.

"But I'm going to be honest with you. If you came back here with the idea of rehashing what happened three years ago with her, I'm going to kick your ass into next week. The girl has suffered enough. You didn't know. She never told you and you dealt with losing her the best you could. I get that. But I demand that you be careful with that girl's heart."

I clenched my jaw against the tears forming in my eyes. "I shut down," I said. "It's what I do. I just..."

"I know, son. You haven't had it easy either."

"I'm sorry," I said

"I know that too," Marty said, bringing me back into his embrace. "And so is she."

"I don't know what comes next," I said, pulling away and wiping my eyes against the crook of my arm. "You're the director, Marty. Direct."

"Her parents are throwing a party for us at the Renaissance in Braxton. Watch the play, and then come with."

"Her parents?" I asked. I shook my head. "No. I need to see her alone."

"It would be better, methinks, if you saw her in public place. She can decide for herself if she wants to talk alone, or remain with her friends. Her support. Fair?"

I hesitated and Martin gripped my shoulders.

"Don't waste one more second," Marty said. "Every second that goes by is another mile between you. The distance is long enough already."

"Does she want to see me?" I asked, feeling as raw and exposed as I ever had in my life. The kind of naked emotion I'd turned into silence, to bury and protect myself.

"I don't know," Marty said. "But if I had to guess…" He held up his hands, his smile kind and full of hope. "I'd say it's never too late."

Marty had a cancellation from a ticket-holder in the front row. Me sitting there was out of the question, so Marty played a little musical chairs and got me a seat in the last row where Willow couldn't see me.

The houselights dimmed. The murmured talk of five hundred people quieted. The lights came up onstage and I laid eyes on Willow for the first time in three years.

I sucked in a breath. She was so beautiful. Almost twenty-one years old now, she carried herself with the grace and dignity of someone much older. Someone who'd been through hell and back and was still standing.

Over the next two hours, she took her character from a naïve, hopeful young wife, to a woman ready to stand on her own in a society where being married and having children was the ultimate goal.

She was brilliant. Electrifying and subtle at the same time. But it was in the final scene that she mesmerized. She sat in a chair, her hands folded in her lap. Perfectly still and straight. The eye of the storm that was her husband. Len Hostetler as Helmer, circling around her in confusion and then panic.

"*Playtime shall be over, and lesson-time shall begin,*" Len said.
"*Whose lessons? Mine, or the children's?*"

They argued. Or rather, Len argued. Willow conveyed her lines with a quiet certainty. And dignity.

"*I must stand quite alone,*" Willow said, her face to the audience. She could've been talking to me. Or to her father. Or Justin Baker or Xavier. To all the men in her life who tried to make her into something she wasn't.

"I am to understand myself and everything about me. It is for that reason that I cannot remain with you any longer."

Len was every man who watched the woman in his life tell him she no longer needed him. The jilted boyfriend. The failed pick-up in a bar. The online rejection after an unsolicited proposition was shot down.

"You are out of your mind! I won't allow it! I forbid you!"

"It is no use forbidding me anything," Willow said calmly *"I will take with me what belongs to myself. I will take nothing from you, either now or later."*

"This is how you would neglect your most sacred duties to your husband and your children?"

"I have other duties just as sacred."

"That you have not! What duties could those be?"

"Duties to myself."

I sank in my chair, my hand pressed to my lips. The pain of losing her, once so sharp, mellowed and transformed as I watched her. As I *listened* to her.

It was so easy to blame her for what happened. For not standing up for us when I was willing to risk everything. But the truth was she'd stood up for me, and I had let her fall. She'd been trying to protect me and I couldn't convince her I didn't need protection. That I would've gladly suffered the slings and arrows her father threw at me.

What I hadn't taken into account was that she could not.

I'd only added my weight to the tremendous pressure she carried. The fact she hadn't been crushed was a testament to her bravery and strength. Sitting there, watching her perform, I felt a fierce pride I didn't deserve. I had nothing to do with her success or talent or courage. She owned every bit of it herself.

The only thing left for me to do was throw myself at her feet and beg forgiveness.

Chapter Forty

Willow

The applause during curtain call was tremendous. It bowled me over and I clutched Len and Lorraine's hands tight as we bowed. The strange tension I'd felt before the show pulled at the air, crackling and ominous. As I stepped out of Nora and back into Willow, I scanned the audience, looked over and around and through the sea of clapping faces.

Who are you looking for?

A pull on my hands made me find a smile as the cast took another bow.

Afterward, I changed into a black satin dress for the cast party in Braxton. Martin was jumpy as hell as we all grabbed our things to head out.

"You go on ahead," he said. "I have to wait for Brenda."

"Marty, what's going on? Did my parents tell you about the surprise?"

"What surprise?"

"I don't know. Something they wanted to give us at the party. Maybe it has to do with the theater plans?"

Marty shrugged. "Haven't heard a word." He kissed my forehead. "Go. I'll be along shortly."

In the lobby, Angie, Bonnie, Yolanda and Benny stood together. My parents milled nearby, on the fringe of the group. After some congratulatory hugs and awkward chitchat and confusion, it was decided I'd drive up to Braxton with Angie and Bonnie. Yolanda and Ben were going to head home.

On the drive to Braxton, Bonnie put on her Therapist Face.

"Are you sure you want to go through with this? It's a nice gesture, but you're under no obligation to attend."

"I know," I said from the backseat. "But I feel like if they're going to be in my life, they're going to be in my life. Otherwise, I should just cut them out, right? And that doesn't feel right either. It might take a while, but I think trying to have a relationship is better than nothing."

"So long as it's not toxic as all hell," Angie said from the front seat. She looked pretty in a 50's style dress that flared at her waist. Bonnie was elegant in a coral-colored pantsuit.

"I think a party in a public place is a good start," I said. "Less chance of a scene. My mother can't stand a scene."

We arrived at the Renaissance Hotel and were directed to a ballroom that was large by Braxton standards, but small by Regina-Holloway standards.

Still, I was touched at my parents' efforts. They obviously spared no expense with an open bar, a small dance floor and a live pianist who played themes from different Broadway shows. The tables held elegant centerpieces of white roses with sprays of baby's breath. Candles flickered in crystal cups.

"This is the nicest cast party I've ever been to," Len Hostetler said, doing a drive-by hello on the way to the bar. He kissed my cheek. "Tell your folks I said grazie."

Angie, Bonnie, and I took a table in the rapidly filling room. I frowned at all the faces I didn't recognize—far more people than HCT cast and crew. Most were older, in fact, and dressed to the nines as if this were some kind of awards gala.

Or a Wexx convention, I thought with a tiny stirring of something unpleasant in my gut.

Angie did her best Seinfeld impression. "Who are...these people?"

"Good question."

My parents approached us. Twin expressions of apprehension. My mother was elegant, if a little overdressed in a silver sparkly floor-length gown. Dad wore a dark suit with a ruby red tie that matched my mother's lipstick. Mom's face was pale and her eyes darted around as if she were trying to avoid someone.

"Mom and Dad, this is Angie and Bonnie McKenzie. Angie is pre-med at Stanford University and Bonnie is a therapist." I looked my father in the eye. "My therapist, actually."

Mom winced at that, and my father's lips pressed into a thin line before he managed a smile.

"Regina and Daniel Holloway," Dad said. "Thank you for coming."

Bonnie and Angie nodded and murmured something polite but no one offered any hands to shake.

"Do you like the party, darling?" Mom said, kissing my cheek. "You deserve it. You were incredible tonight."

"Magnificent," Dad said. "I'm very proud of you."

"Thanks," I said. I wanted to give more, feel more for them but I couldn't. This party was exactly how everyone described: a nice gesture. Kind. Generous. But not enough to fill the gaping hole my parents had put in my life.

All at once, I understood the strange tension I'd felt in the theater, both before and after the show. It was Isaac. Or rather, it was the absence of Isaac. He wasn't onstage with me or in the audience watching. He wasn't here to look beautifully handsome in a tuxedo. To dance with me, hold me close and whisper *never doubt* in my ear.

Dad cleared his throat. Everyone was looking at me.

Quickly, I put a smile on my face. "It really is lovely."

"Well, the party is only one part of this evening's festivities." My father glanced around, but apparently didn't see what he was looking for and turned back. "It's early yet. Enjoy yourself, sweetheart."

Angie leaned in to me after he'd left. "What was that all about?"

"I have no idea. He's been hinting at some sort of a surprise." I glanced around. "Where's Marty? I thought he was right behind us."

"I'm going to the ladies' room to powder my nose," Bonnie said. "Angie, will you get me a glass of white wine please?"

Angie gave a little salute. "If they don't card my ass. Willow?"

"Diet Coke with lime? I'll guard our table."

"Please." Angie dumped her purse on the chair beside me and

walked away. A split-second later, my throat constricted when I tried to call her back. To *scream* for her to come back.

My parents were approaching the table again. My father wearing a satisfied smile, my mother looking straight at me, her face perfectly blank as they walked over Ross and Melinda Wilkinson.

Beside them was Xavier.

The temperature in the room dropped a hundred degrees. I broke out in gooseflesh as the blood drained from my entire body, leaving me weak and cold.

He wore a dark suit with a gray tie. His black hair was slicked back and glinted in the muted lighting of the ballroom. His large, dark eyes raked me up and down, a faint smile curling his lips. He was handsome in the way a vampire was handsome. Dangerous and sexy, but no less a monster that would suck the life out of you and leave you in a state of half-dead, half-alive.

Until he comes to finish you off.

I stared without breathing. An icy boulder sitting on my chest.

"Willow, my dear," my father said more confidently, as if we were standing on firmer ground. "You remember the Wilkinsons? Ross, Melinda and their son, Xavier?" He beamed proudly. "Xavier just finished his degree at Amherst and is set to pursue a career in politics."

"Good to see you again, Willow," Xavier said in his smooth, low voice. I only stared, and in the silence, his smile tilted a little, annoyance around the edges.

My mother's gaze darted between us, her mouth slightly ajar.

My legs shook as I rose to my feet, still unable to tear my eyes from Xavier. If I blinked or looked away, he'd pounce and tear me to shreds.

"What are you doing here?" I managed through chattering teeth.

My father cleared his throat. "It's part of the surprise I wanted to share with you tonight. Is Martin Ford here? No? Well, you can share the news with him when he arrives."

"Daniel," my mother said in a strangled tone. "May I have a word?"

"In a moment, dear." He put his hands behind his back, the way he did when giving speeches to stockholders. "Willow, I was telling Mr. Wilkinson about your endeavors with the Harmony Community

Theater. I had my secretary investigate the particulars of the building and its financial standing. I'm pleased to say the Wilkinsons—by way of the Wexx Foundation for Charitable Works—have agreed to invest in the project. We'll ensure the entire block is preserved and maintained, and we'll establish Martin Ford as the creative director for time in perpetuity."

My vision clouded gray. I didn't think the ballroom could be any colder. Xavier looked angry and nervous now. Hands jammed in his pockets and rocking back and forth on his heels.

The Wilkinsons are going to be part owners of the Harmony Community Theater.

I thought I was going to be sick.

"Willow?" my father asked. "Are you all right? I thought this would be joyous news."

"She looks a little pale, Mr. Holloway," Xavier said, stepping forward. "She's probably so happy it's overwhelming. Come dance with me. We need to catch up."

"What a wonderful idea," Mrs. Wilkinson said.

"No," Mom whispered.

Xavier closed his hand around my arm. I nearly screamed. I *told* myself to scream. But all my nerves were dizzy and numb now. The shock of his presence and its shadowy memories closed around me were like a drug in my drink. I couldn't speak. I could hardly move, as Xavier pulled me onto the dance floor, I thought I heard my mom calling after me. Her voice tiny through a roaring blizzard, far away and unreachable.

The piano played "What I Did For Love" from *A Chorus Line* and Xavier drew me toward his body.

"Don't touch me," I whispered, holding myself stiff. "I'll scream…"

"Scream?" His outward face to the crowd pleasant and unruffled, but his eyes confused. "Willow, what's going on? The way you were looking at me is making me think there's been a misunderstanding about the last time we talked."

"A misunderstanding?" I managed. "*Talked?* We…we didn't…*talk.*"

"Is that what you're upset about? That I didn't call you again after the party?"

I sucked in a breath. The disconnect from reality was so staggering I could hardly comprehend it.

He turned me in a slow circle, and my body recoiled. Gagged. My skin crawled. Xavier in the flesh, walking around, wearing an expensive suit, smiling and talking and living. Graduating college and planning a future. No night terrors. No sleeping on the floor instead of a bed, no marking his skin with black ink to show where 'normal life' used to be.

It repelled me down to my bones.

I sucked in a breath and the drugged, hazy shock drained out.

"Take your fucking hands off of me," I seethed.

His hand on mine tightened immediately. The other, at my waist, pulled tighter.

"I think there's a misunderstanding about what happened that night and I think we should talk it out," Xavier said, still smiling brightly for anyone watching. "I'm open to it. If you'd stop being so dramatic."

"You raped me."

He froze, blinked rapidly, then gave his head a small shake. "I beg your pardon?"

"You heard me, you fucking sadistic asshole. After everyone left, you put something in my drink and you took me up to my room. I don't remember every last detail, but here's what I do remember. You were eating peanuts. They were on your breath when you tried to kiss me. To this day the smell of peanut butter makes me gag. I had bruises on my throat where you choked me. Was it one or both hands? Did you need the other hand to subdue me?"

"Willow, this is crazy—"

"I remember you lying on top of me, crushing me. I couldn't move, couldn't breathe, couldn't speak. I thought I was going to die. It was my first time. Did you know that? Did you see the blood in the morning? Did you even stay that long? I doubt it or you would've covered your tracks. The evidence was everywhere. On my bed and my clothes. Lucky for you, I felt so degraded and humiliated and *violated* that I got rid of all of it."

Xavier's eyes darkened like a snake getting ready to strike. "I have no idea what you're talking about. I gave you something to drink because you were nervous as hell. I was trying to get you to relax." He leaned closer. "You drank a lot that night and don't think no one knows it."

"I didn't drink that much."

"Does it matter? You were dancing all up on me, grinding your ass. Everyone saw it. Who's to say you weren't the same in bed? Nervous for your first time and drinking to take the edge off."

My face paled and my throat threatened to close. "You're disgusting."

He laughed. "You don't remember? I have certain a picture that'll surely jog your memory about how much you wanted me…"

I fought for calm, held myself away from his body. "I know I'll be attacked for that photo. People might not believe me because it took so long for me to report you, but I *will* report you. You make me sick. Looking at you right now makes me physically sick."

Xavier's jaw clenched. "I suggest you stop talking to me that way. I suggest you drop this disgusting story of yours."

"Or else what?"

"I will destroy you and your family."

"My family is already destroyed. There's nothing you can do to hurt me again. I've been to the edge of the abyss and back *twice* now because of what you did."

"Boo fucking hoo. I didn't do anything to you. You're having second thoughts. Regretting you fucked me, so now you're cooking up a rape story. I plan on running for office. To be a senator. If you think I'll let you taint my backstory with your pathetic fantasies of revenge, you—"

"Your backstory is that you're a rapist criminal," I spat. "And I'm done being smothered alive under your X anymore. It's over."

I tried to wrench my arm from his but he twisted my wrist against his chest until I thought it would snap.

"Go ahead," Xavier hissed. "See if they believe you. They won't. In the meantime, I'll tell my dad to buy the whole damn theater. And when he does, I'll have it razed to the ground until it's nothing but a pile of rubble."

My heart stopped for a moment and jumpstarted again. "What? No…"

Xavier's smile was wide even as a sigh of relief hissed out his nose. "You didn't think of that, did you? I'll bulldoze your precious theater to dust. And if your little Harmony Historical Society tries to stop me, I'll still buy it. I'll buy the whole damn block and let it rot. Shut down the theater forever."

"You can't do that," I said. "It's part of this town's history…"

"Fuck your history. This is what happens when you threaten me. Do we have an understanding?" He grabbed my chin. "Save your theater, Willow. Save it and keep your little story to yourself, because no one will believe you anyway."

He let go of my chin and his fingers turned soft, caressing.

"And you know it."

I couldn't move, couldn't speak. The icy weight was back and this time it was poised to crush more than me.

"Good girl." Xavier's cheerfulness came back with a bright smile. "Let's go back and make nice in front of our parents."

He led me on shaking legs off the dance floor.

"You look beautiful tonight, by the way." He leaned into me, his lips brushing my cheek. "Can I get you a drink?"

Chapter Forty-One

Isaac

Martin, Brenda and I drove up to the Braxton Renaissance Hotel, and Marty pulled his old Lexus into a free spot at the back of the lot. We were only fifteen minutes behind everyone else, but it looked as if half of Harmony was already there.

Marty killed the engine but I didn't move to get out.

"Maybe this is a bad idea," I said. "She's having a party. She's having a good time. Then I show up and…"

"And make it better," Marty finished.

"How do you know?" I asked. "She has every right to hate me."

"But she doesn't."

"She misses you," Brenda said, turning from the front seat to smile at me.

I gnawed my lip. This was worse than any audition. This *was* an audition. The greatest most important audition of my life, and if I blew it…

"So what do I do?"

"You go in," Marty said quietly.

"Just walk in, in front of her parents and God and everybody?"

"Yes. And ask her to dance."

I swallowed a sudden lump of pain in my throat. Until now, the idea of touching Willow again, holding her, kissing her, or even just looking at her up close was like a dream that always faded upon waking. I'd been able to shut off some part of me in order to keep going without her. But now that she was here…

"I can't," I said. "It's been too long. I don't want her to feel pressured."

"Maybe it's as simple as watching her from across a crowded room," Brenda said. "Go inside, let her see you, and take it from there."

"Yeah, okay." I nodded. "That sounds good."

I threw the car door open. The time for talk was over. It was time to get my ass in there and find my girl.

My nerves disappeared the second I reached the ballroom and found Willow. She sat in a group—her parents, another older couple, Angie McKenzie with a woman who must've been her mother. Willow sat while they all stood around her chatting, looking pale and stiff, hardly moving at all.

Something's wrong.

The urge to run to her was strong but my heart was pounding in my chest, my nerves jumpy. I needed to calm the fuck down, take a breath, and get this right.

"She's surrounded," I told Marty. "I'm going to the restroom. Splash some cold water on my face."

Or dunk my head in the goddamn sink.

I took a long, circuitous route to the men's room at one end of the ballroom. The restroom was grey and chrome, and smelled like Old Spice. A dark-haired guy in a suit was at a urinal taking a piss, and whistling.

I went to one of the basins at the sink and ran cold water. The guy turned around, zipping up, and moved to the sink to wash his hands. He had a narrow, weasel-like face, and dark eyes. He glanced at me once, then twice.

"Hey," he said, wagging a finger at me. "I know you, right? You were in that movie? *All the Way Down?*"

"*Long Way Down,*" I said, dabbing my face dry.

"Yeah, that's right. Great movie. You kicked ass in that."

"Thanks."

"Isaac…something, right? I'm bad with names."

"Pearce," I said, balling up the paper and wishing this guy would shut up already and let me have a minute to myself.

"Isaac Pearce, right," he said, frowning. "I feel like I know you from somewhere else. Your name is familiar... Wait, you're from around here, aren't you?"

I nodded.

His eyes widened and he smiled with dawning realization. "Oh, shit, I remember! You're the guy my dad told me about a few years ago. The actor. But your family had one of our stations in Harmony, right? The one that exploded?" He shook his head, laughing. "Crazy."

Every muscle in my body tightened and my head creaked on my neck to look at him. "One of your stations?"

"Wexx Oil & Gas? My father is Ross Wilkinson, CEO." he said, and offered his hand. "I'm Xavier."

I stared.

Xavier. X. The rapist. Standing right in front of me. Smiling. *Whistling.* Walking around free as if nothing had happened while Willow suffered for years...

He dropped his hand. "Hey, no hard feelings," he said. "It's not like losing one station is going to break us—"

I flew at him, gripped him by the lapels of his jacket, yanked him to me.

"You..." I seethed between clenched teeth, the blood pounding in my temples. "It was you..."

Xavier's eyes were wide with fear, inches from mine. "What the fuck...?"

I fought for calm, remembering what Willow had said. That hurting him wouldn't help her, though every sinew in my body screamed to fight, to make him hurt, to make him pay for what he did...

I released him with a rough shove. He fell back against the sink and I turned a small circle, raking my hands through my hair, breathing hard.

"What the fuck is your problem, man?" Xavier said, jerking his jacket back into place.

"I know you," I said, jabbing my finger at him. "I fucking know you...I know what you did. To her."

"To who? I don't know what you're—"

"To Willow," I snarled. "What you did to Willow Holloway."

Xavier's eyes widened and his glanced darted to the door behind me. "Look, man," he said, holding his dripping hands up. "I don't know what she told you but—"

"Everything. She told me everything."

Xavier's fake, smile vanished, but his voice was tinged with nervousness. "She told you everything? Did she tell you she sent me a picture of her tits? I still have it on my phone. I haven't uploaded it online for the entire fucking world to jerk off to, but I will. I fucking will, so why don't you get the fuck out of my way."

He started to push past me. I calmly put my hand on his chest and shoved him back. I didn't have a plan; my thoughts were in a tangle of raw emotion. But letting him out of this bathroom to stand in the same room as Willow was out of the fucking question.

"You belong in jail."

"Fuck you," he spat, his voice rough at the edges with fear now. "You better watch yourself, man. I'll sue you for every penny you have."

"I'll take my chances."

Xavier scoffed casually and then struck with a sudden right fist to my jaw. I took the hit, my head whipping to the side, and the pain was like a fire under a fuse. Control fled. All I could see was this fucker on her, choking her, his mouth and body on hers...

Willow...

I drove my right fist into his face. My knuckles smacked the hard bone of his cheek, sending him reeling. Pain from my split skin rocketed up to my elbow.

Xavier staggered back, touched his fingers to his cheekbone and examined the blood on his fingertips. "This right here," he said, "is a lawsuit. This is jail time. For you."

"You keep saying that," I said over hard breaths, "And I keep telling you, I don't give a fuck. I could kill you for what you did to her..."

"Aw, come on," Xavier spat. "You know how chicks are. They fucking tease you until you're hard as a rock and then send you on your way. Fuck that bullshit. She wanted it. They all do. You have to play their game. Take a little initiative."

Initiative.

I charged at him, tackled him to the hard linoleum and we became a tangle of fists and jackets on the bathroom floor. His fist hit my right eye. Mine connected with his nose. Dimly I became aware of the door opening. Footsteps around us, shouting above us. I had Xavier on the ground. I pinned him down, my hands around his throat, squeezing.

"How does that feel?" I raged at him. "Can't breathe? Imagine feeling like that *for years*, you fucking son of a bitch."

Rough hands jerked me off him and hauled me back. Xavier scrambled to his feet, one hand to his throat, the other jabbing a finger at me. He appealed, wide-eyed, to the growing crowd in the bathroom.

"He tried to kill me. You saw it! Someone call the police."

One of the spectators already had his phone out to call, another was taking photos.

Xavier whipped his head to me. "You're done. Done in Hollywood. You're going to jail."

His threats meant nothing. I'd had enough of him. I needed Willow. Nothing else mattered.

I shoved past the small crowd in the bathroom. Xavier screamed after me, but I kept going, out into the ballroom, to Willow.

She sat in a chair, still silent and motionless, like a beautiful statue, Angie and her mother flanking her. Everyone looked worried now, uncertain about what to do, asking her questions and getting no answers.

When I was ten yards away, I slowed and did what Brenda had advised. Let her see me. Let her decide.

Willow looked over slowly and our eyes met, our gazes locked. I froze. The weight of three years suddenly felt impossible to carry any longer. So heavy. Everything fell away as she stood up and left the protective circle of Angie and her mom.

I walked toward her and she walked toward me, until we were face-to-face.

Her eyes swept over me, her fingers tentatively reached up to touch one bleeding cut at my lip, another at the corner of my eye.

"Isaac," she whispered.

"Hey, baby."

She looked so beautiful. Pale but composed. I could've cried because her eyes weren't full of anger or hate, but full of love. She still loved me.

"You're here?" she whispered.

I swallowed hard. "I'm here."

Her eyes fell shut for a moment, and her lips parted with a little sigh of relief only I could hear, even as her brows came together. I could feel the questions and the hurt rising in her. She still loved me, but this moment was only the beginning of whatever was left of us.

Xavier tore out of the bathroom door as the police came in from the front. He waved them over, shouting and clutching his throat and gesturing frantically at me. Everyone turned to stare.

"Arrest that guy. He attacked me in the bathroom. He tried to fucking kill me."

Calmly, Willow left me and walked over to Xavier. I itched to grab her hand, pull her back to safety but I let her go. Watched as she moved to stand in front of him. She tilted her chin, raised her hand, and slapped him across the face. Hard.

The sound was like a gunshot, reverberating through the crowd, sending ripples of gasps and murmured exclamations.

Xavier's head whipped at the force of it and a red handprint inflamed his cheek immediately

"You fucking bitch," he seethed, eliciting more gasps. "It's over. Your precious theater? Gone. I—"

"Yes, it's over," Willow said, her voice impossibly calm. "At long last. It's over."

She turned her back on him and walked to me, took my hand, and led me back to her parents and friends. Marty and Brenda were at the table now too, everyone gaping.

"Isaac, these are my parents, Dan and Regina. Mom and Dad, this is Isaac Pearce. Three years ago, he helped save my life. I got drunk and told him a story. Then I told Angie that story, and I told Bonnie that story. Now I'm going to tell you. Isaac never hurt me. Never. You caught him sleeping in my bed with me and threatened to have him arrested. You had the wrong boy. It was Xavier. The summer before my senior year, I threw a party when you two were away. And at that party, Xavier Wilkinson raped me."

I watched the truth spread from her lips. A poisonous vapor she'd had to keep inside for three years, afraid of how it would affect everyone she loved. Her dad's hard expression crumbled to shock and horror. Her mother's pale face went white. Regina squeezed her eyes shut, then gave a soft, agonized cry as she rushed at Willow and held her.

"Oh, baby. Oh my baby. My sweet girl, I'm so sorry…"

She hugged her, stroked her hair, released her, crying, her hand pressed to her mouth, shaking her head over and over again. Angie and Bonnie closed in on either side of Willow as Xavier, who'd been huddled with his parents, crossed over, bringing the police with him.

"That's the one," he said, pointing at me. "Arrest him."

"Did you do this?" one of the officers asked me, gesturing at the finger marks stark on Xavier's throat.

"He did," Xavier said. He turned to another guy who I recognized from the bathroom. "You saw it, right?"

The guy nodded. "Had him pinned to the ground."

The officer took in my bruised and bloody face, my swollen knuckles, and nodded at his partner. They turned me around and tugged my arms behind my back.

Chaotic shouting rose up from all sides.

"What are you *doing*?" Angie cried. "Isaac was defending Willow. He isn't the one—"

Marty held out his hands for calm. "Now, hold on one second, officers…"

Ross Wilkinson's voice rose above them. "Daniel, what in God's name is going on here?"

Dan Holloway didn't answer, but turned slowly to stare at Xavier.

Xavier, who stood with Willow's handprint like a sunburn over half his face. A mark on his skin, in the shape of her hand, stark and red for all to see.

In a flash of movement Dan broke out of his stasis and tackled Xavier to the ground, taking two chairs down with him, and sending a table teetering, its centerpiece toppling over.

One of the officers sprinted into the fray, yanking Willow's father off of Xavier. Ross stepped in to defend his son. Mrs. Wilkinson shrieked for someone to 'save her boy'. Regina cried. Bonnie and Angie stared, a protective barricade in front of Willow. More police arrived, pulling people apart, barking orders to break it up and threatening to haul us all down to the station. It was something out of a movie scene. Except for Willow, who stood dead center in the storm. Her eyes finally reaching me as a cop grabbed my arm to take me out.

"It's okay," she said, pushing through her friends to come to my side. "Everything's going to be okay."

And I believed her.

Once at the station, I was directed to sit at the booking officer's desk. I sat for ten minutes, still cuffed, watching the hum of precinct business, but none of it directed at me. Not until the Wilkinsons arrived, Ross cursing, his wife clinging to her son.

Xavier was pale beneath Willow's red handprint on his cheek. It had faded from blistering red to pink but still visible.

My imagination told me it resembled a W made from her palm and fingers.

No smug smile, blustering threats or pointing fingers. He stood still and quiet as his father shouted at anyone who would listen that this nothing town would pay for this outrage.

Willow and Regina came into the precinct, followed by Angie and her mother. A female officer led them down a hallway of interrogation rooms. Willow walked with her head high. Our eyes met as she passed me, and the barest of smiles curved her lips.

I sank in the chair, the handcuffs tight around my wrists. Xavier had no handcuffs, but as he was marched past me with his family, he met my eyes too. In them I saw only defeat. He looked like a man on his way to the gas chamber.

A bookings officer finally sat down at his desk and shuffled through some paper. "Turned out to be one hell of a party," he said. "You want to tell me what happened?"

"Four years ago," I said with cold calmness, "Xavier Wilkinson raped the woman I love. I felt he needed to know that was un-fucking-acceptable."

The officer nodded and rubbed his eyes. "Yeah, she's telling her story right now." He took his face out of his hands and smirked. "Four years ago?"

"If you caught a murderer four years after he committed the crime, would you want to let them go?" I spat. "Go easy on him? Or would you be fucking glad a criminal was caught so he couldn't do it again?"

The officer gave me a dry look. I knew the system wasn't going to be fixed overnight with a few choice words. Still, I was shocked when twenty minutes later, the officer unlocked my handcuffs and told me I was free to go.

"They're not pressing charges?" I asked

The cop gave me another look. "You want them to? No, your boxing partner refused to make a statement. He's clammed up. You're free to go."

I went to the front of the station, rubbing my wrists. Brenda sat in a chair while Marty paced around, running hands through his hair. He stopped when he saw me.

"Jesus, Isaac, what happened? What's going on?"

Before I could answer, Angie emerged. Eyes bloodshot and swollen, leaning heavily against her mother.

"Where's Willow?" I asked.

"She's going home," Angie said. "She's dead tired and wants to be alone. Her parents are driving her. They left out the back."

She took a step toward me. "She told them everything. I don't know what good it'll do. The fucker and his parents promised to fight with every weapon they have. But she did it."

I nodded. I wanted to say I was glad, but the battle wasn't over yet. It had likely just started.

"Willow told me to tell you something," Angie said. "I'm supposed to say 'Act Two, Scene Two.'" She cocked her head. "You know what it means?"

I nodded, relief surging through me. "Yeah, I know exactly what it means."

It means we still have a chance.

Chapter Forty-Two

Willow

The ride from Braxton to my cottage was silent. I sat in the back of Dad's BMW and Mom sat with me, all ten of my fingers twined up in hers. It seemed my hand hadn't been out of hers for hours now. She hadn't broken physical contact since we left the Renaissance Hotel and followed Isaac to the station.

Isaac…

He appeared in the ballroom, and at first I couldn't comprehend what I was seeing. My worst nightmare, Xavier, followed by the greatest wish of my heart. Isaac's face had been bloodied and bruised, but in my turbulent chaotic swirl of the emotions, I imagined it was his battle wounds of everything that happened between us.

And like plot twist, the police were there to put handcuffs on Isaac while Xavier's hands were free. It was then a calmness fell over me, the kind that comes when you know exactly what you need to do. Xavier's threats about closing the theater had bought a few minutes of my silence, but seeing Isaac had broken me free. If I wanted a chance at happiness, I had to get the poison out. The price for keeping silent was too high, not just for me, but for any other girl Xavier might've assaulted, or any he'd target in the future.

With Mom holding my hand the whole time, I told the police my story in my own words. No standing ovation at the end. No rounds of applause. But I felt better. Cleaner. Years of black ink seeping out of my skin and washing away. The darkness lifting, my flame standing tall and bright.

I imagined my grandmother was proud of me.

Exhaustion laced my bones by the time Dad pulled up in front of my little house.

"Are you sure you want to be alone?" my mother asked as they walked me to my front door. "I don't know if it's a good idea. Daniel, what do you think?"

"She can make her own decisions," Dad said, his voice gravelly and rough. "Whatever she wants."

The dim porch light made both of them look weary. Tonight wasn't so much a bomb dropping as it was a pebble in a pond. Ripples would slowly spread out, farther and farther. Maybe Xavier would feel the impact one day. Maybe not. Right now, my parents stood at the epicenter of the damage.

"Whatever she wants," Dad said again.

"I'm sorry," Mom whispered. Her mascara was smeared under her eyes. Dark, dried tear tracks down one cheek, her hair falling out of its twist.

"God, I'm a mess," she said.

"I think I like you better this way."

My mother threw her arms around me and held me close. "I think I knew. Or suspected."

I closed my eyes.

"I was so scared to say anything. Not because of your dad's job, that was my cover. I was scared of failing you. Because I did. This feeling inside me right now? It's the worst feeling I've ever known. I didn't protect you, and I'm sorry. I failed you and I'm so sorry."

"It's okay, Mom."

"No, it's not. Nothing is okay."

"But it will be."

She released me and Dad stepped forward, clearing his throat.

"I'm sorry, Dad," I said. "You'll probably lose your job."

"I quit tonight. And you have nothing to be sorry for." His jaw worked. "Willow…"

I felt the enormity of what happened between us pressing him down now, too. He didn't know how to cope with it. There was no memo to write or order to send.

"We'll talk more later, okay?" I said. "Right now it's late and everyone is tired. Let's just try to get some sleep."

Relief sagged his shoulders, but he forced himself to look at me.

"I'm so proud of you," he said. "And I'm... I hope it's not too late."

I smiled and gave him a small peck on the cheek. "It never is."

Inside my little cottage, I stood for a quiet moment, breathing. The weight I'd been carrying for so long was lighter. Halved. I could breathe again. Still, a hole remained in my heart that had nothing to do with my black and ugly past, and everything to do with my future.

A knock came at the door.

My future.

Isaac stood on the porch, his hands in his pockets, shoulders hunched. He'd washed the blood from his face, but blue and purple colored the skin around his right eye. A little slash tore the corner of his lower lip.

"Hey," he said.

"Hi."

"It's late. You must be tired. But I wanted to make sure you were okay." He raised his eyes to mine. "Are you?"

"I'm okay," I said. "I am."

He nodded. "Okay. Good."

"Do you want to come in?"

"Yeah, I do."

I opened the door wider and he stepped inside. A waft of expensive clothes and cologne as he passed, instead of gasoline and smoke. I felt a stab of fear that the Isaac I knew was gone. That three years of Hollywood had turned him into someone else.

I closed the door behind me. "Do you want something to drink?"

"No, thanks."

"Did you quit smoking?"

He nodded.

"I'm glad. Though I miss the smell a little." I swallowed. "I missed you."

"I missed you too, Willow. So fucking much."

We watched each other for a moment. Now that the chaos of the night had died away we were left with only each other and three years of silence.

"I don't know what to say," he said finally. "I don't know where to begin or how to begin *again*… I don't know if it's what you want."

"What I want…" I said, looking up and out as the tears were already starting. "I want to tell you the truth about what happened."

"You don't have to," Isaac said.

"But I hurt you too. And I'm so sorry, Isaac, but I can't regret it. It was the only way I knew to protect you."

"I know. Marty told me what your dad threatened. He told me not to dredge all that shit up for you all over again. Because it would hurt you too much. And he's right. The last thing I want to do in this world is hurt you." His eyes were shining, his voice gruff. "Again."

"I believe you," I said slowly. "But…"

"But what?" he asked, his face pale.

"But it's not what scares me," I said, and the nightmare of that first winter without him came back to me. "The silence, Isaac. The silence scares me. Three years…"

He put his hand over his heart as if my words had stabbed him. He gripped his shirt, the pain constricting his face. "I know," he choked out. "I'm so sorry, Willow. I swear to fucking God, I'm so sorry."

I shook my head, my heart aching. "I know it's how you cope," I said. "You've been hurt too. But if you're asking me what I want, then I'm telling you. It's you. Your presence. Your *voice.* To feel connected to you. To never feel that cut off from you again. Even if things don't work out between us, I can't have…nothing. I can't."

"You won't," he said, his voice thick. "You won't, ever again. I swear. I'll never stop being here for you, talking to you, telling you every day how I feel. Because the only fucking thing I feel is how much I love you. And how sorry I am for adding to your pain when you were already carrying so fucking much." He coughed, his jaw working. "You're so goddamn brave, Willow. Braver than anyone I know. Braver than me. And what you did tonight…" He shook his head. Then he grew very still. He swallowed hard, and lifted his eyes to mine, bracing himself. "Did I lose you?"

My face crumpled with the strain of holding back the tears. I shook my head until I could speak.

"You can't lose me, Isaac," I said in a broken whisper. "You're my *until*. The one that makes everything better."

He held my gaze for a moment, then his head bowed. "Christ..."

I went to him, to hold him in my arms, my tears spilling over now, but he fell to his knees first. Wrapped his arms around my waist, buried his face against my middle, holding tight to me, his shoulders shaking.

"I'm sorry, baby," he said, over and over. "I love you so much, and I'm so sorry."

I cried and reached to touch him. Tentatively at first, my fingers in his hair, remembering the softness. My touch trailed down his back, remembering. His shoulders, remembering. I dropped to my knees, my hands touching his face now, my eyes tracing every part of him, remembering.

His tears were rain in the stormy gray-green of his eyes. A tempest of pain and regret and three years lost. But beneath that, love.

The love was there first.

"I'm sorry, too," I whispered. "I love you. I will never stop loving you."

His hands came up to hold my face. His palms spread wide, remembering. His broken voice wrapping around my name.

And he kissed me.

Isaac...

A little sound fell out of me just as he made a noise deep in his chest.

God, it's him.

My eyes fell shut, remembering the feel of his mouth on mine. A sweet ecstasy. A give and take of himself for me, and me for him. Tasting him—the salt of his tears and a small tinge of blood. The gulf between us finally bridged, letting him come back to me on a flood of sense memories.

Nights in the dim of the theater, speaking centuries' old lines with modern emotion. The block at the amphitheater and his hands helping me down, touching me for the first time. The scent of the hedge maze in our noses as we kissed. The cemetery where I'd told my story and he took it from me without recoiling or thinking me ruined. And our dance on a hill, Harmony laid out below us in the dark.

We kissed through tears. We kissed though we could hardly breathe, arms wrapped tight, clinging to one another because to let go again was impossible. We kissed until the exhaustion of the night was too much.

Isaac slumped against the side of my couch, taking me with him. He pulled me onto his lap sideways, my head to his chest, listening to his heartbeat. His arms held me tight and my hands made fists in the back of his shirt.

"I'm so tired," I said.

"I know you are baby. Me too."

"Let's go to bed."

I led him to my bedroom. We parted just long enough for me to change out of my dress and draw on a T-shirt over my underwear. When I came out of the bathroom, Isaac had stripped down to his undershirt and boxers. Same as he had on that night three years ago. Only this time, nothing would wake us in the middle of the night to tear us apart.

We curled our sides, facing each other, our hands entwined and legs tangled. Kissing until fatigue finally took Isaac under, his lips still on mine.

"You fell asleep on me," I murmured against his mouth. "In the middle of kissing."

I drank him in a few moments more, then rolled over to tuck my back against his chest.

"Willow," he said, against my neck.

"I thought you were asleep."

"I was resting my eyes."

I laughed in my throat, too tired to do anything else.

"Have to tell you something," he said. "Very important."

"Hm?"

"I'll never love anyone but you."

I opened my eyes and sunlight flooded my room. The clock read ten in the morning. I'd never slept so late in my life.

I was still tangled with Isaac, his body pressed to mine, holding me tight. I snuggled deeper against him, letting my fingers trail down his arms, skimming the words tattooed on his left forearm:

I burn, I pine, I perish.

My fingers kept going, down over his bruised knuckles. I told him once that beating up Xavier wouldn't help me. Looking at the wounds now, I couldn't help feel they were physical proof Isaac would hurt anyone that hurt me, including himself.

"No more hurt," I whispered, and kissed his knuckles.

He stirred and his lips brushed against my neck.

"I like your house," he said. "I love you in it. You belong here."

I rolled over to face him. "What about you? Where do you belong?"

"With you. If you want me."

"So much." I kissed his lips, the cut on the corner, his chin. "But can you be happy here? What about your career? What about Hollywood?"

"I'm done with Hollywood. It gave me what I needed and I got the hell out. I'm not going back."

"Broadway?"

"For me or for you?"

I covered my face. "Oh my God, not *me*."

He pulled my hands away. "Yes, you. You're brilliant, baby. The world should know it. But there's no rush. I can stay here. I *want* to stay here. I've seen Harmony through your eyes and…" He shrugged. "It's home. I want to build a life here with you."

"You do?"

"Promise." He smiled. "Marty's already cast us in the next Shakespeare."

I dropped my gaze. "There might not be a theater, Isaac. Xavier told me he'd buy it and have it razed."

Isaac's eyes darkened. "I'll buy it."

My eyes widened. "You can do that?"

He pulled me close. "I can. I will. I'll buy it and give it to Marty. Or set it up with the city so that Marty can run it for as long as he wants."

"Oh my God, he'll be so happy."

"What about you? I want you to be happy, too. That's all I'll ever want for the rest of my life."

I slid my palm over his cheek. "I'm happy. Right now, I don't think I could be happier."

He inclined his head to kiss me, deeply, and I felt his body come awake against mine.

"Sorry," he started to say but I shook my head.

"Don't be." I kissed him again, harder. "Isaac, I don't want to stop this time."

He pulled back to look at me. "You sure?"

"I've never been more sure of anything."

He kissed me again, pulling me closer. My body let go of old fear, leaving only the intense desire to have Isaac in every way. To be enveloped by him completely, skin to skin. Not smothered and choking but holding him and being held. Letting him inside me because I wanted him everywhere.

No more waiting.

My hands slipped around his neck, down over his chest and back up again, greedy for all of him. I didn't want to stop kissing him but I needed to see him.

"Take this off," I said, pulling at his shirt.

He yanked it over his head, tossed it aside, then lay back on the pillows, pulling me on top of him. A shiver shot up my spine at the sheer masculine beauty of his body. He was mine to touch and explore, however I wanted. My hands skimmed over the smooth planes of him, down to the contours of his abdomen. Muscle and power thrumming under my fingers. An energy that drew me toward him, falling forward on my hands and kissing him hard.

His fists in my hair tightened and then slipped down my back to my waist, curved around my ass, then glided up under my shirt. The sensation of his hands on me filled me with need. To touch and be touched. To give him more. Our mouths took back all the kisses we'd missed. Our hands sought to reclaim every lost touch. Our bodies craved the other, starving and desperate and needing to be satiated.

I sat up on his lap, stripped off my T-shirt, letting my hair fall down around my shoulders and breasts. Isaac stared, his pulse jumping in his throat. I waited, trembling, not with fear but anticipation of his hands on me. Or his mouth.

Or both.

He sat up and lifted the mass of hair off my neck. Strands stuck to my sweat dampened skin as the heat of the day intensified in my little house.

"Willow," he whispered, drinking me in, his eyes leaving trails of heat wherever they landed on me. "God, you're so fucking beautiful."

"Touch me," I said.

His hands skimmed up my sides, then covered my breasts. Calloused skin over my sensitive nipples. I bit my lip and arched into his touch.

"Come here," he said.

He lay back and gently pulled me toward him so he could take one nipple in his mouth. I cried out, a hand braced on the headboard as he sucked and licked. His teeth bit just hard enough to make me gasp, then his mouth moved to the other breast. His tongue swirling over my nipple, sending a slow heat down my back where it settled between my legs. A heavy ache of want growing more dire with every passing moment. My hips rolled against his erection, only the thin material of his boxers and my panties between us.

His mouth on one nipple, his hand on the other, thumb circling. Shivers of pleasure slipping down my back. I pulled away, sliding down the length of his body, kissing his mouth, his chin, then down his chest. I pressed my lips to his warm skin and inhaled. Beneath the expensive cologne was the faint sweat of his fight with Xavier, the fainter scent of blood, and everything that was purely Isaac.

I kissed down to the ridged muscles that coiled and tightened under my touch. A small groan in his chest, a sharp gasp as I took one of his small nipples in my mouth. A power I'd never felt before swelled up in me. A heated want of give and take.

I slipped my hand under the waistband of his boxers, wrapped my fingers around the hard, heavy length of him. His jaw clenched and a hiss escaped his teeth.

"God," I said, burying my face in his neck as I stroked him. "You're so hard. For me."

"Fuck, yes," he grunted.

I lifted my head. "I want to see you. I want you…"

He slipped out of his boxers and I stared at him, hard as iron in my small hand. A wetness dampened my panties instantly and I let out a little gasp. "I've never…" The words were shy. I swallowed and tried again. "I've never felt like this before. I need you so bad…"

He kissed me, his hands trailing down my body, over my breasts, my stomach, to my hips, to tug at my panties.

"I'm going to make this perfect for you." Then his mouth traveled down after his hands, trailing hot, open-mouthed kisses over my skin. The stifling heat of the summer laid a sheen of sweat over me he slipped down my body, adding his own heat, licking and tasting mine, pulling my panties completely off. A man dying of thirst about to drink for the first time.

"Isaac…"

His name turned into a cry as he put his mouth on me. My back arched off the bed, the pleasure taking over my body. My hips lifted into his mouth for more, while my hands clutched the top of the headboard. He sucked and licked me relentlessly. My bare heels slid along the sweat-slicked skin of his back, and he growled into me, ravenous.

I tensed and arched a final time, a scream of delirious pleasure locked in my throat as the first wave crashed over. I let it out on a slow moan as I came down on a current of gusted breath, my back coming down to touch the bed as if I'd been floating from a great height.

"Jesus Christ," I panted, and looked down at him between my thighs.

He smiled briefly but I felt his own need tense in him as he crawled back up my body, his mouth skimming quickly now over my skin, up to kiss me.

"Willow, can I…?"

"Yes." My head bobbed, my hands were clutching his shoulders, the nails digging in. "Yes, now. God, Isaac now…" Then my eyes widened as I remembered. "Oh no. Oh fuck, I have nothing."

He blinked at me, eyes glazed.

"I mean, I'm not on the pill."

"Oh shit. Hold on, I might have one." He slipped off the bed to grab his jeans and dig his wallet out. "Jesus, God, please let me have one…"

I bit my lip, as the three years we'd been apart whispered in my ear: *No shortage of women when he was poor in Harmony. Now he's a gorgeous Hollywood movie star. He must have flocks of women at his feet.*

Isaac came up with a condom, his eyes falling shut in relief. "Thank fucking God."

He blew on it as if to get rid of imaginary dust but his smile dropped to see my expression.

"No one," he said. "I haven't been with anyone since our dance on the hill. No. Since before that." His brows worked over the eyes that gazed into the past. "Since I met you, actually. The day you stole my seat in English class until this morning… There's been no one but you."

"No one?" I asked, feeling both relieved and selfish. "I mean, three years is a long time and things ended so badly between us."

"They didn't end," he said. "They never ended, they were just on hold. You never stopped being mine, Willow, even when I was too busy feeling sorry for myself to reach out. I couldn't even look at another woman, though God knows my manager tried."

"You waited all that time? For me?"

"I told you before. I'd been waiting for you my whole life. There's no one else. There can never be anyone else but you."

I swallowed and wiped my cheek with the heel of my hand. "You're doing this on purpose."

He smiled and kissed me, the chuckling turning inward, melting into joy and love.

"I love you, Isaac," I whispered, my heart pounding now. "And I want you now. All of you."

He nodded and kissed me again. He held my face in his hand. "I love you. And I want this to be perfect for you."

"You said that before."

"Because it's true."

I saw the hesitation in his eyes and I wanted to burn it away under my hands. I trusted him completely. No fear in my bed, only nerve-endings on fire with anticipation. I kissed him hard, my tongue delving deep into his mouth, leaving no doubt what I wanted. My hand slipped between us, stroked him hard again. He groaned into my mouth and his own hand traveled down my body. Between my breasts, across my stomach, gliding over wet skin to the center of me. His fingers found the dampness there, and he groaned again, circling the little bud of flesh, coaxing and teasing.

I tilted my hips to him, slid along his fingers and pressed against them.

"Please," I said. "Let me feel you."

Slowly, he slid two fingers inside my wet heat. I bit the slope of muscle between his neck and shoulder, my hand still squeezing him harder, stroking him faster. He hooked his fingers inside me, pressing up and I let out a cry.

"God *now*," I begged. "Isaac...I can't. I need—"

He silenced me with a kiss and braced himself on one arm. His other hand closed over mine, both of us guiding himself to my entrance.

I closed my eyes, letting out a slow breath.

"Don't," Isaac whispered. "Look at me, baby. Open your eyes. Look right at me."

I did. Stared up at his body poised over mine, every muscle taut, the cords in his neck standing out, and his gray-green eyes now dark with want. But the love was there first, over and surrounding us both in this moment.

"I'm here," I said. "With you. Just you."

He held my gaze and pushed inside, one slow inch at a time, watching me until his eyes squeezed shut in an expression of purest ecstasy—as if it were so good it hurt. His brows drawn together and teeth clenched to hold back a small groan.

"Oh God," I gasped, feeling him inside me, more and more, heavier and heavier. I gripped his hips to pull him in deeper. Our mouths clashed in a kiss of moans as he moved inside me completely, my body taking all of him. He held still a moment, breathing heavily against my neck.

"Jesus, Willow," he said. I felt his broad chest expand and shrink against mine in a giant breath. He lifted his head to look at me. "You all right?"

"Yes" I said. "Don't stop."

He kissed me as his hips pulled from mine. I gasped at the sensation of him sliding out a little, then pushing back in. Again and again, our bodies heated and wet with sweat and moving against one another so readily. Perfect. Heavy. Full.

Mine.

He kept a hand on my hip, pushing and pulling me into his thrusts, then his palm slipped under me, to the small of my back. Tilting me up to go deeper, building a sweet pressure inside me. I cried out as he brushed that place inside me where the ache of pleasure began over and over. My legs wrapped around him, pinning him to that one spot. Holding him there.

"Feels so good," I whispered, clutching him to me, my hands in the dampness of his hair at the base of his neck. "God, I never knew…"

"Neither did I."

"Does it feel good?"

"Perfect, baby. You're perfect and so goddamn beautiful."

He moved faster now, our bodies sliding and colliding, his thrusts driving into me. I took every one, took every sound he made. Every gasp, every groan and grunt and curse that slipped between his teeth, along with my name, I took them all.

"Yes," I said. Over and over, "Yes." Body and mind delirious with "Yes."

"So good," Isaac growled. "You feel so fucking good…"

"Yes," I breathed.

This is how it's supposed to be…

I could've let my eyes fall shut. I wasn't afraid of the dark. Or of Isaac's crushing weight on top of me. Or his mouth that kissed mine with equal parts lust and reverence. As I reveled in the feel of him over me and against me and inside me, I kept my eyes open. Not wanting to miss a moment of his face. Needing to emblazon every second on my heart and body. Inking him into my skin. Imprinting this moment on my soul, so I'd never forget how it felt to be this cherished, desired and loved.

His hips moved faster against mine. The exquisite push and pull driving me to another crescendo, even higher than where he'd taken me with his mouth. I tried to hold onto him, his skin slick and hot, my nails raking to clutch at him. His thighs slapped against mine, the heat and wetness between us so much, so good, until the deep ache of mounting pleasure tensed tight for one beautifully agonizing second, then exploded.

I cried out, my legs cinched tight to his waist, my arms around his shoulders, as the pleasure swept through me. Clinging to him as he rode my body under him, taking me over the edge. His thrusts became erratic as our bodies shuddered, the tension flowing out on a tsunami of ecstasy, leaving us boneless, breathless, sweaty and limp.

Isaac collapsed on top of me, his breath gusting hot against my neck. He tried to lift off of me but I held him there. Feeling all his weight along the length of my body. Not crushing but blanketing me. Shielding me.

"I love you, Isaac," I whispered between breaths. "I love you and I always will."

He raised his head and I held his face in my hands. Seeing myself reflected in the stormy gray-green that slowly calmed into a peaceful sea I'd never seen in him before. He breathed my name like a question. A hope that I meant those words and he could keep that peace forever.

I smiled. "Never doubt I love."

"Never doubt I love." He kissed me softly and brushed the damp strands of hair from my face. "But I swear I'll never stop telling you."

Epilogue

Three years later

Isaac

I sat in a corner of the costume tent, turning a little blue velvet box over and over in my hand. This wasn't the safest place to inspect a secret treasure—the cast of *As You Like It* was in and out of the tent at intermission, drinking water and changing costumes. I turned my back to the noise and opened the box.

An old European-cut diamond sat in a nest of smaller diamonds and lacy filigree. The antique dealer called the style "pierce-work"—delicate little cuts and designs surrounding the diamond. "Quite popular in Edwardian times," he said. "My guess is it was made in nineteen ten."

The setting was simple and delicate. Perfect for Willow's little hand. But the diamond was a full carat, and the sunlight streaming through a seam in the tent glinted off the stone, throwing perfect little rainbows on the canvas.

It's perfect for her.

I hoped. Christ, my nerves were bunching my stomach in tight knots. Yanked even tighter when I heard Willow's laugh toward the front of the tent. I snapped the box shut and stuffed it into my light brown costume jacket.

Because we were performing *As You Like It* in the amphitheater,

Martin wanted a picnic-like feel to reflect the lightness of the comedy. The cast wore 19th-century pastoral clothing—smart trousers, jackets, and high-collared shirts for the men. The women wore Victorian-style dresses, except for Willow. As Rosalind, she spent much of the play disguised as a man named Ganymede, instructing my Orlando on how to win Rosalind's heart.

I already had Willow's heart, and for the last three years, my happiness was something out of a goddamn dream.

I spent nearly all of my $7 million on the Harmony Community Theater and its restoration. The City Council approved it quick because my only condition was Martin Ford be named artistic director and manager. He had final say over everything, until such time as he retired or wanted to move on to something else.

I expected Wexx to retaliate, instead they backed off. Or rather, they retreated without surrendering, putting their resources into Xavier's legal team, gathering lawyers like an army. Because the lack of evidence meant Willow's accusation had no bite, Xavier's lead attorney was going with a strategy he actually called "the slut defense."

Little did he know, Willow's single act of bravery started a chain reaction. Her words broke down a wall of silence, leaving her bruised and bloodied, true. But also leaving a hole that more women came through, ready to tell their stories.

Four more women accused Xavier Wilkinson. One of whom had DNA evidence.

Xavier was sentenced to seven years in prison. It was as if the last cloud on the horizon lifted. Willow came alive in Harmony. We bought her house in The Cottages with some backend money from my last movie. We fixed it, remodeled it, and put in some air conditioning.

While it was being renovated, I did a short, six-week turn off-Broadway, playing Tom in *The Glass Menagerie*. Willow played Honey in *Who's Afraid of Virginia Woolf* to intense acclaim a few doors down. But we always came back to Harmony. Came home to the life that was more precious to us than anything in New York.

I always thought being tucked away in this corner of the world would be stifling. Instead, with Willow, I found the Harmony of my youth. The town I knew before my mother died. Recast as my home, with Marty and Brenda as my parents, Benny as my little brother.

And now, hopefully, with Willow as my wife.

My nerves tightened. I had a speech planned out. A declaration of my love, because she deserved all the words of my heart.

Martin came up to me, glanced once over his shoulder, and gave me a grin. "Can I see it again?"

Willow was deep in conversation with Lorraine. I quickly showed Martin the ring.

"It's not too much, right? But not too small either. It's perfect, isn't it?"

Just as they did every time he looked at the damn ring, Marty's eyes filled with tears. "She's going to love it. It's exactly her."

I snapped the box shut again and stuffed it in my jacket. "Holy fucking shit."

Martin laughed. "You're going to wait until the cast party tonight? Please tell me you are. The play's halfway done. Almost there."

"Yeah, I'll wait. If she says no, I'll be the most depressing Orlando you've ever seen. Turn your comedy into a tragedy."

"You know she's going to say yes," he said. "But if you ask her before Rosalind and Orlando are done falling in love, they'll have that… What's the word young folks like to use? Insta-love?"

I laughed. "It took us six years to get here," I said, my voice turning soft. "I could've asked her to marry me the day I came back to Harmony. Or any minute in between. But I wanted her to trust me. That I could be here in Harmony and be happy."

Marty sniffed. "You need to save those words for her."

"I have more. A lot more."

"*After* the show." He looked around behind him. "Someone wants to say hi, if that's okay."

I glanced over his shoulder and saw Benny—Ben, now—at the tent. I grinned. "Send him over."

Martin left and Ben took his place, staring around, his hands jammed in the pocket of his jeans. Nineteen now, he was tall and solid; the kid I'd known was gone.

He's the same age as I was when I met Willow.

"Hey, man," I said, rising to give him a hug. I laughed at his dubious expression as Len Hostetler belted an operatic-sounding vocal warm-up.

"Theatre people are the weirdest," he said.

"You got that right."

A short silence fell. Ben and I had talked when I came back to Harmony three years ago, but it had felt strained. My apology weak. He'd already lost his father and then I'd cut him out of my life. I don't think he'd ever forgiven me for that, and I couldn't blame him. The tension between us had never gone away, and then he'd gone to school. University of Southern Indiana. I could not be more proud, but he wasn't mine to be proud of anymore and that hurt.

"So listen…" Ben's shoulders came up, his arms stiffening. "I just wanted to thank you for all that you've done for my mom and me. Her house…my college."

"You don't have to."

"Yeah, man, I do. It's a lot."

And I don't want to owe you anything.

The subtext was there, all over his face.

Fix this. Tell him the truth. It's what we do.

I glanced around the tent and held up my hands. "All of this? This is a lot. That woman standing over there?" I pointed at Willow laughing with Lorraine. "She's a lot. This entire life I have now is a helluva lot, more than I'd thought I'd ever have."

Ben frowned. "That's not all on me."

"Yeah, it's a lot on you," I said. "You remember how you used to help me run lines for my shows? For *Hamlet*?"

"Yeah."

"Remember all those scenes between Hamlet and Horatio?"

He shrugged. "Didn't understand much of it."

"Horatio is one of the most important characters in that play. He's Hamlet's best friend," I said. "He's the only character who sticks by Hamlet no matter what. And at the end of the play, when Hamlet is dying, it's Horatio he asks to tell his story. Because he trusts him. They'd been friends longer than anyone."

Ben's eyes were brighter for a second, then he shrugged again. "Yeah? So?"

"So you were my Horatio, man. You were my friend when the entire town talked behind my back or laughed at Pops."

"I was just a kid."

I shrugged. "So was I." I glanced around the tent again. "I have this theater, this show, because I hit it big in Hollywood. I made it to Hollywood because of my performance in *Hamlet*. And there's no Hamlet without Horatio. I just want you to remember that."

Ben thought about this for a second, dug his hands deeper in his pockets. "Well, we got to watch out for each other, right?"

I swallowed hard. "Yeah, we do. And you did. Thank you, Benny. I owe you."

His gaze flickered away, and then back. "I should get back. Leave you to it." He turned to go and then swiveled to me instead to pull me in for a hug.

I held him tight, my jaw clenched to keep from losing it.

"Love you, man," I said.

"You too," he said, his voice tight. "Okay, break a leg," he said, releasing me and turning away quickly. "See you after?"

I nodded, lips pressed together. "Absolutely."

He smiled, waved a hand, and went out.

A low buzz of laughter and talk from the audience drifted on a light breeze under the summer sun. It was a full crowd today. Among them were Angie and Bonnie, Yolanda and Ben—my best friend, I thought with a smile—resuming his seat, along with all the friends Willow and I made around town.

Ben had always been enough of a friend when I was younger, but now I had more than I'd ever imagined. Our days were full of socializing, small dinner parties over candlelight and bottles of wine. After the door closed on the last guest, Willow and I reached for each other. We spent the sleepy warmth of morning in bed, talking and kissing, or clutching at the bed sheets in relentless ecstasy.

It was a life a poor kid from a broken house of violence could never have imagined.

The tent cleared out but Willow remained at the entrance, peeking through the flap at the audience. I moved to stand beside her.

"I see my parents," she said. "My mother's hat could provide shade for an entire village."

Dan and Regina still lived in New York but visited Indiana twice a year. Breaking down the walls between us was a slow process, although Regina embraced me more readily than Daniel. He was proud. His apology didn't come in one sentence. It took countless visits for him to finally grasp his daughter's happiness. And the gratitude in his eyes as she laughed or smiled was apology enough for me.

Likewise, the relationship between Willow and her parents was improving, largely because of Willow's generosity. My girl was filled with love. Bottomless. After being dimmed for so long, her light was blinding.

I glanced down at her, then back to the audience. Intermission was almost over. The two of us stood behind a curtain, waiting to take the stage together.

This was the perfect place. The perfect time.

There was no other.

Sorry, Marty, I thought. *I can't wait another minute.*

As I mentally went over my prepared words, Willow moved closer. Her shoulder warm along my shoulder, her hand slipping into mine. "Isaac?"

"Mm."

"There's something I need to tell you. I was going to wait but I can't. Not one more second." Her lips brushed against my ear. "I'm pregnant."

Every thought in my head evaporated as I stared at her. "What?"

She was radiant, joy coming out of her pores, shining in the blue topaz of her eyes. "I'm pregnant. I'm going to have a baby. Your baby."

"My baby..."

My heart. God my fucking heart was going to explode out of my chest with happiness when I already thought it couldn't contain a single ounce more.

She bit her lip, watching my dumbstruck reaction. "Are you happy? Or are you worried it's too soon? Or...?"

"You really are?"

She nodded.

"Holy shit." A shocked laugh burst out of me. "Holy shit, for real?"

"For real."

I laughed again and ran a hand through my hair. "Fuck. I can't remember any of my lines." I took hold of her face, falling into the bright blue of her eyes. "You're going to have a baby?"

She nodded, tears slipping down her cheek. "Yes, honey. I am."

She took my hand and put it over her stomach. "We are. I suspected I was pregnant a few weeks ago, and I took a test this morning." She grinned. "I passed."

"Oh my God." I staggered away, then came back to kiss her again and again. "Is this my life?"

Her head nodded under my chin. "It is," she whispered, and then her shoulders heaved a tremendous sigh. "I'm so glad you're happy. I didn't know how you'd react. I mean, we're not even married."

Another happy, disbelieving laugh burst out of me, and I reached into my pocket. "No, we're not married," I said, bringing out the box. "It's lucky I happen to have this lying around."

I held it up for her to see.

Willow's eyes widened and her hands flew to her mouth. "Isaac…"

"I figured we might need it in case you ever wanted to make an honest man of me. I guess that day is today."

"Oh my God."

I dropped to one knee, my hands shaking as I opened the box. "Willow…I had so much to tell you. I had a whole speech… God, I can't think."

She stroked my cheek, shaking her head. "I hear it, Isaac. I hear it in every look, every touch. I hear you. The words of your heart."

"I need to say it," I swallowed hard. "Will you marry me?"

"Yes," she whispered, sinking to her knees. "Of course I will. Yes."

I slipped the ring on her finger. Still kneeling in the tent, we kissed through tears until Martin called places.

"Oh God," she said. "I can't remember any of my lines now either."

"We'll just wing it," I said.

"Wing Shakespeare?"

Willow stood up and I kissed her stomach, where my child was growing. Our child. A boy or girl who would know more love and happiness from their parents than we ever had. A child who would never, ever doubt that we loved.

On the circular stage, under a blaring sun, Willow, as Rosalind pretending to be someone else, smiled coyly at me.

"What would you say to me now, an I were your very, very

Rosalind?"

"*I would kiss before I spoke,*" I said, and we looked through the characters to each other, and I knew she heard my unspoken words.

And tell you I love you.

The End

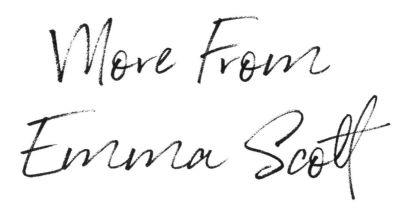

More From Emma Scott

Forever Right Now
You're a tornado, Darlene. I'm swept up.

"Forever Right Now is full of heart and soul--rarely does a book impact me like this one did. Emma Scott has a new forever fan in me." --*New York Times* bestselling author of *Archer's Voice*, **Mia Sheridan**

Amazon: http://amzn.to/2gA9ktr

How to Save a Life (Dreamcatcher #1)
Let's do something really crazy and trust each other.

"You're in for a roller coaster of emotions and a story that will grip you from the beginning to the very end. This is a MUST READ..."—
Book Boyfriend Blog

Amazon: http://amzn.to/2pMgygR
Audible: http://amzn.to/2r20z0R

Full Tilt
I would love you forever, if I only had the chance...

"Full of life, love and glorious feels."—**New York Daily News, Top Ten Hottest Reads of 2016**

Amazon: http://amzn.to/2o1aK1o
Audible: http://amzn.to/2o8A7ST

All In (Full Tilt #2)
Love has no limits…

"A masterpiece!" –**AC Book Blog**

Amazon: http://amzn.to/2cBvM26
Audible: http://amzn.to/2nUprDQ

Sneak Peek

She loves two men—friends and first loves. Her soldiers. But only one is her soul mate. It will take a war to reveal the deepest wishes of her heart and whether or not she has the courage to follow it, even if it means losing them both.

Beautiful Hearts Duet, coming this summer. Add to your Goodreads TBR:

Bring Down the Stars:
http://bit.ly/2BMzZzw

Long Live the Beautiful Hearts:
http://bit.ly/2Bi6TXM

28234228R00201

Made in the USA
Lexington, KY
12 January 2019